The Havana Syndrome

Colin T. Nelson

Rumpole Press of Minneapolis, MN

ISBN: 979-8-218-62361-6

Printed in the United States
June 2025

Rumpole Press of Minneapolis, MN

Dedication

To my wife,
Pamela Nelson

With me forever

Also by Colin T. Nelson

Reprisal

Fallout

Flashover

The Amygdala Hijack

Up Like Thunder

The Inca Code

Ivory Lust

Collection of Short Stories

Taste of Temptation

Acknowledgements

As a writer, I could not have completed this story without the help of so many others. They include my wife, Pamela Nelson, who was such a big part of this process in both the creative side and the editorial side. The following people gave their time and advice reading the manuscript: Brian Lutterman, Reid Nelson, and Christine Husom. Professional photographer and author himself, Wayne Martin, helped create the cover image. Jun Ares created the fabulous cover for publication. And my editor of many years, Jennifer Adkins, gave me her best, as usual.

And to the warm and generous people in Cuba: art historians, teachers, musicians, and guides who told me about their fascinating country and their struggles.

Thanks to all of you.

Cuba: a sunny place for shady people.

—W. Somerset Maugham

Havana is one of the great cities of the world, sublimely tawdry yet stubbornly graceful like tarnished chrome—a city, as a young Winston Churchill once wrote, where "anything might happen."

—Jonathon Miles

The continuing battle between the superpowers will be fought inside the human brain. Control or destruction of the brain will be the new frontier. And when the "cat (the weaponized technology) gets out of the bag," who will get the cat?

—An unidentified CIA agent

Prologue

This story is based on true events that occurred between November 2016 and August 2017 in Havana, Cuba, but still carry consequences today. While stationed there, twenty-four American diplomats were "attacked" by an unknown source, resulting in neurological and cognitive damage. Even though the Cubans categorically denied responsibility, U.S. concerns were strong enough to activate the highest levels of investigative resources.

Many of the victims suffered permanent brain injury. In spite of extensive testing by the best experts in the U.S, no one has been able to explain what caused the "Havana Syndrome" injuries.

To date, the source of the attack, the possible weapon, and who was responsible are still unsolved and remain a mystery.

To better understand the story behind this mystery, it's important to know a brief history of Cuba. Located only 90 miles off the coast of Florida, the U.S.-backed government was overthrown by Fidel Castro and his rebel army in January 1959. Castro promised democracy, but instead smothered the island in a repressive police state with ties to the Soviet Union. In response, President John F. Kennedy instigated a trade embargo in February 1962, preventing commerce or tourism, in order to destabilize and change the Castro government.

After Castro took over, he seized the homes and businesses of many affluent Cubans. In turn, they fled to Miami, where they and their descendants live today. For 60+ years those Cubans have plotted to return and recover their lost assets.

Over the years, attempts have been made by U.S.-backed operatives to seize the island from Casto's government, such as the failed Bay of Pigs invasion, planned by the CIA using exiled Cuban dissidents. In addition, there have been 600 attempts to assassinate Fidel Castro, all of which failed.

Recently, U.S. government policy has vacillated between tightening the restrictions or removing them in an attempt to alter relations between the two countries. It is the longest trade embargo in world history, and in spite of it, the Castro regime is still in power.

Chapter One

Havana, Cuba
2016

Unlike the explosions of weapons of mass destruction or the humph of an exploding improvised explosive device (IED) or even the cough of an automatic rifle, the attack from this weapon began with only a faint grinding sound.

Officer Lou Morales, a member of the CIA's Special Activities Division, sat in an open-air bar in Havana, drinking a small cup of Cuba's excellent coffee. He perched on a stool because one of his legs was an inch shorter than the other—the result of a war wound in Afghanistan. Since the United States' opening of an embassy six months earlier in Havana, Lou had been assigned there as an economist but worked secretly to gather intelligence.

Three of his companions joined him.

The leaves of the royal palm beside the bar fluttered in the breeze off the ocean, allowing the sun to poke between them, warming Lou's skin. The months he'd been stationed there had been pleasant duty. He unwrapped a chocolate-brown Cohiba cigar and planned to spend the next hour enjoying the sweet smell of it while watching the beautiful Cuban women strut by him in their high heels.

A faint grinding sound, like metal scraping against metal, interrupted his reverie. Excruciating pain shot through his skull. He jumped up, knocking the bar stool into the street, almost striking a pink convertible. Falling to his knees, Lou screamed, sure that he was dying.

His three companions sprawled onto the sidewalk, holding their heads and shouting for help. Their skulls felt like they were exploding, jerking their bodies violently in seizures.

By the time the barrage was over, two dozen employees of the U.S. Embassy had been attacked and maimed. There were no reports from other foreigners stationed in Cuba. The symptoms were excruciating pain, memory loss, mental stupor, hearing loss, hospitalizations, long-lasting imbalance and inability to walk, and for some, permanent fear of death. The victims were all airlifted immediately to Walter Reed Medical Center in Washington, where a medical team from the State Department examined them thoroughly. The only conclusion the medical director at the Walter Reed Center offered was that the affliction was not caused by a virus or some exotic strain of mold.

More medical teams tested the patients. The chief physician from the Walter Reed Center told authorities, "They sustained injuries to widespread brain networks without an associated head trauma." The press translated his words into English and called the incident "The Immaculate Concussion." Meaning, no cause was determined.

Florida Senator Marco Rubio, a member of the Senate Intelligence Committee, held hearings from which it was concluded that ". . . the number of attacks caused by an unknown technology could only have been carried out with the full knowledge and cooperation of the Cuban government." He added an ominous analysis. "We're faced with a very sophisticated technology that doesn't exist in the U.S. or anywhere else in the world."

At that point, even the best minds in the American scientific community failed to identify the cause or the possible weapon.

The FBI and the CIA launched investigations. Witnesses were interviewed, scientific evidence analyzed, dozens of agents and hundreds of international contacts shaken down. Nothing. No one was able to solve the mystery. Eventually, new problems and new threats occupied their time.

Finally, with no more information or new cases, the scientists, reporters, FBI, and government defense experts faded away. Silence shrouded the victims like the settling of dust after an explosion.

Until years later, when the attacks started again.

Chapter Two

Dr. Judy McWhorter
Wichita, Kansas
Present Day

"This weather's way too hot for February in Kansas. And the painting is way too peculiar to ignore it. But am I doing the right thing? Will they think I'm crazy?" I'm talking out loud to myself again and stop walking when I stand before one of the few skyscrapers on Main Street in Wichita. The FBI offices are on the fourth floor. Blowing dust pushes against my back and smells of the grasslands to the west. What I've found shocks me. Never seen anything like it before. It's significant enough that I must report what I've discovered.

I'm the executive director of the Wichita Art Museum; I should know about the art we receive, especially since I'm an expert on Latin art. But then, maybe I've read too many spy novels that have affected my perspective. I've even lost sleep over this. My husband thinks I'm seeing ghosts. But here I am, standing outside the FBI office.

The painting is upsetting but intriguing. My mind spins out all the possibilities—none of which have anything to do with art. Is there something sinister going on? Maybe the agents will dismiss me, but I have to at least let them know. Then it's off my plate.

It's cool inside the building, and I feel like I'm entering a different world. A world of spies, intrigue, and mystery. I glance down at my serious brown slacks and plain white blouse. My gray hair and my doctorate in art history should assure them of my credibility. Okay, here we go.

Ten minutes later, I'm directed to a small office in the corner. The view across the plains to the west is impressive. Agent Jones welcomes me to sit before his metal desk. Dressed in a blue suit, white shirt, and tie, he looks about eighteen and has already gotten paunchy. The walls are bare; no artwork anywhere.

"So, you're an art expert here at the Wichita Art Museum?" he says. "I'm impressed. What've you got for us?"

When he leans back in his chair to look out the window, I sense he's not taking me seriously.

"The importation of artistic material from Cuba is forbidden under the American embargo. But if we characterize the art as a 'cultural exchange,' we can circumvent the restrictions. For years, the museum has received paintings from some of the best Cuban artists. Recently, several paintings arrived and were inventoried into the museum's collection of Cuban art. One of them caught my attention. A large canvas by Rodolfo Diaz, a favorite artist of mine."

"Oh yeah? What's it look like?"

"It's a painting of five musicians, full of earthy colors, green and yellow. They each have large brown heads. The most arresting feature is their eyes. Huge white slits with brown irises. The eyes spy on each other with malevolence. There's something odd about the piece that I couldn't identify at first."

The young man sits forward in his chair.

"After several viewings, it struck me. Diaz, or someone, had embedded a code into the painting. Cleverly hidden, so that only an expert like me would discover it. I've never seen anything like this previously. I've taken a photo of it. Can I put it on your laptop?"

"Sure." A blonde thatch of hair falls into his face, reminding me of Kansas wheat. He expands the Diaz painting onto the screen. "Weird," Jones says. "Those eyes."

"Everyone spies on each other in Cuba. This represents the oppression of that system but also draws attention to the beauty and freedom of music. See, they're all holding instruments."

He grunts. "You're the expert. What's that mean?"

I lean across the desk and point at the lower side of the painting. "Look at these items."

He squints at the screen. "Cigars? So what?"

"As you can imagine, Cuban art contains images of cigars, but not often. Here, you see several in one painting. Very odd."

Jones stretches his neck forward to get a closer look.

"I've found a code embedded here. With a message."

"Yeah?"

"In all my years of studying Cuban art, I've never seen anything like it. I think someone is trying to communicate with us."

"This is Wichita," Jones chuckles.

"But what if I've found something important and…" I pause for effect. "…you missed it?"

He swallows and picks up his phone. "Hey, Dave. Maybe you should check this out."

Introduced as the section chief, Dave Winslow squeezes into the office and listens to me. "Okay. For the moment, let's go with your idea, Doctor. Big question: what the hell does it mean?" He's balding, with a gourd-shaped face, and wears a beautifully colored suit.

"Are you aware of the Cuban cigar codes?"

Both men shrug.

"Starting in the 1980s, the Cuban government began putting secret codes on each cigar in an effort to ensure the quality of the product."

"So, we're trying to decipher those codes?" Winslow asks.

"Not exactly. That's the easy part." I point to one of the images in the painting. "It's hard to see, but look at this one." Labeled on the side of the cigar are the symbols: *TOSU = 10/04.*

"What's that mean?"

"The government uses algorithms to choose these codes, which change constantly. They identify which factory manufactured the cigar and when. If there's a defect, the problem can be traced easily. But I've *never* seen them included in a painting. It led me to believe someone did it to leave a coded message." I'm breathing quickly.

Winslow leans back on his heels. "Huh."

"Do you have a paper? Although there are hundreds of cigar factories, there are only a few that produce export-quality cigars. They're well known. In the painting, twelve cigars are depicted, but only nine with a code." I point at the screen again and draw my finger across to each one. "I started by listing each code." I write them on the paper that Agent Jones gives me.

Both agents bend over the desk to examine my notes.

"You can see the factory origin names here. At first glance, it seems ordinary. But if you take the first letter of each code and line them up…

well, see this?" I circle each one and turn the paper around for them to study.

The words leap off the paper.

CONTACT ME

Chapter Three

Pete Chandler
Foggy Bottom, Washington, D.C.

I've almost finished my coursework at the language school in Guadalajara, Mexico, as two uniformed Marines arrive at the school and intercept me outside the classroom. We stand hidden behind a clump of Joshua trees, and I can smell wood fires from the local restaurants.

"We have orders to transfer you to Washington," is all one officer says as they whisk me onto a military transport, its jet engines already whining.

Arriving in Washington, D.C., later that afternoon, I'm dropped off at a narrow townhouse in Georgetown. The cold weather shocks me after leaving balmy Mexico. Snow clutches at my feet as I slip on the sidewalk. I look up at the three-story red brick Colonial with white trim, clutched by fingers of dead ivy. It's quiet, brooding.

I pause at the steps, my hands on the cold wrought iron railing, wondering who issued the order for me. Normally, I work for the U.S. Export/Import bank at their branch in Minneapolis. I've learned that my boss and best friend, Martin Graves, will be present also. That gives me a little assurance.

When I look back, the driver is gone. Across the street, the arthritic arms of oak trees sway in the wind. Before I can knock, the door bursts open.

"Mr. Chandler. Welcome." A uniformed Marine guard taps stiff fingers alongside the bill of his cap.

"Why am I—?"

"Director Sonnenfeld is waiting for you down the hall to the left."

The Marine takes my heavy winter coat. I follow the rich smell of coffee to the library of the house. When I turn into the room, I see an older man seated behind a wide desk. Bookshelves line one wall, as do two other men who stand with their backs against the bindings. One is dressed in a full military uniform. To my left, a cold gray fireplace occupies the opposite wall.

I stop for a moment. I'm in pretty good shape, except for some weight around the middle, but the military guy looks particularly fit. Without thinking, I run my hand through what little black hair I have left on my forehead as if I could coax my hair to disguise my receding hairline.

The older man grunts as he stands and comes around from behind the desk. "J. Winston Sonnenfeld." He offers an extended hand. "Glad you could make it as soon as possible." He looks up at me. He smells like old paper files.

"Who are you?" I've never seen him before.

Sonnenfeld clears his throat. "I know this is unconventional, but so is the, uh, situation we face in Cuba." His thin smile disappears. "I'm with the National Security Agency. This is Timothy Smith from the Defense Intelligence Agency, and that is General Radmer. His involvement is on a classified basis, so I can't say any more."

"What situation?" He makes me feel uncomfortable.

"Sit down."

I hesitate, then sink into a wingback chair that lost its resilience years ago. "Where's Martin?" I sit so low that my knees slope higher than my legs.

"He's on his way. Time is of the essence, so we must brief you quickly." Sonnenfeld settles into the matching chair at an angle from me.

I accept a cup of coffee from a Marine who backs out of the room and slides the two wooden doors closed behind him. I look across at Sonnenfeld. His body, shaped like an egg, settles into the chair, filling it to both arms. Thin shoulders hunch forward, as if tired from working too much. The oddest feature is Sonnenfeld's eyes, slightly protruding.

"We're meeting at this safe house because this mission is top secret. Have you heard about the new attacks against U.S. diplomats in Havana?"

"No."

"A few months ago, two dozen people were struck with some kind of a weapon that attacked and damaged their brains. Extensive testing was conducted by our best scientists, but no cause was determined. In other words, the weapon used is unknown to any of us."

I sip coffee to try and figure out what's going on with all this important firepower surrounding me.

"A similar attack occurred in 2016. But this time, the results were more lethal. Several of our employees have been targeted. We've evacuated them back here, but three are in ICU, and the others still suffer serious health problems."

My chest tightens. "I think Martin's brother works in Havana. What's wrong with the victims?"

"Pain, headaches, chronic fatigue, insomnia, and depression." Sonnenfeld takes a deep breath. "Some of the victims are in wheelchairs, and some have to wear weighted vests to stabilize their balance." He pauses. "The ICU patients may not make it."

I don't say anything.

"Since the first attacks in 2016, we've called it the 'Havana Syndrome.' Our scientists have ruled out chemical agents, viruses, and poison."

"But why am I here? I'm just an investigator for the Export/Import Bank."

"Not *just* an investigator, Mr. Chandler. My sources assure me you are one of the best and toughest. And you just finished Spanish language school, and you were an engineering major in college. Normally, we would use our own resources, of course, but with the delicate nature of our *new* relationship with the Cuban government, we must be extremely discreet. This will be done 'off book.'" His lips become thin. "After all, Cubans have categorically denied all knowledge of the attacks."

"My gut tells me not to believe a damn word they say."

"I know, I know. But many politicians want to open up relations with the island. As do American business interests."

"But I can't do anything about that."

"That's not your mission." He clips off his words abruptly. Sonnenfeld's blue eyes grow larger as he stares at me. "If the United States is threatened by a secret weapon that we cannot identify or stop, the consequences could be extremely perilous."

I ask the obvious question. "What about the FBI? The CIA?"

"After their recent investigation failed to turn up any evidence, they moved on to other pressing investigations. We don't have a clue about the Havana Syndrome. I suspect both agencies saw this as a no-win waste of resources." He sighs.

I still don't understand why I'm here. "If none of you can figure this out, why me?" I look around at the silent men along the walls. Normally, at this point, I'd argue with them. But I've learned to be patient. For once, I keep my mouth shut.

"Because our intelligence assets in Cuba have been consistently and thoroughly compromised by the Cubans." Sonnenfeld leans forward and drops his voice. "Because we suddenly have a possible clue to open a door." He looks from one of his colleagues to the other, as if to ask permission to continue. "A few weeks ago, the FBI office in Wichita received a very odd tip from a reliable source. They 'ran it up the chain of command,' where two agencies' analysts pored over it. They gave us an eighty percent probability the tip and information were legitimate and therefore, critical to our national security."

My stomach knots, but I don't let it show on my face. This sounds way above my pay grade. Sure, I served in the military in Iraq, but this is too far out there for me.

"It looks like someone in Cuba is trying to make contact with us."

"Doesn't that happen all the time? People trying to get out of the country?"

"Yes, of course. But this message had significant differences that convinced us it should be investigated."

"Like what?" The chair digs into my back and hurts.

Sonnenfeld explains the coded message in the Diaz painting. "By itself, we wouldn't be interested, but three things made this an immediate, high-level concern." He raises one finger in the air. "The message arrived in Wichita right after more attacks on our diplomats." A second finger goes up. "It was directed at one of the few persons in the country who would be able to decipher it."

"That's it?"

"No, the final clue convinced us. When we took possession of the painting, our labs used the Art Innovation ARTIST system to perform forensic UV scans to see what was beneath the surface. The 'gnomes in the basement' got to work." He smiles and waits a minute. "We found another clue: the word *HSynDrom* embedded in the back side of the canvas."

"Havana Syndrome?" I look at the cold gray fireplace.

Sonnenfeld nods. "At first, we thought the message could've been a single artist asking for asylum, but the fact he hid that particular word represents a higher level of sophistication and planning. We're convinced this person could be a 'cut-out' for us, giving us valuable intelligence we've been missing."

I take a deep breath. I'm not a spy. "Will you contact him?"

"You will. Your mission will be to enter Cuba and find this person. We'll do the rest."

I frown at them.

"You're perfect for this because you can get into Cuba and do your work under the radar. Who would suspect someone like you? It's a perfect cover."

Timothy Smith adds, "I understand there is a branch of the bank in Havana, set up years ago to promote the mission of the bank, which is to lend to high-risk international companies with the intention of creating new markets for American business. Am I correct?"

"Yes."

"Your cover will be a trade representative. Assigned to negotiate new business, allowed by the embargo, for the bank," Sonnenfeld says.

"This doesn't sound well thought-out."

Sonnenfeld flicks his hand at one of the men behind him, who retrieves a laptop from the desk and hands it to Sonnenfeld. He scrolls through screens. "Let's see. You are forty-seven, single, worked as an investigator for the Criminal Investigation Division with Special Forces when you served in the Iraq war." Bulging eyes rise to focus on me.

"My Spanish isn't good enough. That'll blow my cover."

"You've worked for the bank in many dangerous spots in the world."

I stand abruptly.

Sonnenfeld pats the air in front of him, motioning me to sit down. "Our due diligence on you said you could be prickly."

I'm more than "prickly" when I'm forced into a corner. I'm sure I could do it, but the whole plan sounds like something for James Bond. Not me.

Nodding while he scrolls through screens, Sonnenfeld finally says, "You don't understand the fear this has caused. I have a certain senator from Florida calling me every day, threatening to invade the island to install a more 'friendly' group of people willing to work with the U.S." He bends back to the laptop, the glow of the screen coloring his face in a ghostly pallor. "This is the only clue concerning the Havana Syndrome we've had in months of work. If it's the least bit legitimate, we've got to go after him."

I don't say anything.

"Yes, here it is." Sonnenfeld frowns and starts to read the screen. "Recent testing was done at the Center for Brain Injury and Repair. The director gave this report. I quote, 'The victims of the Havana Syndrome suffered neurological changes that are not like anything we've seen before. Using advanced neuroimaging technology, it is clear something structural in the brain was damaged permanently, but we don't know what that is or what caused the effects.'"

Sonnenfeld hands the laptop to the man behind him. "But you're a damn good investigator. These attacks started again a few months ago and are continuing. The fact that we are defenseless against them scares the hell out of a lot of us."

My body feels very heavy.

Sonnenfeld pauses and focuses on me as if he were inspecting a bug. "You're good looking and your Asian heritage has colored your skin, so you'll blend better."

"My mother was Vietnamese. My father was an American soldier during the Vietnam war." I'm always conscious of my darker skin, black hair, and black eyes.

"Because the U.S is sponsoring you, diplomatic immunity will apply. Diego Arnaz is the director of the small branch of your bank in Havana. We did our due diligence on him and got good reports. We've vetted him, and he comes back clean and seems reliable."

"You want me to find this artist. Okay." My tone of voice doesn't mean I agree.

"We also have a 'sleeper cell' that was planted there several months ago. We don't want to expose the asset unless it's absolutely necessary to help you."

I twist to the left in the chair. I'll serve my country, but their plan doesn't sound thought-out enough to work.

"I've reviewed your record of service to our country. I'm convinced that service will continue with this mission. How can we be secure against something we can't even identify? If this contact can help us, we must pursue him."

I nod. Duty to my country is very important to me, but this job seems like it's been cobbled together too quickly.

"We've got a flight booked for you today. You will be provided with a briefing book that should prepare you for most of what you'll encounter there. We'll also give you some technological tools to help. Secret ones." He raises a finger in the air again to draw attention to his words. Staring into my eyes, he says, "Our biggest fear is that the president is scheduled to arrive in Cuba in only eight days. Therefore, we need this problem solved before he visits. We have very little time."

"Maybe—" I think about Karen, my daughter. Our relationship has just been patched up. What will happen to that if I leave suddenly? But then, everything Sonnenfeld said tugs at me. I've been an investigator almost all my life. A professional snoop. I feel kind of sluggish unless I'm chasing a mystery, even though I'm certain they're not giving me the full story.

There's some commotion at the front door, loud voices, and fast clopping of feet over the wooden floor. My boss at the bank in Minneapolis, Martin Graves, bursts into the room. He was instrumental in saving my ass on the job in the past. Therefore, I owe him a lot. He's shorter than me with a large middle. His thick hair is blown apart from the wind outdoors and falls over his forehead.

Graves's face flushes pink, and he leans forward to catch his breath. "Sorry I'm late." He smells cold and fresh.

"Martin. What is it?" Something's very wrong. I stand and hurry to my friend's side. A dusting of snow melts across his coat.

"My brother's still at the embassy in Havana. He hasn't been pulled with the others."

"What?"

Sonnenfeld comes over to stand next to us. "Don't worry, I'm sure he's okay." He rests a hand on Martin's shoulder to console him.

Graves bobs his head in apparent agreement and even smiles briefly. But I know him well enough to see his eyes twitch with fear. I want to help. And if the president is threatened in any way, I must help. I straighten up, step back to Sonnenfeld, and ask, "What time does the flight leave?"

In a desperate attempt to "think outside the box," the U.S. Defense Department officials hired a team of psychologists who had extensive experience with trauma victims. After conducting interviews and testing of the Havana syndrome victims, the team concluded they were suffering from "conversion disorder." Although their physical symptoms were real, the cause was a mass psychogenic illness. Suggestive phenomena cause people to psychologically convert stress and fear into actual physical trauma.

Robert Baloh, a professor at the University of California, wrote: "Such illnesses have occurred for centuries and continue to occur around the world on a regular basis. For example, as telephones became widely available at the turn of the 20th century, numerous telephone operators became sick with concussion-like symptoms attributed to 'acoustic shock.'"

—Professor Robert Baloh, University of California
Published 2017

Chapter Four

Pete Chandler
Eight days before president's visit

One of the Marines returns to the chilly room with a plastic crate stuffed with various items. Sonnenfeld takes it from the officer and carries it over to me. "Besides these items, we have some, uh, tools for you. But we must review them quickly." The other two security people leave, having said nothing.

"Wait a minute. How the hell am I supposed to 'make contact' with an artist in Cuba? Google the address?" The mission suddenly sounds ludicrous.

"Relax, Pete. We've worked out an operational design, and you'll have Diego Arnaz to help you." He waits for me to calm down. "Here's an encrypted SAT phone to contact me. Although phone connections are spotty in Cuba, this phone will get through."

I hold a larger-than-usual smartphone. Turn it over and see that it's a Sectera Edge, made by General Dynamics. I know that only the top people in the government are entitled to have one of these.

Sonnenfeld points at the phone. "It meets the stringent requirements of government agencies and the military. It uses hardwire-based encryption to protect both voice and data, and it can be remotely wiped or the settings changed if necessary."

I push it into my front pocket.

"But to be even more secure, we're using another tool called Twofish. It's a symmetric encryption algorithm."

"I've heard of that."

"It's a cryptographic method that uses a secret key for encryption and decryption."

"Who's got the key?"

"Only you and me." Sonnenfeld smiles as if he were a boy sharing secrets with his best friend behind the garage.

Next, Sonnenfeld hands me a special black diplomatic passport, the rarest of passport colors. He pauses and glances at me. "This should be easy for someone with your background."

"No problem."

Sonnenfeld lowers his eyebrows. "I'm your control here. Don't try to contact anyone else; they've never heard of you. Just like they say in the movies."

I nod and shove the chair away. "Got it."

"Have a seat. There are more tools."

I sit down again.

Sonnenfeld circles behind his desk and returns with an odd-looking backpack. Setting it on the table before me, he opens it.

"Here are a few 'toys' for you to use." Sonnenfeld points at each item as he identifies it. "Start with a power cord, add a write blocker, one two-terabyte Seagate hard drive, boot disks, two Tableau clones, FTK imaging software, and two iSCSI-to-USB cables."

"What's all this for?"

"It's cutting-edge technology. With these tools you can hack any computer you find on the island. Instructions are included in your briefing material on your phone. With your engineering background, this should be child's play for you."

"Okay."

"And we've uploaded our own proprietary artificial intelligence on the laptop and on the phone. Use it with the FTK imaging software, if you need it."

"Got it."

He reaches in again, like he's Santa Claus, and pulls out a small plastic square colored to look like a package of Marlboro cigarettes. "A KAXYUYA RF detector. It can find wireless mics and cameras. A bug detector." Next, he pulls out a slim tube, silver metal with a thin point on the end. "This is fun. The Kronos electric lock pick gun. The beauty of this new tech stuff is that it looks like a big pen." His eyes light up. "And here's a Sabre Tactical stun gun with an LED so it mimics a flashlight. This one is my favorite." He opens a tiny box and gently lifts out what looks like a dragonfly, painted black and green. "A miniature drone." He chuckles. "The software is loaded on your phone already."

Eyes on me, Sonnenfeld continues, "I almost forgot." He flips open a hardshell case to reveal a small automatic pistol. "The Taurus GX4. Subcompact, 9mm ten-cartridge magazine, and even comes with a TORO red-dot optics slide."

I hold the weapon, surprised at how light it is. It has the sweet smell of gun oil. "Sure."

"Remember, you've got a diplomatic passport and something called the diplomatic pouch, the backpack. Anything you carry in it is private. You won't go through customs."

"Right."

"There's one more tool you'll need, but I'm not the expert with this one."

Sonnenfeld calls someone, and I hear a door open in the back of the house. In a few minutes, a lone man enters the room and closes the door behind him. The man is pasty white and has small brown eyes. His fingers are long and thin like the legs of a praying mantis.

Sonnenfeld doesn't introduce him. "What you're about to hear is not official government policy. You will never divulge this information to anyone. Understood?"

I swallow hard.

"Have you ever heard of Pegasus?"

"Uh, it's some kind of a cyberweapon, I think."

"Very good. Since the U.S. government has officially banned its use because of privacy issues for our citizens, we can't acknowledge using it."

"But you still have access to it." I leave some sarcasm in my tone of voice.

A brief smile flits across Sonnenfeld's mouth. "You see, the days when we used aircraft carriers and supersonic jets to protect our country are an anachronism. Things have gone dark. Drones and cyber warfare and AI are going global, and we intend to be at the cutting edge, regardless of what the politicians must tell the public." He turns to the other man and says, "Tev can explain it better than I can."

Tev sits in the chair in front of me. He speaks with a foreign accent. "About ten years ago, an Israeli surveillance software firm developed this technology." He waits as if to emphasize the next revelation. "We can consistently and reliably crack the encrypted communications of any smartphone in the world."

I frown. "I know that agencies have listened to phones while people are talking. What's different about this?"

"We can punch through any encryption barriers and hack the phone without the owner knowing about the breach. We developed what's called a 'zero click exploit.' The owner no longer has to click on a link or email in order to allow the malware to enter the phone."

"What data can you get?"

Tev laughs for the first time. "Everything."

"Everything?"

"We can even take control of the camera and microphone, see and hear what the target is experiencing in real time. Nor does this require cooperation from AT&T, Verizon, Apple, or Google."

"And I suppose you have powerful artificial intelligence software to analyze what you scoop."

"Of course. We utilize a network of servers around the world and our proprietary AI programs."

I lean back in the chair. All I can think of is an unscrupulous government spying on its own people. "So, how can the government, or you folks, use it?"

Sonnenfeld interrupts. "We don't—officially. And we only use it for foreign intelligence work. As you develop a network there, give us their names or phone numbers so we can hack them. We'll analyze the intelligence."

I stand up. This stuff scares me because I've been in government long enough to not trust anyone.

Sonnenfeld reaches up to put his hand on my shoulder. "For obvious reasons, we want this cleared up before the president arrives in Cuba in eight days."

As I'm led toward the door, no one says anything more. It opens and an assistant takes me to the back of the house. "We will escort you to the airport," the man says and opens the last door, letting a blast of cold air hit me. I am determined to approach this the way I approach any investigation—my way.

I leave in the afternoon, carrying only a suitcase filled with clothing assembled by the handlers and the special backpack, called a Faraday bag. It blocks all electronic signals so no one can hack the tools I've stuffed inside.

I've read about Cuba's history and the shady events that seemed to always occupy the island. Spanish conquistadors, rum running, the Mafia, and all the elegant nightclubs with gambling and American entertainers. Cuba's history haunts and dominates the island as the ghosts of its past keep returning from the tropical mists.

My ticket directs me to the warmth of Havana, where I will slip in quickly and quietly. I realize that I'll bring along a few ghosts of my own, including the guilt left over from Iraq for my participation in an unreported crime.

I buckle into the narrow seat on the Aeromexico flight and prepare to read all the briefing files while I squeeze the backpack under the seat. Hidden within the suitcase and the diplomatic pouch backpack, Sonnenfeld has stuffed the tech tools for me to do forensic snooping.

In Miami, I make a quick phone call to my daughter, Karen. Although we've had our problems in the past, I am relieved for the truce between us. During the call, the parent in me comes out even though she is in her twenties. Especially since her mother and my former partner died. "Remember to be careful driving. The black ice," I tell her.

"Yes, Dad."

"Do you have enough money to get through the month?"

"I'm worried about you. Did you get your stupid long hair cut? Makes you look like an old hippie."

"As a matter of fact, I did. The woman cutting it said I looked like Tom Cruise."

"Shut up."

"Uh, Karen. I can't tell you where I'm going, but it shouldn't take too long."

"Heard this before." She's quiet for a while, then says in a quieter voice, "Will you come back?"

My throat tightens. "Uh, I'll be okay, but if something happens, remember that I, uh, love you." I pause. "If there's a problem, contact my boss, Martin Graves, who has all my directives and papers."

She hangs up, and the flat silence in my phone makes me feel lonely. Her mother, Barbara, and I never married. We loved each other but realized we got along better when we had less contact with each other. Undoubtedly, that fractured relationship affected Karen and made her life more difficult. Especially since Barbara died recently. Karen was forced to become independent long before she needed to do so. Now I feel overly responsible for her, and guilty. Both are bad for creating a good relationship. I bear my share of the responsibility for that and have been trying to patch things up for a long time.

Karen and her former boyfriend tried to start a restaurant. Reluctantly, I lent them money. Now the money and the boyfriend and the restaurant are gone. It's still a sore point between Karen and me. But it seems like we're finally making progress. I'm hopeful.

I'll get this problem in Cuba wrapped up quickly and be back to see her soon.

As the plane climbs in a low arc that will bring me into Havana in less than an hour, I scroll through the briefing file on the phone. I'm anxious to meet the director of the bank in Havana, Diego Arnaz, and I feel a familiar tightness of excitement in my chest. A pure and simple purpose to move forward. I open the first report.

U.S. Department of State
Washington, D.C.
Myron T. Gilbertson, Secretary of State
Circular No. A-36, Cuban Desk

Fidel Castro and his bandits toppled the corrupt, U.S.-supported government in 1959, promising huge reforms. Sadly, few of the promises came to fruition. Instead, Castro initiated a reign of political terror, executing all his adversaries and instituting a secret police force called the Committee for the Defense of the Revolution. Headquartered in a small green building with blue shutters on a quiet street in Havana, it was rumored that all interrogations and torture occurred in the basement.

See also: *Country Reports on Human Rights in Cuba,* (CRHR), amended 2014.

Castro had successes, however. Literacy rates in Cuba are some of the highest in the world, higher than in the U.S., thanks to free education at all levels. The Cuban medical system offers well-qualified doctors and nurses, but Cuba has limited access to medical technology due to the 60+ year embargo by the U.S. In contrast, their pharmaceutical industry leads other nations, producing many of the drugs used across South America.

By literacy measures, Cuba is a first-world country; by almost every other measure it's still a third-world country. (Further sections deleted. Requires security clearance, JSC-24b)

With Castro's recent death, observers thought the country might change to allow more freedom and openness. But when Raul Castro, Fidel's brother, took over, Raul immediately increased the secret police effort while reducing personal freedoms to assure no one got any new ideas.

I receive a text from my boss, Martin Graves. Through his contacts in the federal government, he's verified that Sonnenfeld does work for the National Security Agency in a high-level position. That makes me feel more confident about him—a little.

Before I can finish reading, the plane banks to the left and starts its descent into Jose Marti International Airport. Internet and cell phone service are available in Cuba, but only for the elite members of the Communist party and a few others. Common people have some coverage, but most likely it's surveilled by the government.

An image of Janette creeps into my mind again. Blonde hair and a large smile that came to her so easily. I think back to my recent investigative assignment in South Africa. I fell in love with Janette Koos, a local investigator on the same case I worked on. We talked about marriage until she went to London for her daughter's surgery. Then a few weeks ago, I received her email. Janette was sorry, but she'd patched things up with her former husband and they were back together.

Of course, everyone gets hurt. Loses people dear to them. That's part of life. But several people I trusted betrayed me in the past. So Janette's rejection hurts badly. It leaves a hollow feeling inside me.

I know exactly what draws me into the sky toward Cuba. Sure, I accepted the assignment to find the artist, but this is also a way to keep the latch fastened on the door to some bad memories, including guilt, even if it's only temporary.

I feel the plane descend toward the island. As we come down through a puff of clouds, I spot the Prussian blue color of the Caribbean and a long stretch of land, green for as far as I can see. When the plane approaches the airport, Havana spreads across the window. I notice the white crown of their national government building, modeled after the U.S. capitol. The jet bounces once on the runway and coasts toward the gate.

I exit the plane and walk across the tarmac, smelling the sweet warm air of the tropics. To the left, I spot an American C-17 Globemaster cargo plane lumbering over the runway next to us. It must be delivering equipment or limousines for the presidential party that's arriving soon.

Along with the other passengers, I walk into a one-story reception area. The crowd shuffles over worn linoleum tiles. The lighting is dull, but at least there's no smoking allowed, although it smells like too many human bodies squeezed into one place. I feel claustrophobic.

Along with me, it looks like every news agency in the world is congregated here. Bulky cameras clog the floor so I can't walk in a straight line. There are dozens of young people, attractive enough that they must be the on-camera reporters, all struggling in the airport chaos.

Armed soldiers carrying ugly Russian AN-9 Nikonov assault rifles stand around the exit kiosks and scan the crowd. I walk toward the special diplomatic kiosk. A woman in uniform behind a glass barrier asks in English for my passport and papers. I slide both through a slot in the glass over the red counter and make eye contact. Assertiveness works all over the world. She smiles and waves me forward immediately. I head for the exit.

Another man in uniform smiles at me and waves a welcome. He has a sharp, prominent nose and shoulder patches that read Dirección General de Inteligencia, Section 3, the Cuban Foreign Intelligence Service.

As I pass the officer, he suddenly touches my shoulder. In perfect English, he says, "Follow me, sir."

I look around. All the other diplomats have moved beyond me toward the exit. "Why?" I raise my voice.

"There are some, uh, irregularities we must clear up."

In many dangerous places in the world, I've experienced these kinds of petty men. "I'm not going."

"It is simply routine." The man grips my arm tightly. I shake him off and start to walk again when a second officer appears from behind an opaque glass door. He has a shaved head and a funny, thin mustache that makes him look like Charlie Chaplin. He also carries an old Russian rifle over his shoulder and moves to cut me off.

I yell at him. "Get the hell away from me. I'm an American diplomat. You have no right to stop me." I push my face close to the intelligence officer's face, raising my chest to meet his chest. I crowd him, stare him down.

A third officer approaches. Old and overweight. "I'm in charge here," he announces. "You must come with us, Mr. Chandler."

"Get out of my way," I shout. "I'm a U.S. diplomat." Fighting my way out isn't a possibility, especially when the one with the rifle moves to block me.

I face off against the three of them. We are alone. No one speaks. I feel sweat moisten my sides, feel the weight of the contraband I carry in my luggage, including the illegal gun resting in a holster on my back. An image of a damp, cold Cuban prison flashes through my mind. Even though I have diplomatic protection, it doesn't mean anything when I'm alone against force and guns.

Cheryl Rofer, a former chemist at the Los Alamos National Laboratory, has taken the view that, "The evidence for microwave effects of the type categorized as Havana Syndrome is exceedingly weak. No proponent of the idea has outlined how the weapon would actually work. No evidence has been offered that such a weapon has been developed by any nation. Extraordinary claims require extraordinary evidence, and no evidence has been offered to support the existence of this mystery weapon."

—Cheryl Rofer, Los Alamos National Laboratories
Published in *Foreign Policy*, 2021

Chapter Five

Ava Alvarez
Havana, Cuba
Eight days before president's visit

I enjoy my last *tacita, a* small cup, of one of Cuba's finest products: coffee. Like everyone else, I mix in lots of sugar and cream to offset the bitter taste. Meanwhile, I'm waiting for my son, Tomas, although he insists on using the Anglicized "Tom." This coffee reminds me of the mixed feelings about what I must do to him.

Long ago, I gave my life to the Cuban revolution and worked for decades as an officer in the Cuban secret police, Dirección General de Inteligencia, Section 2, which handles internal Cuban security. I hold onto my high rank in the organization and survive by being careful, ruthless when necessary, and by paying attention to even the smallest pieces of intelligence. A little bit of paranoia has also kept me alive.

What I've recently discovered in my position will be catastrophic for my country. I can't stop worrying about a secret plot by traitors and, if it succeeds, what will happen to Tom.

His help will be crucial to help me plan a response. I love him and dote on him, maybe because he resembles his estranged father in many ways. Geraldo was lean, muscled, and so attractive that I was unable to resist his need for constant sex even though I never really loved him. Tom is his clone, but also very intelligent and well educated.

Now, I'm facing the biggest challenge of my life, and I need his help. The plot I discovered rocks me to my deepest core. I don't know all the details yet. At first, I thought of alerting my superiors, of course. But the threat is so audacious it must necessarily involve some of the top people in our government. Because of that, I have to act in secret for now.

I have expansive plans for Tom's future. I'll stiffen him like the stalks of ripe sugar cane to ensure his success. Pushing away the coffee cup, I notice my legs are already dancing in jittery twitches. *Comiendo un cable*, I'm having a really hard time.

Thanks to my position with the secret police, I'm entitled to a guard, stationed in a car in the street during the night. He just left. Of course, his real purpose is for the party to spy on me, as we all spy on each other. I must meet Tom here so I can maintain secrecy. The house is fairly secure from any eavesdropping or surveillance, unlike my office downtown.

My black maid, Solana, comes in from the kitchen. "Would *Señor* Tom like chips?"

"I'm sure he would."

She looks at me for a moment. "You're still so attractive, even in your late fifties. You don't have a wrinkle in your face. How do you do it?"

I think of my looks and am proud. Lighter skin color, hazel eyes, and short hair. My nose is the only odd thing, smaller than most Cubans'. I thank Solana and tell her she can have the rest of the day off. I don't want her listening to me and Tom.

I think back to my childhood. I was born in the middle of the country in Santa Clara. My father was a shoemaker. *Mamacita* was illiterate, but she had one thing that transformed my life from a destiny of poverty, work in the cane fields, ox carts, and early death. *Mamacita* owned the only phonograph in the neighborhood. I listened to American show tunes. In our small kitchen with the smell of fried plantains, I invented dances to match the rhythms of the songs.

When I was fifteen, a school teacher told me I was beautiful and talented. The nun encouraged me, "You should attend the studio in Havana. Get trained and audition to be a dancer at the Tropicana." So I applied and, against all odds, was accepted.

It was so glamorous. The rich of Havana, famous tourists, and even some international financial tycoons. I was strong, disciplined, and obsessed with my life as a dancer—all good traits, it turned out, for my conversion later.

But the Communist Party ran the club, really. That included the *barbudos*, the bearded ones, as the old loyalists were called. Many were crude men who had been soldiers before settling into their positions in the party. To commemorate the revolution, they wore soiled olive green Army fatigues and stank of cheap cigars. Their ignorance was disgusting.

Except for one man.

Fidel Castro. Taller than the others, he attended occasionally. Our revolutionary president who often wore black horn-rimmed glasses while his eyes constantly shifted from side to side behind the lenses. In his early 60s then, he rarely smiled. Elegant in a rough way, he had small feet and moved with the grace of an athlete. It was hard to imagine him carrying a rifle.

It was my eighteenth birthday when he first talked to me.

A car horn honks outside, interrupting my reverie.

Since my promotion to lieutenant comandante, I am also entitled to live in a restored mansion in Miramar at the west end of the city near the ocean. I hurry through the open mahogany doors to the veranda in front. On the way, ceiling fans move the humid air in a failed effort to cool the house.

Tom parks at the curb and climbs slowly out of the car. He shakes his shoulders and starts up the sidewalk toward the house. When Tom looks up, he sees me, arms folded across my chest. He hesitates and drops his head.

I stand on the veranda, waiting for him as I have so many times before. How should I approach him to finally get his cooperation and make him understand the seriousness of the mission? He looks thinner than usual. Of course, he parties all the time and lives on a young man's diet—mostly rum and *Medianoche* sandwiches.

"Tom," I call, trying to be cheerful yet firm.

He nods but doesn't say anything.

When he reaches the front step, he stops and looks up to survey the expansive house. Tom repeats a joke he's made many times before, to poke fun at my many privileges. "Nice house, *Mamacita*."

The house was built for the grandchild of the original owner of Bacardi rum. It reminds my visitors of decaying tropical aristocracy. Untrimmed vines, doors that don't lock well, a broken window frame with a faded, bitter shade of blue paint that reminds me of the faded power of all those original owners. I "liquidated" the latest ones, and now I own it—a zealot child of the revolution that overthrew those capitalists.

I give Tom a restrained hug. Study his face. "How are you?"

"*Bueno. Un poco cansado.*"

"Come in. I have yucca chips and a cold Hatuey beer." The day is unusually hot for the season, and I'm sweating in spite of the feeble breeze.

Before she left, Solana had laid out the food and drinks on the patio outside my office. Though it's supposed to be secure, I always suspect my house is bugged, even though my assistants sweep for them regularly. For safety, we move outside. Tom flops into the nearest chair and stuffs himself with chips. He stops only long enough to drain the beer. "*Una mas?*"

I wait for him to finish.

He notices me watching him and says, "Hey, I fucked up." He burps. "I know you wanted me to get the formula. But I don't want to do this."

"Normally, you're quite dependable, Tom. I got you the job at the medical lab after you earned your chemistry degree. You have privileges that only a few Cubans could dream of having. You must do this."

He waves his hand in the air to dismiss my desperation.

"Tom, listen to me," I shout, wiping sweat from my forehead.

He stops chewing and gives me a half grin. It reminds me of his father's expression, and I hate Tom for a moment. He also has his father's insouciance, the easy way his body drapes over the chair. Opposite from his mother's intensity. My discipline.

"Stop eating your food like an ox chewing grass." I point a finger at him. "This is serious. The future of our country is at stake—and so is your privileged life."

I can't reveal everything to him about the plot I've discovered—a possible attack on the American president when he visits. It's so audacious I have a hard time believing the data I received. But so far, I don't know who's involved, where it might happen, and when. From my experience in the secret police, I know it probably won't occur long-range, using a sniper, for instance. Too obvious, and the Americans will have manpower to prevent it. That leaves a closer attack, so I may have a chance to also get in close and stop it. And with the product Tom will produce, I can avoid getting caught.

"I don't want to become what you are." He turns back to pick at the remains of his food.

"What happened to you? You were raised to be a good revolutionary."

"There is a new Cuba, different from yours. We want to work with the U.S. It's our only chance to improve the situation here."

"You don't understand." I shake my head and pick up a fan from the table, fluttering it across my face.

He grins as if my words are no more serious than the rehearsed words of a tourist guide to the capitalist pigs.

"Tom! You didn't even bother to show up at the meeting to get the formula."

"Dammit," he shouts, pushing back from the table and standing up, his shoulders stiff.

"Time is running out." I grab his face in both hands. "I can't tell you any more now, but I was lucky that my second cousin discovered this crisis and reported it to me."

He slides away from me. Studies himself in a large mirror hanging on the wall while rearranging his hair. Pretends to ignore me.

He's hopeless. I reach into my side pocket and grab my cell phone. At my rank, I warrant phones and cell service. No messages yet. From over my shoulder, I yell at Tom, "Don't be stupid." I'll have to manipulate him.

From the open windows, a breath of air hints at a coming storm. Like all tropical storms, sudden and heavy and loud, with pounding rain that rattles the loose tiles on the roof and always leaks in somewhere.

"Want me to become what you are?"

"At least I believe in something more than myself. The revolution—"

"So that justifies all the killing you did? I know about your slaughter of everyone in that small town down south. Lining up the women and children of the town while the men looked on as their families were shot. You personally fired the machine gun. The only thing that stopped you was the gun overheating."

I don't know how to respond. The truth about ridding the island of lingering traitors to the Revolution? It was so beautiful and brutal at the same time. "I don't want you to do the things I had to do." Waiting for a moment, I continue, "But in your entire life, you have never thought of anything except yourself."

Tom smirks at me.

"And even with that slut Lucinda you—"

"Don't say her name." His face contorts in broken lines.

I finally see some passion in Tom. Something deep and strong inside of him. It gives me hope.

We quit yelling. The anger seeps out of the space between us, dissipating into the humid silence.

"*Lo siento.*" I try to reach for him, but he squirts away. "*Comiendo un cable.*"

Tom's head dips forward, shakes a bit until he lifts it, tears threatening to overflow his eyes. "You don't understand. In all my life she's the only one who's meant something to me. I love her."

Suddenly, I believe him. My body shudders. Does Tom really love Lucinda in the same way I once knew love with a man? Maybe this is a lever I can use to move him. "Okay, I have a deal, Tom."

He looks at me, still sniffling.

"Is Lucinda still working in the chicken factory?"

Tom nods.

"What if I get her a much better job? Something clean, where she can use her education." I watch his face for his reaction. "Would you finish the formula and production?"

"*Bueno.*" His face tightens for a moment, then releases. A forced calm. "I'll go back to work and get it done."

"Good boy, *Tomacito.*" I cradle his shoulders in my arms. So big now, but still so much like the little child I held years ago. His face dampens my cheeks.

I let out a big breath, and my shoulders relax. My work on the delivery apparatus has moved into the final stages, and with Tom's help, everything will be ready. But after all those years working in the shadows, I don't trust anyone. Except my longtime aide, Ricardo Pena.

While Tom gets ready to leave, I call headquarters in the green building. "Give me the reports for today," I demand. Although I'd like to be free of the cords that tie me to headquarters, I have learned to supervise every detail, every day. Many of the new agents are lazy and uncommitted.

"We received a call from the airport. From the security people."

"What? I can't believe those bastards would share anything with us."

"They noted a new American diplomat arrived. We have no data about him and he came in alone, but there was a problem. Although he had diplomatic privileges, he was stopped by those idiots."

I perk up. "Um. I want you to follow him."

"What? We normally don't do that."

"I want this one followed. This is an order." I wonder who he is and why he's really here. No American diplomat comes to Cuba for any legitimate reason.

"Yes, Comandante." Headquarters also gave me a short list of people and events I've been monitoring. A few new problems. "Of course, those damn Ladies in White are protesting their missing family members again."

I sigh. They aren't dangerous, mostly a pain in the ass for security. "Already working on that."

Tom comes into the library. His face is washed, and he smiles at me. I hold the phone to my side as he gives me a quick hug. "*Adios, Mamacita.*" He kisses me on the cheek and saunters through the front door, leaving me with an empty feeling that is as big as this old house.

I talk on the phone again. "Keep infiltrating those women and give me what intelligence you get." I shift my weight onto the right leg as I wait again. Because of the Communist Party's demands for larger numbers in the secret police, they recruit increasingly unqualified candidates. Not like the early days when I began my service with a core of dedicated, disciplined, and ruthless spies.

I lift my face to catch a feeble breeze coming off the veranda through the open doors. It agitates the palm leaves before reaching me.

Headquarters continues with their updates. "We've been working closely with the American Secret Service on the security details for the president's visit, but we could use more officers."

"I'm trying to get more manpower." I gaze over the veranda, through the bright heat of the sun, past the fainting bougainvillea flowers, to finally lose focus as I feel another pinch in my gut. After years of spy work, I have a sixth sense of trouble. The plot I uncovered scares me because nothing about it surfaced in any reports, even the secret intelligence from headquarters. That proves the conspiracy is deeper and more dangerous than I first thought.

So far, the intelligence I have is still unfocused. But when I learned the plan is somehow connected with what the Americans call the "Havana Syndrome," that convinced me the mix of enemies goes beyond just Cubans. Who else is involved? Russians? Even Chinese? But if they succeed, the repercussions will destroy my country.

I think of the American trade representative again. Why is he really here? Is he a part of the plot? An operative linked to a larger, foreign force deployed here to help the traitors? Or is he here as a spy?

Whatever his purpose, I'll find him and force the truth from him.

American neuroscientists studied the Havana Syndrome victims, many of whom continued to suffer extreme debilitating effects from the attacks in Cuba. Initially, the scientists thought an "infrasound" (below the sound waves that can be detected by humans, below 20 hertz) weapon could be responsible. However, they concluded such a weapon would be difficult to focus and would require very large speakers to generate enough waves to damage.

Next, they researched the possibility of a weapon that used "ultrasound" waves (sounds with frequencies higher than the upper audible limit of human hearing, starting from 20 hertz up to several gigahertz). They realized such a weapon could easily be focused on a victim, but the waves dissipated quickly, which meant the weapon must be activated very close to the victim. Of course, there was no evidence of that, so the theory was dismissed.

—National Academy of Sciences, 2018

Chapter Six

Miguel Garcia
Havana, Cuba
Friday noon. Eight days before president's visit

Most of the weaklings employed in the Cuban Communist Party, the PCC, would be hesitant, even scared, to be going upstairs like I am. In fact, I'm anxious to meet with my boss, a senior member of the Central Committee of the party. He was a legend in the Revolution and is still feared around the party.

I have an appointment with Comrade General Manuel "Redbeard" Fernandez—something Fernandez rarely does. I ignore the tingling in my chest because I need his help badly.

To get to his office, I climb the stairwell. Even though I work out at the gym, by the fourth floor I feel my forty-eight years dragging on me, and near the top I plod up each step. But I must meet with Fernandez because a threat to my work—not my official job, but the work I hide from the party—has occurred. I've got to fix it immediately, and only Fernandez can authorize what I need to do.

In my early years, I shot up in the party apparatus because of my brains and ruthlessness. I'm taller than most Cubans and strong across the chest. Consequently, I was chosen initially as an enforcer. Not every Cuban agreed with the official party policies, so I made sure they obeyed. I did so well, the top people recognized my abilities, and that led to several promotions, including my present position as Commissar of Party Organization. The only remnant of my early work is my nose, still crushed from a fight. But unfortunately, my profile mirrors my career.

I guess my career also mirrors the state of the Communist Party and government. Stale, stagnant, and overly oppressive.

Now, at my age, I fear that time and life have passed me by. I dread repeating the failure of my father, who toiled in a minor post in the party in the old colonial town of Cienfuegos. He died penniless and was buried in the red soil of a cemetery that had only wooden crosses and shallow graves. Tired nuns occasionally raked dead leaves off the graves.

So, when a small group of men approached me secretly for help in their plot, I listened. It seemed ludicrous and impossible, but the more they talked, the more I could see it working. An attack on the American president when he came to Cuba? Ridiculous, and of course, extremely dangerous. My role would be to set up a structure, using my knowledge of the Cuban bureaucracy, in order to construct a new regime. I'd do it with one or two dependable men. If successful, I will be rewarded with a high status and an important position—my last chance for the ultimate success I deserve.

And it's a chance for me to free my country from the morass of widespread failure.

It has taken months to recruit the necessary Cuban operatives and assemble the weapons to carry out the plan. But now, my network of contacts in the party has alerted me about a threat to all that work. To stop it, I need the ability to act independently of the party restrictions —something that's impossible with the layers of bureaucracy.

That's where the old general comes in. Only he can authorize more freedom to carry out the necessary defensive actions.

Getting his approval will be tricky since I can't reveal what I am really doing. However, I'll base my request on something that could threaten our plan: the arrival of an unusual American diplomat. Somehow, I'll have to convince the general it's a threat to him also for different reasons.

With a membership of over 500,000 people, the Communist Party is the only legal political party allowed. Castro himself often visited the far corners of the country to visit the loyal members, usually small farmers who didn't care about the ideology but enjoyed the extra money the party paid them. Over the years, Castro expanded the authority of the party so that today, we control almost all aspects of Cuban life. And when I look around me, I see the unfortunate failures of all the idealism Castro started. The repression, the corruption, and the suffering of people like my mother must change.

When I finally reach the fifth floor, I push through a solid wooden door into a long hallway. It smells stale and closed up. As I start for the general's office, clerks, agents, and military officers part to give me room, saluting me as I catch my breath.

I think back to the first meeting with Felipe Garcia, my cousin, to explain the secret cabal and their plot to recruit him. Felipe had argued, "This is a really dangerous idea. Don't even speak the words."

"You are smart and cunning," I insisted. "You will be trained."

"What if I'm caught?"

"No one will suspect an engineer, the vice comrade of Marti Foods, of doing something so big and significant. You won't attract attention." I threw my arm onto Felipe's shoulder and squeezed to convince him. "Think of the rewards you'd get and what a free Cuba would be like."

"It's too crazy to succeed." Felipe had always helped me in the past, going back to our early years when we committed crimes together.

"I know, but what if it does work?" I whispered to him. "If Fidel could pull this off years ago, isn't it time for another revolution? It's our destiny."

Still, Felipe hesitated until I handed him a thick wad of new American dollars that had been supplied by the cabal. "This make you feel better?"

From down the hall at the general's headquarters, I see Antonio approaching. A childhood friend whom I have helped over the years to navigate the Byzantine labyrinth of the party, Antonio is one of the few people allowed to use my nickname. "Hey, Chucho, what the hell you doing up here?"

I look down on my friend and push him into a quiet corner. "I'm meeting with Redbeard."

Antonio frowns and glances around the hall to make sure no one is close. "Even you should be careful."

I shrug while flexing my shoulders. "I'd like to 'kick him out of the cane factory and put him under the trees in the back.' I can handle him." I'm careful to whisper.

"*Buena suerte, mi amigo.*" Good luck, Antonio says. He drops his voice also. "I've heard rumors about something you're working on. We've been friends for a long time. I want in on this."

"Shut up, you ass!"

"Okay, but I know it's something about the U.S. president's visit."

My chest tightens. If even this idiot knows something, who else does also? I'll draw him off. "I can't say anything now, but when the time is right, I'll cut you in," I lie to him.

"You can trust me." He reaches up to my head to point at the few strands of hair left there. "You're still good looking, Chucho, but you'll need a wig soon." Antonio laughs. "And that beard—you look like a burro's back end!"

I fake a smile and leave quickly. Only an old friend could get away with such an insult. Cuban men pride themselves on luxurious, thick hair. My premature balding embarrasses me. To counter it, I have a thick beard, which doesn't compensate either.

He secretly hates the regime as much as I do, but if he gets too close to the operation, I'll kill him.

Turning the corner to Fernandez's office, I take a deep breath. I'm confident I can persuade the comrade to give his approval.

I knock on a mahogany door. A secretary calls out permission to enter. An Afro-Cuban woman sits behind a metal desk. Short red skirt, narrow waist, and pendulous breasts. She has several *bolitas*, lottery tickets, spread out before her. With an embarrassed look, she mumbles, "For the general." Although it's officially illegal to bet on the numbers, everyone in Cuba does it, including me.

She points toward the couch along the wall. She bends down to her work again, studying the tickets. Silence settles around us.

When the inner door squeaks open, Comrade General Fernandez ambles out. "Garcia?" He's wearing pressed green fatigues, like all the old revolutionaries who try to tickle their brains into remembering the mythic times in the mountains with Fidel—even though most of them have never been there.

"For the Revolution, Comrade General." I stand and salute sharply. Even though the party is not the military, Redbeard still insists on being called General.

He grunts and gives a brief bob of his head and turns to stare at the secretary's cleavage, exposed where her blouse gapes open. Fernandez waves me into the office. It's enormous but smells of mildew, sweat, and age. Stale. A panoramic window behind the desk frames the languid ocean beyond, and the beautiful weather that has followed the rain from last night.

The general sits heavily in a leather chair with thick padding. He props his boots on the desk and retrieves a half-smoked cigar from the ashtray near his elbow. A CZ-75 automatic pistol sits beside the soles of his boots. Scratching a wooden match to flame, he takes a long time re-lighting the cigar. Blowing a cloud of smoke above his head, he turns to look at me. "You have some suspicious information? Why didn't you go through channels? Why do you bother me?"

"Yes, sir." I set the file on his desk. When Fernandez squints at me, I start, "I normally wouldn't be here, but this is an unusual situation that requires your authorization."

"Oh?" Lines crease the old man's face. Lines he always said were there because of the weight of the Revolution. More likely, lines caused by the mindless weight of the Communist Party bureaucracy and oppression.

"I need the authority to expand my responsibilities."

Fernandez's feet clomp onto the floor. "This is wasting my fuckin' time." He waves his arm to the side toward a tall pile of paper files balanced on a table that fills the entire corner. "See how busy I am? It's killing me."

"Yes, I understand. But this is different." A cloud of smoke descends around my face. I turn away and notice a door in the corner beside a file cabinet. I bet it's an escape hatch in case of trouble.

Picking up a different file from on top of a stack of papers on his desk, the general opens it. He spreads it on top of my green file and mumbles, "I've got your 2601 File, personal background. You achieved cadet status by your fifteenth birthday, then a rapid rise in your career. Over many years, you've left several bodies in your wake."

"For the Revolution."

"But it looks like you've had some trouble in the past."

"Uh—"

"Fighting. You get in lots of fights, huh?" Fernandez flips the pages.

"No more than, uh, any other soldier," I insist.

"Says here you killed a comrade. Ten years ago. Knifed him in the back."

"Self-defense. Even my supervisor agreed."

Fernandez' eyes pop up to stare at me, but he doesn't say anything more. His intelligent eyes hint at his past capabilities. He closes the file slowly.

For a moment, I want to jump over the desk to sink a knife into this old fool. The grip of anger slices through my stomach. I take a deep breath and remember that I am already too far into the operation to risk anything now. I paste on a smile and stare back at Fernandez. "Do you want to talk about what's in the past or what the threat is now?"

The general sighs. "Okay, just because I got a few minutes before my lunch break." Propping his boots on the desk again, he adds, "But I like someone with the balls to fight. All we got around here now are pussies. Weak and stupid." He looks up into the cloud of smoke above him. "Not like the old days. Today, Cuba's going down the shit hole. I'm too old, but we need something to change."

I agree. The party spends so much time and resources on repressive measures, the basic needs of the people go unmet. I slide forward on the chair. I've planned the presentation to set the hook at the end. "Today our security agents at the airport reported that a new American diplomat has arrived."

"So what?"

"Normally, with our new 'relationship' with the U.S., this wouldn't attract my attention. But he said he was a trade rep, working with a branch of the U.S. Export/Import bank here in Havana."

"And?"

"The agents were suspicious and detained him."

Fernandez nods.

"I made a quick check with my reporting groups, including the women in the Federación de Mujeres Cubanas. You know how women are; they gossip all the time." I force a chuckle. When Fernandez doesn't blink, I continue. "Luckily, I have an informant at that very bank."

"I'm hungry."

"Perez is her name. She told me something astounding." I speak slowly to watch the effect my words have on him.

The general tries to get a final drag out of the cigar, then drops it in the ashtray to smolder to death. He stands and points to the party mission statement tacked on the wall.

> The Communist Party of Cuba is the superior guiding force of the Revolution that organizes and orients common efforts toward the high goals of equality, fulfillment, and peace through socialism and the advancement toward a fully communist society.

"Can you read this, Garcia? See those words, 'high goals'? Are you talking about goddamn high goals here?" His eyes cross and make him seem deranged.

"What Perez reported could be serious."

"She's probably another stupid Cuban woman. We have an island full of them."

I push on, mindful that my country will never be free unless I succeed here. What my informant reported scared the shit out of me. "The new American, Chandler is his name, will work with the president of the U.S. Export/Import Bank, Diego Arnaz."

"That's it?"

I dribble out more of what I've learned from my embedded spy. Fernandez frowns.

"I forgot to tell you something else." I did not really forget. "Perez reported that she overheard Diego Arnaz talking to another woman in their office about doing some 'secret' work with Chandler." I watch the general's face screw up. "Something that may be connected with the American problem of the 'Havana Syndrome.' Remember when that issue went directly to the Council of State, of which Raul Castro himself is a member."

"I remember."

"So, why is an American trying to get into the country, snooping around about something that could be dangerous to us?"

Fernandez turns to look out the window. "With your seniority, can't you handle this?"

I purposely wait, remaining silent. A tree branch taps on the outside of the window, a metronome that clicks to pace the growing worry in Fernandez—what if he screws this up?

I know the general's mind will churn through the possibilities: is there really substance to the woman's report? Worse yet, if he doesn't respond, will he be in trouble later? I wait in more silence. The fear of retribution from the leadership will dominate any doubts Fernandez has, even for someone with his reputation.

I speak quietly. "Even at my high position, as a loyal Revolutionary I need expanded authority to act. The American's in the country. Certainly, he's a spy but has diplomatic protection."

"Yeah, maybe you should check into this." He points a thick finger at me.

"Of course. I have your authorization to investigate Chandler and others who may be—"

"Yes, yes."

"And because of the top secret nature of this threat, I may need to work, uh, outside the party's rules of engagement."

"Okay."

"Of course, I'll report for your eyes only," I lie to him. "I may need to neutralize the threat without blowback on us."

"My secretary will give you the official paperwork. Now get out." Fernandez leans over the desk and pokes through the debris in the ashtray, looking for more cigar stubs.

I hurry across the hall to the staircase. I drop down two steps at a time. Weightless. It was easier than I thought, and now I can move forward. I still need continuing intelligence from the Perez woman about Diego Arnaz and the American. And if the threat grows, now I have all the tools to crush it immediately.

I'd like to go to Gabbie's and get laid, but I have just enough time to make it to the *toque de santo,* the Santeria drumming ritual that will call my *oricha,* my god. He will possess me for direction and power, enabling me to communicate with my dead ancestors for support. Outside, I stop to think about the remains of my living family. Separated from my wife for years, we have two grown children. Neither of them contact me unless they want something I can give them from my official position. When I succeed, they'll see what I've done for them and, finally, be grateful.

Waiting for my driver, I remember my initiation into the Santeria religion years ago. Brought from Africa to Cuba, the practices are secret and even use a secret, divine language, *Lucumi*, to communicate with our gods.

In twenty minutes, my driver drops me off at an old apartment building, the *Casa*, where the rituals have occurred for decades. The leader, the *Santera*, waits on a small patio close to the front door. Shaded by palm trees, it offers a much-needed green space among the piles of concrete structures towering over the patio. Several older people sit near her, many listening to boomboxes from which they strain to hear crackly mambos and *son*, the folk music of Cuba.

Under the arbor at the entrance, I pause and look at the *Santera*, Maria, slouched on a bench. My chest always tightens every time I see her. She has luxuriant ebony hair that descends in swirls over her narrow shoulders.

Maria turns and her face brightens when she spots me. With a faint smile, she calls, "*Buenas tardes*, Chucho." She stands and wraps her arms around my shoulders, and I inhale the smell of soap. "You are just in time. All the *creyentes*, believers, are inside."

I glance to the right. An old man smoking a cigar creaks to a standing position. Wobbles and starts for the door, planting a cane ahead of him with each step.

"We've done this as often as there are stalks of cane in the fields." She laughs with her head thrown back. "Follow me."

We enter the long hallway with peeling squares of linoleum on the floor and go all the way back to her apartment. The drumming sound is faint but insistent, drawing us inside. In the corner, among dozens of people crowded into the space, is an altar. A shrine to the *orichas* containing two burning candles and several stones. Each divine stone represents a god, and the stone has become the god. Here's an ocean stone for Yemaya, river pebbles for Ochun, and ten black stones for Chango. All of them have been baptized to consecrate them.

Cigar smoke hangs in the air, its pungent odor reminding me of all my ancestors who stood in this *Casa* to be initiated. A jug of holy rum is passed from one believer to another.

I blend into the swaying group as the drumming intensifies, louder, insistent, calling for the *orichas*. People sing and chant, hands above their heads. I do the same and begin to feel the power flow through me as the drumming penetrates my body. The heat becomes intense, and sweat runs down my face.

In the corner, a *matador* lifts a squealing chicken high into the air, chanting and offering it to the *oricha*. The ritual climaxes when he twists the neck of the chicken several times until he rips it off, releasing its blood for the *oricha* to eat and, in turn, enter our bodies to strengthen us.

To help even more, I bet the entire amount of my last paycheck in the *bolita*, the illegal lottery based on numbers. I picked number seven for Yemaya, the god of the sea, who has always brought good luck to me in the past. Now, in the midst of the sweating crowd, the shouting, and the throbbing of the drums, I feel his strength possess me. My *oricha* is riding my back like he'd ride a horse, always guiding me.

I am ready.

Chapter Seven

Pete Chandler
Friday afternoon. Eight days left

Two of the officers whisper between themselves. Everyone glares at each other. Getting a breath is hard. Then I decide, screw it. "Dammit. I'm an American diplomat. Get out of my way!" I start to walk toward the sunlight that fills the exit door. Long strides, head up. Step by step, I keep going.

The security officer with the gun closes on me. I thread my way through two of them, coming to the gun that is now leveled at my chest. His face is screwed up with fear—which is worse since scared people tend to act irrationally. Finally, the older officer says, "Enjoy your time in Cuba." He opens the way for me to leave.

I walk deliberately toward the exit. I'm anxious to meet Diego Arnaz and start the investigation.

I finally get outside the building, looking for the driver who will pick me up. It takes a moment for my eyes to adjust to the light outside, but I don't see anyone waiting as promised. While I stand there, a large black Suburban pulls up to the sidewalk. Several people in dark suits come out of the terminal, heading for the car. They're Americans, and I call hello. After identifying myself, I ask, "Setting up security for the president?"

"Attached temporarily to the Secret Service," a young man responds. "AIF, Augmentation in Force. We're just the tip of the iceberg, prepping for the visit. He'll be arriving in eight days. This place is gonna get crazy." He waves and pulls out a large briefcase from the vehicle.

The warmth of the sun and the drooping palm trees remind me of the stories my mother told me of her life in Vietnam. My father served there during the war and brought her back to Minnesota, and she soon gave birth to me. I have the body of an American, but aspects of my Asian mother in my hair, skin color, and the slight slant of my eyes.

Asians often seem peaceful on the outside, but I know they can be tenacious and tough on the inside. I inherited that also.

Growing up, I never felt much overt racism, but then again, I never felt like I fit in completely. Still feel that way. My mother worked hard to raise me, but she never fit into the culture of Minnesota. While I was in high school, she divorced my father and moved to San Francisco, where she still lives. Their inability to maintain a long-term relationship probably passed on to me. And being the only child didn't help either.

So, as an adult I stumble through relationships, trying to make them work. I have hope with Karen that I'll break the pattern.

In the military, I discovered my skills as an investigator and I thrived. Returning from Iraq, I was hired as an investigator for a U.S. House committee to uncover any corruption by the members. It gave me a cause to work for, something that would improve the government body. I am much more successful with my work than my relationships.

I sit on a bench outside the terminal and resume reading the reports.

Cuba has tractors, but since the Soviet Union fell and stopped propping up the economy with gasoline and cash, many farmers are forced to use oxen to till their fields. See also the *Annual Economic Report* (AER). Beginning with FY 2017, UNESCO designated nine spots in Cuba as World Heritage Sites, including the old part of Havana. And there are the old cars: American convertibles from the '50s painted wild colors and held together with wires and homemade parts.

I look up and spot the hawk-nosed man from the foreign intelligence service who stopped me indoors. He must've followed me out. While lighting a cigarette, he stares at me. In a few minutes, a jeep pulls up next to him, and he climbs into the front seat. They wait as blue exhaust dribbles out from the back end.

From across the street someone calls to me, "Mr. Chandler. Over here."

I wave and hurry toward a young woman. She wears blue jeans and a faded green t-shirt with the name of a band across the front: Isoderm. Brown hair gathers into a ponytail to settle over her shoulder. Bouncing along the side of her leg as she walks to meet me is a cloth bag of rainbow colors.

"Amy Cardiff," she says quickly, extending her hand to shake. "I'm from the embassy. I'm your 'designated driver' to your hotel. Welcome to Cuba."

"Thanks. Is it always this hot?"

She laughs. "You'll get used to it. Remember, we're on a tropical island."

The morning sun lights up the low buildings in golden colors, unlike the white glare in the northern climates. Palm trees flutter in the breeze, each green frond glistening with reflected sun. While underneath them I smell a pile of garbage, greasy papers, and the carcass of a chicken, surrounded by thin dogs who take turns poking their snouts into the pile.

"How long will you be here?" Amy asks.

"Not too long."

"It's a beautiful place but with lots of problems. I'm thrilled that Obama opened relations in 2015. Otherwise, I'd never be here."

"What do you mean?"

"I'm working on a doctorate from Johns Hopkins in international relations. This posting is perfect for me. And so exciting."

She reminds me of my own daughter. Ambitious, bright, and a little too confident for their short life experiences. "How are things at the embassy?"

Amy rolls her eyes. "Bad. Everyone wants to get out. These attacks have put people on edge."

"Sure."

"The worst part is that no one knows how to protect themselves."

Across the street a group of men surround a car, laughing with each other. The car's hood is propped open, and the men lean over the fenders to study the engine. Behind them, a wooden shack with faded blue boards offers flavored ice cones for sale. A fat young woman sits in the doorway, smoking a fat cigar.

Amy and I stop at a small car with a dented fender. An old Russian Lada. She warns me, "Cars are hard to find in Cuba, so this is the best I could do. The right door is loose and comes open sometimes. Hold it closed with your arm." I get into the passenger seat while Amy starts the engine. It coughs twice, then catches with an irregular grinding.

"I feel like I'm back in college." I laugh.

Amy follows the left lane to exit the airport. We pass a billboard with large red letters that reads *Socialismo o Muerte!* Socialism or Death.

Amy turns toward me. Large brown eyes tug up the corners of her eyebrows on either side when she smiles. She looks intelligent. "Mind if I give you the 'tourist guide' while we drive?"

"Of course not."

"Things are different here, to say the least."

"Okay."

"So, my advice to you is, be careful. The secret police are everywhere. Every Cuban is an informer." Amy looks out the window again.

I listen to her advice because I've been in many dangerous places, and the locals usually know what's going on.

"Castro calls the system socialism, but it's really Fidelism, his one-man party. In 1960, at the time of the Revolution, he promised all kinds of freedoms and people followed him, anxious to get out from under the economic control of the U.S. When he took over, the opposite happened. He created an oppressive, dictatorial police state."

"As it is today."

"Yes. But I hope that a younger generation in Cuba can make a difference." She looks up in the rearview mirror a second time.

"Maybe, but I've dealt with dictators like Castro all over the world. The last thing they let go of is power."

"You've done your homework." After she glances in the mirror again, I look back to see the jeep with the intelligence officer following us. It pisses me off.

The Lada labors forward on the Avenida de la Independencia as we drive toward the center of Havana. I watch the green countryside slowly get crowded out by buildings. Schools, car repair shops, one-story offices, and fruit markets. They're all open-air, and people sit on stools around the doors, talking and drinking. When the road curves, I see a large blue soccer stadium. Around it, a chain-link fence leans to one side as if it were tired.

She glances at me. "What's your assignment here?"

"I'm a trade representative, looking for business opportunities now that things are opening up between the countries."

Amy slows as traffic becomes more congested. With the narrow sidewalks, kids in colorful clothes, some wearing flip-flops but most barefoot, are forced into the middle of the street. They part just as our car reaches them. Paint peels off every one of the ancient stone buildings, and many balconies have pots overflowing with bougainvillea like frozen red waterfalls.

We turn onto the Paseo de Prado. Buses with dirty windows lumber beside us as bicycles thread among the cars, many of them the famous vintage cars I've read about. Painted in tropical colors of banana, pomegranate, and mango, they look well cared for.

I look at the Edge phone, see that it's working, and check the time. I've ordered Diego Arnaz to meet me after I get to the hotel.

Amy points to a white building that dominates the corner on the left. Royal palms surround it as if guarding the delicate architecture. "Look at that."

I glance to my left. Impressive. Three stories of intricately-carved stone facade support four ornate cupolas on each corner. It looks like it should be set on top of a wedding cake.

"El Gran Teatro de la Habana. The Grand Theater, their opera house." Amy's face brightens. "Our president is scheduled to give a speech there in a week, on Saturday. Cubans are really excited about his visit."

"I know."

She glances back at me, her eyes squinting. "You seem a lot friendlier than most of the diplomats I pick up."

"Thanks."

Amy turns right and heads into the old part of the city. I know from my earlier reading that UNESCO designated the entire area, bordered by the city walls of the seventeenth century, as a World Heritage Site. The change from the rest of the city stuns me. It's as if we've driven from a deteriorating third-world country into a charming and beautiful living museum.

The jeep behind us with the security officer is closing on us. It makes me mad all over again. I turn to look and see the hawk-nosed officer has his hand out and is waving us over to stop. I tell Amy, "Can you make a quick turn to the right and let me take over driving?"

She frowns at me but nods. Two blocks later, she leans into a sharp turn and stops. We change places quickly. I search the street behind us to see that the jeep has disappeared.

"What are you doing?"

"I'll handle this."

Street musicians set up on the corners sing in the syncopated beat of Latin music. The sidewalks are full of people. Cars honk, friends on the street call out greetings, and grinding truck engines protest the heavy weights loaded onto their old backs.

I make a U-turn and get back onto our original route. "You tell me where to go." I drive fast. "I want to let those cops know they can't screw around with me."

"But they're very dangerous. And they follow us all the time."

"Not me." I accelerate and swerve to avoid a slower car on the right. In five minutes, we're deeper into the old city, and when I look in the mirror, I see the jeep has found us. I start making evasive moves. Switching lanes abruptly, turning corners without warning, alternating our speed. The jeep hangs on and edges closer.

"Stop. They'll kill us," Amy yells.

I see a roundabout coming up and tell Amy to hang on. I hope the old car can handle what I intend to do.

Chapter Eight

Martha Rodriguez
Havana
Friday afternoon. Eight days before president's visit

I wake up early in a spacious room in the same hotel where the presidential delegation stays in Havana, while the president and his family occupy a mansion in the Miramar area that was once considered for a winter White House by Franklin Roosevelt.

The delegation fills all the rooms in my hotel and two others, because almost 1,200 people accompany the president to Cuba. I'm thrilled to be here with all of them. I think back to all the years I've done advance work for this president and find it amazing to still be so excited. I'm the exception to the old saying that politics is a young person's game.

Today my experience will also benefit the president if things work out as I've planned so carefully.

The fact that I graduated from the University of Ohio, where the president attended briefly, and the fact that I am fluent in Spanish got me onto his staff. Of course, the years of advance work I've done for other politicians helped also.

Months ago, our team traveled to Havana and helped with event planning, although security's not our jurisdiction. Instead, we scout out the locations and activities the First Family will participate in. My team of assistants briefed me on their progress and warned me of something called the Havana Syndrome. When I researched the issue, I worried about the president. But then, I'm sure he'll be well protected.

This work is so much easier today. For instance, I've been using ChatGPT to cover the hundreds of details and decisions to be made. Advance work is fun, but complicated. On the one hand, I must find resources in a foreign country; make sure the White House is in agreement; get the media lined up; and consider the political ramifications of the activities.

The president himself spoke of his top priority just a week ago: "This is a historic opportunity to engage directly with the Cuban people."

If he follows my idea, that will happen.

My parents were *Braceros*, Mexican workers allowed to enter the U.S. during World War II in order to fill jobs vacated by Americans serving in the military. Luckily, both obtained U.S. citizenship, raising me and my brother in Los Angeles while they labored in the fields until their deaths. I admire their grit but not their end. That wasn't going to be mine, and here I am working for the president of the United States. With my top assistant Oliver's help, we have every activity planned, always in cooperation with the multiple levels of security agencies. Two days ago, the Secret Service canceled one of the most important events. I'm working on reversing that.

The presidential party will arrive Thursday night for the three-day visit. We set up the motorcade to travel through an old section of Havana. I also suggested the president eat at one of the *paladars*, the privately owned restaurants allowed by the Communist government.

Not only will he engage directly with Cuban people, but he will see how private capitalism is working in Cuba. I feel damn good about that.

The media images will be perfect: the president supporting private industry under the noses of the autocratic, oppressive regime—without actually confronting the leaders head-on. Even the president's chief of staff, always stingy with compliments, congratulated me.

The First Family is scheduled to eat at San Cristobal, which is run by an Afro-Cuban family. I'm sure there will be lots of laughter, music, and handshakes.

Today, the weather's still humid, leaving everything sticky. This coming Saturday morning, the president meets with several high Cuban government officials. Then at noon, he will give a speech at the Grand Theater, a beautiful, ornate building next to the Cuban national capitol building. The setting is perfect continuity since the last president to come to Cuba was Barack Obama in 2016. He also spoke at the Grand Theater. Then the president goes to a baseball game between a U.S. team and a Cuban team. I don't know how he's able to keep up a schedule like that.

Far above my pay grade, the political officials around the president set up a meeting with Raul Castro, but not with older leaders in the party, to occur after the speech. In fact, the "old bulls," as I call them, blasted the president's visit in the official propaganda newspaper, *Granma*, saying, "We don't need the empire to give us anything."

I also suggested that he meet with Cubans, some of whom are dissidents. Again, as the TV cameras of the world follow the president, they'll film him with the oppressed people. The message will be clear and beneficial to the administration. The president agreed and asked specifically to meet with the Ladies in White.

I researched the group and made contact six weeks ago. The leader, Berta Soler, assured me the Ladies would be in the plaza outside the Grand Theater and would very much like to meet the president after his speech.

Berta told me, "There will be over forty of us. Dressed in white from head to toe. We formed in 2003 in opposition to our relatives being jailed by the Castro government. Many husbands have simply disappeared. We march every week to remind the world."

This seemed perfect for the president, until I learned the Secret Service canceled it.

"I want that meeting back on the schedule. The TV cameras of the world will be there," I tell Oliver.

He raises his voice. "It's so damn complicated because of all the security agencies from home who have to coordinate with the idiots here. I can't believe how many layers of security Cuba has, including their secret police. It's not my call, but I guess it's a cluster-fuck, to say the least."

I nod, understanding the importance of protecting the president. Still, I know how powerful the TV images would be for the administration. "Oliver, we must let the world know what's really going on here."

Propping his hands on his hips, Oliver says, "You know the president's not really here to talk with dissidents."

"It's a photo op—"

"Do you know how many lobbyists are here?"

"Lots of them."

"Hundreds. Let me remind you they're representing hotels, agriculture, telecoms, personal products, and entertainment. The administration hand-picked hundreds of Cuban business people to meet the lobbyists. For God's sake, even the Tampa Bay Rays' lobbyists are here. This is a pure example of power politics."

"Don't lecture me, Oliver. I out-rank you by about ten levels. I know thousands of businesses want the island opened for commerce. The possibilities of investment and profits for U.S. companies is incalculable. But Congress won't lift the embargo. If these lobbyists can get enough business deals set up, that may force Congress to reconsider."

He thinks for a while, then adds, "Once the embargo is dropped, our government needs reliable Cubans to work with not only in the business community, but also in government positions."

"That's all true, but the president wants to demonstrate how our country cares about human rights, as an example to all of Latin America. The photo op with the dissidents will be a real plus for him."

Oliver pauses. "I know. But I've also heard there will be pro-government demonstrators present in front of the Grand Theater who will try and break up the Ladies in White as they march. What if there's violence? I can't imagine the safety issues if we put the chief into that mess." His stiff finger stabs in the air. "Or try to get him out."

"Who are the pro-government protesters?"

Oliver says, "Some people say they're a front for the secret police so they don't get blamed for violence. The Cubans say they are funded by American groups whose real purpose is to embarrass the Cuban government." He pauses. "So, the meeting with the women is off for good?"

"I shake my head. "Not if I can help it. I'll use some juice to get this moving again."

Oliver grins. "You always win."

Later, I find Oliver in the restaurant of the hotel, waiting for me to find out if the Secret Service have changed their minds. I sit and finish a cup of the rich Cuban coffee.

He slumps into the chair across from me. He drops his head for a long time, then looks up and when he sees my expression, he produces a huge smile. "You got it, girl."

"I convinced security to allow the president to walk out into the plaza next to the theater after his speech and meet, briefly, with the Ladies in White. Just a couple waves from him, maybe a handshake."

Oliver tries to hug me, but he always stinks like cigarettes. "I'll contact Berta Soler, the leader."

"Don't promise her too much." I watch him pat his back pocket, looking for a pack of cigarettes. "Our security details will accompany the president as he walks out of the theater. Side door. He won't have much time in the plaza."

"Got it."

"Oh, and you alerted the press like I told you?"

He smiles again. "I'm all over it."

"But here's the deal. I have to be in the plaza to identify the leader and get her over to the president for a quick meet."

Oliver stands and is about to leave when I remember one other problem. "Hey, what've you heard about the Havana Syndrome?"

"The what?"

"You know, those attacks against Americans. Are they still happening?"

Olver tilts his head while he's thinking. "Don't know. But I'm sure someone's got it covered."

Chapter Nine

Pete Chandler
Friday afternoon, Eight days before visit

As we enter the circle, I stomp on the gas and the engine growls but lurches forward. As I hoped, the jeep responds equally and pulls up beside us. The driver waves us over to stop.

We careen around the circle, horns honking to warn other drivers. The jeep stays next to us. It tries to cut us off by crowding the right front end of the Lada. It taps our fender, and the old car shivers from the impact. But we keep speeding around the circle. Amy screams to stop. After one more circuit, I agree and hit the brakes. The Lada screams in protest but slows down as the jeep hurtles forward. Glancing behind me to make sure we have an open window in the traffic, I press the gas and shoot off to the right, exiting the roundabout.

Amy's face glistens and she yells, "That was crazy. You don't want to mess with those guys."

I make random turns at each corner until I'm sure we've lost the jeep. Then I slow down. "How do we get to the hotel?"

Amy faces out her window and won't talk.

"Hey, I'm sorry. I don't like to be pushed around."

She shakes her head. "I don't want to do something like that again. At the next corner, turn left."

We stop before the Ambos Mundos Hotel, and I let the Lada idle.

Amy takes a deep breath and looks at the building. "Totally renovated. In Spanish the name means 'both worlds.' Hemingway stayed here."

"Okay." I start to get out of the car to grab my things from the back seat. "Thanks for all the advice."

"Who are you, really? I've never met a diplomat like you." Then Amy grabs my forearm, holding me back. "I'm just a clerk at the embassy. No one even sees me, so I get to observe lots of things without raising suspicions."

"Like what?"

"Mr. Chandler, don't mess with these security people." Her eyes survey the sidewalk. "Just because you're an American diplomat, that won't protect you completely. It's even worse. Everyone spies on everyone else."

"Neighbors and friends?" The heat builds in the car. It imprisons me with a clammy and claustrophobic feeling.

Amy nods. "Yes. And they report to several government agencies. So, if your neighbor is mad at you, they report a fake violation to get you in trouble. Cubans are wonderful, warm people, but you put eleven million people on an island where they're desperate for food, clothing, and clean water, and you have problems."

"Like *Lord of the Flies?*"

Amy frowns. "Not that bad." She gets out of the car and wrenches open my door with a creak. "Don't be offended, but if I were you, I'd check on any possible anger issues you may have." She pretends to laugh. "By the way, I'm never going to ride with you again." Her ponytail flips across her back as she smiles and leaves.

I set my luggage on the sidewalk, and my eyes travel up five stories of the hotel to discover the rooftop bar. The first floor is painted pink on the outside. Above that, the walls look the color of wheat, with stone balconies at the corner windows. Walking under the loggia, I find a series of floor-to-ceiling doors running along the length of the hotel. All of them stand open, welcoming the warm air of the street along with the smell of overheated flowers.

Inside, high on the wall to the right, hangs an immense portrait of Ernest Hemingway. Below that, several photos of him posed in various parts of Cuba cover the wall.

I cross the lobby in several strides, my feet noisy on the marble floor. At the desk, I check in. The cinnamon-colored receptionist speaks flawless English. "Your room is ready, Mr. Chandler. The lift is to your left." Pointing in the direction of Hemingway, her arm floats out from her side slowly, as if time is irrelevant.

Before I walk away, I remember. "Any messages for me?" I wonder if there's any chance Janette may have contacted me.

"There is one. Mr. Diego Arnaz said he would be here in twenty minutes. We have conference rooms."

I ride the lift to my floor and turn down a narrow hall with a cool tiled floor. At the door, I open the ornate handle and step inside. Very plain. Tile floor with rugs, simple bed, but a stupendous view over the orange roofs of Havana. I do a quick check of the inside of drawers, underneath lamp shades, behind doors, and drop to my knees to study the fascinating underside of the bed. Nothing unusual. But to be sure, I pull out the LM-8 bug sweep Sonnenfeld included and point it in every corner. Before leaving for the lobby, I put my luggage on a stand in a specific position, which I remember for future reference.

Then I pull a chair over to the corner by the window. Standing on the chair, I place a tiny Jiasen IP video camera just above the frame of the window. The camera is another gift from Sonnenfeld. It's the size of a bottle cap. The adhesive tape holds it in place, and I get down from the chair. I use the app on my phone to activate it.

I carry the Faraday bag containing all my "tools" with me. The gun also stays with me in a holster in the small of my back.

Forty minutes later, Diego Arnaz steps through an open door into the lobby, his shoulders rolling with his small steps. Diego wears a light blue *guayabera* frayed at the cuffs and a Panama hat with a drooping brim. He ambles toward me and swings out his hand to shake. Then he grabs my shoulder and shakes it. Diego isn't tall, but his thick body gives the impression of greater size.

"*Bienvenido.* Welcome to Havana," Diego says. "I am privileged to meet you." He has a shiny black mustache, dwarfed by a round face, and moisture across his cheeks. He studies me for a moment.

I nod and smile back but still ask him. "Pardon me, but I gotta do this. Can you show me some identification?"

Diego frowns, then reaches into a battered leather satchel he carries and pulls out two pieces of thick paper with official seals attached. They name him as president of the U.S. Export/Import bank, Havana Branch, and show his official Cuban ID that everyone carries.

"One more thing. Gotta check for wires." I wand him with the bug detector. "Thanks. Just being careful."

Diego shrugs. "I hope you're enjoying our beautiful weather."

"Thanks." I drop my voice. "I want to find the artist."

"Yes, of course. Later. Now, we take our time and get acquainted. Nothing is rushed in Cuba."

"I want to go outside to avoid being overheard. We'll sit with our backs to the wall so I can see who comes in, and we will order coffee first."

He smiles slowly. "Mr. Chandler, you've learned quickly. The secret police, the Dirección de General Inteligencia, are everywhere."

I glance around the lobby. Tourists puddle in small groups, wiping their faces repeatedly. "So I've heard." Undercover spies can act like tourists, so maybe Diego's right. A large group of Chinese tourists enters the lobby and takes photos of everything, including Mr. Hemingway.

"You are in a country with many, uh, mysteries."

After we sit in low chairs behind a table just outside the doors, Diego orders coffee. Quiet salsa music reaches us from the PA system. Soft air drifts through the doors, waking the palm fronds that slumber along the walls until they sway in response.

From my bag I pull out another gadget Sonnenfeld gave me: a Cicada TinyTx transducer jammer. It can jam any listening device operating in the area, even if it's not close to us. It rests in my palm and I set it on the table, switching it on.

"Thanks for your help," I begin. "Especially on such short notice." I study Diego closely. He has brown eyes that sag to give him a worn-out look. Even though he seems competent, after all the people who have disappointed or betrayed me, I don't trust easily.

Diego starts, "We are excited to have your president visit our country. Hopefully, relations between us will improve. Our contact in Washington told me about the artist you seek." He chuckles, a nervous tic that seems inappropriate. "You need my help, as there are several forces working underwater here." His voice becomes quieter.

"You mean *undercover?*"

"Yes. Since Cuba is only ninety miles from your country, we have spies from all over the world doing their shadowy work. Russia, China, Israel, and even the anti-Castro groups from Miami." I smell cigars on him.

"Diego, my only job is to find that artist."

"Of course." Diego wags his finger close to my face. "But we must move carefully."

A uniformed waiter interrupts us at the table with two small cups, a silver coffee pot, cream, and sugar. I taste it black and find it rich and flavorful.

"Cubans love their coffee," Diego brags. He holds his head at an angle, posing like a sad prince from a vibrant country. "But don't be so quick to judge us; your country has its own problems also." He smiles.

"I want to get started right away." I ignore the comment.

Diego looks from one side to the other, then drops his voice. "Be quiet. I am in a difficult position by helping you. If your cover doesn't work, I am in very much danger."

I hope to find the artist quickly. But the slow pace of life here gives me a hint of how complicated this job could become. I feel wary. "You speak good English."

"Everyone except the *ancianos*, the old ones, speaks English in Cuba." Diego traces his finger across the stone facade beside his shoulder. "You will enjoy this hotel. One of our best. Hemingway stayed here many times."

"How could I miss that?" I set my cup on the small table. "Diego, I want to get this done quickly." When Diego blinks like he doesn't understand, I add, "Time is running out as we wait here."

"Of course." Diego swallows his coffee slowly. Dabs at his lips with the cotton napkin. "There is an art market in an old, renovated warehouse near the rail tracks. Hundreds of artists show their work at the warehouse. We will start there."

"So, we'll just wander around?" I am surprised at how lackadaisical he sounds.

"Correct." He pauses. "As if I'm showing our newest trade rep what's available for sale."

Behind us, I hear the brakes of a tour bus wheeze as it settles to a stop in front of the hotel. In a few minutes, a Cuban woman carrying a stick in the air with the Cuban flag attached to the top leads a group of tourists into the lobby. Some of the men wear Hawaiian shirts and sandals. Many faces are pink with sunburns, and they drag enormous suitcases that clatter across the marble to clash with the elegant music.

I watch them swarm like a school of fish to the north end of the lobby and hold up phones toward the portrait of Hemingway on the wall.

Diego continues, "Consider this. When the Soviets stopped supporting the country and when the Americans tightened the embargo, we suffered extreme shortages of everything, including food. The average Cuban lost twenty-five pounds during that 'special period,' as Fidel called it." Diego opens his hands. "We survived all that. We are resourceful people."

The information troubles me. I don't respond but study him. Diego appears capable and trustworthy. But the cogs in my brain creak into action in an experienced fashion with a depressing conclusion. The investigation will be harder than I imagined. "Once we find Diaz, let me do the talking. I can speak Spanish."

"May I suggest that I start the first conversation." His voice goes soft, hinting at hidden resources and shady connections. "Mr. Sonnenfeld suggested we may use my assistant, Raquel Sanchez, on occasion, if we need extra help."

"Who's she?"

"She is very bright. I've worked with her for years. She's Cuban and had an American grandfather, and she's also a good lawyer. After the Revolution, lawyers were abolished. Since then, the party recognized they needed some and opened up the law courts again."

"She was a government lawyer? Why the hell would I work with her?" My breathing comes faster.

"She works full time at the bank." Diego's eyes narrow, but he continues, "Everyone uses whatever connections they have to survive. It doesn't mean Raquel is compromised. In fact, I recall she had some bad problems with the party. Something about her late husband. A mystery that will bring me trouble if I try to dig into it."

I take time finishing the coffee. The more I discover about the situation here, the worse it becomes.

The group of tourists shuffles from the portrait of Hemingway to crowd around the lobby bar. Three men order Hatuey beers. Most of the suitcases in the middle of the floor are so large the women call to the porters for help.

In spite of the coffee, my mouth feels dry. I say, "Let's get going." We step back through the open door into the lobby.

"We must be extremely careful." Diego tangles his fingers together around the small cup. "In the past few years, we have had, uh, disruptions in our country."

"Disruptions?"

"Fidel died and his brother, Raul, has taken over. He is part of a very old and conservative faction that is worried about the new freedoms the people are asking for. The response of the government officials is to press down: more censorship, more repression, and especially, an anti-American propaganda effort." He sets the cup on the lobby bar.

We stand back from each other. Diego takes a deep breath, his chest puffing out. "Tomorrow, come to my office and we will proceed to the art market." He smiles at me, but his handshake is limp. There's an awkward minute of silence. Then we walk into the shadows created by the loggia. Saying goodbye, Diego plods off, the bottom of his pants legs puddling around his ankles and threatening to trip him.

I can't relax. The investigation is delayed until tomorrow morning. Diego's slow pace concerns me, but I've worked with all kinds of people in my investigations. I'll push him harder or do it myself somehow.

I turn back into the lobby while my eyes pick out various people. A hollow feeling carves into my belly. Against my usual instincts, I find myself trusting Diego. But then, at this point, I have no one else to depend on.

After picking up my tech tools, I ride the lift back to my room. Already tired from all the intrigue, I decide to take a shower and wash the dust of travel off me before dinner. I enter the room, open the windows to a cooling breeze, and check the luggage.

The precise alignment I left them in has changed. I unzip the pieces. Don't find anything missing. But there is no doubt someone has searched the room thoroughly. So, I use the bug detector again. Nothing.

I leave the room with my bag and tools and go outside the hotel. I open the Sectera Edge phone and call Sonnenfeld. When he answers, I ask, "Why the hell did you pick Diego Arnaz? He moves slower than the federal bureaucracy."

"So, how are things going?"

"They're not going. I want to start looking for Rodolfo Diaz today. All Diego wanted to do was drink coffee."

"You must get into the tempo of the people and the country. Don't arouse any suspicions." Sonnenfeld takes a raspy breath. "But you must complete the mission soon. Since the president decided to visit Cuba, the spooks over at CIA have received excessive chatter from other players: Chinese, Russians, and Cubans. None of us want this to blow up."

"Of course not."

"And give me Diego's phone number. We'll run him through Pegasus."

"You told me he was vetted."

"Apparently, in our rush to initiate the mission, we didn't do our usual due diligence." Sonnenfeld hangs up.

My chest tightens. I'm harnessed to a group of incompetents.

The JASON Defense Advisory Panel is an independent group of elite scientists that advises the United States government on matters of science and technology, mostly of a sensitive nature. Although much of its research is military-focused, JASON also produced early work on the science of global warming and acid rain.

Trained to assess new threats to national security, the group learned of the Havana Syndrome and leaped into action. Their experts assessed the victims and their bizarre symptoms. The initial conclusion was that the vestibular (inner ear) systems in all the victims were seriously damaged—by something. But they couldn't identify what had caused it, and the group was unable to solve it. The enigma remained.

—JASON Defense Advisory Panel, 2018

Chapter Ten

Pete Chandler
Saturday morning. Seven days before visit

The taxi dodges through the morning traffic in Havana on its way to the Plaza de la Revolucíon, the largest city square in the world. I'm anxious to meet Diego at his office and finally find my guy.

On the way, I open the app for the Jiasen IP camera and fast forward through the video until I see the person come into my room. He hunches over, probing into my items, and then he turns to leave. Unfortunately, he's got a hoodie on and keeps his head down. I can't make out a face.

Southwest of the old city, the plaza begins at the elevated statue of Jose Marti on the south end and flows in a series of asphalt cataracts across an open space that looks more like a giant parking lot than a memorial to the success of the revolution. Fidel gave his speeches here, surrounded by tall office buildings.

The bank is located in a small building at the north end.

"Here you are," the driver shouts over the salsa music beating from the cheap radio. "Please get out quickly."

I understand most of the driver's Spanish. But it's difficult because I've been trained in North American Spanish, while the Cubans speak a dialect of Caribbean Spanish. When I talk, the driver understands me.

Then he switches to English and repeats his request.

"Why?"

"I must hurry. This is my second job."

"What else do you do?"

"I am a medical doctor."

Stunned, I ask, "Why are you driving a cab?"

"Everyone in Cuba is guaranteed a job, but they only earn thirty U.S. dollars a month. Some people, like engineers, doctors, teachers, get more. Thirty-five dollars. Clearly, it is not enough to support us, so every-one—how do you Americans say it? 'Moonlights'?"

"Yes, that's how we say it."

The doctor slows on a tree-lined street beside an office building. The fare is three dollars, but I pay him ten. His story gives me added respect for the Cuban people.

A breeze scatters last night's fallen palm leaves while the pungent scent of jasmine brushes around me, so powerful it stops me for a moment.

I walk along a short sidewalk to the office building. The doorknob is missing, so I simply push it open. Inside, a female guard sits at a small desk in a warm room. She reads something that looks like a Hollywood gossip magazine. In a few minutes, she looks up and jerks her head toward a second door before going back to her reading.

Inside that door, I find a list of offices that directs me to the U.S. Export/Import Bank on the third floor. The elevator creaks upwards, and I slide back the metal screen to get out.

Entering the office, I think I've been transported back in time. A low ceiling spreads over an open space dotted with steel desks, all Army green. Iron columns support the ceiling and separate the desks. A few women sit at them while their fingers stab at electric typewriters. Steel balls twitch back and forth in the middle of the machines. Lazy ceiling fans rotate to remind me that I'm in a tropical climate.

A receptionist smiles feebly at me. "I'm Connie Perez, *Señor* Arnaz's secretary." She waves me into a metal chair along the wall. "Diego will be right out."

While I wait, I check my phone and read a text from Sonnenfeld. "Preliminary background research on Diego Arnaz looks good."

A door beside me opens and Diego steps out. Once again, he breaks into a broad smile and shakes my hand vigorously. "Welcome, welcome. Do you like our modern offices?" His arm sweeps off to the side toward the open area.

"Very nice." I run my hand over my forehead, an old habit, to cover up the hair I've lost.

"Since we have American funding, we enjoy a few nice things here." He starts to lead me toward another door in the back. "Let us share some coffee first."

"Uh, Diego, I had breakfast. Let's get going."

Diego stops. "Uh, of course. If you insist. One of my jobs for you is to get you to relax. In Cuba, we move at a sane pace, not the North American rush."

Diego continues toward the back of the office, his shoulders rolling from side to side as he walks. From around the corner, a tall woman about my height runs into us. A moment of awkwardness. Stepping back in a polite move, Diego introduces Raquel Sanchez. She looks to be in her late thirties.

She hesitates, then reaches out to shake my hand. Slim fingers, caramel-colored skin, pink nails, tendons and sinew. She wears a blue skirt and a white blouse open at the neck to show off a modest gold necklace. I notice her eyes first. Dark brown, intense, and looking directly at me through red-framed glasses. "Mr. Chandler," she says in a low voice while she lets my hand slip away.

"Diego told me you work together," I reply.

"Welcome to Havana." Her eyes hold mine for a while until she turns to walk away.

Diego interrupts. "We'll start in my office."

I follow Diego. His office feels cramped, with large windows overlooking an enclosed courtyard outside. Diego cradles a thick file of paper under his arm, balances a notebook on top, and says, "Let's go outside; it's so pleasant this time of the morning. Besides, no one can overhear us." He wears the same frayed *guayabera* that he wore yesterday.

Diego leads us outside. Two chairs offer a comfortable place to sit in the courtyard, and a tired fountain in the middle spits water a foot in the air as if it didn't have the energy to lift the water higher. Palm trees along the edge offer us shade. And in the corner, moving in jerky steps, a rooster ducks into the bushes.

"Can I trust Ms. Sanchez?"

Diego nods. "Your friend in Minnesota recruited me first. I insisted that I needed her help, so Mr. Sonnenfeld did some kind of a background check on both of us. You can trust us."

"Okay." While he adjusts his files, I text Sonnenfeld on the SAT phone to confirm what Diego said.

"How do you like the hotel we picked?" Diego asks.

I look around the small area, wondering how many microphones are hidden in the palms in spite of Diego's assurances. "Fine, except my room's already been searched." I poke my bug detector toward him but find nothing.

Diego frowns. "I warned you." He changes the subject. "Did you come across our famous plaza?"

"Yes."

"When I was a little boy, my father took me to hear Fidel's speeches. The plaza was full of people because the party made everyone attend. He would speak for eight hours, so my father brought food and games like chess to play throughout the day."

I sit down in one of the surprisingly comfortable white wrought-iron chairs. From my bag, I pull out the Cicada transducer jamming device, activate it, and put it on a small table. "Just to make sure," I say.

Raquel Snachez walks out and silently joins us.

Opening a large file, Diego leans forward to read it, page by page. Finally, he looks up at me. "I found a listing for Rodolfo Diaz. He's a painter of some note who displays at the Almacenes San Jose Artisan's Market. It's an old warehouse that was used when trains came into Havana. Now, it's been converted to an art market."

"Is it close to here?"

"Not far." Diego closes the thick file. "Our approach to him must be very careful. I will do the talking. The best skill one can have in Cuba is the ability to improvise."

For the moment, I agree. I have worked with many different kinds of people, especially during my military tours in the Middle East when I worked with the Criminal Investigation Division. Coming home, I worked with the congressional committee in Washington, whose chairperson was from Minnesota. I met and fell in love with one of the members from Wisconsin. During a reelection campaign in which she was smeared by hackers and misinformation, I investigated to find the perps. I failed, and the toll was too much for her. She committed suicide. I failed her. After that, the chairman offered me a job in the Export/Import Bank in Minneapolis. I was forced to improvise through that pain. I'm still improvising, for that matter.

And there's the guilt for what I did in Iraq with Judd Crowe.

Diego interrupts my thoughts. "If we are stopped by any security people, your diplomatic protection will get us through. I will explain that you are a trade rep looking for business opportunities." He pauses. "The promise of jobs, any jobs, is a powerful tool." He slaps the arm of his chair. "I forgot something." Diego walks back into the office.

I check my phone and find a text from Sonnenfeld, assuring me both of these people are not security risks.

Raquel asks me, "How do you like Cuba so far?"

"I like the warmth of the people and the beauty of the old city." I hesitate for a moment. "But your government is awfully repressive. As if no one is worth anything here."

"That is why I became a lawyer. Individuals *are* important. We were all betrayed by the Revolution." She takes a breath. "And you are here for justice for your people?"

"I'm here only to find an artist."

"So, you have your struggles also." Her mouth turns up in a sarcastic manner.

I shrug. "I'm trying to do a small part. And sometimes it actually works."

"You'll need help here."

"I've been around," I say dismissively.

"A little arrogant, Mr. Chandler? You're an American, used to getting your way. Cubans don't have that luxury, even if our cause is good." Sanchez glances at her wrist watch. "I must leave soon."

The water in the fountain looks soft as it rises and turns over on itself, the sun sparkling through it. Diego comes out again, while Raquel passes him on her way.

I don't like her, but at least she seems competent.

Ten minutes later, we get into a new Toyota Corolla. When I comment on it, Diego says, "Because our bank brings in desperately needed foreign capital, we are allowed to have one new car."

"So, most Cubans don't have a car?"

"Ha! Most Cubans don't even have enough food or clothing. I'm lucky, although I have worked hard to get these advantages."

We drive across the Plaza de la Revolucíon and enter a densely populated area. People move everywhere in the streets. Kids kicking soccer balls, elderly women carrying umbrellas for shade with big cigars in their mouths, and young men clumped on corners, sitting on folding chairs while listening to battered boomboxes. Salsa music echoes faintly among the walls like ghosts speaking from the past.

Diego glances up at the rearview mirror. "We're being followed. That green car looks like a government car." He drives faster. "We're only a block off the Malecon." He points out the window to the right.

"The road that runs along the edge of the Caribbean?" I remember the map of Havana. The city sits on the north side of Cuba on a long bulge of land that thrusts into the ocean. The Malecon, a four-lane road, runs like a wide belt around the bulge of land from one end of the city to the other, separating it from the water.

I turn to Diego to tell him how beautiful it is but stop while I study him. Diego's face relaxes, and he looks like he's enjoying this ride. What is his story? On the surface, he seems jolly, but I detect hints of intrigue and survivor skills. I've noticed that he seldom makes eye contact with me.

Meanwhile, the humid air, the ocean, the palm trees bending with the wind to wave the car forward, and the yellow sun splashing on ancient stones give me the illusion of peace. After all, we're still being followed.

The road curves around the city to the left. We pass several old American cars, still running thanks to Cuban ingenuity and homemade parts. Most are convertibles filled with tourists.

"We call those old cars 'rolling museums,'" Diego says. He takes a sharp turn onto Avenida Paseo and drives into a residential area of broad lawns, spreading magnolia trees, and large white mansions covered with orange tile roofs. Turning right on Calle 17, we come to a small park covered by a carpet of grass set among the mansions.

"Why are we stopping?"

Diego frowns. "We have to play the role." He glances in the rearview mirror to demonstrate his point. "This is a stop all visitors to Cuba make."

Near the sidewalk I see a bronze park bench with a man sitting at one end. A flamboyant tree spreads over him, dropping pink petals on the bench. The man is a life-size bronze statue of John Lennon, hair to his shoulders, legs crossed while he rests his left arm on the back of the bench, as if he were inviting friends to sit next to him and talk about how he wrote "Strawberry Fields."

We get out of the car, Diego reaches for his Panama hat, and we stroll toward the statue. When I stop before the bench, Diego urges me, "Go ahead."

I glance to both sides and sit down, slightly embarrassed. Lennon's head tilts toward me, ready to laugh about the absurdities of life, while John peers through oval wire-rimmed glasses.

The moment feels unreal. The pleasant scent of flowers surrounds us, and the statue is so lifelike it makes me uncomfortable. Yet I want to remain there, a small cocoon amidst the noisy city, inviting me to relax and be at peace, but it doesn't work. I feel anxious to get moving again.

Diego laughs and turns to face the park. "See all the lovers here? This is our 'privacy.'"

"Privacy?" I notice the couples lying on blankets. "Aren't you afraid of the government spies?"

Diego frowns. "There's fear, of course, but now there's also more anger. The government's reality looks different from our reality. It's like we're all wearing glasses with the wrong prescription." He glances backward. The men from the government car are following us.

Twenty minutes later, Diego parks a block away from the Almacenes San Jose market. The streets bustle with people and tourists recently disgorged from two buses idling near the entrance.

I follow him across old train tracks embedded in the street toward the front doors. Several antique rail cars guard the entrance, including an old steam engine. Made of tan sandstone, the building is three stories tall with several cloudy windows along the sides.

At the door there are guards, but I wedge us into a clot of tourists who burst past the security before we can be questioned.

Inside, an immense two-story warehouse spreads out. Steel trusses support the second floor above, while the large windows admit dull sunlight. I recognize a market like so many I've seen all over the world. Noisy and crowded, with intriguing smells that lead us from one stall to the next.

It looks like hundreds of artists show here. Paintings, t-shirts, toys, ceramics, wood carvings, and several food kiosks occupy row after row of space. Much of it is simply tourist trinkets, but I spot some very fine art also. "How will we find Diaz?" I ask.

Diego shakes his head. "This isn't the Louvre. We'll stop at the office over there."

I follow him to a tiny cubicle occupied by two men, a low desk, and stacks of paper. Diego introduces us. One of the men speaks English.

"We look forward to more open trade," the first man tells me. He has a mouthful of golden teeth.

I shake his hand and say, "I'm representing several businesses, including medicines, agriculture, art products, and even cement. All of these are exempt from the U.S. embargo." I stretch the facts a little.

Without drawing attention to Rodolfo Diaz, Diego asks for a directory. The man removes a stiff board hanging from the wall and hands it to Diego. After scanning the curled pages, Diego says thanks and we leave.

Diego strolls among the endless aisles. He nods at some people, waves, and says hello to others. He tells me, "One thing Fidel and the Revolution did right was to support the arts. Of all kinds. Dance, music, painting, sculpture. All kinds. Although there are few opportunities to sell, at least we Cubans can enjoy our wonderful art."

I have trouble walking as slowly as Diego. From stall to stall, we check the name of the artist whose work is displayed. How long will this take to cover the entire building? I'm growing impatient. I raise my phone to take photos until Diego stops me. "Careful," he warns, speaking out of the side of his mouth.

Then I begin to notice Diego's plan. His feigned friendliness conceals a calculated effort to find Diaz without attracting unwanted attention. I slow my pace to match his and even understand much of the Spanish spoken to us.

We stop at random stalls while Diego introduces me. I play my part as an earnest trade representative. Look serious, nod several times, smile, and pretend to take notes on my phone.

After forty-five minutes, Diego stops at a coffee kiosk and orders for us. He sips slowly and talks softly. "Two men behind us on the left, about fifty feet back. When we finish, we'll duck between the sides of this stall to come out on the far aisle. It won't get rid of them, but it will buy us some time."

Glancing behind us, I see the man with the big nose from the air-port. Following Diego, I slip between the canvas wall of a stall selling body lotion and fragrant soaps. We pop out on the parallel aisle, and Diego repeats the tedious work of meeting artists.

Glancing behind us, Diego steps into a narrow kiosk. Large paint-ings of pop stars hang on the walls: Marilyn Monroe, Bob Marley, and of course, Elvis Presley. Diego drops his voice and speaks to a man with mahogany-colored skin. "I want two for Olodumare and five for Ellegua. They're always lucky."

The man turns to the corner and comes back to slip something into Diego's hand as if they're doing a drug deal. "I recommend Ye-maya." Then the artist nods and points to the end of the aisle.

"What was that about?" I ask as we hurry along the stalls.

Diego whispers, "Our secret religion, Santeria. Can't talk now."

We reach a series of more stalls, each of them displaying huge paintings in vivid colors. Many of the subjects are Revolutionary images, many are of beautiful women, but there are mostly portraits of sad peo-ple. It's beautiful work, and I'm impressed.

I look up to find the name Rodolfo Diaz printed on a sign above his kiosk. Finally, Diego actually came through for me. The stall is crammed with paintings of excellent quality, but Diaz is not here.

Diego steps next door and talks to that artist for a long time. I wait and check out the aisle behind us. The two secret police have found us again. They come at us quickly. Putting his arm around my shoulder, Diego hustles me away from Diaz's stall toward the back side of the building. We hurry outside into the hot sun, keep walking until we find the shade of a palm tree, and stop. I don't see anyone following us.

"The artist next to Diaz told me something very troubling." Diego looks back over my shoulder.

"Where is he?"

"Like many Cubans, he has two jobs to make ends meet. He's also a scientist at the Cuban Neuroscience Center, CNEURO, lab here in Havana."

"Never heard of it."

"It's a research and production program dedicated to neurosci-ences, especially the development of technology and new drugs. It was founded in 1969 as one of the first facilities in the world to use informatics for the analysis of the brain's electrical activity. Fidel wanted to incubate some of the best scientists in the world. He considered the work done there so important, the CNEURO lab reports directly to the Council of State. That's our highest governing body in the country."

"So what?"

"When the attacks on the American diplomats happened, the CNEURO scientists were the first to analyze the cases."

"The lab studied the Havana Syndrome?"

"Yes."

"And Diaz is a scientist there." The coincidence can't be stronger. "So, where the hell is he?"

Diego whispers hoarsely, "The artist in the stall next to Diaz said he's been missing for three weeks."

In 2016 The Senate Intelligence Committee subpoenaed the director of the University of Pennsylvania Center for Brain Injury and Repair, Dr. Coretta Banfield, to testify about her analysis of the Havana Syndrome victims' symptoms. She appeared before the committee with a retinue of assistants, assuring that her testimony would be taken seriously.

Between sips of water and repeated frowning, Dr. Banfield said, "Clearly, it was an electromagnetic pulse generation and/or a hypersonic sound generation that utilized the architecture of the skull to create an energetic amplifier or lens to induce a cavitational effect to do damage."

"Can you tell us what weapon caused it?" the senator from Florida asked.

Dr. Banfield looked behind her and scanned her row of assistants, all of whom lowered their heads. She turned back to the committee. "I'm sorry, I don't know. We can't even speculate about that."

—*Journal of the American Medical Association*, 2018

Chapter Eleven

Pete Chandler
Saturday afternoon. Seven days left

Waiting for Diego back at the hotel, I call Sonnenfeld on the Sectera Edge. He answers immediately. "I've got good news and bad news." I talk fast. "Diego's finally moving forward, but when we went to the artist's market, we couldn't find Diaz. He's been missing for weeks."

"Damn. And the good news?"

"He works full time as a scientist at the Cuban Neuroscience Center, with the scientists who initially analyzed the Havana Syndrome. That can't be a coincidence."

Sonnenfeld is silent for a long time. "Yes, there's definitely a connection between the artist and the Havana Syndrome. He's our guy. The one who sent the code."

"By the way, you told me I can trust Diego and this other woman, Raquel Sanchez?"

"Yes. We've vetted both of them." He takes a breath.

"Diego set up an appointment for us at the CNEURO labs. I'll pretend I'm investigating trade opportunities. And I'll see if I can find the artist there."

In the lobby, a group of tourists come toward me. They're laughing and when they spot me, they wave.

"Isn't it great the president will be here?" The middle-aged man wears a golf shirt and a baseball cap with "Astros" written on it. His face is flushed. "I've never seen so many reporters in one place before. They're from all over the world."

"Yeah, it's a big deal."

I walk outside to wait for Diego and notice two men dressed in green army fatigue uniforms. They look at me carefully. Tailing me.

A half hour later, we're back in Diego's Toyota, driving west to reach the CNEURO headquarters. The Malecon ends, but the road still parallels the ocean. We pass by vacant lots of rubble, potholes, and dead cars. Another billboard urges Cubans to *Vaya al Futuro con Fidel!* Go into the future with Fidel!

"Sorry we couldn't go to the lab immediately," Diego apologizes, "but this is Cuba. It was difficult to even get an appointment for today. I reminded them you are an American trade rep, looking for new opportunities for importation of medical devices."

I shrug, getting used to the slow pace here.

Green plants grow in profusion along the streets. Mahogany and cedar trees, fruit trees bearing mangos, and cup-of-gold vines that curl around every vacant corner of the buildings like groping fingers. Warm air returns, along with the usual humidity.

Diego interrupts my thoughts. "We are in luck. Remember I told you Raquel Sanchez worked as a lawyer? She told me there is a scientist there whom Raquel represented many years ago. When I made contact with him, he refused to talk with us."

"So, what's the luck?"

"Raquel called him. I don't know what she said, but now he will meet with us. Of course, we must meet with the director of the facility first and talk about trade to maintain your cover."

"I hate being dependent on such flimsy plans."

Diego glances at me. "Now you're getting a taste of life in Cuba."

In ten minutes Diego drives into a quiet neighborhood of office buildings. To me it resembles a suburban office park in the U.S. I'm surprised at how modern they look. Steel frames with large glass windows, parking lots surrounded by flowering bushes. "I feel like I'm at home," I say.

After checking his rearview mirror, Diego turns onto Avenida 25 and enters a parking lot of a three-story building covered in bright blue glass panels. "I told you Fidel spared no expense in this 'scientific pole' area. It's our own Silicon Valley."

"Impressive."

"It's rumored that Raul Castro has a mansion near here."

We leave the Toyota in the lot and walk around a row of trimmed bushes and under a carport to the sliding glass door in the front, flanked by beautiful stone walls. Other cars pull up underneath the overhang to unload men and women wearing white lab coats. A low wall surrounds the entire facility, but there isn't any military presence or outside guards. But there are more cameras than palm trees.

I follow Diego inside, where the sharp slap of cold air conditioning surprises me, rare for most buildings in Cuba. A sleek counter blocks our way forward. Diego talks to the security people and waits for several minutes. We're both required to show identification.

I notice about a half dozen Chinese men enter the lobby. Dressed in business suits, they all carry cameras. When they reach the guard, they are waved through quickly and disappear behind an opaque glass door into the facility.

One of the guards motions us to move to the side of the counter. He asks us to bend forward and spread our arms over the top.

"I'm an American diplomat." I don't move.

"Sorry, sir, but it is our requirement," the guard says.

Diego looks over at me and nods. I still don't obey. I notice cameras hanging from every corner, their black eyes capturing everything, and I feel claustrophobic.

A few minutes later, a man in a lab coat comes through a door from behind the security desk. He takes long steps, stops before us, and shakes Diego's hand. After being introduced to me, he shakes my hand also. It's damp with a firm grip. He waves to the guard, and we walk into the facility.

"Welcome to our headquarters and laboratories, Mr. Chandler. I'm Comrade Director Litchenko. We are encouraged that the U.S. is interested in our products. You will find that our research is excellent, and we produce some of the finest quality medical drugs. After all, we have scientists working here from all over the world. Except the U.S." His smile disappears quickly. "I understand that you have a connection to one of our scientists? Sergio de la Vaca."

Diego answers, "He is a friend of my associate, Miss Sanchez."

We follow Litchenko back through the side door into the lab. He's tall and walks awkwardly, as if his arms and legs are too long for his body and don't know where to go.

Diego asks him, "Litchenko is a Russian name?"

"Yes. My father came here when the Soviet Union helped Cuba in the '80s. He married a Cuban woman, and here I am. As you know, there are still many Russian scientists here, even though the Soviet Union officially left the island years ago."

Diego glances at me with hooded eyes. Something's wrong.

Litchenko leads us through several more locked doors. He speaks English. "We were founded in 1969 to diagnose and produce technology for brain disorders."

We cross through several labs where both men and women bend to their microscopes. Mostly young people, they stop to stare at the two strangers who pass by. I see lots of chrome, steel, and white plastic, with complicated tech machines resting on the tables. Even the air conditioning smells metallic. I'm impressed by what I see.

Litchenko continues, "We have some of the best neuroimaging technology in the world. For example, we have a neurostimulation device that seems to be successful against depression."

After the tour, Litchenko brings us to a spacious office on the second floor. He offers coffee and pastries. We all sit around a long, low table. Various science magazines lay on the top. Diego begins by explaining how the bank could help finance American trade projects.

"We look forward to that possibility," Litchenko says. "We have many investors from around the world. Today, we are hosting a contingent of Chinese businessmen."

For almost an hour, I field questions about pricing, quotas, which products are allowed under the embargo, particularly medical devices, distribution networks, and manufacturing possibilities. I exhaust the material Sonnenfeld coached me to say but fake it for another fifteen minutes. Sweat dampens my sides, and I run my hand over my forehead. What if this guy asks more questions? But then, it appears I've convinced Litchenko. He leans back in his chair, arms crossed over his chest. He's finished.

Carefully, I ask, "Can we meet any of your scientists here?" I feel Diego stiffen next to me.

Litchenko purses his lips. Shakes his head. "That would be difficult, Mr. Chandler. We welcome your business opportunities, but with our security, you know." He nods, assuming I understand and agree. "Besides, they're on the third floor, which is difficult to reach from here."

If it were up to me, I'd keep pushing. A good investigator doesn't stop at the word "no." Diego shifts uncomfortably in his chair. I give it one more shot. "It would be important to be able to tell our American business executives we had actually talked to your scientists."

"You're in my country now. We must follow protocol." Litchenko lowers his voice and looks at the ceiling, as if to remind me and Diego of the cameras and microphones. "Wait here." He excuses himself and leaves the room.

I look at Diego and whisper, "What's he hiding?"

"Be careful."

Reluctantly, I sit back in the chair. This isn't the way I'll try to find Diaz.

Comrade Litchenko returns and says quickly, "I am very busy and must end our meeting. It has been productive, and we will remain in contact, Mr. Chandler. My assistant will show you out."

We wait for fifteen minutes. No one comes for us. I stand and look around. Litchenko said the scientists are on the third floor. When I see a white coat hanging in the corner, I get the idea. I slip into the coat and start for the door. Diego hisses behind me, "Don't."

When I turn into the hall outside the room, I'm near an elevator. I step into it and press the button for three. I'm alone but figure if I'm stopped, I can always bluff my way out with my Spanish.

Turns out Litchenko lied about getting to the third floor. It's easy. I find an open space with labs and equipment set up along the outside walls. Several desks clog the middle of the room. About ten people are bent over microscopes or computer terminals. I know I don't have much time before it's discovered I'm missing downstairs. Walking up to a young woman, I ask her in Spanish if Rodolfo Diaz has an office here.

"Yes." She points to the back corner. "Second on the left." She hesitates for a minute. "But—"

She doesn't say anything more and drops her head to her work. I hurry to the corner. There are four offices in a line; the third one is empty. I find a small plaque which says "Dr. Diaz." I turn the knob and step into the deserted office.

There's a wooden chair, a clean desk, and a computer table next to the desk with a black laptop resting on it. Silence and dust settle around me. On the wall are a few framed photos of a man with his family and a dog. It must be Diaz. I pull off one photo and pocket it. Trying to open each drawer, I find them all locked. Time ticks away while I fumble around.

I glance out the small window into the hall but don't see anyone.

Back at the desk, I pull out the Kronos electric lock pick gun that Sonnenfeld gave me. It looks harmless. A metal tube with a pointed, thin screwdriver attached to the end. Placing the point in the first lock, I activate the gun. It vibrates violently but finally, the drawer pops open.

A small stack of papers rests on the bottom, and I lift them. Scanning them, I find receipts for groceries, a parking permit, and what looks to be an instruction paper for some equipment. My Spanish isn't good enough to interpret it, so I take photos. There's nothing else in the drawer.

I glance into the hall again. Quiet.

Using the lock pick gun, I hit all the other drawers. Most are empty, and what few things I find are worthless to me. This isn't the desk of a working scientist. Someone must've cleaned out anything critical before I got here.

I hear voices in the hall, and I duck underneath the window behind the door. The voices pass me slowly and disappear to the left. When I stand and look out, the hall is empty. But I've wasted lots of time here. At the last minute, I lift the keyboard of his computer. There's a folded piece of yellowed paper. I open it and see what appears to be a schematic diagram. I don't understand it, but the fact that it was hidden makes it important to me. It goes into my pocket.

Hurrying back to the second floor, I stop to catch my breath before the reception room where Diego remains. I open the door and find Litchenko standing with a scowl on his face. Diego cringes in the corner, looking sick.

Litchenko glares at me. "Who are you?"

With my arms out to the sides, I assure him, "I told you, Director."

"Why are you sneaking around in my facility?"

"I decided to check things out myself. Now I can tell my government that it is an excellent operation." I smile, hoping he'll fall for this.

His face colors red. "You and your friend will remain here until I can get security up here. There is much you have to answer for." He gives me another hard look and leaves with his lab coat flapping around his legs.

Diego's voice is low. "I warned you. What will my family do when I don't come home tonight?" His face dampens with sweat.

"You're going home. Come on." I grab his arm and pull him to the door.

"You don't understand. After Litchenko brings his guards, they'll call the secret police."

"We won't be here." I wrench the door open and pull him behind me. At the lobby, it looks like we've beaten Litchenko, since the guards wave us out.

Within five minutes, we're outside. Diego runs to his car. Once we get there, he looks up at the building. "That was very foolish. And dangerous."

"I've been in worse spots before. Will Litchenko come after us?"

Diego drops his head. "I don't know. Most of the Russians don't get along with Cubans, so maybe he'll let this go. And there are rumors."

"What?"

"Oh, that the Russians are returning quietly and setting up spy networks around the island." He moves closer to me and pushes his finger into my chest. "You must be more careful. You can't be a cowboy here." He looks at the paper I found again. "I've got an idea. Hopefully, I can get an internet connection." He calls someone on his phone. Tries two more times before he has a brief conversation and tells me, "Sergio, Raquel Sanchez's former legal client, is willing to meet with us at his next break. He will meet us around the back side of the facility."

Once again, Diego surprises me. In spite of his fear, he comes through better than I thought he would, and I'm impressed. I survey the parking lot. People come and go, so it's impossible to pick out anyone following us, but I assume they're lurking around. We start a leisurely stroll along the sidewalk, then duck between a thick stand of sea grapes to follow a narrow path behind the building.

No one follows us. We wait for a long time. Then a single door in the building opens, and a small black man approaches us. He wears a lab coat that's too big for him. Without saying anything, he passes us, leading us into deeper cover underneath the dark blue pine trees at the edge of the property before he stops and turns to face us. We're surrounded by the pungent smell of pine needles.

"Sergio de la Vaca," he introduces himself. He doesn't offer his hand to shake. "This must be quick. I owe Mrs. Sanchez a lot, so I agreed to meet you." He glances back at the building. Sergio begins. "I know the man you're looking for, Rodolfo Diaz."

"Can we talk with him?" I ask.

"Uh, no." Sergio's shoulders twitch.

Diego asks, "What does Diaz do here?"

"He is part of the team that investigated these incidents about the American diplomats in January, what Americans call the 'Havana Syndrome.' The team consisted of neuroscientists, physicians, and physicists. They interviewed witnesses, inspected the buildings, and ran some experimental tests with our own sonic equipment."

"What did he discover?" Diego asks.

Sergio's shoulders drop. "Not much, I'm afraid. Rodolfo told me they tested audible sounds. But to inflict damage to humans, it would have to be very loud, therefore heard by everyone. That was not the case. They tried infrasound waves, that is, below the hearing range of humans. That's hard to focus on one person and would require giant speakers. Then they tried ultrasound that could be focused, but it dissipates quickly. None of these would cause any damage to humans."

"But clearly, something happened to those people," I remind him. "And whatever caused it is dangerous."

Sergio adds quickly, "He did not find evidence of Cuban government involvement. My question: are radical American politicians creating a fake crisis? Something to crush Cuba?"

I start to wave my hand to dismiss the idea. But maybe he's got a point. There are lots of crazy people in both countries.

"You know that Mrs. Sanchez saved my life. To be black in Cuba, there are many doors closed to you. I was in despair and committed a crime. She defended me, helped me to avoid prison. I owe her my life." He nods and continues, "I returned to school, and here I am today."

I pull out the paper I found underneath Diaz' laptop and show it to Sergio.

He studies it and looks up. "It's old. This is strange, but I don't recognize what it is. I will study this further." He takes a photo with his phone.

"Can you help us meet Dr. Diaz?" I ask. "We must make contact."

Sergio starts walking back to the door.

"Sergio, what's wrong?"

He stops abruptly. "Rodolfo Diaz has been missing for three weeks. And whatever he uncovered, I fear the worst for him." Sergio opens the door and disappears inside.

Diego and I retrace our steps between the bushes and jog across the parking lot to reach his car. Two guards at the front door spot us and come toward us.

"Shit. I knew we should've gotten out of here earlier," Diego yells at me. We both run for the car. When he rounds the front, he stops and screams.

I hurry to his side, feel his shoulders shaking. On the ground beside the driver's door, a decapitated turtle lies on its back in a pool of dark, wet blood, its left leg still twitching. Diego gasps and stumbles backward like someone smashed him in the chest.

"What the hell is that?" I look back at the lab and see the guards leap over the low bushes, running toward us.

"Get out of here. Now!" Diego shouts. His face glistens with sweat, and he steps carefully around the turtle and jumps into the driver's seat. With the engine racing, he guns it out of the lot.

Chapter Twelve

Ava Alvarez
Saturday afternoon. Seven days left

The high-level meeting at the headquarters of the Dirección General de Inteligencia (DGI) began late, at eleven. This has been my working home for years. Our agency is tasked with gathering intelligence, espionage, and counterintelligence disinformation. I sit among twenty other officers waiting for our assignments. The American president is scheduled to visit Havana in less than a week. I try to act calm, but I'm more scared about what's going to happen than I've been since I was first recruited for the secret police. I look around and wonder how many of these officers are in on the plot. It smells like too many men in a closed space.

We meet in the old green building with blue shutters that served as the first headquarters of the secret police. Over the years, the facility spread across many blocks to encompass one of the largest campuses of the Cuban government.

The interior is constructed to the highest degrees of security and furnished with all the up-to-date technology available. From the start of the Revolution, Fidel himself stopped by many times a week.

Still, it's dull, metallic, and reeks of stale Communist bureaucracy. The walls are pea green, and the only art are portraits of the heroes of the Revolution. Once I attained sufficient rank, I refused to office here.

I fidget in the hard plastic seat. Tom called and told me he's finally working on "my project." And then there's the top-secret report from my agents embedded in Miami, which I read last night.

The "chatter" is up again among dissident groups about invading the island. Of course, that kind of talk has swirled around the Cuban-American colony since Fidel kicked them all out in the 1960s and confiscated their capitalist thefts of property. So many crazy ideas since then have never turned into action. Still, in my experience, I listen to everything.

Our commanding officer, Captain Alfredo Mendoza, interrupts my thoughts. "Comrades, we are continuing to cooperate with the chief of the Revolutionary Armed Forces to assist in the security measures when the president arrives on Thursday for a series of events that culminates seven days from now at the Grand Theater." He's wearing a full dress uniform, resplendent with ribbons on his full chest. "It's a momentous opportunity for us to show the world the success of the Revolution." There is vigorous applause from the crowd.

"It is a great honor that you have brought to our agency," the captain's adjutant shouts. He can always be counted on to suck up to his boss, which is why he got the job in the first place. I hate these people. Of course, Captain Mendoza is the worst of all of them.

He's tall for a Cuban and handsome. In his younger years, he had a beautiful smile and thick black hair with a few curls that fell across his forehead. Like a lot of men, he worked his way up the ranks while, at the same time, working his way through most of the females on the staff. Except me.

Mendoza raises his chin. "Yes, thank you. As I detailed in the operating papers, Form 237, the president will visit a *paladar* for dinner after he arrives on Thursday, tour the Hemingway house on Saturday morning, and then give his final speech at the Grand Theater that afternoon. Then it's off to a ball game and meetings with our esteemed leaders. The transfers between events will pose the greatest threats for us. Some personnel will be assigned to each of the locations the president will visit. As for the rest of us, our strength has always been to find the subversives and traitors to the Revolution before they can become a true threat and disrupt this important, historic occasion."

Comrade Officer Mata says, "As the chief liaison officer with the American Secret Service, I can report ongoing success. They are very demanding, but our security agencies are working to complete the mission."

I almost get up and walk out. It's hard to sit still, knowing all that I must do. But right now, I don't have any clues to follow up. So, I may as well stay and see what I can learn here.

The captain ignores him. "We will spare no expense or effort in our mission. I will not risk my command for any of your mistakes." He glares at the group. Most officers in the audience nod in agreement.

My fingers explore absentmindedly through my short hair. It's gone steel gray but remains a symbol of the sacrifice of my femininity for the sake of the cause. I wear an olive green fatigue uniform like everyone else in the room, polished jump boots included.

I've programmed my cell phone to vibrate when the call comes in with official updates. I cross and recross my legs. Waiting.

I don't have any problem accepting the luxuries that come with my position. Like a cell phone that has service all the time—unlike ninety-eight percent of other Cubans. But then, they don't deserve the perks I enjoy. Most of them are lazy, undisciplined, and have gone soft after Fidel's revolution matured throughout the years. Now, people just get drunk and dance in the streets.

Like the discovery of the planet Neptune, when scientists noticed the irregular behaviors of Uranus but couldn't see the new planet, I've detected odd "data warps" in my security network. A dangerous force is out there, but I can't see it clearly yet.

At first, I thought of reporting to Captain Mendoza. But his high-level connections are suspect. What if he's in on the plot? So, I go forward on my own. The threat is extraordinary, which requires me to take extraordinary risks.

"Here are the assignments." The captain's voice rises, and the murmuring around the room falls silent. "Obredor, you will provide back-up security to the army at the airport. Jimenez, you will scout the motorcade route into the city. Do not overlook anyone, and use whatever force you must to get the information we need. Alvarez, you meet the president's party at every *paladar* they eat at. Castro, your assignment is to do surveillance at the Grand Theatre every day."

One of the few Russians still allowed in the secret police, Anatoly, raises his hand. "My assignment?"

The captain frowns. "Yes, yes." He lifts a laptop from the desk beside him and swipes his finger across the screen. "You will scout the area on Paseo de Marti, especially the bus station. It is only one block from the Grand Theatre. I want you there twenty-four hours a day." He pauses to light a cigarette. A gray cloud circles his head.

"Yes, sir."

I arrived at my office early in the morning and picked up the files of new intelligence reports. Now they nestle between the daily security reports and all the informer networks, bulging the sides of my old leather briefcase. I have to get through all of them today. Mundane, for the most part. Not the excitement of years past, when I was still protecting the gains made by the Revolution, ferreting out the traitors, and cleansing the island of the last of the pigs who opposed Fidel and progress.

Last night, I received more intelligence about the American. I paid close attention. Most curious was the fact he visited CNEURO. That couldn't be a coincidence. I immediately instructed my trusted officer, Ricardo Pena, to go to the lab and interview the director. Pena reported the American was looking for trade opportunities, which I still question. What is Chandler really doing here, and how should I handle it?

Can he be a foreign resource for the Cuban traitors? Or for some other reason? But the timing of his arrival coordinates with what I expected.

"Okay, comrades." Mendoza's voice is deep but scratchy from all the smoke he's swallowed over the years. "Our department has never failed when called upon to defend the Revolution."

I look around the group. Eyes glaze over; a few heads bow. Most don't believe a thing about the Revolution anymore or even remember it. But underneath, I know each of them is spying on one another.

The meeting breaks up as people shuffle to the cafeteria for the morning coffee break. I follow, folding the paper Mendoza handed out detailing the president's itinerary. Of course, we've all been working off that for months in our planning. Since I discovered the plot against the president, I've tried to figure out where it might occur. So far, I still don't know.

"*Mi corderita,* my lamb." The hoarse voice of the captain comes softly from behind me. Close to my ear, which makes me cringe. "Your uniform fits you like a glove."

Nevertheless, I turn with a smile plastered on my face. "Alfredo. Nice talk. The troops admire you."

"I have dinner plans which include the very best grass-fed beef from Argentina. Difficult for anyone but me to obtain. You will join me?" He sips papaya juice.

I lean briefly into his outstretched arm. When I smell the overpowering stink of too many cigarettes, my body clenches. "Oh, I would love to, but I must execute my duties. I am very busy." When he tries to kiss my cheek, I squirm away. I fantasize about kicking my boot into his crotch to finally convince him to stay away.

From the outside, Alfredo appears relaxed and nonthreatening. But I know he's a cunning and fierce fighter when he's cornered, like the wild pigs who ravage the island. He can still be dangerous to me. As I look at him, my mind spins. His outward appearance would be the perfect cover for him. Who'd ever suspect Mendoza of masterminding such an audacious plot to destroy Cuba? And he certainly is ambitious and ruthless enough to carry it out. Keeping a straight face, I hide my disgust for him: a lazy, lapsed revolutionary.

He scowls at my resistance. "I know how you got your position here, but Fidel's gone. We're sinking in bureaucracy now, and that has to change. A new day's coming for Cuba and for DGI." The tone of his voice carries an obvious warning.

What does he mean by "a new day for Cuba"?

For a moment, I feel a touch of pride to still be attractive enough to engage men's attention, even someone like the captain. Should I play along with him for information? It's too disgusting to contemplate but could be helpful for me.

Could Alfredo be part of a "new day for Cuba"? The present leadership has been seduced by the glittering of the beaches at Varadero and all the easy money flowing into their corrupt pockets from the European tourists. In order to protect those gains and keep the lid on any protests, the rulers tightened security everywhere. So, there are constantly new subversive movements percolating around the island. Is this what Alfredo means? As I often do when I'm at a difficult crossroad, I think about what Fidel would do.

I was eighteen when I first met El Comandante backstage at the Tropicana. Gloria Estefan, the Cuban/American singer, had finished her act. Fidel came back to welcome her to the island. Fidel noticed me and, in an odd way of introducing himself, shook my hand. His handshake was firm but not especially vigorous, and it seemed to be the hand of a man who spent his time behind a desk, not holding a machine gun.

His eyes captured me immediately. Luminescent, deep brown, and searching until they reached someplace inside of me. My breath caught and I tried to say something. He laughed at my nervousness and waved good-bye as he left.

A month later, a bearded soldier appeared at my small apartment. "You must come with me," he commanded. I stiffened and gripped the door frame, because in those days a knock on the door usually meant trouble. The man must have sensed my fear and said, "Don't worry. Fidel wants to meet you." That made me even more fearful.

We began an affair that lasted for a few years. Always at the last minute, clandestine, and in different houses around Havana. Besides the sex, I came to love and worship this unusual man. I even left my dancing to follow him.

As he promised, Fidel helped me. He placed me in a high position in the DGI, the secret police. They trained me, and I found skills and a determination to do whatever it took to protect the Revolution and Fidel. I brought the same discipline and hard work to the new job that I had learned dancing at the Tropicana.

Though he's gone now, I never imagined what the outcome of my brief affair with Fidel would be, but it transformed me, gave me a higher purpose.

Now, I face Alfredo, a dangerous piece of ox dung compared to Fidel. "Oh, Alfredo, you know I'll always be attracted to you," I purr. "Perhaps I won't be able to keep up with a bull like you in bed." I laugh and watch his face relax as he falls for the fake praise.

He winks and smiles with yellowing teeth. "I know you're the woman who successfully recruited the American spy, Ana Montes. Still one of your most illustrious successes."

I feel a surge of pride but don't show it. "Thank you."

"Seventeen years, wasn't it?"

"Yes." I tilt my head back, remembering how I ran the most notorious spy for all those years. "She worked as an intelligence analyst in the U.S. Defense Department."

"You were her control."

"She fed me secrets about American defense workers, defense strategies, and gave us advanced listening platforms."

"Unfortunately, Montes was exposed and arrested." His expression changes, and it worries me. "All traitors are eventually caught." His voice drops to a whisper.

I stare into his eyes. "But never forget, Alfredo, decisive action and ruthlessness are most important."

He doesn't respond at first. His jaw clenches. "I appreciate the agents you run within the U.S., but I also suspect you've been working on something new—something you're not authorized to do."

My body shivers, and I try hard to not let it show. "I'm very busy with many assignments, as you know."

His soft eyes poke around my face. "Be very careful, *mi corderita*."

Wiping the crumbs of the pastry from my hands, I turn to leave. Alfredo's never been subtle with his words. Now, I want to get away.

Outside of the headquarters, my driver brings the car around and I get in. Air conditioning cools the interior. I head for my private office. In front of it, I pass a Soviet SU-100 tank stationed on the front lawn. Legend says that Fidel himself sank a U.S. ship by firing the tank's cannon during the failed invasion of the Bay of Pigs in 1961.

From the underground garage, I climb up one floor to pass through a reception hall on the first floor. It's been converted to a museum of the Revolution. I feel the lack of air conditioning immediately, but in many ways, I feel most comfortable here. Nearby a table displays pieces of shrapnel, old rifles, some cryptic battle notes written by Fidel Castro, and even the broken remains of Che Guevara's pipe still packed with tobacco.

I ride the elevator to the top floor and hurry past life-size photos of Fidel and his brothers, Raul and Che, before reaching my expansive office. Two male secretaries hunch over their desks. Both salute me. I glance out the windows overlooking the old city with its orange-tiled roofs reflecting the dull shine of the sun.

I can't wait any longer. Calling the officer in charge of the American's investigation, I demand an update.

"Sorry, comrade. Reports are slow in coming." He hangs up.

I remember Tom and his girlfriend. If this will motivate Tom to get back in the labs and continue his work, it's a simple thing to do.

When I call, Lucinda says hello. I explain how I can get her a job in the film industry. Although the Cuban film industry is very successful and renowned throughout Latin America, Lucinda certainly wouldn't qualify. "I will check with my friends and let you know."

Suddenly, I feel old and tired. Too many fights, and all the struggles, even though they were leavened with hope. I recall moments of joyous excitement. Victories. But now, the country is turning to a younger generation. Idiots like Lucinda. Even former heroes like Raul Castro became corrupt. Maybe it's already too late. *Comiendo un cable.* What a fucking tough day.

But then, I feel an old, familiar excitement rumble low in my body. One more time? This last mission will be all I can do to save my beloved country.

My work would be much easier with computer access, but the security in this office is abysmal. My home computer, in contrast, has been protected by some of Cuba's best experts.

I sip coffee that my assistant left. My cell phone vibrates like an excited cricket. When I set down the cup, coffee slops over the rim. "Yes?"

"Comrade Comandante." The agent's voice is strong. "Are you aware that we spotted the arrival of a Russian Improved Kilo II attack submarine outside the harbor?"

"What's it doing?" I sit up stiffly.

"It's just cruising back and forth. But it's being shadowed by an American Perry-class frigate."

The Americans are probably here because of the president's visit. Or is there a more sinister reason? Silence settles between us for a long time until the agent changes the subject.

"We've found a suspicious comrade. Antonio Lopez."

"Who's he?"

"He works at the Central Committee of the Communist Party. Almost by accident, our undercover agents heard him bragging about helping a friend on a secret plan that will shake the country."

"Anything else?"

"Remember, he works in the same department as Redbeard."

Everyone in the intelligence community knows Redbeard and his reputation. Is he behind the plot? Lopez might yield some valuable intelligence. In my position, I have authority to arrest and interrogate almost anyone except the top Cuban officials. I'll call my enforcer, Cortez, the big guy. I use him for these kinds of missions. I'll instruct him to do a pickup of Lopez and bring him to the basement.

My agent continues, "And we have new intel about the American, Chandler."

"Tell me."

"As you ordered, we've been following the American and the Cuban national, Diego Arnaz."

"Get to the point."

"Their destinations have been odd, to say the least." I hear paper rustling. "Their first stop was the art market, at the old train station. They remained there for approximately an hour and a half. Our agents followed them continuously until the two slipped out the back entrance."

"Idiots."

"But we picked them up the next day. They went to CNEURO."

"I know that."

He cleared his throat. "One of our agents followed them inside and later interrogated the director, an old Russian holdover."

"What did you find out?"

"When Chandler was in the facility, there was a period of time when he went into a restricted area without the director."

I thought for a long time. Then it struck me. I tell my agent, "The U.S. embargo does allow some trade in various products. For instance, the U.S. ships tons of meat here, and art can be exchanged, but not the export of our drugs."

"Then why did they go to CNEURO?"

My stomach rumbles again. Can he be a foreign resource for the Cuban traitors? Or is he here for some other reason? But it's the combination of his arrival at the art market and CNEURO that spikes my suspicions.

The University of Pennsylvania Center for Brain Injury and Repair produced a report signed by the director, Douglas Smith. They tested forty Havana Syndrome victims who showed tangible neurological changes that "are not like anything we've seen before," he said.

White-colored fatty substances commonly wrap around fibers in the brain to protect it. Advanced neuroimaging machines used by the center showed the volume of white matter in the victim's brains was significantly smaller than in healthy adults. Director Smith wrote, "It is clear something structural in the brain was affected, but we don't know what that is and what caused the effects."

—University of Pennsylvania Center for Brain Injury, 2017

Chapter Thirteen

Pete Chandler
Saturday afternoon. Seven days left

Four blocks away from the lab, Diego finally slows down. He breathes heavily and says, "Do you know what Santeria is?"

"I'm not sure."

"It's a widespread Cuban religion that involves hypnotic trances. People possessed by spirits not of this world."

"What?"

"It was imported by African slaves when they came to Cuba in the 1500s. The gods are called *orichas*. In some respects, it's like voodoo in Haiti. Of course, the Catholic church condemned it as witchcraft."

"So it's practiced secretly?"

"The government prohibited any practice of it until a few years ago. Even so, aspects of it are still shrouded in secrecy and rituals. Believers use music, dancing, chanting, with cigar smoking and rum, to create a trance-like state of mind as they ask an *oricha* to take possession of them, enabling them to communicate with their dead ancestors for help."

"You believe this stuff?"

Diego doesn't answer directly. "Cubans all understand it. To encourage communication, animal sacrifices are offered to the dead. The scary part is that sometimes, their extreme practices lead to violence and murder."

"Animals like turtles?"

"Birds, pigs, and yes, even turtles."

"What's the big deal?" The air conditioning vents shiver as they attempt to pump out cool air.

Diego licks his lips. When he looks over at me, he's got a strange expression on his face. He whispers, "It's a warning. It means someone very high up knows you are here, which makes your search much more complicated and dangerous than I imagined."

In spite of the air conditioning, I feel hot and claustrophobic again. The surveillance everywhere, guards, and intrigue make me twitchy. After all, it's just a damn turtle. Can I trust Diego's warning?

Diego drops me at the hotel and shoots off quickly. He assures me he will be back tonight with some suggestions. I can't sit still, so I ignore his warnings and walk into the old section of Havana, dodging tourists, and marveling at the preservation of buildings and the complicated mixture of cultures in Cuba that stretches back to the 1500s.

When I reach an open plaza, I look for a group of tourists. By embedding myself in the middle of them, I can block any long-distance shotgun mics that Cuban police may be using to overhear me. Their suntan lotion stinks, but the protection of the crowd is necessary.

I call Sonnenfeld on the Sectera Edge phone and report our failure to find Diaz.

"Um, this is becoming more difficult than I anticipated," Sonnenfeld says. "What's your next move?"

"I'm meeting with Diego tonight. At first I didn't trust him, but I've changed my mind, and he's courageous."

"I'm getting intel from several sources. Warnings. And with the presidential delegation arriving there in a few days, you need to get your job done and let us take over. Then you get the hell out."

I tell him about the dead turtle and what Diego explained about Santeria.

"What? You, of all people, should know to listen to the locals. If Diego's afraid, you should watch your back constantly."

As we talk, I rotate in different directions within the crowd to further block anyone trying to listen to us.

Sonnenfeld pauses for a long time, and I hear him mumbling to someone else. Finally, he comes back on the phone. "Uh, Chandler, I don't think we'll need to activate this option, but—"

"What option?"

"With the diplomatic passport you have, there shouldn't be any problems for you to get out of Cuba, in case things get too hot."

My chest tightens. "What the hell are you talking about?"

"Considering events there, we must plan a second exfiltration option for you."

"You don't have one?" He's made many promises to me; now I realize how few he's actually accomplished.

"Of course we do," he lies to me. "I'll get the details to you soon. From now on, to communicate, we will use Twofish, the symmetric encryption algorithms, for added security. It's already on your phone."

None of this reassures me.

"Don't worry. All you have to do is find Diaz." Sonnenfeld hangs up.

I look around the plaza, trying to spot the secret agent with the big nose, or anyone else. I'll have to rely on Diego even more than I want to.

I leave the crowd and head back to the hotel. I think of Janette and others, like Judd Crowe, who let me down or worse. Crowe led me into an unforgivable tragedy in Iraq that still haunts me. Maybe if I accomplish something here, I'll assuage the guilt.

The old yellow stone buildings seem to lean in toward me. Heavy. It adds to my sensation of entering a time warp, a crease in reality that allows me to glimpse what the past looked like seventy years ago and how great the city once was. All that antiquity is juxtaposed against the ultra-modern facility at CNEURO. The contrasts unsettle me.

I realize that Cuba is one of the few places on the globe that's immune to the passage of time. Even in the twenty-first century, technology has made almost no penetration into the country despite a few spots like the science labs. For the majority of Cubans, Zoom, artificial intelligence, video games, Instagram, sharing Google docs, and spreadsheets are passengers in time that missed a stop at the island.

But I'm coming to understand how Cubans, even under the harshest conditions, manage to live and work and enjoy life. I could learn something from them.

Back at the hotel, I find Diego waiting for me. He's still nervous. "I need to go back to the office before I leave you for the night."

I agree and get into the car with him. Turning to look at Diego, I feel my shoulders loosen. "I believe you about the turtle." I add a reassuring pat on his shoulder.

He nods but doesn't say anything, concentrating on the rush hour traffic. Then he sighs. "We were there for over two hours. I'm certain every move we made was observed. Someone would've had the time to plant the turtle."

"Litchenko?"

"No, someone much more powerful." He pauses, then continues, "Pete, I'm not sure I am the person to help you."

"Afraid?"

"You don't understand our life here. We are not as free as you. I hate this, but I can't change it."

"Got it."

"Now I'm the one who is sorry." He turns away from me.

"This has happened to me before."

Diego slows for the traffic and slaloms through a sea of Chinese bicycles, their bells pinging as people try to get ahead of one another.

"I understand if you want to drop out."

He glances at me and turns forward quickly. "I don't know."

"What can I do now?" I ask.

"I have to think about everything."

"I don't want you to quit."

Diego sighs again. "You have a very direct way about you, but also a passion for justice and hope for the future. Many Cubans stopped hoping."

He stops in front of his office. "Come with me. I have to drop off my notes and files." Diego leads me up the three flights of stairs to the bank office. Inside, he asks Connie Perez if Raquel is in. We find her in the office next to his. I follow the two of them to the outdoor courtyard. I put the Cicada transducer jammer on the table between us and turn it on, just to be careful.

Diego tells her about the lab and the turtle.

"No." Raquel's face blanches.

I still can't fully understand it. The warning is based on some ancient folk religion. But if it scares them, I will be more careful.

We all stop talking, sinking into our own thoughts for a while.

Finally, Sanchez removes her glasses and looks up at me. She doesn't smile. "I must be honest with you, Mr. Chandler. We are not happy with this development." She wears sandalwood perfume.

"Call me Pete. I'm sorry for you, but I have to find Diaz." Smiling broadly, I try to disarm her.

She nods but doesn't answer me for a few minutes. "This is not the way we usually work at the bank. I am the vice president of Personnel and Comrade Satisfaction."

"I don't want to get involved in anything more than finding the artist."

"Ha!" A forceful burst comes from deep in her body. Her eyes expand. "You don't understand the risks to us, Mr. Chandler. If we continue to help you, we must thread the needle between the threats your investigation has aroused and what you are looking for. Your 'mission' is putting us in a precarious spot and extreme danger."

"Why?"

"Navigating Communism is like walking on a cobblestone street in high heels. We try to act like we're moving gracefully, but in the end some of us twist our ankles and fall."

"But the consequences are far worse than a twisted ankle," Diego adds grimly.

"And you?" I ask Sanchez.

"I have, uh, problems from my past with the party, so I must be extremely careful."

Her expression tells me whatever the problem, it's serious. I lean forward. "Diego told me you were a former prosecutor."

"Yes." Her eyes cut across the space between us to find my eyes. "I came here as a child and became one of only a few of the new Communist women selected to attend law school. I have fought hard to get to where I am now. Almost all other lawyers are men. My entire life has been a struggle."

"Why did you quit that work?"

"Oh, *Maria, madre del Dio*, you don't know anything about us. It is typical of Yankees to think they can dominate us—"

"Wait a minute. I'm only here to find one person. Anything else, I don't care about."

She doesn't say anything as we both negotiate the silence between us. Sanchez shifts in the chair. "I loved my work as a lawyer, but like all other professions here in Cuba, it doesn't pay well. I'm able to get extra pay at the bank because it's affiliated with the U.S. Simple as that." She crosses her arms over her chest.

Diego tries to talk to Sanchez, but she ignores him.

"I'm impressed."

She sneers, "The Revolution taught us the greater good for the people was more important than the good for an individual."

"You believe that?"

"When I was a teenager, I was assigned to the state art school for Pioneers, promising young party members. I boarded in a coed dormitory, all of us dressed like soldiers. You can't imagine the smell." She raises her face. "My femininity was taken from me by the party. Female beauty, aloneness, and even our sense of self were all taken for the good of the party and the future of Cuba. We all believed it fiercely."

I don't know what to say. I lean back in my chair and feel her intensity.

Sanchez waves her hand in the air. "But you don't care about any of this."

I sense her anger and some hopelessness. "Do you still believe in justice here in Cuba?"

She stares into my eyes. "I don't believe it anymore. That's my point. Fidel promised a free and equal life where everyone shared and worked together. The Revolution would throw off the yoke of American imperialism and move us into a glorious future."

"And?"

"He lied."

The collapsing sun drops shadows in the silence between us.

I steal a glance at her. Although Raquel rarely smiles, she's attractive. Maybe more like oleander, whose lavender petals are incredibly beautiful yet is one of the most toxic plants on earth. And I've learned through painful experience to always be cautious.

Back at the hotel, I find a text from Karen. Her humor makes me laugh and, for a moment, lifts me from the discouragement I feel. Diego tells me he'll meet me at the rooftop bar since he has to park the car.

The concierge waves me over to his desk. "Sir, there was an officer of the secret police here, asking about you."

I frown. "Oh?"

"This is not good. Will you be staying with us much longer?"

"I hope not. What'd he look like?"

"Uniform, sharp nose, like he has Spanish heritage. His name is Comrade Captain Cardozo." He reads it off a business card and drops his voice to a whisper. "You must be very careful. He works for DGI and has ordered me to report on you, but if you don't stay too much longer here, I will stall him."

I nod and pass him some American dollars. "Thanks."

The sky darkens with threatening rain clouds coming in from the ocean. In contrast, the lights in the lobby shine golden against the walls. Taking the lift to the sixth floor, I enter the rooftop bar that stretches across the entire floor, open on three sides and covered with a reinforced blue canopy roof. It appears that no one followed me up here.

Silver cocktail shakers click with diamonds of ice. Lining the top of the bar, stemmed glasses brimming with daiquiris tempt the tourists.

"*Buenas tardes, señor.* May I help you?" a uniformed bartender offers. "Would you like a Hemingway daiquiri?"

"Uh—"

"All the tourists love them."

"Then I'll have a gin and tonic, extra lime." I take the sweating glass to a far table, and when the bartender turns around, I wand the area with my bug detector, which doesn't register anything. I still don't trust the location. I turn on the Cicada TinyTx transducer jammer in my pocket to effectively create a hushbox around me.

I look across the red- and orange-tiled roofs of the restored part of the city. Pushed by winds off of the ocean, storm clouds invade the ancient harbor, hiding Morro Castle behind them. The earthy smell of damp air surrounds me. I order another gin and tonic.

"I see you found the bar," Diego calls to me as he walks from the elevator. He pulls out a chair while he sets his Panama hat on the table. Grunting as he sits, he waves a waiter over to the table. "*Un Cuba Libre, por favor.* Did you know they were actually invented by American soldiers during the Spanish-American war?"

"No."

"Did I tell you I attended graduate school in Rhode Island?"

Since no one else is in the bar and with the protection of the Cicada jammer, I feel secure in telling Diego, "I want to talk about the investigation."

"Unlike most Cubans, I understand the Western ways of Americans."

I sit back in the chair, preparing for a long conversation. A small votive candle inside a translucent glass glows in the middle of the table. It lights up our faces from below, making us look grim. "I need to find Diaz or his home."

The waiter returns with a rum and Coke and places it on a small brown coaster on the table.

Even though we are sitting at the far side of the bar and the bartender disappears into the back, Diego whispers, "It's obvious that we have been compromised. Someone has done more than just follow us. I suggest we stop all activities for a week."

"No. Now we fight back."

Diego sighs.

"Can you find out where he lives?"

Diego turns the coaster to face me and says, "Here's your first lesson about our history."

I pick up the coaster, which profiles a strong human face, leaning forward from the shoulders as if looking into the future. A long feather extends from behind the head.

"That's Hatuey, an indigenous chief who fought against Spanish conquest. We consider him our first national hero." Diego nods. "Since all Cubans have some indigenous blood in them, we remember his bravery against oppression. Keep it as a souvenir."

I pocket the cardboard circle, wondering where Diego is headed with this story. Outside, the rain arrives with a sudden pounding rattle against the canvas roof. I need to get Diego back to the investigation. "Can Sanchez help us?"

"Yes. What do you think of her?"

I shrug. "Seems competent. All business."

"Did you know that she is supporting her husband's parents?"

"Why?"

"I'm not sure. Something serious from her past, I suspect, hushed up like so many things here. It's common for the children who can manage to get good jobs to help the parents who live on meager pensions."

I want him to focus. "I need to interview Diaz's family."

Diego scans the room, then looks at me. "Yes, but we must be more careful than before."

I thought about the turtle. "Do all Cubans practice Santeria?"

Diego looks closely at me. "Not formally, but many Cubans still play the *bolita* or *charada*. It is closely associated with Santeria."

"What's the *bolita*?"

Diego sets down his glass and rotates it in a circle on the coaster. "It's a national lottery, originally introduced by Chinese immigrants. Declared illegal after the Revolution, everyone still bets on it."

"The Chinese?"

"Yes. They brought a new world of numbers, symbols, fire dragons, red moons, and elephants with golden trunks."

"What the hell are you talking about, Diego?"

"The *charada* uses combinations of numbers that are associated with people, animals, things, and even dreams."

This information surprises me.

Diego's eyebrows become animated, as if he's a cartoon character. "You don't understand Cuban culture. All of us have a veneer of Western rationality. But underneath, we are like the Cuban stew, *ajiaco*. Everything is mixed together. All the different people who came to this island. It's created a unique conception of time and reality." Diego smiles. "Even Fidel, when he came down from the Sierra Maestra mountains to claim victory in the Revolution, changed from a green uniform to an all-white suit. Babalu's colors, the most powerful of the *orichas*."

The lights in the bar come on.

"I have studied in the United States," Diego tells me. "Western reality is square, bounded by rational thought, with nothing outside that square. Nothing else is even considered. But we see reality in a far larger sense, as it can break out of the usual boxes. And it's an incredibly powerful weapon to help us face life. Relying, to a degree, on the supernatural gives us inspiration and hope to go forward."

I apologize because I didn't realize the depth of their cultural beliefs or the suffering of even the privileged people. "Are there any problems with this?" Thunder rumbles after my words.

Diego's eyes float to the canopy above. "Who knows what happens in the darkness of these rituals conducted in hidden rooms? Violent crimes have certainly been committed." He waves the waiter away. "It's real to us, and that's what scares me about what happened at the lab."

What have I gotten myself into? Elephants with golden trunks, red moons, secret death rituals. Dead turtles. It's a crease in reality that gives me a peek at something deeper, dangerous and much more ominous.

The wind blows across the candle on the table. The flame twists to avoid its fate but is overwhelmed and flickers out.

Diego stands. "I must be going. Tomorrow, we look for Diaz' home."

"I want to go there tonight."

"There are various curfews we can't violate. We will go at first light tomorrow."

I step back reluctantly to let Diego pass by. He pauses and we exchange glances. His eyes are unusually soft, and I feel something pass between us. A shared melancholy? I find myself wanting to help him instead of the other way around.

I scoop up my tech gadgets and return them to my Faraday bag. Only a few tourists remain sitting on the high stools at the bar. We ride the lift down to the lobby. From the speakers in the ceiling, soft Cuban music contrasts with the noisy storm outside.

Diego takes a long time saying goodbye in a formal way so common in Latin countries. Finally, we lift umbrellas from a stand near the door and step outside into the night. "My car is over there." Diego points around the corner. I follow him, bending forward into the driving rain. Two black umbrellas camouflaged by the darkness. At the last minute, Diego remembers he left his hat in the rooftop bar.

"I'll get it," I offer and start across the street.

"No. You're a guest here." Diego tilts his umbrella over his shoulder against the wind and passes me in the street on his way toward the lobby.

From out of the shadows to our right, an engine roars. A large truck bursts into the light, charging up the street at Diego. I yell a warning to him. I dash forward, but the truck beats me. It hits Diego with a wet splat that heaves him over to the far curb, in front of the hotel doors. The truck squeals around the corner and disappears.

I run over to Diego. The stink of exhaust hangs in the air. His crumpled body lies on the cobblestones, the lights of the lobby bathing him with a golden glow while his life washes away in the transparent rain.

Chapter Fourteen

Pete Chandler
Saturday night. Seven days left

The police wear yellow rain slickers. Long enough to cover their ankles. As two of them walk me back into the Ambos Mundos Hotel, I smell stale rubber, like the raincoats I'd worn as a child.

There are two squad cars angled among other cars in the street. An ambulance with a siren that sounds like a braying donkey stops next to Diego. They cover his body with a gray blanket. A medical person lifts the side of the gurney and follows it up into the interior of the ambulance. The doors close, and it leaves quietly.

The older cop instructs me in English to wait in the lobby. A few tourists, wearing flip flops, stand to the sides and jockey to get a better view. Smartphones are up and clicking photos of whatever appears in front of them. Their sunburned faces stare at me.

"It is too crowded here," the cop says. "We will go to the station. I'm sure you can help us, no?" He looks about fifty, yet his shoulders slope forward like the remains of a squeezed grapefruit.

"No, I'm not going with you." I pull out my diplomat's passport. The cop studies it for a long time, sighs, and hands it back. "I've got diplomatic immunity," I remind him.

The cop shakes his head. "Just a few questions to help us?"

I've seen death many times in many places all over the world. I even caused one when I was deployed to the desert in Iraq with the Army Criminal Investigation Division. "I really don't have much information for you." I tell the cop I am working with the bank on trade opportunities and met Diego Arnaz earlier. Other than that, I don't know anything else or why someone would want to kill him. The cop nods and walks away.

I look down at the spot where Diego's body fell. A muddy stream of water sluices along the curb, carrying a paper bag of soggy French fries that scatter in disoriented patterns before washing away into the darkness. No matter how often I've witnessed death, it always strikes me hard. Occasionally, the world is better off with the death of some, but when people like Diego die, the injustice of it leaves me feeling hollow.

Then there's the death of Judd Crowe that I caused, still haunting me with guilt.

I turn toward the lift, thinking I should call Sonnenfeld and ask him what to do now.

A second man, dressed in an American golf sweater, interrupts me. The man folds a black umbrella closed and calls hello. "My name is Benny." He speaks English with a slight Spanish accent. He's tanned, middle-aged, and has several creases across his forehead. The cologne he wears is overpowering.

We wait in silence while water runs off his umbrella onto the lobby floor.

Starting for the lift, I glance at him and see thin lips that tug up in a reluctant smile but are betrayed by cold eyes, searching all over my face. I don't like this guy.

"You okay, Pete?"

I stop to face him. "Who are you?"

"Benny. From Miami. I'm Cuban-American." He grins. "I'm known as Benny the Axe."

"I haven't got time."

"You will have time if you listen to me."

"How do you know who I am?" I move my hand back over my forehead.

Benny's lips tug upward again. "We have, uh, associates here who know about you."

I frown. "And who are 'we'?"

Glancing to the side, Benny continues, "My team has been contracted by various organizations, including an agency of the U.S. government. Which one is unimportant." He drops his voice to a whisper. "Can't say any more, but I'm here because of the Havana Syndrome."

I look around the lobby. Other than small groups of tourists, Benny seems to be alone.

Benny nods his head to move outside. I activate the jammer in my pocket as we walk, capturing his phone number. Curious, I follow him to stand under a blue awning that shelters us from the ebbing rain. A foghorn groans from a ship, disappearing into the harbor of the city.

"Our contract work has taken me all over the world. We specialize in 'correcting dysfunctional situations in target countries.' In other words, we do the dirty work no one else wants to do." He hands me a card that reads, "Red Dog Associates. Miami, Florida."

"Know what 'red doggin' ' means?"

"No."

"It's an old football play. It's called when the defense gets more aggressive and blitzes the quarterback—to take him out." He grins for a long time. "Here, we call it the Havana Syndrome."

My back stiffens although I don't let that show to him. "I don't know what you're talking about," I tell him.

Benny nods but says, "Maybe. But we noticed when you entered Cuba. Why are you really here?"

"Why should I talk with you?"

"We may have the same goal." He has a small mole in the middle of his forehead. He touches it absentmindedly while he talks.

"I don't think so. I'm a trade representative." I lean away from the wall and start to walk back toward the lobby.

"Diego Arnaz's death wasn't an accident."

I stop. "That's not a surprise."

"I'm sure you were the target."

"Oh?"

"I'm sorry about what happened to your friend."

"Uh, Diego wasn't my friend."

"Right."

"He worked for the U.S. Export/Import bank and was helping me."

He touches the mole again. Pulls out a small cigar and lights it.

"What the hell do you want? I don't have time."

Benny looks up into the clouds. "Let me tell you a story. Since Fidel Castro stole this country, there have been over six hundred attempts to assassinate him. They all failed." He looks back at me again. "Unbelievable, huh?"

"I guess."

"But the goal behind all that failure is still valid."

I shift my weight. "I can't help you."

Putting his hand on my shoulder, Benny says, "This will be of value to you."

"I don't think so." I shake off his hand.

"There's a reason the Havana Syndrome exists."

"I don't care." This guy is starting to piss me off. Too cocky. An amateur gangster. But maybe there's something I could learn from him. "How long have you worked in Cuba?"

"For two years."

"Let's say someone wanted to find a Cuban person. And the person had disappeared. What would you do?"

"I'd go to the secret police headquarters at Linea Street and Vedado and ask to visit with him in the basement." Benny's head rocks back as he laughs hard.

"Fuck off." I start to walk away again.

"Wait. Sorry. But that, actually, is the correct answer to the *Jeopardy* question. Most people who disappear are grabbed by the secret police."

"Okay. I get the joke. Beyond that, what would you do?"

Benny looks into the lobby. "You can't knock on the door to the police and ask for help. The secret police are insanely suspicious, and they'd kick you out of the country. You could try family, but see, things are tricky here. If your friend's been grabbed, the family won't know anything. Besides, you need someone who can grease your way into the situation. Especially with Cubans. As you can imagine, they don't trust anyone. Especially *Americanos*." He pulls on the cigar again.

"Sure."

"Fidel and his fucking thugs have created the worst, most oppressive police state in the world."

"Uh, I gotta go."

Benny's eyes open wider. "But that's gonna change." He pokes his finger into my chest to emphasize each word.

"I'm not tracking."

"Don't you want to open this country again for American business?" The sweet smoke of the cigar hangs around his head.

I step into the edge of the lobby.

Once again, Benny holds my arm. "I've worked in some shitholes all over the world, and I can tell when someone else is in the same line of work as I am."

I'm tempted to pull out the Sabre stun gun and let him have it. "Not me, pal." I brush off his hand.

Benny follows and continues talking. "I haven't got your gig figured out—yet, and I don't care much as long as you don't fuck up our op here. In the meantime, let me give you a warning. As one American stuck in this circus to another." He tries to stop in front of me, but I sidestep around him. He calls, "Hey! You're like a virgin prostitute in a whorehouse. You don't have a clue what's going on here."

"Yeah?"

"Why don't you have a few margaritas, fuck a couple women, and leave."

"Leave?"

"I'm warning you. Get out. Now."

I turn to laugh at him.

Benny points a finger at me. "'Cause there are people who don't want you here. Don't end up like that idiot Diego. And very soon, this island is going to explode. Believe me. And when the dust settles, you don't want to get choked to death." He steps out of the lobby, throws his smoldering cigar into the water flowing by the curb, and turns to walk into the darkness and misting rain, disappearing around the corner of the hotel.

I wait for a minute. The rain is tapering off and the air smells clean, especially after Benny left. I walk into the lobby, which regains its previous festive mood. Soft music fills the room while the cocktail shakers clatter furiously at the bar. Two overweight tourists sitting on bar stools turn to study me as I walk toward the main desk.

Taking a deep breath, I lean on the desk, trying to relax my shoulders. I've met jerks like Benny all over the world. Independent military contractors, cowboys who usually screw up the situation they're hired to fix. "Any messages?" I ask the concierge.

She leans forward while her fingers crawl over a small wooden box filled with yellow papers. "No."

My body sags. More exhausted than I thought. For a moment, the weight of hopelessness pulls my shoulders forward. I've been trapped in many dangerous situations in the past. Usually, I can fight my way out or, at least, use my brains to invent a way out. This is different. All plans and my contact for help have died with Diego. I linger for what seems like a long time.

When I look up, the woman frowns, and her hand hesitates against her chest. Cocoa fingers spread across the white cotton. "Are you okay, sir?"

"I'm okay." With my left arm, I prop myself on the edge of the desk.

"Do you want to send anything?"

Absent-mindedly, I reach into my pocket. Find the Hatuey coaster Diego gave me. I pull it out and look closely at it, feel the coarse, dry cardboard, and fold it open. It has broken in half right through the face of the chief.

"Sir?"

"Nothing to say."

Fatigue wilts my body. I face the lobby, trying to orient myself toward the elevator. I shuffle to the left for several steps until someone touches my arm.

Benny? I start to throw it off and look up.

Raquel Sanchez stands beside me. I can smell her sandalwood perfume. Tall, shoulders squared, dark eyes reaching out to me. "Mr. Chandler?" She squeezes my forearm with her hand. "I just heard the horrible news."

I nod. "I'm sorry for you." I add, "And me."

"Cuban drivers drink too much rum, and these accidents happen."

She doesn't understand. Doesn't get that I was probably the target, not Diego. "Yeah, it's too bad." I start to leave, but her hand on my forearm tightens. Holds me steady.

Raquel moves directly in front of me. I sense the warmth of her body. Someone turns up the music in the lobby, and I hear the upbeat rhythms of a bossa nova. I'm wary, but too tired to walk away.

"What can I do to help?" she says.

I take a deep breath. Could she replace Diego? We didn't get off to a good start together. Could I rely on her? "Okay, maybe. I still have to find Rodolfo Diaz."

"I've got some ideas about how to do that." Through red-framed glasses, her eyes convince me. "I can set up a meet with Sergio de la Vaca, for a start."

"Why…?"

Still looking at me, she says, "Because I'm the sleeper cell."

Of course. How could I have missed the clues? I chuckle at myself. Maybe she can help after all.

After agreeing to meet in the morning, I take the lift to my room. Exhausted, empty. I turn down the hall and hear the hollow clapping of my footsteps on the marble floor. When I open the door, I spot a piece of paper on the floor. Picking it up, I unfold it. So low-tech. Printed in letters like a child would make, it reads: *Do you like Cuban art? Meet with John Lennon tomorrow at 10 am. Alone.*

Chapter Fifteen

Miguel Garcia
Sunday. Six days left

Gabbie's black hair hangs over her shoulders, puddling onto my chest as she straddles me. I love to watch her breasts sway back and forth when we have sex, so I reach up to drape her hair to the sides. She's bent forward in concentration. She gasps each time she plunges her hips down onto me. I lift up to meet her thrusts. She's insatiable, and I hate myself for being so dependent on her.

But I need to relieve the tension I feel from my frustration at the men who are funding and plotting this operation. I'm also dependent on them and hate the lack of control. I know what position I want in the new regime, but they won't commit to my ideas yet.

I think of the work I must do today, the meeting with Benny to get things finally straightened out. But when Gabbie rocks faster, my breath clogs my chest, struggling to come out in ragged gasps. All other worries disappear. Now, Gabbie directs each move, which is okay with me.

"Kiss me, *bebe*," I moan while my entire body is rigid with pleasure. Her release comes with a long scream that causes the neighbors to pound on the walls until they shake back and forth and people yell, "Quiet."

After it's over and Gabbie flops to the side, sweating and panting, I hear the sputtering of the neighbors' TVs. Indistinct chatter that reminds me that in spite of the miracle that has just occurred, life around me continues in all its banality.

When she regains her breath, Gabbie rolls onto her back. "You are my *perrito*, little puppy." She sits up and leans forward as she inches off the bed while I reach for her. I miss and she stands, shoulders thrown back, and shakes out her thick hair, running both hands through it in a fruitless effort to straighten it.

The mingled smell of sex and her perfume keep me in a stupor. I wallow in the damp sheets, my body still vibrating.

"Get up, *Perrito.* You told me you have good news," Gabbie says from over her shoulder as she pads into the bathroom. In order to fit through the door, Gabbie inches sideways. She turns on the water. It sputters for a moment until it trickles steadily in a crinkled cadence.

I get up from the bed and stagger toward her. I see her hand resting on the edge of the bowl, ruby-colored fingernails contrasting with the bone-white sink. Gabbie glances at me with a bone-white indifference. Looks back at her image in the mirror and runs a finger across her eyebrow.

My body still aches for her, yet I recognize my dependence. It makes me angry. "Get out here and listen to me," I demand.

"Can't you see I'm busy, Chucho?"

"*Mierda!*" I spin away and trudge back into the bedroom. I hate her sometimes and kick at the tangle of sheets dripping off the bed onto the floor.

In ten minutes Gabbie returns, wrapped in the silk robe from China that I bought for her. "Chucho, Chucho." Her fingernails trail over my cheeks, then linger for a warm moment to feel my skin. "You are so strong and smart. *Mi toro* in the bed."

Wrapping my arms around her shoulders, I pull her tightly against me. When I try to cup her breasts in my palms, she pushes me away.

Gabbie asks, "What is the news? You promised to get me out of Cuba someday."

I grin and from the chair, I lift my briefcase and flop it onto the bed. Opening it, I dig deeply inside. Pull out a wad of American dollars and hold it out to her, high in the air.

Of course, she grabs the cash. As her eyes soften, she lifts her face and kisses me deeply. "For me?" She pretends to be surprised and thankful.

"Our plans are moving quickly now."

"With Felipe?"

"He's only the point man. I'm in charge of the operation."

Gabbie turns in a circle, grasping the cash between her breasts. She stops and faces me. "He's a fucking electrical engineer in a dead-end job, as we all are. Is that why you're using him?"

"He's more clever than you think. Besides, it's top secret." Her lack of respect makes me furious.

"Get me to Miami. At least I'll be free of the secret police there."

"I promise." I have no intention of doing that. "I'll be in a high position, one of new authority."

"If you won't tell me more, it's time for you to leave."

"I'll leave when I'm damn ready."

She flips her hand as if to dismiss me.

I grip the handle of the briefcase while heat rushes up from my chest to spread across my face. Heating it as much as the sex did. "You're a bitch, Gabbie."

She glances back at me over her shoulder. "You talk like a *burro*."

"Go to hell." I whip my briefcase through the air toward her, which surprises me, but it feels good when she jumps to the side. I want to smash her face for her lack of respect. Instead, I jerk the door open and stomp out.

I pound down the stairwell to come out onto the small plaza, hurry past the old men, and cross under the grape arbor to try and cool off. The sex is great, but she must obey me. A Cuban man must be in charge of his woman. I think of my kids. Like Gabbie, they only call when they want something, usually luxury goods that only I can get. They all make me angry.

I wait for the limo that will take me toward the central city. I've set up a meeting to finalize the operation. I only know him as Benny the Axe, like an American gangster.

He's half Cuban, but I don't trust that or his American half either. But everything he's told me about the mission has worked as he said. And I really don't give a shit who's helping me so long as I get the chance to rid the island of corruption and stagnation. So far, he's set up several clandestine meetings with his underlings as we jointly plan for the transition and what my permanent position will be.

But Benny must understand that in Cuba, I'm in charge. I'll straighten him out when I meet him.

The rain from last night has cleared but threatens to return later in the day. A bus stops at the corner, settling with a wheezing sound like the old men at Gabbie's plaza make when they sit down to play domi-noes. From the open windows I smell the odor of plantains fried in the cheap oil that's available to Cubans. Someone has a boombox in the back, playing Cuban hip hop music. The bus rocks from the corner, its engine grunting with the effort, while inside, bodies are packed so tightly no one needs to hang onto the overhead strap. Thank God I don't have to travel like that anymore.

In forty-five minutes, my limo drops me off in the outskirts of the old city. I walk a few blocks to a quiet street of car repair shops. I've ordered Felipe to meet in front of a one-story shop called the Havana Motor Club, named after the famous Cuban car races using the rumbling vintage cars. In turn, we will meet two of our allies, one disguised as a truck driver and then Benny.

In ten minutes, Felipe gets out of a taxi and limps over to me. The limping comes and goes, depending on who's present at the time. "Sorry I'm late."

Felipe is one of the smartest people I know. From our childhood criminal activities, I know he's reliable and crazy enough to do dangerous work. We fist bump.

"When's the action?" Felipe asks.

"Any time now. We're waiting for a truck driver."

"A fucking truck driver is the top guy?"

"It's a cover, you idiot." I stare at him. "And he's not 'top guy.' I am. He and his people provide the money and the tech support. Don't be an ass when he gets here."

"Antonio's been calling me. That friend of yours. He's bragging that you've included him in our plans."

"Shit. He's heard rumors about our work and wants in."

"No."

"Of course not. I'll meet with him and tell him to fuck off."

The driver is late but finally turns the corner in his truck. The cab is faded red with a divided windshield, cracked in the corner, and has a flat wooden bed behind. It lumbers up the street toward us, breathing black smoke from its asthmatic engine as the driver tries to make it far enough to reach us. Stopping before the Havana Motor Club, the brakes squeal. There are two men in the cab.

Like most Cuban shops, the Motor Club has open doors in front. Two mechanics sit on plastic milk crates in the shade of a palm tree. One smokes a cigar. In their quiet street, the arrival of a strange truck breaks up the monotony of work. Both men stand to see what activity will occur.

To get away from the spying eyes, I walk around to the far side of the cab and wait for the men to get out.

"*Hola, amigo.*" He calls himself Leonid and waves over the top of the truck's hood.

I nod and rest my hand on the flared fender, itself hot from the work of the old engine. This guy looks like a loser, but I can see someone else in the passenger side.

Leonid has a black mustache that grows down on either side of his mouth until it's lost under his chin. "I'll never get used to the goddamn heat here."

"I've got a lot of questions I want answered. Hurry, it's clouding over." I glance up at the sky. The man has a Russian accent and certainly doesn't look Cuban.

"You don't give us orders, dude." A second man climbs out of the truck's cab. It's Benny. Middle aged, wearing a golf sweater and a stylish straw hat pulled low over his forehead. He doesn't offer to shake hands, and I notice a mole in the middle of his forehead, which he touches absentmindedly. "Hey, bro." He wears too much cologne.

"Yeah?"

"Back up."

"I want to finalize what happens after the operation with the president." I'm not going to let this guy push me around anymore.

Benny clears his throat and spits into the dust of the street. "You'll be briefed when you need to know the final details."

"What about our equipment, weapons, location, and timing for the op?" I demand.

"We'll take care of all that, including the final intel. Saturday we go."

"Saturday?" I'm surprised to actually hear the day.

"Which one of you is going in?"

"Uh, this guy's point." I look at Felipe.

"The cripple?"

"He's tougher than he looks."

"How about you?" The American stares at me as if he's sizing me up.

"I'm running the operation, remember?" I draw out the words to emphasize my sarcasm. "Of course, I'll back up my cousin."

Benny laughs and touches the mole in the middle of his forehead. "I can't believe the B-level help I gotta work with. My investors would pull their support if they knew."

"Fuck you," I shout. I've had enough frustration for one day. This guy's an asshole.

"Calm down. Without my group's money and our planning, you'd still be sitting behind a desk. You want to come out on top of this?" He pauses. "Then you do what I order."

My stomach tightens. Like Gabbie, this prick doesn't respect me. "But I have the authority and connections here to get it done. Without me, your plan is nothing but talk."

"Don't threaten me." Benny's face is damp, and he pulls a silver handgun from his back pocket, exposing it for me to see. I've put down punks like him many times.

As the clouds increase, the shadow cast by the truck evaporates like water in the heat.

I stare at Benny, drop my arm to my side, and move closer, taking an angle toward the man. "You don't seem to understand who you're talking to."

When Benny shifts his weight, his back bumps up against the fender of the truck. He points the gun at my chest. "Back up, you dickheads." The cooling engine ticks rhythmically.

Without warning, I ball my hand into a fist and swing upward to catch Benny in the gut with a powerful punch. He bends over with a groan, gagging for air. That movement exposes the side of his head, defenseless to my other fist that crashes into his face, driving the man to his knees and then sprawling him on the ground. His straw hat spins off, creating a small tornado of dust until it loses energy and flops into the street.

The men from the shop wander out. When I glare at them, they retreat to their milk crates and sit down.

Benny stands up and stumbles around the hood, hanging on to steady himself. He points at me and screams, "You're a dead man." He heaves himself into the cab. Leonid follows. Even though the engine growls in protest, Leonid pushes it hard to make a sharp turn to the right, crushing the straw hat in the dust of the street.

I straighten up to watch them leave. I know they'll be back, because in the end, they need me to execute everything successfully.

Felipe and I walk to the pickup point with my limo. I flex my hand to make sure it's okay after the head shot. The two-punch combination works best if done by surprise. I feel the anger seep out of my chest. Hitting Benny was stupid, but it sure felt good.

Felipe's words punch through my thoughts. "Why'd you do that?"

"Guy pissed me off."

"You stupid fuck. You also probably blew the whole op."

Thirty minutes later, we're sitting at a curbside bar under a canopy of bougainvillea flowers to protect us from the impending rain. The flowers are white and pink. I sip a Cristal beer and cool off. All my life, my temper has gotten me in trouble. Have I destroyed everything now? My left heel taps repeatedly on the tile floor. Thanks to my temper, I feel exposed now.

Felipe limps back from the bathroom, stops at the open-air bar next to the garden, and orders a Hatuey. He's always told me the disability came from a gunshot wound he suffered while fighting as a young man in Angola with the Cuban Liberation Army. I don't believe it; he's too young to have been in that war, but Cuban men all crave masculine glory in whatever form they can get it.

Felipe grunts when he sits across from me and takes his time drawing on a long cigar. A cloud of smoke rises to choke the birds. He wears a green Armani sport shirt, opened to expose his bare chest covered with black hair. Finally, Felipe says, "You fucked up, Chucho. I've warned you about your temper. Hopefully, you can fix things. After all, they need all your connections to make this work."

I nod and lean forward, dropping my voice but keeping it steady. "Guess I showed 'The Axe.' Yeah, I'll patch things up with them." Raindrops whisper on the flowers above us. "I'm in tight with his lieutenants, and we've already made good progress."

"We need Benny to help us execute the final mission." Felipe blows smoke up into the arbor. "After all, it's the logical outcome of the Havana Syndrome. But you can't fool around with these guys."

"We're taking all the risks; I deserve to know the entire plan."

Felipe wipes moisture from his face. He wears his hair long, and damp curls fall across his forehead.

I shrug. "This is about our future." I look around the small garden to make certain no one can hear me. "When we're done, everyone in this country will know who Miguel Garcia is." I push up each sleeve toward my elbows.

"Saturday?"

"We have to get ready."

"What happens afterward?"

"I'll be in a critical position, and we'll clean out the old bulls. We'll have freedom."

"You always say that, but it's an illusion. Nothing will improve." He looked up at the flowers. "I want out."

My face flushes. "You can't back out now. This is my last chance."

Felipe stubs out the cigar in the ashtray. Raps his fist against the table top. "In the meantime, I want the *chance* to live a long life and not be killed by Benny and his thugs."

I'm surprised at the sharp edge to Felipe's voice. I lick my lips and gulp at the beer. "I got it under control."

"And that stupid friend of yours, Antonio Lopez. He's telling people that you recruited him to work with us." Felipe stares at me. "You gotta shut him down right now or he'll end up getting us killed."

"Goddammit. I'll take care of him today. I told you."

Felipe changes subjects. "What about the new American that's snooping around?"

"I've got to be careful. He's got diplomatic privileges." I keep my voice light. Confident. "Maybe the American's secretly working with Benny." I don't want to tell Felipe that I already tried to get rid of the American. Felipe's teetering on the edge. I need him to be dependable, at least for a few more days. After that, I'll let him go.

Rain finally breaks through the trellis and drops in random splats on the table.

Felipe's eyes protrude like he's taken a gut punch from me. They lift slowly to stare into my eyes. "I'm worried. These people we're working with will kill me, you, Gabbie, and everyone else we know."

I don't say anything while I twirl my beer bottle in my hands. Then I smile slyly at him. "Yeah, he's tough, but we're tougher. And smarter." I lean closer to Felipe. "I've got a plan of my own."

"Yeah?"

"In the end, we'll fuck Benny. I'm gonna double cross him."

"You're crazy." When he slams back his chair, it scrapes across the tiles of the floor to violate the silence left in the wake of his words. He leaves quickly.

A dying whisper of smoke wiggles up from the ashtray, stinking as it passes in front of me.

In 1961 U.S. biologist Allan Frey discovered that irradiating the human head with microwaves produced sensations of sound—even from thousands of feet away. Tiny pulses of microwaves aimed at the ear raised the temperature inside the ear by an amount so small it couldn't be measured. One millionth of a degree. But enough to rattle the moisture molecules to cause structural harm.

When government officials from the national security establishment investigated the Havana attacks, they learned of the "Frey Effect." But they had little evidence to confirm or deny it. All they could do was scratch their heads. One of them asked, "So, a microwave popcorn popper was responsible for all the human damage in Havana?"

—*Journal of Applied Physiology*, 2020

Chapter Sixteen

Pete Chandler
Sunday. Six days left

I call Raquel to postpone our meeting. Diego's death hit me harder than I expected, even after the deaths I've seen in my line of work. I was beginning to like him.

After breakfast, I tell the concierge of the hotel to order a taxi. I don't tell Raquel about the note or that I plan to go to Lennon Park tonight. A "coconut" pulls up and the driver waves at me. I lean down to peer inside and see someone who looks about twelve years old.

With no other immediate choice, I bend down and crawl into the back seat. The coconut is simply a motor scooter with a round plastic cab attached to the rear of the cycle. Colored yellow and green, it resembles a ripe coconut. The driver twists the throttle on the handlebar so the engine whines like a lawn mower. The young kid picks up speed, dodging clots of people who stroll into the middle of the street.

"I have to be there before ten." There's a lightness in my chest.

The driver speaks English. "'No problem,' as you Americans say." The engine cries as if in pain, while giving all the power it's got. The kid leans around a corner and shoots forward in the straightaway.

My breath comes quicker. In many circumstances and places in the world, I have followed clues like this. Usually, they're dead ends. But someone went to the work of placing the note under the door. It's the first promising opportunity I've had to find Rodolfo Diaz—I hope. Just in case, I carry the automatic in a holster nestled in my lower back.

Traffic is heavy and slow. Bicycles dart in front of us without the riders looking. The coconut stops and waits for another red light. I smell cooking odors, exhaust, and an occasional whiff of a woman's perfume from an open convertible that crowds next to us.

"Isn't there a faster way?" I shout to the boy.

He raises his palm in the space between us. "Nothing I can do. This is Havana."

When the light changes, he charges ahead to the next corner before being blocked by a double bus. Its engine grumbles, but the boy curves around it and finds a clear lane ahead. He turns to me. "Now we should be okay."

"Good. I can't be late." I think about the timing. Sunday morning will probably be busy at the park and offer lots of cover.

We fly across the Plaza de la Revolución, dip down into the Vedado section of Havana, and turn onto the broad Avenue Paseo. Two blocks later, the coconut skids to a halt to allow a cart piled with water jugs and pulled by a donkey to cross the street.

I check my phone for the time. Thanks to the kid, I should make it.

One more left turn and we arrive at John Lennon Park. I pay double the fare and thank him. After I crawl out, I survey the park, looking for suspicious people—either following me or trying to make contact.

I stroll to the bench with the statue of Lennon in the middle of the park. I gaze at the mansions that flank the north side, now pure white in the sun. Branches of magnolia trees, heavy with large, dark leaves, bend toward the ground, creating islands of shadows. I hear faint music from boomboxes. No one approaches me.

Looking behind me, I check for tails. I don't see anyone that's obviously watching me. But then again, there are still dozens of people walking around the park. Across the sparse grass, couples lie on blankets. I hear birds calling for their partners. I look at my phone. I still have five minutes, so I take a quick walk through some groups of people to confuse anyone who may be following me. Finally, I approach the bench where the statue of Lennon sits. There isn't anyone around it, and after circling it again, I sit down. A cooling breeze whispers across my face.

How will contact be made?

Once again, I feel uneasy sitting next to the bronze statue. So lifelike. It is as if Lennon is about to say something to me.

I wait for fifteen minutes. Couples walk by holding hands, an older woman pushes a stroller with a baby nestled in it along the path in front of the bench, and a woman sits in the grass to eat a *torta*, a sandwich, probably for her breakfast. Sun bathes the houses at the far edges of the park until they disappear into the glow. I stand up and take photos with the phone, turn in a different direction, and take some more.

I wait. This is Cuba, so maybe even the contact will be late. Or this is another dead end.

A lone man in a trench coat walks by. He slows and glances at me but keeps walking. Later, he circles back. He looks promising. I try to make eye contact, but the man doesn't respond. He pauses with his back toward me. Should I say something? Without turning around, he walks away.

Five minutes later, a young man comes from the right side of the bench. He's short and carries an old guitar slung over his shoulder, long hair hangs around his face, and he wears a striped wool *sarape* that looks too hot. He stops before me.

"*Tu eres un Americano?*"

I look around then say, "Yes." My mouth is dry.

"You like John Lennon?" His English is good.

"Sure." I look behind the man. "I'm waiting for someone. Can't talk now." I flick my hand to wave him away.

"I don't meet many Americans, so I like to practice my English."

"Sorry, but I don't have time."

"Do you think John Lennon was the greatest pop composer?"

The guy looks like a '60s hippie, Cuban style. "Yeah, he's good," I respond by running my hand over my forehead.

"If he hadn't died, can you imagine how many new songs he would've written?"

"Got a point." I expect him to move on, but he stands to the side. Adjusts the guitar over his shoulder. When I look closely at him, I notice something odd about the young man's hair. It doesn't look real, as if he's wearing a wig. Why would he—? At that instant, our eyes meet.

The man continues, "I like Lennon's words to my favorite song." He swings the guitar from over his shoulder and strums it. It's out of tune, but he sings along with it. "Imagine there's no countries, nothing to kill or die for, and no religion too, imagine all the people, living life in peace." He sings them slowly.

I nod. "He's talking about freedom."

"Yes."

Neither of us speaks for a while. A blue hummingbird hovers over Lennon's bronze head for a moment before flitting toward a row of petunias along the sidewalk.

"I also like art. Cuban art," I say as casually as possible.

The man smiles. "So do I. Who's your favorite artist?"

My chest tightens. "I like Rodolfo Diaz."

He looks up and across the park. Turning around, he searches the path that leads out through the middle. He swings the guitar back over his shoulder.

Did I say too much? I take a deep breath.

Then he turns back to me and whispers, "I know him."

"Can I meet him?"

"It can be arranged."

A voice from far behind the bench shouts, "*Vaya, vaya,* move along, you dirty dog."

"We're talking about music," the young man yells back.

"We don't allow bums like you in the park. Forbidden. Move along now." The voice comes closer.

I turn to see a Cuban officer in full uniform, with gold epaulets on each shoulder. The uniform is buttoned, causing it to stretch across a bulging stomach. I recognize the insignia for the foreign intelligence service, equivalent to the CIA, and when I turn fully around, I recognize the man.

A hawk nose, small mustache, and heavy eyebrows. It's the security officer who has followed me since I arrived at the airport. The officer kicks at the man with the guitar and forces him to hurry down the path and out of the park. He returns to me, smiles, and says, "Enjoy your time in Cuba, Mr. Chandler. We don't want the local bums to bother you."

I turn around and see two more of his henchmen coming toward us. Without saying anything, I get up and join a crowd of passing tourists while we leave the park.

Chapter Seventeen

Pete Chandler
Monday morning. Five days left

I sleep fitfully as several pale faces float into my dreams. Faces of people who have disappeared from my life. Julie, the congresswoman, Janette, and Barbara, the mother of Karen. Some dead; some still alive but gone. And I've done little to get them back. I can even hear Diego's nervous laugh, hollow now, like listening through an old Cuban rotary telephone. I finally wake up with damp sheets tangled around my legs and the window open. I stumble toward it and gulp fresh air that carries the scent of gardenias from somewhere far below.

Because of the warm weather, much of Cuban life is lived with open windows. So different from where I live. I could enjoy this lifestyle.

The musician in the park was probably legitimate, and hopefully, he'll contact me again. I'm not used to hitting brick walls like this. I think of Raquel's offer to help and that I agreed to meet her at the U.S. Embassy after a meeting with my boss's brother, Frank, who works at the embassy. Maybe he can open a few doors for me.

After breakfast, I walk through the lobby of the hotel. The staff has folded open the louvered floor-to-ceiling doors. Warm air, humidity, the hum of traffic, and people talking entice me into the new day. I head outside to call Sonnenfeld. The shock and anger from the night of Diego's death is fading, allowing me to think clearly again.

From the street, church bells clang with hopeful sounds.

Sonnenfeld answers immediately. "Have you made contact?"

I report the attempt in Lennon Park and what happened.

"Dammit! Any way to find him again?"

"No. Raquel told me you recruited her. She's got a plan to find Diaz's home and interview his family."

"Chandler, we're running out of time. This MUST be wrapped up before the president's visit! Whatever it takes!"

After I calm down, I explain that I'm going to the U.S. Embassy and afterward, the "crime scene" in front of the building. Over the years, I've learned the hard way to control my temper.

"My boss's brother, Frank, has some 'critical data,' as he calls it. Won't take long." I hang up before Sonnenfeld can respond.

I grab a taxi outside the hotel. We wind through narrow streets, slowing for bicycles swarming like metal bees and a group of boys playing soccer in the street. A dirty ball kicked by dirty feet. They part for us with a few waves of hands and many smiles.

At ten thirty, the driver drops me around the corner from the embassy on Calzada Avenue. A six-story white office building that houses the United States Embassy is pockmarked on its exterior with recessed black windows. Like dozens of black eyes, they look out over the street at the Caribbean across the Malecon.

When I reach the front of the complex, Marines in blue and red uniforms are guarding the steel gates. I present my identification.

"Welcome to the U.S. Embassy," the guard says. "Mr. Frank Graves is on the third floor. Look for the Senior Data Analysis Section." He salutes and stands aside to allow me to go inside.

The air conditioning feels good after coming inside from the heat. I ride the elevator up and find Frank's office; he comes out and shakes my hand for a long time. Frank resembles his brother in Minnesota. Bulging in the middle, balding, sandy hair, and serious eyes.

Years ago, my misbehavior almost got me fired from the bank in Minneapolis. My boss, Martin Graves, saved my career. Today, I'll do anything for him, including meeting with his brother. Maybe I'll learn something.

"Get you something to drink? American mineral water?" He's slightly buck-toothed, which makes it look like he's smiling all the time.

I accept the water while Frank steps a little too close to me and says, "I'm so damn glad someone's come back here to help." He talks fast while he leads me across the office. "We'll go to the Sensitive Compartmented Communications Facility."

"The 'quiet room'?" I follow him into a sealed room with a large polished table, six chairs, and five computer screens hanging from the walls. He closes the door behind us.

"After the FBI and CIA couldn't find anything, they disappeared and we've all been left here. Scared, to say the least. And goddamn angry at the government for abandoning us," he explains.

"You're scared?"

"Hell, yes. The State Department has posted me all over the world, and I'm happy to serve my country. But I don't get paid enough to work in a combat zone. None of us do." He waves his arm toward the other offices.

I don't tell him that his brother, Martin, is even more scared. "Frank, I'm not here because—"

"Martin says you're the best investigator he's ever had."

I nod.

"Thankfully, none of these attacks have happened inside the office, so we're all nervous when we leave the building. It's like we're trapped in a prison." His hands clench in his lap. "If the Communists want us to leave, they're giving us a hell of a shove."

Although I don't care to talk about the Havana Syndrome, I decide to at least engage in the subject to calm down Frank. "Have you seen any of the attacks happen?"

Frank shakes his head.

"Any witnesses?"

"No. That's because they've picked us off when we're alone."

"Anything else?"

Frank pulls his chair closer. "It's the Chinese."

"The Chinese?"

Frank takes a deep breath. I'm worried this may take longer than I first thought.

"My job here is financial data analyst. As you probably know, both the State and Commerce Departments monitor the financial situations in many countries. Until the embassy opened in 2015, Cuba was a black hole. Now we have the ability to attempt to analyze things here."

"What do you mean?"

"We have state-of-the-art artificial intelligence software. We use AI surveillance to detect fraudulent transactions in real time by recognizing patterns. Or I should say, anomalies in the patterns. I measure lots of statistics, like national revenue, cash flow, foreign currency reserves, debt levels, production numbers, and stuff like that. The Communist Party publishes data, but of course, it's highly suspect. I try to get as close as I can to accuracy." His voice is hoarse.

"But we do very little trade with Cuba."

"Correct, but at this point, my analysis is important for political and military reasons."

I sip the water. "So why China?"

"Recently, AI alerted me to anomalies in the financial data—numbers that couldn't be explained by simple fraud or corruption."

"Anomalies?"

"Right. AI augments my ability to track changes with dependability. Suddenly, that data skewed badly. For instance, the level of foreign currency reserves rose twenty percent in six months instead of the normal four percent drop."

I frown.

"There wasn't any corresponding increase in revenue or trade to justify the data."

"Meaning?"

"Someone is pumping tons of foreign cash into the country." Frank laughs, hands held out to the sides with his palms facing me. "And I can tell you it wasn't Bolivia or Borneo. It had to be a big player, a superpower."

"Why would they do that?"

"Simple. Influence." He leans forward in his chair. "Pete, I was posted in Hong Kong until the Chinese government turned the screws on the island and started to take it over. Their tactics are brutal."

"I know."

"But since Cuba is only ninety miles from the U.S., the Chinese have to be very careful. They're secretly giving the Cuban government massive amounts of cash."

I stand up to think. It's the first theory I've heard about the Chinese being behind the Havana Syndrome. Walking to the end of the table, I say from over my shoulder, "Do you have proof, Frank?"

"Not something you could use in court."

I've also noticed lots of Chinese tourists, but then, they're all over the world now. I turn around. "Okay, but here's the big question. Why would they attack American diplomats? They certainly don't want to start a war with us."

"No, of course not. But this has got China stamped all over it."

"But how would they benefit from such a damaging attack on us?"

"Destabilization. Just when America is trying to establish better relations with Cuba, the Chinese are trying to get a foothold here. That strains our relationship to the point we'll be back to Cold War relations with Cuba, allowing the Chinese to step in, unopposed."

"Maybe the money's coming in from Russia."

He thinks for a minute. "Possibly."

I walk back to my chair but don't sit. "I'll keep it in mind."

"Please do more than that." Frank stands and grabs me by the shoulders with both hands.

"Okay." I feel sorry for Frank but can't tell him that I'm only in Cuba to find an artist.

I look at my phone.

"Are you going to the trade reception?" he asks.

"No. I've got work to do."

"You may meet people who can help you with your investigation." Frank walks to the door but doesn't open it until I agree to attend for a short time. At the end of the hall, we take the elevator up to the sixth floor. It opens onto a spacious room decorated with prints of American artists and a long window that overlooks the sea. We find the bar, and Frank orders a Bloody Mary. Telling him I have work to do, I drink mineral water.

He introduces me as a trade rep to many Cubans who manage businesses for the government. They are friendly and interested in increasing sales to the U.S. that are allowed under the embargo.

A thin blonde woman approaches me, reaches out to shake my hand with her dry one, and introduces herself. She wears a brilliant white full-length dress. "Claudia Martinez. I'm actually Comrade Director General of the Sugar Secretariat."

Whatever that is.

"I'm so charmed to meet you." She leans close enough to my face that I can feel her warmth. She has full red lips and a beautiful smile. "Are you enjoying Cuba?"

"Yes. Very friendly people, and the natural beauty is astounding."

"It's a beautiful island."

I try to turn away, but she touches my shoulder with her hand. "Let me introduce you to our sugar industry. We may have mutual interests for the future."

I nod as I learn more about how the system operates. She probes me with questions about my work and the possibility of future trade. I pull out all the answers I was coached to say, and it seems to satisfy her. She's obviously intelligent, so I hope the questions end soon as I've run out of rehearsed answers. I can only imagine the people she knows who could make my stay in Cuba even more difficult.

She hands me her card and passes me off to a squat man in green combat clothing. He wears a red beret like Che Guevara wore. His voice is brusque, commanding, and he introduces himself as the Chief Counselor to the Commissar of Internal Affairs. Their government bureaucracy must be ten times worse than ours. We talk about trade also until he leaves. I notice a few Asian people heading toward our ambassador. Chinese?

I appreciate Frank's intelligence but doubt his conclusions.

When I glance at my phone, I see it's almost time to meet with Raquel. I remember my mission and decide there's no one here who can help in any way. Setting my water on a nearby table, I head for the elevator. I look over my shoulder to wave goodbye to Frank but don't see him.

When I turn back, Comrade Director Litchenko from CNEURO stands in front of me.

I stiffen but look him in the eyes. "Hello."

I'm surprised when he nods at me. I extend my hand, but he doesn't shake it. "Ah, I get the pleasure of meeting you again, Mr. Chandler." He grins and asks, "If that is your real name."

"Uh, yes, it is. I've got to run." I try to step around him, but he slides sideways, still grinning at me.

"When are you leaving Cuba?"

"I don't know."

"I would suggest that it is soon."

"I don't take orders from you." I move to the left toward the elevator.

This time, he steps aside but hisses at me, "If I ever see you near my facility again, you will be killed as a threat to state security."

At first, I think he might be joking. "I'm a diplomat. I'm sure you wouldn't want the international repercussions from something like that."

Leaning close to my face, he responds, "That won't be a problem if they can't find your body."

Chapter Eighteen

Ava Alvarez
Monday noon. Five days left

Cortez and Miller bring Antonio Lopez to Workroom Number 7 in the basement of the secret police headquarters at Linea Avenue and Vedado. I always liked the shade of green on the outside, set off with blue shutters, and have spent years of my life in this old building.

I reserved the room near the end of the basement so no one would get too nosy.

Having already been worked over earlier by my men who scooped him, Lopez looks exhausted. He's dragged face forward to the straight-backed wooden chair in front of an intense light. They fasten the soiled straps on the arms and legs of the chair to stabilize him and finally position him over the floor drain.

He looks around and, finally, up at me. He's thin and ugly, but he flashes a defiant sneer. This kind is the easiest to break.

My team has gone through this so often, I don't even have to order Miller to wheel in the cart. It's a two-tiered old medical cart, white enameled with a polished chrome frame. Long ago, one of the wheels rusted, causing it to squeak each time the wheel came around. At first, I wanted it fixed but realized the sound was more unnerving to prisoners than the sight of the instruments and tools on top of the cart. It smells of old rubber.

Pliers, tweezers, a steel band with a notched strip that can be tightened, soldering irons of various sizes, picks, slim knives, electrical prods, a stack of clean towels, and even a long, curled length of brown rubber hose with a nozzle attached at one end. I never use the hose, but it suggests torture so vile, its presence alone usually convinces even the hardest of prisoners to cooperate.

There are also simple things to prepare a prisoner: strip off their clothing, turn up the air conditioning to freezing levels, flash the strobe light into their faces to disorient them.

Miller parks the cart just inside Lopez's line of sight. Then, at my order, they both leave the room. I don't even trust them with the information I need, although they've proven to be loyal to me over the years. The chair is positioned over a floor drain so any residue can be washed away easily.

I've done this so often, it's become routine for me. But not this time.

I take my time lifting various tools off of the cart and showing them to Lopez. I don't speak but let the silence unnerve him even further. I pick up the pliers while twisting them in my hands to suggest how I'll rip off his fingernails or squeeze his balls. I show him various knives, making sure to let them glisten in the bright light. An effective technique is to bring the tip of each knife close to the prisoner's eyeballs. Then I laugh softly.

The strongest psychological tool is to convince the prisoner that I alone can kill him or let him live. By flipping back and forth between these two approaches, I create a dependency on me for survival—which comes only when I get what I want. I take my time, watching for the signs of weakening resolve. At this point, some people give up immediately and tell me what I want. Then there are others who hold out longer.

With Lopez, I tap the tip of the knife on his left cheek while staring into his eyes. He tries to avoid my look, but I don't let him. "Do you know where you are?"

"I can guess." His voice is still defiant.

I'll have to proceed to the next steps. Of course, I don't care about this piece of cattle shit, but I have to convince him that I do. "This can be very easy and you can be home in a few hours with your family." I walk around behind him, tapping the top of his head with the knife. "I want some information from you. That's all. And the truth, of course."

"I don't know why I'm here."

"Oh, I think you do. My agents overheard you bragging about your work with a project that will 'shake the island,' as you said."

Lopez struggles against the straps for a fruitless moment. "That was all a joke. I'm not involved in anything."

"Then where did the idea come from? People who say things like that get in trouble."

"I don't know."

I poke the tip of the blade into his hair, gently but enough to hurt. "Who is behind this project?"

He yells. "I'm a loyal Communist. Talk to General Fernandez."

"You know I will, so why not make this easier for yourself? What is the project?"

"I swear by my mother's blessed heart, I don't know anything."

"Your mother wouldn't be happy to know you're lying."

"I'm not."

I'm tired of this session, like so many hundreds of others, and I don't have the time anymore. I lay the knife on the cart, pick up the soldering iron, and plug it into a wall socket, hoping the electric current will work today. It does, and I feel the tip warm immediately. I hold it up to Lopez' cheek, close enough so he can feel the heat.

His face brightens into a crimson shade, and his eyes bulge.

"Tell me what will happen."

He screams a long, loud cry but doesn't answer.

Normally, I'd play him a little longer, give him time to confess, but I'm in a hurry. I press the glowing iron against his fingertip and hold it there until his finger starts to flame. It stinks, but I'm used to the smell.

The screaming is intense. I'm practiced enough to block it out. I splash water on his finger and wait for his pain to subside. "I can help you if you tell me about the project."

He collapses into crying, begging. He's getting close now.

I use a different angle of interrogation. "Tell me who is working on this with you."

"I can't say. They'll kill me."

"I'll kill you right now, and your mother also if you don't tell me."

His head flops forward. I wait, knowing I'm almost there.

"Fuck you," he mumbles.

Another finger bursts into flame. His body convulses, but the straps do their job to hold him upright. I douse the finger with water again and wait. Then, I go for a third finger.

"Okay, okay. Please… Mama… have mercy on me."

I step back. "Who is it?"

"My old friend, Michael Garcia, and his cousin, Felipe Garcia."

"Where do they work?"

"Miguel works with me."

"When will it happen?"

He mumbles something.

I step back and assess the situation. Can I squeeze anything more out of this traitor? "How will they do it? Where?" When I set the iron in a holder on the cart, I hear a gasp behind me. I turn to see his head has fallen forward onto his chest. He's very still. Dammit. He must've had a heart attack, and sooner than I expected, he's gone.

Cortez and Miller return, and I nod once to them as I leave the room. They'll clean up thoroughly, as they always do.

Chapter Nineteen

Pete Chandler
Monday afternoon. Five days left

When I step outside of the embassy, I immediately see two men converging on me. My usual tails. I duck back into the embassy and work my way to the far side of the building. When I look out the door, I don't see anyone following me.

I hurry across a narrow sidewalk and find a row of coconuts waiting to give rides to embassy personnel. Approaching the first one, I offer him one hundred dollars to "borrow" his vehicle. The young man agrees and I climb inside, hiding my face behind the yellow shell. With a twist on the throttle, I take off, circle the building, and race past the two men waiting for me at the front entrance.

Within two blocks, I spot Raquel and the bank's Toyota waiting for me. I park the coconut and transfer to her car. It feels sad since Diego always drove the same car. "Sorry, I have to do this." I wave the KAXYUYA bug detector around the inside. Nothing. It goes back into my Faraday bag.

Raquel frowns with a little shake of her head. "I can't stop thinking about Diego," she says in a soft voice, reading my mind. She looks at me carefully, as if she's searching for anything broken. "He was such a happy person, loved his family."

My chest tightens. "Raquel, listen to me." I find her eyes and say, "Diego was murdered."

She remains expressionless but asks, "Why?"

"He was probably mistaken for me." Silence hangs in the space between us. Finally, I tell her, "You can leave the case now. I'll make sure you get paid in full."

"Uh, I want to help."

I study her for a moment. She's attractive, smart, and tough, but probably not tough enough for what might come as I continue looking for Diaz. "You should get out of this."

Raquel's eyes lose their focus. "Are you going to keep investigating?"

"Yes. I have a job to get done, and with Diego's death, it's become personal for me now."

"I understand, but how will you get around?" She glances at the abandoned coconut.

"I'll be okay."

Her hand grips my forearm briefly. "We got off on the wrong foot, as you Americans say, but I know you need me." Pushing back her hair, she stares out the windshield, shoulders squared.

"Thanks, but I don't think so." I still don't like her condescending attitude.

"I have my reasons to help you."

"Like the money from Sonnenfeld?"

She scowls at me. "Pete, sometimes people can do things for more important reasons." She crosses her arms over her chest. "You should think about this."

I finally agree. "All right." I reach down and lift my backpack with the laptop off the floor. "I've got all the data from the previous investigations by American officials."

"Where should we go?"

"Closer to the embassy. I know American investigators have been all over this, but I still want to check it out for myself."

Raquel starts the car, the air conditioning huffs into action, and she drives a few blocks away and stops. We leave the car and walk to a low stone wall, where I set down the laptop underneath the shading branches of an ancient ceiba tree. I activate all my jamming tools. While booting up the computer, I share Frank's worries with her.

Raquel blows out a lungful of air. "Wow. There certainly have been a lot more Chinese visiting, but the government tells us they are here for trade and scientific missions. But then, I don't trust anything our government tells us."

"I've got the encrypted wifi code for the embassy," I say, "so we can get the reports here." In a few minutes, I access and scroll through numerous screens while Raquel shoulders next to me to watch also.

"Will you investigate this instead of looking for Diaz?"

"No, but I hope by looking at this data, I may learn something that'll help. I just want to get a feel for the evidence." I scroll through the reports. "Here's something about the flagpoles."

Raquel points across a wide boulevard to a large area studded with dozens of tall flagpoles that face the embassy. "Over there." They look like a forest of bare trees several stories tall. Row after row, so thick it's difficult to see through them.

I read aloud from the FBI reports. "Investigators questioned if those metal poles could be used as antennas to project some kind of a sound wave around the embassy. This says the scientists used specialized sonic equipment to create loud sounds behind the poles, aimed at the building. They concluded that to be harmful, the sound would have to be loud enough that everyone could hear it. Besides, it couldn't selectively target an individual."

"Is this the kind of work you normally do?"

"I don't have expert knowledge, but yes, I investigate crime scenes, talk to witnesses, and act like I'm a cop." I look up at the poles and run my hand over my hair. "But this is impossible for anyone to investigate."

"Why?"

"The FBI arrived days after the attacks occurred. Unlike a normal crime scene, there was no physical evidence here, no shell casings, dead bodies, footprints, or blood spatters."

"Where were the Americans attacked?"

"Around here, at the Hotel Nacional, and on the street."

"Anything suspicious at the embassy or the hotel?"

I squint at the computer screen again. "Looks like the FBI went to the hotel and found wifi routers and security cameras that hung in every room. So far, the Cuban government has refused to provide any data retrieved from the devices." I turn to the side on the low wall, looking over the Malecon. A bank of cumulus clouds billows across the sky like white sails on Spanish galleons, pulling before the wind. "Of course, there wasn't any evidence inside the embassy either. That tells me whatever did this was portable." To my right, I notice movement. A man skirts behind a palm tree, but it's too narrow for him to hide. Luckily, he's also too far away to hear us. Still, I pack up the laptop and my tools.

"Could it have been some kind of poison in their food?"

"The medical exams of the victims ruled out poisons, viruses, or any weird mold." I shake my head. "Everyone was attacked by some portable device while *outside*, on the street, which could explain how they would be accessible to the attackers."

Suddenly, I realize something that should've been obvious from the start. "All the American experts couldn't find one single piece of evidence even after weeks of investigation. Every crime I've investigated leaves something, some clue, some evidence of the perpetrator. But in this case, the *absence of evidence* is proof of a very sophisticated operation —that didn't even leave a faint footprint."

I face Raquel. "Even though they deny it, could the Cuban government have attacked us? Stricken the U.S. in retaliation for the embargo? That could explain how the attacks were covered up."

Raquel's eyebrows pinch together. "I don't think so. Raul and the old men who run the country and even his son, Alejandro, have enough problems with the new freedoms that Cubans are demanding. The response has been more repression and censorship. Why would the rulers want more trouble from the U.S? What possible reason could they have?"

"And what about the CNEURO labs? That would be the perfect place to do the research for a weapon."

"So now you're going to investigate the Havana Syndrome?"

I shrug my shoulders. "No, but deep down, I'm tempted. This crime is so unusual, and there's part of me that wants to solve it. Also, there is the hint that Rodolfo Diaz left in his painting, tying his message to the Havana Syndrome."

"Now what?"

"Can you find where Diaz lives?"

"I've already contacted Sergio to get it from the lab's database. But the government monitors the scientists constantly. We'll have to figure out a clandestine way to meet him."

"Great. I'll go out there."

She laughs for a moment. "And how are you going to blend into the neighborhood?"

"I speak Spanish."

"—like an American. No one will even open a door for you. Instead, they'll call the secret police to pick you up."

I hate the smirk on her lips. "Okay, okay."

We walk back toward the car. The enormity of the roadblocks I face hits me again, as does Diego's death.

The heat of the morning triggers a memory of another ghost from the past. I try to keep it locked up, but the strength of the memory forces it out. I remember the hot room in a cinderblock building in Iraq and my fellow officer, Judd Crowe, in the Criminal Investigation Division. The uncooperative prisoner drove us beyond frustration and rage. But our reaction could never be justified. I carry the guilt with me, as oppressive as the heat surrounding me now.

Chapter Twenty

Pete Chandler
Monday, early afternoon. Five days left

Raquel says, "I'll contact Sergio again. See if he's found Diaz's home address." She smiles and says, "While we wait, I'll buy you a drink at the Hotel Nacional. Besides, I need internet access there."

I shake my head in a futile attempt to forget the memories that stick to me like the heat. We pass flamboyant trees that scatter petals across the sidewalks like pink snow and smell the salty ocean air.

"If you text Sergio, will the secret police catch that?"

"Sure, but over the years we've established codes to talk with each other. All Cubans do this."

"Okay. Let's get going on that."

"The hotel is one of our most well-known landmarks. Everyone famous or even those people trying to hide, like American gangsters, stayed here. Hollywood people, Winston Churchill, South American dictators, and famous performers all liked it. But Americans are forbidden to stay in hotels in retaliation for the embargo." She parks the car a block away, and we approach the front entrance.

The pale yellow walls of the hotel cover nine stories of rooms with the finest dining, dancing cabarets, bars and, before Fidel Castro, glamorous gambling dens and prostitution.

We stroll through a shallow lobby and come outside again onto a wide space of grass decorated with palm trees and a swimming pool next to the blue Caribbean. At a veranda she finds a table, sheltered under another series of arches.

I open a menu and find dishes I recognize, but I'm not hungry.

Raquel notices and says, "All of that food is reserved for tourists."

"What do you mean?"

She reaches into her purse and pulls out a limp red notebook. She opens it to show me pages with check marks next to food supplies "allowed" for each person. "Every Cuban except those in the Communist Party is issued ration cards with subsidized prices for basic food."

"You must eat well."

Raquel sneers, "If you call getting one chicken a month for a family of four 'eating well,' yes, we do. Or one liter of cheap Venezuelan cooking oil to last a month."

"So, how do you survive?" A waiter sets a cloudy mojito on the table. Out on the lawn, pretending to study some old Spanish cannons still "guarding" the hotel, I see the same man who stopped the exchange in Lennon Park.

"There's a dual economy in Cuba. The government sets prices, which are high because there are shortages of everything—thanks to the American embargo." She sips her mojito. "But we depend on wide networks of family and friends to get what we need."

"How does that work?"

"Let's say I have an uncle who lives in Miami. He buys a microwave or underwear or a lamp in the U.S. He's allowed to send in a limited amount of goods to 'family' every month. Once on the island, I get the microwave, but if I don't need a microwave, then I contact everyone in the network to offer it in exchange for something I need."

"Does the party know about this?"

"Of course. But they also know it's the only way Cubans will survive, and so long as we pay tax on the goods, the party ignores it."

"Why don't Cubans rise up against the government?" I sip the mojito and enjoy the tart taste.

"People will never do that."

"Why not?"

"We have no guns, and for many, Fidel is like an old grandfather who made many mistakes but is still revered as the founding father of our independence. Besides, everyone gets free medical care and free education. We are hungry, but Cubans have learned *sonriendo de vida*. Smiling through life."

A breeze blows shiny black strands of hair across her face. Raquel looks at her phone, and her face lights up. "He got the address."

In a few minutes, we're back in the Toyota as Raquel drives to the west of the central city. "The Cuban government rewards its scientists, so they are allowed to own homes in the Miramar section of the city. One of the nicest."

She turns into a quiet section with big white mansions baking in the heat along the clean streets and green lawns. Some fly the Cuban flag. I remember Raquel's explanation of the food shortages here. I feel sorry for these people. Most of them I've met are warm and intelligent.

"Many foreign embassies are located here." Raquel points to a squat building. "That's the Canadian Embassy." She makes many turns as if she's lost. "I'm going to lose any tails we have." Twenty minutes later, convinced we're in the clear, we take a left onto Calle 34. We drive away from the ocean and creep along a quiet street, looking for house number 248. I look behind us. Don't see any obvious tails. All the turns Raquel made must've lost them.

"There, there it is." She points as we slide to the curb in front of a small but elegant house. One story, whitewashed stucco with an orange tile roof. Two palm trees shade the flushed facade. The outside looks bare by American standards, but I know the important part of a Cuban home is the open-air courtyard, hidden from the public in the middle of the house.

I jump out of the car, but Raquel cautions, "Slow down. Let me do this."

It's hard for me to let her take over, but I realize I'm out of my element here. "Okay."

A breeze carries the smell of the ocean, and a red macaw balances on the edge of the tile roof, watching us. It's quiet in the neighborhood. Raquel strolls across the lawn to the side of the house, looks around, and comes back. "Guess it's time to try the door."

We both approach a blue door with an arched top. Raquel knocks several times. No answer. Knocks again. Jiggles the doorknob, which is locked.

She leads us around the side of the home again. As we approach the back, we hear someone call to us from the backyard garden of the house next door. "*Buenos días.*"

An old man pushes a straw hat back over his forehead. Dark face with silver hair. "Hot, isn't it?" He walks toward us, jerky steps. Hesitant.

Raquel agrees and introduces both of us. "We're looking for Rodolfo Diaz. Does he live here?" She smiles.

The man seems to shrink backward. "Who are you?"

I'm about to say something in Spanish, but Raquel interrupts. "I believe Rodolfo may be a distant relative of mine."

"Don't think I can help you." The old man turns to pick up a rake.

"Do you know him? His family?" Raquel persists.

"I shouldn't be talking with you."

I sneak a quick glance at Raquel. Her eyes signal: something's wrong here.

"What's the problem?" She strolls closer to the man.

"I don't want to get involved."

"We're not from the government."

The old man pulls out a red handkerchief and wipes his forehead. "You're not the first ones looking for him."

"Oh?"

He takes a few steps toward us. "Two days ago, there were some men here who circled the house and stayed for a while before they left. A couple weeks ago, some of the officers from the DI came to the house."

"Did you see what happened?" I ask in Spanish.

"Of course not. I hid inside my own house. I don't want anything to do with them. I'm not a troublemaker." His eyes blink rapidly.

A breeze ripples the palm leaves.

"No one has been there for several weeks."

"Did you see them leave?"

"No. It must've happened at night, like so many of these things happen. They're all gone. The wife, kids, pets. The only one they forgot is Chico, the macaw." He nods at the bird still perched on the roof, looking down on us.

"Were you friends with Rodolfo?"

"Sure. He was a gifted artist and a scientist, I think. He never talked about his work. I always suspected it was something secret, some work for the government that he couldn't talk about." He pauses, looking up into the clouds sliding across the sun. "Maybe even something dangerous."

We both nod. "By any chance, do you have a key to get in?" Raquel asks.

Lifting his rake, he disappears around the corner of his house toward the garden. We follow him to the shelter of a small courtyard.

He looks around and drops his voice. "Something odd. I didn't tell the secret police, but I saw Dr. Diaz getting picked up."

"Oh?" Raquel asks.

"Normally, the police come at night and throw people in the back ends of trucks. Only one person showed up for this. A middle-aged woman with gray hair. Late afternoon. I couldn't see her clearly because I was hiding, but the entire family left, and it didn't look like a police grab. They were friendly."

Only the clatter of the palm leaves interrupts the surrounding silence. As we leave for our car, the macaw watches us closely.

Neither of us speak as we get back in the car. Inside, Raquel lets out a big breath.

"What?" I look at her pale face.

"I don't know if I can keep going, Pete."

"I understand."

"I don't know why you're really here, but it's getting quite dangerous."

I prop my elbow in the open window. My face feels moist. "When I took this assignment, it seemed so simple and easy for someone like me, with my experience."

She looks over at me, eyes dark, intense. "How do Americans say it, 'You stuck your finger in a hornet's nest'?"

"Yes, that's how we say it."

We wait for five minutes in silence until Raquel says, "But we must keep working on this."

"What?"

Her lips tighten. "I have my own reasons." Starting the car, she drives toward the Malecon.

I ask her, "Why are you still helping me? Can you tell me?"

She turns slowly. Her eyes search around my face until they focus on my eyes. "It's none of your business, but I've grown to respect you." She faces forward again.

I wait for her to say more. She's silent as we turn onto the Malecon, and I feel the spray from the crashing ocean spill into our open windows. In spite of that, the heat in the car is uncomfortable.

"I was married for many years. My husband was an ophthalmologist but secretly worked for an underground group that tried to influence the media to make it more open and free." Raquel swallows. "Until he was caught and disappeared one night. I have not seen him for eight years."

My breath catches in my chest.

"I also helped in his secret work, but they didn't arrest me with him. Thank God we didn't have children. Inevitably, the secret police came for me and questioned me for days. The worst one was an attractive woman with short gray hair. Alvarez was her name. I knew about my husband's activities, and I directed many of the campaigns. But I lied to Alvarez, defied her, and finally persuaded her that I was innocent. Eventually she believed me and let me go with a warning: if I screwed up in any way, they would make my parents-in-law disappear also. I couldn't bear that." Anger sharpens the edge of her words.

I speak softly. "So why would you risk working with me?"

Raquel turns toward me, lowering her voice as if someone could overhear us in the car. "Because I hate what they have done. The memory of my husband is still with me, but they've taken him and everything else I loved."

Her intensity pushes me back into the seat. Maybe she will be tough enough to follow through with the mission. But an unanswered question hangs in the car like the heavy humidity. Without Rodolfo Diaz, now what do I do?

In twenty minutes, we arrive at the Export bank. Without speaking, we trudge up to her office and walk out to the patio in back. Diego's memory tumbles around us like the water in the fountain.

Raquel checks her phone, scrolls through screens, and frowns. "This is strange."

"What?"

"Sergio texted me again."

"About Diaz?"

"No, he would never put that information in a text. This is personal." She stares at me. "He insists we meet him immediately, tonight, at a music club."

"Why?"

"He must have something important; we must not take any chance of being overheard."

In a 1976 top secret report to the Pentagon from the Defense Intelligence Agency, they warned of Russian scientists who were conducting secret, non-thermal testing by exposing animal brains to microwaves. Building on the 1961 research of the American scientist, Alan Frey, they changed the frequency at which neurons fired and, as a result, the neurons went out of sync. Brain cells withered, nerves were damaged, and a complete "alteration of brain functions" afflicted the animals. "Their brains turned to mush," a Russian scientist was reported as saying.

The Pentagon ignored the report, considering it "science fiction," a product of the Cold War, and nothing worth pursuing.

—U.S. Defense Intelligence Agency, 1976

Chapter Twenty-One

Ava Alvarez
Monday afternoon. Five days left

I pace across my living room, turn and walk back with uneven steps. My neck tightens. I'm waiting, again, for Tom. And I'm not happy. He still hasn't delivered the poison products I need.

Tom has finished production of the necessary chemicals. My defense against an attack by the traitors is unusual, but it's the best I can prepare. Even armed with the chemicals, I ponder my next step. At least I've got the two names Lopez spilled before he died. My most trusted aide, Rico Pena, is already running down their backgrounds quickly.

My maid lays out chips, freshly fried, and their smell entices me. She also leaves a beer for Tom. She hovers around the table, straightening items that don't need it.

"What is it, Solana?" I snap at her.

Solana comes as close to being family without blood ties, as most domestic help does in Cuba.

Solana touches my arm. "My seventh child was just like Tom, until I told him to come to the Santeria rituals."

I nod, but I don't have any religion. For years, I fought to suppress Santeria as a dangerous opiate of the masses. "Maybe I'll try that." I dismiss her for the day.

The coughing of a taxi's engine in the street causes me to turn toward the front door. Tom saunters through the open mahogany slab carrying a leather briefcase carefully at the side of his body. "*Mamacita.*" He hugs me. "I'm hungry." When he sees the food on the table, he sits down.

I circle him. Waiting. Finally, I yell at him, "Do you have it?"

Tom grins. "Of course." He lifts the briefcase off the floor and places it on the edge of the table. "Here are the pellets. This is nasty shit to work with." He drinks half of the bottle of Cristal beer before setting it down.

"So, the old Russian formula still works?" I ask.

"*Sí, sí.* It's ricin poison, a toxic protein from castor beans. But when I formulated and purified it in the lab, it became truly toxic. There are no antidotes, and it never fails to kill those injected with it." He pauses and tilts his head. "Are you satisfied?"

I reach over and hug his neck. "I know this was hard. You have done a great service for the Revolution."

"Bullshit. You're the only one who even uses that word anymore."

"How many pellets did you prepare?"

"Twenty-four." He slobbers ketchup over the chips. "How do you plan to deliver it?"

I back up and laugh. "We have several 'Bulgarian' umbrellas that are still serviceable. With our shortages in Cuba, I use whatever technology is available."

"Umbrellas?"

"They've got several strategic advantages—"

"Can't you just use your gun?" he sneers.

"No. Wherever this happens, the security will make it impossible to use conventional means."

"I don't want to know anymore. Did you get a job for Lucinda?"

"She is meeting with Eddie Pacheco in a week."

"Hey, you really did come through." Tom looks into my eyes and smiles. Finished eating the food, he stands up. "She's got real talent. You'll see." Tom looks at the clock on the far wall. "Hey, I've got the afternoon off. Beach party."

He wipes his sleeve across his mouth and leans down to kiss my cheeks, one after the other. With a wave, Tom saunters to the front door. "Pepe's picking me up. *Ciao.*" Before going through the door, he pauses. "Hey, Mama, be careful with that stuff. There's no cure if it gets into your body."

I appreciate his concern for me and follow him out and give him a hug. He ducks through my arms and is gone, leaving only a faint scent of himself.

Inside, I cradle his leather briefcase in my arms, as if it were filled with expensive crystal glassware, and go into the office next to the living room. I open the outer flap of the case slowly but don't touch anything with my bare hands. Ricin is most effective if injected under the skin, but I don't want to risk anything. The umbrellas are hidden in a secret closet in my office and can be accessed quickly.

I review the president's itinerary. He'll land with his family on Thursday and tour Old Havana, followed by dinner at a *paladar*. On Friday, he meets with Raul Castro in the morning and local business people in the afternoon, followed by a state dinner at the Revolutionary Palace. The final day he will give a speech at the Grand Theater followed by an appearance in the plaza next to it, and end the day at a baseball game between an American team and Cuba's best.

Of course, the American security forces will be massive at each step, so where do the traitors plan to strike? And how? Anyone even remotely suspected of carrying a gun or any weapon will be arrested. So how can I prepare to stop them?

Rico Pena should be calling soon with his progress report.

I breathe slowly and look across to the open window that faces the garden outside. White mariposa lilies crowd the windowsill and lean into the room. Pale yellow stalks droop as if they are tired. A breeze blows through the window, fluttering the petals and blowing a few inside to scatter on the wooden floor. I stand and let the wind cool my face, strengthening me.

The phone in my office rings. I sprint back there and push aside my laptop to pick up the heavy receiver.

"Comandante, this is Agent Pena."

My shoulders straighten. "What've you got?"

"I found both of the suspects." Pena stops to clear his throat.

"Excellent work."

"Miguel and Felipe Garcia are cousins."

"Stop. I want your report in person." I thought of all the possible agents who could be listening on the phone right now. "Come to my house."

When Pena arrives a half hour later, I bring him back to my office.

I leave Pena standing but tell him, "As you know, my home is secure. Speak freely."

A small man, Pena is dressed in green army fatigues that Fidel made a necessary part of the uniform of the Revolution. Moisture covers his forehead and clings to his body so I can smell the outdoors on him. "Miguel has worked for the Communist Party for years. He's high ranking but has a violent history. Felipe was educated as an engineer and works at a factory."

"Oh?"

"But he seems to have lots of cash. Also, I was able to follow him to a secret meeting with Miguel." He pauses to wipe his hand across his forehead. "I don't know the significance of the meetings, but they're not secret to us anymore." Pena chuckles. He removes several photos of the suspects from his inside pocket and lays them on the desk for me to study.

I cut him off. "Could he be part of the plot?"

"I'll continue to shadow them. Felipe's easy because he walks with a limp. There is some evidence Miguel's also met with one of the suspect groups here in Cuba that we have under watch."

"Which one?"

"Red Dog Associates out of Miami."

I nod. My gut tightens. This is why I trust Pena completely. He is not only competent but could take the lead on his own. "What an *ajiaco*, Cuban soup, this has become."

"The Americans, Cuban traitors, and mercenary gangsters are an explosive combination. But why would the Americans be involved?"

I answer in crisp words. "The traitors will cooperate with the Americans or, worse, give up our country to them again." I stand up. "This must be what all our intelligence has pointed to. You've done great work, and the Revolution thanks you."

He smiles.

My chest tightens and I breathe faster. The combination of these players proves that we've discovered significant clues to the plot. But because of Miguel's work with the party and his high rank, I must move very carefully. I certainly can't approach him directly or arrest him. Although it was small in the early days, the Communist Party has grown to the behemoth it is today, controlling much of Cuban life with their own spies and stifling bureaucracy.

Pena adds, "And when we interviewed people at the CNEURO lab after Chandler and Diego Arnaz had been there, one of the guards told me that Miguel Garcia was probably there at the same time."

"That can't be a coincidence. Could they be the masterminds?" The wooden chair creaks when I lean back into it. Why would they be involved with the American?

"I recently intercepted a phone call from Miguel to Felipe."

"One?"

"They are very careful about communicating."

"What did they say?"

"Miguel said, 'It's going to happen this Saturday.' In five days." He pauses. "In downtown Havana."

I frown and lean forward. I review the president's itinerary again. On Saturday, he meets with Cuban officials, gives a speech at the theater, and goes to a baseball game. The smallest crowds will be when he visits the officials. He'll be most vulnerable at the transfer points, so I calculate that's when Miguel and Felipe may strike.

Pena shrugs. "There was nothing else in the intercept."

"You didn't search further? What the hell are you doing, eating plantains all day?" I yell at Pena, who backs up two feet.

"I am working overtime, Comandante. You know we must move carefully against the two men."

"Unfortunately, we must wait until they act, then take them out." I breathe slower while I think ahead of Pena. Discovering these two is a stroke of luck. I pause. "Anything more on the American?"

"As you know, I tried to make clandestine contact with him in the park by Lennon." He drops his eyes. "Unfortunately, it was not successful."

My mouth is dry, and I sip some water. Disappointed. "As I've warned you, we must be extremely careful. If anyone discovers the secret police contacting an American diplomat, the international repercussions would be a disaster." I also thought of Alfredo Mendoza. If he suspected anything, he'd pounce on me like a mongoose after a rat in a cane field.

"After Arnaz's death, Chandler's been working with a woman named Raquel Sanchez. She's also an employee of the U.S. Export/Import Bank."

I vaguely remember Sanchez from a case I broke years ago. Husband and wife subversives? I can't pull the details out of my memory. I tell Pena, "Pull the file on Raquel Sanchez." Everyone in Cuba has a file on them, maintained by my agency. I retrieve Tom's briefcase.

"Of course." His posture straightens.

Five days. I tug at my hair absentmindedly. How will they do it? Where exactly? But this is clearly the final play. I must act.

Before I can do anything more, the phone rings. I hear the familiar voice of my boss, Alfredo, which almost causes me to drop the briefcase. I hide it underneath files in the bottom drawer of my desk as if he's present in the room and reluctantly say hello. What the hell does he want now?

Alfredo takes his time. "Ava, my beautiful little *trogan*." He refers to me as a bird.

His breathing sounds like a pig snuffling for scraps of food.

"Why are you calling?"

Alfredo clears his throat. "We could be close friends, you and me. We want the same things in life."

"I'm not sure about that."

I can imagine his face coloring from the neck upward as it does when I don't bow to him. "You know what I want."

I hold the phone away from me for a moment to collect my thoughts. He rarely calls me; what does he want? There's an insistent aspect to him that I've never seen before, so I decide to cooperate. "You're right. What a pleasure that you called."

"Don't disrespect me. I'm still your commanding officer."

He must've detected the cynicism in my voice.

"Things are going to change in this country. And I can protect you from that."

"I'm sorry if I sound rude. I'm under so much pressure because of the upcoming visit of the president."

"That's exactly why you need sex with me. To relax."

"I'm sure we will have the opportunity soon." That placates him for now. I hope to never have to face the prospect of getting in bed with him. But he's clever and ruthless.

"In the meantime, I have a question to ask you."

I notice a change in his tone of voice. Something dangerous. "I am aware that you are doing work that I did not authorize."

"I have many projects that are authorized by my position. You know that."

"Yes, but this involves something in deep cover."

I pretend not to understand.

"You see, I am still capable even for an old man." I hear him swallow. "Don't play stupid. I have my own sources of intelligence, and what I'm hearing is not good. What is not good for me is especially bad for you."

"What do you hear?"

"Hmm." Alfredo pauses. "I cannot jeopardize my agents."

Too bad I don't have the opportunity to slip a ricin pellet into his coffee. It's too risky to upset him any further now. "I understand." Is he the mastermind of the plot, as I suspect? It certainly sounds like he's fishing for information in order to stop me.

"You force me to take a closer look at your activities. You will meet me alone tomorrow at ten o'clock outside of the Church of the *Espiritu Santo*, the Holy Spirit. And remember, in the meantime, if you interfere in activities outside your assigned duties, it won't be only your career that ends." He hangs up.

My chest collapses and I have to sit down. He's a pig but still dangerous. Is Mendoza bluffing? Does he really know what I'm doing? This time, I'll do what I've never done before when I've met with him. I'll bring my service weapon, the Belgian revolver that Fidel gave to me.

Chapter Twenty-Two

Pete Chandler
Monday night. Five days left

Late in the evening, Raquel drives us to a second-story nightclub in the area only a few blocks from the Hotel Nacional. The sign in front, neon green and written in English, reads "The Treetop."

My search for Rodolfo Diaz has hit a dead end. I'm not surprised, because if his efforts to make contact with U.S. officials were discovered by the secret police, there's little doubt he has "disappeared" for good.

Before Raquel picked me up, I called Sonnenfeld on the special phone. I told him about Diaz.

"Too bad, but that's it, Chandler," he says. "Time for us to pull you out. I'll arrange it as soon as I can."

I pause, thinking. I've rarely failed in my work as an investigator. I don't want to accept failure now. And I think of the American victims, the fear that Frank Graves spoke of, and I tell Sonnenfeld, "I'm working on a new lead."

"I'm telling you it's over. You've been unable to complete your mission. This is no different than rotating you out of a combat zone."

"I'm staying. You told me there was a second exfiltration option if I need it."

Sonnenfeld sighs. "Uh, we're still working on that, but I don't want to activate that resource yet. Only if we have an extreme situation. You're not authorized to investigate any aspects of the Havana Syndrome, so your assignment is finished."

Telling me that is like telling a dog he can't run. Sonnenfeld's pressuring my withdrawal. "No." I think back to the private contractor, Benny. Lots of people are telling me to quit. I don't like that, and I usually do the opposite. I end by informing Sonnenfeld of my upcoming meeting with Sergio de la Vaca.

Later, in front of the club, Raquel stops the car and says, "There are dozens of clubs all over the city. It's one of the joys we Cubans love. Music, drinks, and dancing to Latin bands from all over the world."

"Except the U.S."

"Yes, unfortunately." Then she grins. "Come on. Let's see if you can dance." She takes off her red glasses and folds them into the glove compartment.

Because of the loud music and crowds inside, it will be difficult for the police to overhear what Sergio has to say. A perfect cover for our meeting.

A narrow stairway leads up to the second floor and turns into a surprisingly large room with a short bar along one wall. The other three walls have French windows, all opened to the warm evening outside. I follow Raquel onto a worn wooden floor. An avocado tree thrusts a branch through one of the windows, hanging its shiny green leaves over a section of the floor.

Raquel insists on a table in the corner as a waiter takes our orders. From the small stage, a band plays the infectious music of Cuba.

While Raquel looks across the room for Sergio, I glance at her. Black hair puddles around her shoulders while her head bobs to the beat of the music. She's smiling and looks beautiful.

"I love music and dancing," she tells me.

"Where's Sergio?"

"He's late. Not like him." She frowns and looks toward the door again. Then she turns back to me. "We all need an escape from the difficulties of life, especially in Cuba. Music is mine. Maybe it's time for a dance lesson." Her eyes tease me.

"I don't think so."

The band stops to introduce a special guest. A large Black woman steps onto the stage, dressed in bright red high heels and a yellow dress. Her face shines while her rich voice fills the entire room. The crowd moves in response to her caressing voice.

"Come on, let's dazzle the boys." Raquel stands and pulls at my hand.

I don't want to do this, but the music and the moment also pull at me. We press our way through the crush of people. The music surrounds us, as alive as the dancers moving beside us while the trumpeter cries into the humid air.

Raquel grabs my shoulders as she shouts into my ear, "Follow my lead. You'll take two steps forward, then two steps back." She pulls me forward, then her right leg presses against the inside of mine and forces me to step backwards. "Watch." She parts from me and demonstrates the move.

I look down to see her bare brown leg step toward me, move back, and forward again with a slight bounce. At the same time, her hips slide from side to side, effortlessly. It looks complicated but beautiful. The faint smell of sweat surrounds us.

Raquel faces me. "The key is to listen to the music. Let your body flow with it." She lifts my arms in her hands and continues the steps, pulling me back and forth.

I lumber after her, feeling like an American clod, my feet heavy and slow.

"Good. Now swing your hips to the sides."

I try but feel even more embarrassed, envying her effortless grace.

She laughs. "Okay, you look like Frankenstein's monster, but you'll get it."

After twenty minutes of dancing, I imagine I might look passable. But my confidence flags and I feel stupid again. We stop dancing and work our way back to the table. She lifts her hair from around her face to cool off. "You're more fun than I thought when I first met you."

"Thanks to you."

Raquel smiles at me. She looks happy for the first time since I met her. For a moment, I also feel good and can ignore the haunting guilt for a while. The warmth of the room touches my skin with damp fingers, relaxing my shoulders. We leave the dance floor as our shoulders bump against each other. I'm more aware than ever of her body next to mine. The sensation feels good.

In ten minutes, we spot Sergio pushing his way through the dancers, coming toward us. He greets Raquel with a long hug and shakes my hand. Sitting opposite us, he looks around for a long time and finally pulls his chair closer.

"Thanks for coming," Raquel says.

Sergio nods. "Sure, but I can't stay long." He waves off the waiter when he approaches.

"What've you got for us?" I ask.

"I owe so much to Raquel." He crosses and uncrosses his arms.

I lean forward over the table, my breath bottled up in my chest while I wait for Sergio to share his information. The song ends and the band moves into another one. I turn quickly to Sergio. "What can you tell us?"

"Shortly after you left the facility, the secret police showed up and questioned me."

"Did they ask about me?"

"Yes. They wanted to know what you were doing at the lab."

"What did you tell them exactly?" Raquel asks.

"That you were exploring trade opportunities."

Raquel says, "What did the agents do after that?"

"Nothing." He looks over his shoulder to survey the room before turning back to us.

I'm surprised. "Anything else?"

"When we met at CNEURO, I wasn't free to tell you, but there's a lot of information you should know."

"What?" I say. My stomach tightens. Hopeful.

"Rodolfo Diaz told me his research took him back to 1961. The American biologist, Allan Frey, discovered that when he irradiated the human skull with microwaves, it produced a sensation of sound. Even from a thousand feet away. He altered the frequency and intensity to produce a range of different sensations."

"So, the Americans are responsible—"

Sergio shakes his head. "When the Soviets were in Cuba, they learned about Frey's research and invited him to Moscow, where they treated him like royalty. They were fascinated with the idea of 'directed energy weapons.' They conceived of a microwave weapon that could cast an invisible wave."

"Sounds like science fiction. Give me hard facts."

"Remember, the Soviets dominated Cuba for years," Sergio says. "While they were here, they conducted extensive research on weapons like this at CNEURO. A few of the records remain."

More patrons squeeze into the room, and in spite of the cool breeze coming through the open windows, the temperature rises.

I push for more details.

"The Russian scientists exposed animal brains to microwaves. When they changed the frequency, the neurons in the animal brains went out of sync. Brain cells withered and nerves were damaged. Basically, they turned to mush."

"Did they make a weapon?"

"I don't know. After the Soviet Union collapsed, their troops left Cuba in 1991, but many Russian scientists and officials remained. But as far as Rodolfo could tell, their research probably stopped."

Raquel says, "Do you think such a weapon could exist now?"

Sergio shrugs.

I wait for more information.

"Diaz thought the Russians were trying to develop a device that emits sonic bullets along an intense beam up to 145 decibels."

Raquel asks, "That's a lot?"

"Fifty times the human threshold of pain."

"Did they build a weapon?" I ask again.

"Lots of theory. I even saw a diagram of some kind of a weapon mounted on a truck. But as far as I can tell, nothing was actually built. When I was part of the team studying the American diplomats affected by the 'Havana Syndrome,' I remembered the Russians' research. I found some of the old schematic diagrams." Sergio's face pinches.

"So much of what the Russians did failed. But sometimes—" He wags his finger in the air. "Sometimes, they succeeded brilliantly. Unfortunately, my security clearance doesn't allow me to search any further in the recorded diagrams."

"Do you think Rodolfo Diaz knows more?" I ask.

Sergio shrugs. "Probably, but now he's disappeared. I'm afraid to dig any deeper."

The musicians take a break, which leaves the churning sound of dozens of people talking with an occasional cackle of female laughter. Raquel and I each order another drink. I think of the computer hacking tools I have in my bag, and an idea comes to me. I lower my voice and explain it to the others. "But I need access to the lab." I don't want to put Sergio in a risky position, so I ask him, "Would you clone the director's security card for me?"

Sergio starts to shake his head.

"It's simple, and he'll never know." I reach into my Faraday bag and pull out a tool that is small enough to fit in my palm. "It's called the Flipper Zero. All you need to do is get next to the director for less than a second. Leave it in your pants pocket so he doesn't see it. It'll copy RFID, NFC, or even sub-GHz. Once you have it copied, we can meet secretly."

Sergio finally agrees. "I must leave." He slides back his chair.

The waiter serves us two daiquiris.

Sergio stands up, shifting his weight from side to side. Anxious. "Okay. Give me the Flipper." He slips it into his pocket, nods once, and jostles his way through the crowd toward the door. I decide to tell Raquel about the message at my door and the incident at Lennon Park. "My hope is that if Diaz tried to contact me once, he'll try again."

An hour later, she drops me off at the Ambos Mundos Hotel and follows me to the edge of the lobby. Before leaving, Raquel looks at me, a somber expression on her face. "I hope we can succeed, but remember what happened to my husband." The hair around her face is still damp, curled into irregular patterns, and her eyes are intense.

"Of course." I also remember Sergio's words about Russian scientists, brains going squishy, and some kind of a secret sonic weapon. Crazy stuff, but obviously dangerous enough to possibly have hurt our diplomats.

She walks me to the corner near the elevator. Hesitating for a moment, she steps closer to me. Against my instincts, I lean forward and kiss her. Both of us are surprised at this development, but she doesn't move. We kiss again for a longer time. Our breathing builds until she pulls back.

I follow her across the lobby, and as Raquel turns and steps down onto the sidewalk, I watch the bunching of her hips under her skirt. Her skin looks golden in the glow of the lights from the lobby. Then she turns sharply and disappears into the darkness. Against all my caution, I want to trust her.

Chapter Twenty-Three

Miguel Garcia
Tuesday morning. Four days left

I told Felipe to meet me at La Necrópolis de Cristóbal Colón, the cemetery of Chistopher Columbus, in Vedado, just east of the Miramar section of the city. The largest cemetery in Cuba cradles the bodies of over a million Cubans, squeezed into plain flat graves or in soaring private cathedrals built by some of the wealthiest and most famous families in the country.

Of course, there are tour groups gawking at the spectacle, but it also offers wide open spaces where I can avoid any spies. I have our final orders. Today, I need Felipe's absolute commitment to follow this to the end.

Luckily, Benny and his contractors haven't killed us yet. Maybe they won't. I've continued to secretly strategize with the top people involved from both countries to set up the new infrastructure.

For security purposes, my limo drops me a few blocks away, so I walk along Calzada Zapata to reach the brown stone arch at the entrance. The plan is in motion, and I'm worried that Felipe will back out when faced with the reality of what he must do. I lean against the cool stone wall but find that I can't stand still.

In a few minutes, an old Russian Zil taxi grumbles to the sidewalk in front of me, and I smell the exhaust from the cheap gasoline. Felipe scrambles out of the back seat. He stands for a moment, looking up at the rolling clouds that cast fleeting shadows across the steeples of the largest mausoleums. He limps toward me, wearing a new red *guayabera*. From his throat three gold chains hang down, flopping against his chest.

"*Hola*, Chucho. *Qué pasa?*" Felipe plugs a large unlit cigar into his mouth.

"Quiet!" I take a deep breath and put my arm around his shoulder as we walk into the cemetery. "It's a 'go' for sure," I whisper. "Remember, it's Saturday." Pressure fills my chest, and I struggle to slow down my pace to match Felipe's limping.

We pass underneath an immense stone arch, heavy with an impressive bulk. At the top, like on every other edifice, marble statues of the Holy Family and various saints all hint at the path of salvation. Some of the statues are so old, black moss has grown around the sharp edges to leave them softer than the hard message they proclaim for the sinners who pass below.

We pause inside, deciding which direction to stroll. For as far as I can see, there is marble piled onto more marble fashioned into steeples, houses, crypts, and monuments. Next to us, a slight breeze teases the roses, causing a few petals to seesaw onto the ground like a dusting of red snow.

"No one is over there." I point toward a tall, lemon-colored church at the far end of the road. I glance at Felipe, trying to read his reaction to the news that we are finally going into combat.

We move slowly past simple, flat slabs of gray marble, edge to edge, with names of the dead chiseled into the tops. Lopez, Morales, Perez, even an occasional Smith.

Still, I notice, among the stones and gravel, several decapitated birds. A pile of glittering coins and dried oranges. Secret offerings. Obviously, the surviving families have hedged their relatives' bets on Catholicism with a healthy dose of Santeria, just in case.

Felipe stops and cups his hand around the end of the cigar, firing it until it glows red. He draws in deeply and lets out a fragrant cloud with a sigh. His face clouds over. "What about the cowboys from Red Dog Associates?"

I smile broadly. "*Tranquila.* Don't worry. The transition planning is almost done. But it all depends on us lighting the fuse."

Felipe's nervous laugh sounds like a horse. He swings his arm toward the sunlit statues next to us. "With our positions in the new regime, we can afford to bury you here. You bet on the *bolita?*" Felipe squints as he looks back at me.

"I always do. Number seven and, lately, number fifty-two."

"Oh?"

"The gods of thunder and valor. So we will be brave."

Felipe nods and starts limping again. "They will help us." His face relaxes. "What's my assignment?"

"For security purposes, I can only tell you what you need to know right now," I assure him.

"Russians, Cubans, Americans—it's a combustible fucking combination." He barks a quick laugh. "What's the next step?"

"We'll carry out our prep on Friday in order to be in place by Saturday."

"Sure."

We shuffle through a trail of dead brown leaves at the edge of the road. They crackle under our feet. "It's all about timing." I lower my voice. "And luck."

"Oh?"

I speak faster. "I have other news."

"What's that mean?"

I pause to make Felipe think he's special and chosen. "We've even figured out a way to get us close enough."

Felipe's voice rises. "Close enough?" He continues to move but stops limping.

We reach a marble mausoleum with a marble fence surrounding it, and I put my arm on his shoulder again. "Settle down. It'll be dangerous, but only a man of your courage can handle it."

"Sure." He swallows hard. More of his hair falls across his forehead.

My mind spins ahead to think of what will happen if Felipe refuses his role. Those contractors won't waste time coming for me. That's okay; I'll fight to the end. Worse, the freedom of the country will also die with me. The rewards that hang before me like the clouds above will disappear forever.

We continue to walk toward the church until Felipe asks, "What about the American spy? What did you find out?"

"I ordered him eliminated, but the stupid driver hit the wrong guy. I'll have to eliminate that problem myself." I smile in a big way to reassure him.

We approach the yellow church at the end of the street, neither of us speaking. We pass a clump of tourists standing before a Cuban guide, popping open umbrellas to shade themselves from the sun. Most of them listen while the guide explains, "These graves look impressive on the outside, but many things in Cuba aren't always what they seem. Some families cut costs by building with cement, then covering it with a very thin layer of marble."

Fifty feet past the group, Felipe asks, "The same kind of weapon?"

I grin. "Don't worry, it's similar to the one you used before."

"Okay." He puffs several times on the cigar.

"But you'll be highly exposed."

Felipe's face contorts. "But I'll get out, right?"

I stop and look directly at him. "You'll have cover and a disguise. Benny and his men will extract us. That's also part of my plan to double cross him."

Clouds scud in from the ocean across the blue sky as they have rolled over Cuba for centuries. A breeze ruffles Felipe's hair and lifts it off his head. "I don't know. That sounds too dangerous."

"We'll catch him when Benny's alone so nothing can be traced back to us."

"I don't trust any of them."

"Remember, I've been meeting with these guys. Red Dog has had successful black ops experience in many countries. When it's over, we'll put our people in a free world. If Fidel could change the country with only a handful of farmers and a couple rifles, we can also succeed."

Felipe drops his head, thinking. Finally, he looks up. "I don't know, Chucho."

I hold my breath, try to remain calm and keep working on him.

He limps into the church, carrying hints of his mortality within his damaged leg. "So, what's my assignment?"

I remain silent.

"I deserve to know."

We stop at the door. The nave is octagonal, with wings of sheltered walkways extending out to the sides. The faint odor of burned incense lingers in the air. I step underneath the loggia in one of the wings and enter the deserted church. Three stories high, the cupola rides on top of pale green walls that give a feeling of peace.

"You will be assigned as the field commander. But I can't tell you any more right now. The outcome of your success will have repercussions that will shake the entire island. So, you can understand why we have to stay compartmentalized right now."

He bobs his head.

"We will take private transportation to avoid detection. We'll receive the necessary cover to get access—"

"I'm worried."

"Shut up, Felipe, and listen."

"And the money?"

I sigh and watch him tap ash off his cigar onto the polished floor. "You'll get paid more than you can imagine. And when I'm in charge, you'll be the *caudillo,* the strong man, at my side."

"Sure, but—" Felipe clasps his hands.

"Like any secret operation, we've all been isolated in separate cells so we don't compromise the op. But I can assure you, we've got this all figured out. I'll get the logistical intelligence soon."

He squares his shoulders. "I will do it."

Relief fills my chest. "That's why they chose you. You're the best we've got."

"My *orichas* will protect me." He looks at me. "And the double cross?"

Three tourists poke their heads into the church. They take dozens of photos without looking at what they shoot and leave.

I look at Felipe and nod. "I'm still working out the final details. I'll need your brains and help."

"Okay, but don't leave me in the dark."

I laugh with Felipe for a long time until I glance at my watch. "Don't worry." Now that I've got him committed, I don't have any more time for this. I look around the nave to make sure no one is present and push Felipe toward the door.

"Let's get it done." He blows out a huge cloud of smoke that hangs around us.

I'm relieved that he feels so cocky. He'll need every ounce of courage. Still, he's family, and I have to warn him or all our relatives will hate me. "We'll be going into the heart of the beast." I turn my back on him and start for the door.

"But Chucho—" Felipe calls after me.

I feel him clutching at my arm, but all he catches is a cloud of cigar smoke.

Chapter Twenty-Four

Ava Alvarez
Tuesday morning. Four days left

At nine fifty, I walk slowly to the intersection of Calle Cuba and Acosta. The Church of the Holy Spirit hulks on the corner, the oldest in Cuba, built in 1635. It looks medieval with its square block simplicity and little outside ornamentation. Once pure white, it now slumbers with gray walls from centuries of wear. Why the hell is Mendoza wasting my time to meet here instead of the office? I'm determined to get rid of him as soon as I can.

He told me to wait in the coffee shop across the street, Café de Cuba. I sit at a small round table and listen to the fans whirring in the humid air. The door is open and I can see the streets, still wet after the early morning shower that has passed but left a heavy cloud cover in its wake.

Next to my feet is my briefcase. Revolutionary women never carry a purse. In the briefcase are reports I must read and also the Belgian revolver.

Twenty minutes later, Alfredo strolls through the door, pulling his own cloud of stinking smoke in his wake. He turns to throw the cigarette butt into the street. He smiles at me with stained teeth. "My little parakeet."

"*Buenos días,* sir."

"Come now, we go back so far there's no need to call me that. Alfredo is okay."

He looks at my *tacita* of thick coffee and walks to the counter to order his own. Back at the table, he flops into the chair and drinks it in one gulp. "Ah, nothing better than our coffee, no?" His bulk and presence are still imposing.

"Cuba offers many good things." I have to wait for him to get to the point of our meeting, and it makes me nervous.

170

"You look beautiful, as usual. You've maintained your youthful figure."

"Thank you."

"Have you ever been to the Iglesia del Espiritu Santo?" He looks across the street at the silent church.

"When I was a school girl, we came to Havana on a trip to see the colonial sites and some of the churches." In spite of drinking the coffee, my mouth is dry.

"Good, because you'll be impressed when I show it to you now."

"Oh?"

He leans forward over the small table so I can smell the cigarettes on him. "I have a special pass to visit the catacombs underneath. The only remaining preserved catacombs in all of Cuba."

"I saw them years ago as a child, so I don't need to go again." I force myself to smile. "Alfredo, is there something you want to talk about?"

"Yes, but it can wait."

I frown. "But I'm very busy now, carrying out my assignments before the American president arrives. The *paladars*—"

Alfredo waves his hand over the table. "As your commanding officer, I will decide what you do with your time."

Underneath the table, my hands clench. Whatever bullshit he's up to, I don't have the time. I think of Ricardo Pena, waiting for my instructions, and all the details that must be uncovered before we can act.

"Are you finished?" Alfredo adjusts his tunic, heavy with medals he never deserved, and stands up.

"Yes, let's go." I follow him out the door and walk across the street. This early, only a few tourists mingle at the door, pointing up at the square bell tower on the left side.

"Did you know this was built by Afro-Cuban ex-slaves?" He leads me to the massive door with an arch over the top.

From the Havana harbor, a couple blocks to the east, I hear the clattering of anchor chains dropping into the water. "How long are we going to spend here?"

He looks back at me. "Not long. My tour will be short and to the point." A dark expression passes over his face that makes me more cautious.

The door creaks as he pulls it open and we enter into the dry, dark interior. There are windows along the side facing Calle Acosta, but they're so old that little light penetrates through them. A nun in a black habit nods a greeting, and I drop a few pesos into a silver bowl next to her. No one else is inside.

Alfredo raises his arm to point at the ceiling. I look up to see ancient beams crossing the space, still holding up the roof in spite of all the years they've been asked to do so. I would be impressed except I'm too nervous to appreciate the architecture.

Then Alfredo reaches for my hand. The thought of touching him disgusts me, but until I figure out what he's after, I decide to go along. I let him hold my hand as we stroll down the aisle, our footsteps echoing off the stone floor. We pass arched loggia to the left and scattered wooden chairs for parishioners.

"The bell tower outside was constructed in the 1800s," he lectures.

Ahead of us, the altar is simple, with a faded painting of the Madonna on the back wall behind it.

Before we reach the altar, Alfredo turns to the left, ducks under an open doorway, and leads me along a short hall. It's silent back here, and we're alone. Thank God, he drops my hand to pull on yet another door that opens to a narrow set of steps going down into darkness.

I hesitate and try to stop him from going forward. "I don't like small spaces, Alfredo. I have claustrophobia." I lie to him.

"Don't worry."

What the hell is he doing? I remember the handgun in my briefcase. If I have to defend myself, I'll do it. And maybe even enjoy it.

He flicks a switch on the wall, and a feeble light goes on. Starting down the stairs, he balances himself by touching the wall. I follow.

"Alfredo, this is interesting, but I have so much to do at the office. Is there something else you want to talk about?"

He shakes his head and keeps going down. "Very few Cubans have ever seen these. Thanks to me, you'll be one of the lucky ones."

The last thing I feel is lucky.

We finally reach the stone floor, and I look into the gloom. The ceiling is low, muffling any sound from above. Along each wall are dozens of crypts with stone arches above each one. Deteriorated bronze plaques attempt to identify the ancient occupants of each tomb, but it's impossible to read them anymore. We're alone in the tiny space, and Alfredo has to duck his head to avoid hitting the ceiling.

I open my briefcase, reach in, and feel for the position of the gun.

Alfredo walks to one crypt and runs his fingers over the cold stone. "Imagine. All these people thought they were important, could ignore the orders of God, and look how they ended up." He turns to stare at me.

I don't know what to say. He's acting weird. I glance back at the steep stairway to calculate how long it would take me to run there. The space smells damp, like mold.

"This is a good lesson about pride and arrogance."

"Yes, of course." I agree with anything he says.

The yellow glow from small light bulbs barely illuminates the space. What the hell are we doing down here?

"Ava, you know how I feel about you."

I swallow hard. "Yes, of course."

"And you feel the same, don't you?"

Somehow, a garbled "yes" escapes from my mouth before I can think of a true response.

"Then why aren't we closer?" He leans toward me and I see the face of a boy, but if I attempt to cross him or disagree, a very dangerous boy.

"You know how busy I've been with my duties for the Revolution."

"You and your damn Revolution," he snorts. "It's long gone, and this country needs a fundamental change. You know it." He points his finger toward me.

"Oh?"

"Yes. The winds of change are blowing." He straightens his shoulders while his voice gets louder. "I want to know, Ava, what you're doing behind my back."

"I don't know what you're talking about."

"Don't fuck with me!" Alfredo screams, his voice echoing off the low ceiling.

I back up a few steps and look him in the eye. I cannot let him know how worried I am. "What is it you think I'm doing?"

"My own spies tell me you are working on something that I never authorized."

How much does he know? I suspect he is one of the traitors. "I'm working on my duties to prepare for the visit. That's all. What do you mean by the 'winds of change are blowing'?"

"I can feel it. This country is about to explode. And I'm the one who can keep you safe when it's all over."

I push a little harder. "Are you part of that change?"

His face contorts, he hesitates, then turns away from me without answering. I have to be careful. He takes a few steps and stops, looking at the tombs. "You know, Ava, it would be a shame if something happened to you in the future."

My body tenses.

Alfredo continues. "And it would be a shame if something happened to your son, Tom."

My face burns. How dare he threaten me like this. My brain scrambles, trying to out-think him. He's a lazy man but a brutal survivor. I have to be extremely careful. "Yes, I love my son." My fingers close on the wooden grips of the pistol.

He turns to me again. "You will stop what you're doing."

I shrug as if I'm innocent.

We don't speak for a long time. From somewhere in the back, I hear dripping water, like a clock ticking off the time before I must kill him.

Finally, Alfredo smiles at me. He starts for the stairs and I follow, my hand still in my briefcase on the gun. Just before starting up, he turns back to me. He leans close to my face. "Or, there's another way."

"What do you mean?" I shouldn't ask that question.

He leers at me. "You could make me happy by having sex with me."

My throat tightens. "Uh—"

"I would protect you and Tom."

Even the thought of that act makes me gag. But that's soon replaced with fury.

His smile stretches across his face.

I've done some horrible things for the sake of the Revolution, but I refuse to do this.

"You don't seem to understand, Ava." He blocks my way up the stairs. "The choice is simple."

Anger builds in my chest in a blaze of heat. I've fought people like him all my life, and I won't take it again. He turns toward the stairs and I reach into my briefcase, pull out the gun, and point it at the back of his head. In such a small space, the explosion is loud.

His brains splatter across the low ceiling as his body collapses on the stairs like a puppet whose strings have been cut.

I pause for a moment to make sure he's dead. His skin has already gone pale, and his stomach sags toward the dirty floor. I step over his body. Racing up the stairs, I worry someone heard the shot. But as I work my way back through the church, no one is present. I'm lucky since I forgot my silencer.

Outside, I take deep breaths and look across the street to the coffee shop, now filled with tourists. I don't know how long before his body will be discovered, but once that happens, a full-blown investigation will occur. I don't have time to worry about that now.

From behind me, three priests come out of the church, single file, through the wooden door that squeaks when it closes behind them. They all wear black neck-to-ankle cassocks with a peek of pious white at the collars. Some of the people in the café wave to them and make the sign of the cross as they pass. One of the priests catches my eyes and nods at me, as if giving a blessing. Leaning forward from their waists, their faces down, hands clasped behind their backs, the priests shuffle across the cobblestones, trailing hope in their wake.

Chapter Twenty-Five

Pete Chandler
Tuesday night. Four days left

At the soft knock on my hotel room door, I open it and Raquel slips through. She's brought the items I requested. A blonde wig and a light *serape* that hangs down below my knees. This should be enough of a disguise to fool the thugs following me constantly. Raquel will wait in my room.

"You gave Sergio the meeting point?" I put on the items.

She frowns. "Of course."

I put on a pair of sunglasses and take the elevator down to the lobby. It's quiet and I don't see anyone. To be safe, I slip out the back entrance and work my way around to the front of the hotel, then cross the street.

As usual, a small band is playing music on the corner. I slide alongside the conga drummer and smile at him. He nods and continues to tap the drum with his fingers. After a while, I ask if I can play the shaker.

"*Si, si,*" he says.

Shaking it on the off-beats, I wait.

In five minutes, Sergio ambles along the street. When he reaches the corner, he stops and listens to the music. He edges around them to stand next to me. Without looking at me, he hands me the Flipper Zero. "That will get you access to the outer doors. I'm not sure if it will work for any other door."

I whisper to him, "Thanks. I want to see the diagrams you found in the records. Where can I get access?"

"The computer center is on the fourth floor." He bobs his shoulders to the beat.

"I can hack into the lab's computer and search all over the system."

Sergio frowns. "Sure. Why not stop by Raul Castro's home nearby and say hello?"

After a serious silence, he says, "There is a time gap between the shift change in security personnel that you can use. Here are the schedules." He tells me the details. "But there are cameras all over. How——?"

"If I can get access to the computer system, I'll take care of that."

Sergio leans forward to drop some coins into the band's tip box on the sidewalk and disappears around the corner.

Hours later, at night, Raquel drives me into the Miramar area of Havana. She drifts down a quiet street sheltered by drooping mahogany trees. The air is still and moist and reminds me of the smell of Florida in the summer. I can hear an occasional radio playing American country music. Otherwise, the neighborhood is silent.

We park four blocks away from the CNEURO labs. I'm dressed in black, with my hoodie drawn over my head. I can tell Raquel's uncomfortable. Luckily, the sky clouds over.

"Not like appearing in a courtroom, huh?"

"I received training from your boss, but nothing like this. I'm scared." She's not wearing her glasses.

"You stay in the car."

Raquel steadies herself. "Okay."

I leave the car in the shadow of the ceiba trees and skirt along the edge of a row of bushes behind the facility. The row is impenetrable except for a small gap next to an open parking lot. I assume cameras are spying on me with every step, but at this distance the images will be distorted. I keep moving quickly to further blur any digital film.

I reach the gap and squat close to the ground, hiding under the edge of the bushes. Two feral dogs circle me, heads low. I check my watch. I have twenty minutes to wait for the shift change Sergio told me about, but the dogs come closer. One starts to bark.

I have to move. Turning my shoulders, I slip between the gap in the bushes. The second dog begins to bark, but the sound fades away.

I run in a low crouch across the parking lot to reach the back side of the CNEURO labs. In the gray light, the main tower looms upward, looking the same color as human bones. Climbing over a low wall, I dive into the middle of some pine trees and rest on a bed of soft needles. I rest against my backpack containing all the gadgets Sonnenfeld provided me.

I wait in the trees. Even at night, it's still warm, and I feel sweat running down the sides of my chest. I pull back my hood to cool off, and I listen to every odd sound. Check my watch. Ten minutes more. Somewhere high above me, two owls call in lonely hoots to each other.

Sergio assured me that when the security people changed shifts, they did so in a sloppy manner. Considering the lab had never been broken into, there was no reason for them to be particularly careful, which would give me a crack of an opportunity.

Two minutes before the shift change, I scurry across an open lawn, head down, hood up again. Luckily, there's just enough light to guide me forward. As I near the door, I trip on something and roll over onto the ground. My ankle hurts badly.

I get up and stumble forward. This will slow me down, but I'm too exposed in the open, so I limp forward. Thoughts of battlefields in Iraq creep into my memory. Soldiers exposed to enemy fire were cut down quickly. In the lawn beside the lab, the enemy's cameras will capture me. I hurry as best I can.

When I reach the protection of the wall and flop against it, I look at my watch. It's 1:26. I made it.

Now is the time. I pull out the Flipper Zero and hold it against the lock on the back door. I hear a click, grab the handle, and turn it to open the door and duck in. Coming from outdoors, it feels cold inside.

I limp through dimly lit hallways. I wear running shoes to avoid any noise. The main lights are off, but each room and laboratory glows with soft blue night lighting. The only sound is the hiss from the air conditioning. At every corner, I spot the hanging black globes of security cameras, recording every step I take. My plan to deal with them should work.

I pull out a small flashlight and probe deeper inside. I cross a cool tile floor that spreads over an immense area. Potted palm trees track my movements from the shelter of the corners. I can almost hear them breathing in the silence.

I'm working my way to the fourth floor to reach the main computer terminals. I'll take the stairs, hoping to avoid any guards. To get there, I turn to the right and start down a hallway with doors staggered along the sides. I'm still walking with a slight limp, slowing me down. I hear something from behind me. The clopping of shoes on the floor. Getting closer.

I'm trapped in an open, long hall. If the guard enters it, he'll spot me easily.

One after another, I try door handles to rooms on the side. All locked. I could use the tech tools I have to open them, but I don't have time. I hobble as fast as I can to the end of the hall. The sound of the guard echoes off the walls behind me.

At the next door I have a moment to use the Flipper Zero. Will it work on this one? The door clicks loudly, and I jump through it. I hear the guard whistling. I collapse on the floor, panting quietly. The guard comes down the hall slowly, checking doors as he goes, and stops before my door. I stop breathing as he rattles the handle, checking to make sure it's locked.

As his footsteps recede, I get up. I crack open the door, don't see anyone, and make a break for the stairwell at the end of the hallway. Inside of it, I climb to the fourth floor but am slowed by my bad ankle. The window of opportunity is a short time, and I worry my injury will jeopardize that time.

At the fourth floor, I open the door and peek out. The door yawns wider and I step through, looking back and forth. I move into an open area and find the computer room.

The overhead blue light makes the room look surreal, like I'm in an alien world. In the middle is a glassed-off smaller room. I can see it's filled with computer terminals and steel tables, each crowded with technical devices. Wires snake over the tables and floor. Stacks of monitors blink with colored lights like Christmas trees, and the air smells faintly stale.

I walk to the small room in the middle of the floor. Starting above a low wall and rising up to the ceiling, a glass wall separates it from the rest of the room, with a door in the middle. Holding the Flipper Zero, I reach for the handle. Then stop. An alarm?

I set the machine close to the code box. It clicks and the door swings open.

Inside, it's cool and dry. I hear the faint hum of several computer fans, working tirelessly. I sit in front of one terminal.

Careful not to disturb anything on the desk, I set down the backpack and lift out my laptop and the special equipment. The steel table feels cold to my touch. First, I have to get access to the computer, which is the easiest step. I repeatedly press the F8 key until the screen flashes "Safe Mode with Command Prompt." I navigate to Administrator, Net User and, using the CMD, I change the password. After rebooting, I attach the iSCSI to a USB cable and then insert it into the side of the computer. It gives me access to storage devices and networks. Plugged into the cable, the Seagate hard drive waits to store the data I hope to discover.

Next, I'll use the FTK Imager. Sonnenfeld told me it is widely used in forensic investigations to acquire and examine computer evidence. The best part of the software is its ability to mount and examine any collected data and analyze the captured evidence. It would enable my search to be fast and accurate. And I can save it for proof.

While I labor on the laptop, I glance out through the glass walls. Then I look at my watch. Seven minutes left before I have to exit.

I'm slowly making progress. After dozens of pages, I catch on to the organization of the notes and can determine which pages are more valuable. I can understand most of the Spanish in the data, but it's technical information, so that slows me down. I scroll through dozens of diagrams, back and forth through the screens. If my chest wasn't pounding, the blue glow in the room would almost be peaceful.

A door opens somewhere on the floor, and I freeze. I roll off the chair onto the ground. And wait. When no one appears, I get back to work. The data has increasingly more "Top Secret" stamps on it.

At one point, my software crashes. I have to go through the bootup procedure again but get back to the search quickly. I send multiple probes in different directions, testing different sites for more diagrams. The FTX Imager records everything I find immediately.

My watch says five minutes left.

A new screen blossoms on the monitor that looks significantly different.

That leads me to several more screens, each one overlapping the previous one. It's obvious these diagrams are old, created by crude software. Faint lines intersect in shapes that are unrecognizable. These must be from the old Russian research that Sergio said Rodolfo Diaz had hinted about.

I initiate the recording of each screen and scroll through several more. Then the software stops opening screens. I frown and realize that even my programming is stumped.

"What the hell?" I say softly.

I remember the AI software on my laptop and open it, keying in questions for it to solve. In a short time, I'm up and running again as the AI figures out the route through all the data to reach what I need.

I see something odd on the next screen. When I lean forward to study the shape, it leaps out at me. A weapon of some sort, but nothing I've ever encountered. If Rodolfo Diaz found this, I can understand why he disappeared.

My watch talks to me louder: two minutes.

I scoop as much of the data as possible in the little time remaining. Then I navigate into their security system and find the camera feeds. Asking AI for help again, it directs me to bring up a real-time digital clock and purposely wind it backward, then delete footage from the security cameras to cover all the time I've been here, including extra time to allow me to escape safely. I find the exact time when the deletion ended and attach it to the point from which I erased the images to create a loop that will show the camera's video without a gap. Of course, none of my images will appear on it.

I also get AI to erase any hint of my hack.

One minute left.

I close down everything and stuff my equipment in the backpack. Throw it over my shoulder and stand up. I push the chair in exactly as I found it and glance around the room to make sure it's left undisturbed.

I can't believe what I've just seen. Could they really have manufactured such a weapon?

I'll get this to Sonnenfeld to be analyzed immediately. I'm feeling good. A successful operation, and I have proof also.

Now, I have to move.

Looking through the glass, I open the door of the computer center. I hurry toward the door to the hallway when an incandescent flare of white light floods the entire floor, blinding me with its brightness and exposing me like a scurrying ant.

Chapter Twenty-Six

Pete Chandler
Tuesday night. Four days left

The lights flash on across the entire floor, blinding in their brightness, especially after I've been working in the subdued blue glow.

I duck back into the computer room and flatten onto the floor along the length of the inside wall and wait. I think of the gun in my backpack and will use it, if necessary. But that's a last resort, as the power balance is certainly asymmetrical in the hands of the lab security forces.

I feel a little dizzy, and my ankle still throbs with pain. Forcing myself to calm down, I try to think of what to do. I could get up and confront the guards. After all, I have diplomatic immunity; I can't be charged with a crime while in Cuba. They'd have to release me and kick me out of the country. But then, I know those kinds of legalities mean nothing in the small spaces where none of the lawyers and politicians are in control.

Assuming the guards will use the elevator to make their rounds, I trace the route I used into the building from the back door, reviewing the points of exposure.

I wait for ten minutes, frozen onto the floor.

My chest pounds again while I force my brain to engage. With the exception of the whirring of the computer fans behind us, silence surrounds me.

Then, a door scrapes open from somewhere at the far end of the hallway. A sense of defeat edges into my brain until I push it away.

I get up on my knees and peek over the low wall through the glass. I can't see far enough down the hall to find the door. It's off to my left, which is good since the stairwell is to the right.

The hall is vacant.

I'm about to leave for the stairwell when footsteps echo along the hall to the left, and I duck down again. I hold my breath to make sure I can hear everything. I feel around in my backpack to find the Sabre

183

tactical stun gun. I grip it, thinking I may have to use it if the guard discovers me. The footsteps shuffle closer, stop, then start to recede. I wait for a few minutes and peek over the wall again. The hall's empty.

Even if I can get to the stairs, I'm not sure of the exit route. Then I remember my phone has AI programming on it. I pull out the phone. Luckily, the wifi connection here is strong. Sonnenfeld's instructions were brief and I haven't had much time to work with the program, but I open it.

More footsteps sound from down the hallway. They move erratically, as if someone is checking doors, stopping, and moving again. I work to get the program operating.

I lie on the floor again and wait. The steps come closer. I have to act. I rise to look over the wall. I don't see the guard but know he's still on the floor. I've got the AI program running, and I ask it questions.

The footsteps move again, coming closer.

I key in more questions for the AI. Can it find the schematic diagrams of the facility? It takes a while, but finally it looks like AI has found the layout of the floors. I can use that to plan an escape route. I'm frankly shocked when the AI finds the diagrams for the entire building. Every stairwell, hall, office, heating ducts, air conditioning vents, locks, and doors are displayed. I key in more questions to narrow the data to something I can use.

I key in a request for the alarm systems in the building. AI responds immediately. I decide that the new shift change has probably also changed where they're located. I'll have to use a different route to get out. And I've got to hurry.

I ask AI a series of questions. What's the safest exit? Avoid security cameras? Which doors are open? I don't know if this will work, but it's all I have. The program flashes several colorful screens. I try to read them, but they change quickly until one screen pops up. It tells me to head for a new stairwell at the north end of the hall.

Carefully, I open the door of the computer room, step out, turn left, and I limp to the end, where I find a closed steel door. I touch the handle but stop. What if an alarm is connected to it? Checking with AI to make sure, I try the handle. Locked. I use the Flipper Zero card and swipe it over the lock. It doesn't work. I remember that Sonnenfeld embedded an app on the phone that can hack smart electronic locks. After all, they're just mini-computers. I switch to the app, hold the phone close to the lock, and wait. I can see it searching for the correct device. It finds the lock and, within a minute, opens it up. No alarms sound that I can hear.

Through the door, AI instructs me to descend for three floors. It's quiet in the stairwell as I follow the instructions. I hear noises from behind doors on each floor but keep going. At the bottom, I reach another closed door. Where does it lead? AI tells me to open it and move along a corridor for about fifty feet. Again, I hesitate, wondering if I'll open a door into the heart of the security center. Cautiously, I pull on it. It's unlocked and scrapes loudly. I peek around the corner to find a brightly lit corridor. It runs between two walls of glass which house several labs. They are all fully illuminated, but no one seems to be in them.

My ankle feels better, and I hurry to the far end, where I take a right turn and find another closed door. I reach for it and tug, but it doesn't open. This is an old-fashioned lock, with spindles and cylinders. I've got the tool to get through, but now I'm stopped. From somewhere behind me, I hear noises, people moving, getting closer.

Did AI screw up? I scroll through the screens quickly until I realize that in my hurry, I've misread the instructions. I should've turned left instead of right. I rush back across the corridor and try another door. It opens. I wonder how many damn doors I have to get through.

AI leads me into the basement, which smells of old, stored paper and scares me as it seems to be the worst way to go. Nevertheless, I follow what the screens tell me. Now I go up one floor and have to cross an open, brightly lit area. I move across it as quickly as my weak ankle will allow. When I hear loud voices, I almost stumble but keep going. It's as if the building is waking up and someone will certainly discover me. But I keep moving.

A voice calls something, so near I can make out the Spanish words, just as I duck around a corner. One more door ahead of me.

"Over here." The voices come closer to me.

I hustle toward the door and find another old key lock. Once again, I reach into the backpack and retrieve the Kronos lock pick gun. Inserting the point, I turn it on. The vibration is loud, and I worry it'll alert the guards. Then the lock clicks open. I push on the door and it sticks. Won't open. I check AI again. Correct door. The stranger's footsteps are louder now. I heave my shoulder against the door, and it pops open as I stagger outside into the dark, damp night.

I have to rest for a moment, so I crouch over in a stumbling run until I reach the shelter of the blue pine trees. I relax for a moment and congratulate myself for a successful mission. I'll get the data to Sonnenfeld as soon as I can.

From here, it's a quick walk to the car where Raquel is still waiting for me. She gives me a brief hug and starts the car. With the lights off, she makes a U-turn and heads out of the neighborhood.

"Thank God you made it. Did you find anything?"

With a big grin, I tell her, "I found more than I expected. I can't wait to hear what the boys in Washington make of these diagrams."

Then I feel a punch to my gut. I realize the mistake I made.

When I was on the lab computer and looped the security camera digital images to delete my entrance into the building as well as my exit, I gave myself ten minutes of extra time to cover the exit. But because of the guards and the delays getting out, the cameras started running before I escaped. Images of me working my way through the building are all recorded now.

Chapter Twenty-Seven

Pete Chandler
Wednesday morning. Three days left

I didn't get much sleep. Last night, I sent all the data and diagrams I found at the lab to Sonnenfeld using the Sectera Edge phone and the software Twofish to encrypt the data. Later, I'll meet Raquel at her office.

Thanks to the tech-gnomes who work for Sonnenfeld, the Twofish algorithm has been integrated into the app on my phone. The most critical part is getting the encryption key from him. Only he and I have it, in order to protect the contents of my message. I receive it now using the protocol, Diffie-Hellman key exchange.

It takes a while for the Sectera Edge to digest the key and encrypt it into ciphertext. With all the diagrams, the file is enormous, so I wait while the phone works away. Knowing the Sectera Edge phone is a secure channel, I send the ciphertext to Sonnenfeld.

He told me that for additional security, he had included end-to-end encryption, meaning not only did my program encrypt the data, but it would be encrypted a second time before Sonnenfeld could open it. That protected against the possibility that my transmission channel was compromised. Okay by me. After all, it seemed that everyone in Cuba was following me or listening to me.

Once again, he orders me to return to the States. Considering all the people after me, he's probably right. But I tell him no, there are a few ends to tie up.

Hopefully, no one will have a reason to look at the night's video where I stumbled my way out. And if anyone does look at it, I'll be long gone by then.

On my way to the lobby, someone taps me on my shoulder. I spin around to see Benny, the contractor, standing behind me. He still reminds me of a two-bit gangster.

"What the hell do you want?" I say as I turn from him toward the lobby.

"Benny. Remember?" He smiles broadly.

"I'm busy."

"I'm sure you are, pal." He steps in front of me. Looks me in the eyes. "I'm trying to help you."

"Oh?" This time, I reach into my pocket and activate the phone to capture his phone number and record our conversation.

He touches the mole on his forehead absentmindedly. "We can get you out of here before it's too late."

"Too late?"

He follows me into the lobby. The doors are wide open as a warm breeze wrinkles the palm leaves. It's early and quiet, and we sit at a small table near one of the louvered doors. Benny lights a fat cigar and blows the sweet smoke out the doorway. He sighs with contentment. "The only good thing to come out of this fucked-up country are their cigars."

"You got about three minutes."

He rolls the chocolate-brown cigar between his fingers. "Ah, where should we start?"

My knee bounces up and down.

"The most important intelligence I need from you is an answer."

"Oh?"

"What are you really doing here, and who sent you?"

"None of your business."

"Oh, but it is my business, or will be when the 'balloon goes up,' as we used to say in the military."

"What are *you* doing here?"

"I already told you that. Red Dog Associates has been contracted for our expertise in correcting dysfunctional systems."

"Which means?"

He grins. "Top secret, for now."

"Of course." I push back my chair. "Gotta go." When I was in Iraq, these black ops guys were hired by the dozens by the U.S. government. Secret and ruthless, many of these gangsters ignored all the rules to get their jobs done. Because they weren't technically part of the U.S. military, none of the rules applied to them.

"Maybe if you knew what's really going on in Cuba, you'd understand something about the Havana Syndrome."

"Doubt it."

He gets up and steps outdoors. Curious, I follow.

Benny tells me, "It's a short lesson. See, we got a United Nations of players involved in this island, all trying to get an advantage. And these boys are not peacekeepers like the U.N." His laugh honks like a horn. "Consider these facts. The Cuban population is highly educated and has a higher literacy rate than the U.S. Since the embargo, they have almost nothing in the way of consumer goods. Can you imagine the huge market they would provide for American businesses if they could start selling here?"

I wait and decide to hear him out.

"The Soviet Union took advantage and moved into the island. Although Fidel hated them, he also realized how much Cuba needed Russian financial help. So, he maintained a relationship of sorts." He touches the mole on his forehead.

"So what?"

"When the Soviet Union fell, most of the operatives left. But now, the Russians are back."

"What do you mean?"

"As Cuba sank under the American embargo, Russia emerged as an alternative source of trade and investment. For instance, Putin forgave 22 billion dollars in debt and began shipping oil to Cuba again. Trade doubled, and Russia is building four power stations on the island and an extensive spy network."

"So, what does this have to do with me?"

"When Putin first came to power, he publicly announced the closing of Lourdes spy station, which had been the largest Soviet military base in the Western hemisphere."

I look at him closely.

Benny lowers his head and voice. "My intelligence suggests the base has been secretly opened again."

"So what?"

Benny shrugs. "Sorry, pal, you're not on my team. Can't say. But anyone with a brain knows that Putin is the leading exporter of instability and chaos against our country."

"You think he wants to take over Cuba?"

He tilts his head. "Don't know, but we can't let him accomplish that, can we, buddy?"

"What else can you tell me?"

"I can warn you. What you're seeing is only the tip of the iceberg."

I wait.

He looks at me. "Chandler, get out of the country. We're going to win with a knockout punch, and it won't be pretty. A guy like you will be an obvious target."

"For what?"

"Top secret." He grins and puffs on his cigar, blowing circles of smoke through fat lips out the door.

"So why are you telling me?"

"Because we're friends?" He laughs with his head thrown back. "I don't want you fucking up our op here. The stakes are higher than you can imagine." He slips his hand inside his jacket pocket and removes a fresh cigar. "That's on me. Smoke it as you head for the airport." He tries to fist-bump me, but I ignore his outstretched hand.

I watch him walk across the lobby with a swaggering, side-to-side movement as he turns out the door. I'll send all the new data about him on the phone to Sonnenfeld.

An hour later, a taxi drops me in front of the U.S. Export/Import Bank, Cuba Division offices. I've come to respect things about Raquel, like her brains, her discipline, and her guts as a woman in this police state. And I'm more attracted to her than I expected.

On the second floor, I enter the 1950s again—steel desks, electric typewriters, and cigarette smoke pushed into patterns around the rotating ceiling fans.

Raquel comes out to meet me, extending her hand in a firm shake. We talk for a while and she seems rested, at least. Her secretary, Connie, stops typing and sits silently next to us. I follow her to the small garden outside her office and activate the Cicada jammer. The water struggling to climb into the air above the fountain, then tumbling over in failure, reminds me of Diego and how I sat with him out here in the hot sun. And how I failed him.

Thoughts of others I've failed threaten to intrude. My fiancée, Julie, who died by her own actions, causing me to feel like I failed her. And the prisoner in Iraq.

I look at Raquel. She's wearing designer blue jeans. I comment on how stylish they look.

She laughs for a moment. "My uncle. It took him three weeks to find them. Thanks."

We both watch the water in the fountain. "You certainly like to take risks."

"I don't, but the information we got is essential, so I had to do it."

"Now what are you going to do?"

"I've pretty much completed my work. But depending on what the techs in Washington find on the diagrams, there could still be a threat to Americans here. If not, I'm going to get the hell out of here."

She looks up at me. "It's so simple for you. For me it's about surviving and trying to 'smile through life' as best I can."

I nod and am beginning to understand the difficulty of trying to survive in Cuba. The resourcefulness of the people amazes me. "There's still something that's going to happen on Saturday." I tell her about Benny and that he's serious about whatever his company of cowboys is going to do here. The thought of leaving her behind causes my chest to tighten.

Her face brightens. "I've got an idea." Standing, Raquel moves to a corner of the garden and returns with a small transistor radio, like those Americans used in the '60s. She turns it on and sets it next to me on a wrought iron table. A tinny voice talks fast.

"What are you doing?"

"The government censors everything, but Cubans have figured out ways to pass news in coded ways that we all understand. Maybe we will learn something about the weekend." The radio was loud with chattering voices. "It's the news. Your president will visit a *paladar* and give a speech at the opera house. And there's a protest scheduled for later this afternoon. It'll start right next to here in the Plaza de la Revolución."

"People have to schedule a protest?"

"Only a few years ago, it was illegal to protest or gather for any reason. Now, they occur often. So far, the government has arrested them routinely but not reacted violently."

"So, the people protest for more food?"

"No. Something more important. The group they're reporting on is called 'The Ladies in White.' They all have relatives who are imprisoned for political reasons."

"So, they march for their release?"

"Yes. And they all dress in white. They don't ask for the government to be overthrown. They simply want the secret police to find and release their families."

"As do you?"

"There's a line the protesters must not cross, or the police will get violent. People disappear and never return." She raises her head.

"Do you ever participate?"

Raquel looks at me. "Uh, with my past, I have to be extremely careful, as it would be a high risk for me. I could never march with them, but I support them financially."

"Risky, huh?"

"The government is embarrassed, so they claim the ladies are supported by American funding in order to disrupt the government."

"Is that true?"

Raquel shrugs. "The Americans have participated in all kinds of disruptive activities since Fidel took over."

"None ever succeeded," I say.

"I carefully weigh the risks and what is most deeply important to me."

I nod. "Sure. I've been in situations where I had to weigh the risks. Sometimes, the cause is important enough to get involved."

"For me, it always comes down to the personal. Not a cause, but who is the person in trouble."

"Did you hear anything else that might be helpful to us?"

"The protestors will also be present near the theater when your president speaks."

We leave the patio. I want to hold her hand, but that would be improper here. We go back into Raquel's office when she gets a phone call forwarded to her. She answers, and her face drains of color. "Yes, yes. You want both of us to come? Okay, Mr. Chandler will come with me." She talks for several minutes and asks many questions and then hangs up. Taking a minute to compose herself, she tells me, "It's a high official from the Communist Party."

"Why is he calling you? Is it about last night?"

"No, thank God. But it's very odd." She frowns. "He said his name is Colonel Miguel Garcia. The Communist Party members don't have any rank except 'Comrade.' I think he's really from the DGI, the foreign intelligence service. And he wants to meet with us."

"That's risky. Do we know anything about him?"

"If we stay outdoors and he's alone, I think we can take the risk."

"We don't have any other leads, so why not? What does he want?"

She looked at me. "He wants to meet with both of us this afternoon. He has information about the Havana Syndrome."

Chapter Twenty-Eight

Miguel Garcia
Wednesday morning. Three days left

It's Connie Perez who alerts me to the danger.

The American and his associate came back to their office and talked in front of Perez. What I learn makes my neck go stiff. The dead turtle warning didn't stop them. Diego's death didn't stop them. In fact, Perez overheard talk about CNEURO again and diagrams before they left her. They've come too close now. The next step will lead Chandler, the spy, to expose our operation, and I cannot let that happen.

I think about my response and finally decide what needs to be done. Closing the door to my office, I sit at my desk and reach for the phone. A new one, it's black, heavy, and even has a rotary dial on the front.

Connie Perez answers the phone at the office of the Export/Import Bank. She's surprised to hear from me so soon again. "Yes, sir," she whispers.

"*Perdóneme, mi amiga.* Your help will be noted in my report."

"What can I do?"

"I must talk with the *Americano's* friend. The woman."

"Raquel Sanchez?"

"Yes, yes. That's the person."

"Okay, Comrade." Connie clicks the phone as she forwards my call.

Thanks to my god Yemaya, the woman is still there and I have her name. This proves that my plan will work. I grin and push forward.

"Hello, this is Raquel Sanchez."

I lean forward and hunch my shoulders. Should I use a false name? No, at this point, I don't fucking care. "This is Colonel Miguel Garcia. I am the senior officer of the Ministry of the Interior with the Partida Comunista de Habana." I hear Sanchez take a breath, and I know I've got her attention. "I have learned that you are, uh, working with an American that we have an interest in." I lower my voice.

She hesitates. "I don't know what you're talking about."

"You don't want to cause any trouble, do you?"

"What are you talking about?"

"That is classified at a level I am unable to reveal to you now. I propose we meet with Mr. Chandler at a quiet place near your office. I have information that will be very helpful for your work."

"But why are you offering this?"

I whisper the truth to her. "Because I don't always agree with the direction our country is going. We all need more freedom."

Sanchez covers the phone with her hand, but I can hear her talking fast with someone else. Probably the American. Several minutes later, she says, "Okay. We will meet with you in the small park outside the performing arts theater across from my office. Do you know where?"

"Yes." Sanchez has many questions, and I worry that at any minute, she'll refuse to meet. But I give her an answer for everything.

"You will come alone. If we see anyone else or another car, we will leave immediately."

"Agreed. You will bring Mr. Chandler with you?"

"Yes. Meet us at three o'clock."

I hang up and stand, shoulders thrown back. Before I can celebrate my deception, the phone rings. "Garcia," I answer.

My boss, the general, yells at me, "What the hell have you been doing? Your reports are late. I could easily move you to a less patriotic duty." He stretches out his words to indicate the unfavorable alternative.

My body tightens. "Of course, sir. All of my reports will be on your desk by Monday."

"They will be on my desk or it's your ass on my desk." He hangs up.

How long before I can get rid of that piece of ox shit? I calm myself with the thought of what I'll do to him when I gain power.

From the lower drawer in my desk, I pull out the Soviet Makarov pistol I've used for years with great success. I screw on an old silencer. Looking at my watch, I see that I have just enough time to stop by my mama's home before I finish off the other two.

Coming down the stairs, I hurry through a long hallway. Slabs of faded sheetrock hang at loose angles from the wall. Built by the Soviets, almost everything they made in Cuba fell apart in a short time. But then, almost everything in Cuba is falling apart now.

If I don't finally stop the American spy, like the Soviet buildings falling one after another, the outcome for me will fall toward a crisis. If the American discovers what I'm doing, other authorities will be pulled in, and even though I wield great power in Cuba, I'll be executed immediately.

I also promised Benny the American threat would be eliminated.

Time runs faster now toward Saturday. Besides getting all the technology assembled, Felipe needs more training on its use.

I push my way through the crowds and the humidity that has come in the afternoon with the full sun. My mama, Clara, called three times yesterday, pleading with me to see her. Even though I don't have time to do so, I will stop at her flat.

Years ago, when I started stealing more money from the party, I was able to buy her a modest flat in a partially renovated building near Old Havana. It's nicer than all her friends have, so she's grateful to me. Climbing two floors and opening the old door, I hear her from the kitchen. "Chucho, finally you come home. You never talk to me, and you always leave in a rush."

I stop to look at her. Arms buried deep in soapy water in the sink, her shoulders look more narrow than ever. Once glossy black hair now hangs limp to her shoulders. For a moment, I feel the ache of guilt. "Mama, I've told you to let the maid do this. I hired her so you can relax and play checkers with your friends." I can smell her cheap perfume.

She waves me off. "I've washed my own dishes all my life. I'm not going to let someone else do it for me." She looks up at me, dries her hands, and comes over to curl into my open arms. I hug her tightly. Her body feels like I've scooped up a scattering of dried cane stalks from the roadside.

In a moment, she leans back to scrutinize me. "And I've told you to get rid of that damn beard. You look like a starving goat."

"I'm busy with the most important work of my life." I feel the urge to tell her, to make her proud, to promise her a huge mansion when I get in power, but catch myself and don't say anything else. "It's top secret."

Her eyes search my face. "I have black beans and rice for you. A Materva?"

I accept the soft drink from her and drain it in one long swallow.

"When all my friends talk about their children and what they do, I never have anything to tell them about you. I wish you'd let me know how successful you are."

"Soon, soon," I assure her. Wiping sweat from my face, I walk into the living room. There's a family shrine in the corner of the room. In a nook in the wall, a doll which represents my favorite *orisha*, Yemaya, stands amid offerings of an orange and a candle. I light the candle and ask Yemaya, "You of infinite power, come to my aid now. I need your wisdom and strength." I bow my head and, although the *orisha* has nothing to do with the church, I still make the sign of the cross over my chest.

I remember the ritual two weeks ago, the *tocque de santo,* in which the drummers started early in the evening as more people arrived with offerings, liquor, and cigars. I participated fully, as never before, letting the drumming sound enter my body. I drank, danced, and breathed in the clouds of cigar smoke. Chanting rose and fell as people became possessed by the spirits of dead relatives. The climax came when I felt the power of the *orishas* take control of my body. I jerked and flopped on the floor like I was a sweating puppet. Then I felt the blessing of power from the god giving me strength to do anything.

Now, in my mother's flat, strength fills my chest again. I hurry back to the kitchen.

My mother gives me a kiss on each cheek, then shakes her head but smiles at me. "You are destined to be great. I bet on number twenty-two last week. And now it will come true." I look down at her. If I fail, she'll probably be executed along with all the members of my family. But if I succeed, I will make my mama proud of me.

Once on the street, I wave for a passing taxi. In twenty minutes I sit on a bench next to the new performing arts theater at the edge of a park. The bench is missing a few slats but still holds me. The Makarov pistol digs into my back where it presses against the wood of the bench. To my left, Norfolk Island pines grow in a clump near the back. Perfect. I'll lure the two of them into the hidden area. The trees will also muffle the sound of gunshots.

To hide my identity, I wear a wide planter's straw hat.

I look to the north side of the Plaza de la Revolución and see a crowd gathering in the large space. Probably another goddamn protest. These criminals are becoming bolder in their demands on the government. Soon, the secret police will appear and crack a few heads, thank God. I feel some sympathy for them because the crowds are mostly hungry. But we all have struggles.

Then I realize I forgot to bring a file or report that I could use to fool the American and the woman. I'll have to dig deeper and use my confidence to convince them, although they're both probably smart and cautious.

At ten minutes past three, I see them come from my right. Walking side by side and looking around, they come across the street. The woman is prettier than I expected and has beautiful, latte-colored skin. They move close to each other. The American walks with an athletic stride and looks in good shape. Glancing around, he's clearly a professional spy; I'll have to be careful with him.

They stop several feet from the bench. Sanchez speaks in Spanish, asking if I can use English, to which I agree. With an open palm, I offer them a seat next to me. She wears red glasses and stands in an elegant manner, like the upper-class bitches I always hated. When I glance at her dark eyes, I see intelligence. Chandler stands next to her. Taller and thin, he looks down on me with arrogance on his face. I could rip him apart with my bare hands right now, like pulling apart a dead chicken.

"What have you got?" Chandler demands. He studies me carefully.

Right away, I don't like the white guy's attitude. Killing him would actually be easy. "I need to know what you know first," I say.

Chandler turns to Sanchez and asks, "Is this the way things work here?"

She speaks in a soft voice to me. "For obvious reasons, we need some trust."

"Of course, *señora.*" I stand and look across the street. More protesters gather next to the building, fanning themselves with yellowed palm leaves. "But we should be careful." I nod toward the crowd. "Let us go over to those trees."

Sanchez and Chandler exchange a look but follow me at a distance.

Halfway to the trees, they stop me and demand, "Tell us more about yourself."

Turning to face them, I lie about my position to convince them. "I have been assigned by some top-level officials in the party to investigate the same weapon you search for."

"Tell us more."

"It uses microwaves."

Chandler lifts his head. "Do you know if a weapon like this really exists?"

Once again, I try to get them into the trees by pointing at the people across the street. "We can't talk here. We need privacy." I angle toward the trees again.

"Wait. How do we know some of your officers aren't hiding in there?" Sanchez asks.

"I am all alone, as you can see."

Still, the two won't move toward the trees. Chandler holds Sanchez back with his hand. I try a different lie to convince them. I drop my voice. "See those protesters over there? They are hungry, and so am I. So is my *mamacita*, my aunts. What kind of a repressive system allows its own people to starve?" I pause to look at their faces. "And now someone has attacked innocent Americans. I want to help you stop it." I fold my eyebrows down to appear more sincere.

"Why do you care about that?" the man asks.

"That's what I have to share with you. It is a twisted plot," I answer as I cock my head toward the stand of pines.

Chandler turns to the side.

"Over here. Quickly." I glance at the protesters, who come closer. Finally they follow me. I step between two trees and push through into a small opening surrounded by a circle of pines. I'm close enough to smell the woman's sandalwood perfume. I turn around to make sure we're alone. This will be a perfect place to finish it. I try to keep my breathing at a normal pace.

"Ok, partner, what have you got?" With his legs spread, Chandler stands before me.

His demanding attitude pisses me off. It'll feel good to kill him. "It is still too open here. Why don't we go a little farther." They are hesitant to move. Instead, I point to the spot and wait for them to look toward where I'm pointing. That gives me the correct angle for two head shots from behind.

Both of them turn as I want them to do. At the same instant, I reach around my back and grab the Makarov. I pull it out, thumbing off the safety, and point it at them.

Chandler's head jerks back toward me. He sees the gun.

I fire, the splat of the silencer echoing among the trees.

Chapter Twenty-Nine

Ava Alvarez
Wednesday afternoon. Three days left

Mendoza's body has been discovered. Of course, a full investigation will start, but it'll take a long time to get any results. In the meantime, I'll complete my mission.

The French doors to my patio are open, and I watch the palms bending at their waists in the wind. From the back of the house, I hear a crash. Probably another roof tile falling off. If I ever have the time, I'll replace the tiles before the entire roof collapses. *Comiendo un cable.*

I think of the painting my cousin Rodolfo Diaz doctored for me and sent to his usual art dealer in the U.S. in Kansas. Did anyone get the message? If so, there's a chance I may work with the authorities in America to stop the plot. I laugh to myself when I think of what Fidel would say if he knew I was working with the capitalists! I'm still not certain Chandler is my contact, but I must find out. He has diplomatic status, and contact with the secret police could cause an international uproar if I'm wrong—the last kind of attention I need now.

Pena tried to make contact at Lennon Park but failed. And since many agents are following Chandler closely, I have to be more careful than ever.

Solana returns and picks up my empty coffee cup. "Wind is blowing harder today," she warns. "Something's coming off the Caribbean."

I nod in response but don't hear any more of her words.

In my deepest core, I worry the Revolution has finally failed. With Fidel gone, the new leadership has gone soft, selfish, and is rotten like spoiled mangos. It has made the country vulnerable to the kind of destruction that's going to occur. *Comiendo un cable.* We're broken.

Then I think of Tom and Lucinda. Because of my relationship to him, if I fail, he will be arrested, tortured, and executed. I really don't have a choice but to fight.

Pena knocks at the front door, and Solana lets him in. He salutes and stands at attention until I tell him to follow me out to the patio for complete privacy. Once again, I dismiss Solana for the day. He's dressed in his uniform, carrying a standard issue briefcase, and his cheeks are moist with sweat. He has the bad teeth of a poor upbringing, but years ago I selected him as my assistant for his courage and his brains. He's never disappointed me, and he's almost as tough as I am.

"*Buenos días*, Comandante," he says. He tries to smile until he looks closely at me. "You look upset."

I wave my hand in the space between us. I've warned Pena of the increased surveillance on both of us. Leading him around the fountain, I sit on a wicker couch in front of an immense bougainvillea bush. Slightly wilted pink flowers drop across my shoulder as if trying to comfort me. "What do you have for me?"

He sits at an angle to me. His chest swells as he says, "I have reports that you will be glad to hear."

"I need something good."

"We have been working with the U.S. liaison officers about the president's dinner at the paladar, The Fields of Cuba. The Americans want to seat about fifty people; however, the restaurant can only hold twenty."

"I know; I've been there several times already."

"We should be able to get the list pared down by Thursday morning."

"And the route of the motorcade?"

Pena reaches into his briefcase and pulls out his laptop, booting it up to show the seven possible routes the presidential group could take to get into Viejo Habana, the oldest center of the city.

I scroll through the options. "I recommended they use Avenue Salvador Allende. That is the widest road and the fastest."

"And the easiest to protect," Pena reminds me.

"Is there a problem?"

"The American security people think that route is too obvious. Instead, they propose a circuitous route through more open streets. Easier to protect, they claim."

I raise my hands and slap them against my thighs. "Do they know how broken up some of those streets are? It will slow down the motorcade."

"We're working on it."

For twenty minutes, we study the president's various routes through the city, trying to anticipate where the terrorists could strike. There are so many options, I feel discouraged for a moment. "What about Chandler?"

"Yes, well, there are some problems—"

"Goddamnit, Pena. What've you got?" I scream at him, surprised at my own anger.

"Uh, I know you ordered two loyal teams to follow the American, which they've been doing," he adds quickly. "There were some delays."

"So, their reports are late?" His silence answers me. "Shit! I thought I could trust these new recruits." I try to catch my breath. "I want confirmation of what he's doing in Cuba."

Pena interrupts me. "But remember, we tried before. The note. Lennon Park."

I pause for a moment. "I can still see you in that 'hippie' outfit. Was the wig hot?"

Pena frowns. "After we missed that chance, our agents continued to track him. Here's a list of everywhere the American has been."

Glancing at it, I say, "I remember this."

"Then, he and Sanchez tried to find Diaz at his home."

I sit up and shake the flowers off my shoulder. "Diaz is hopefully enjoying his new life in Mexico with his family that I paid for. But if Chandler is that intent on finding him, it means our long shot worked."

"And it could also explain why Chandler went to CNEURO. To find Diaz."

I agree, and my chest feels lighter. After all the possible things that could've gone wrong, this is proof my message got through and the American authorities sent someone: Pete Chandler. The clock tolls from the other room, sounding hollow at this distance, and it reminds me of how little time we have left to act. "It's him, isn't it?"

Pena, who helped when Rodolfo Diaz approached me with the diagrams he found in his work at CNEURO, nods silently. That intelligence led me to dig deeper and, eventually, uncover the plot to attack the president.

I stand, run my hands through my hair, and listen to the wind off the ocean. I have no idea if Chandler can help us, but I must try to make contact again and find out.

But how?

Besides my surveillance officers, I know there are probably several more from different agencies, all following Chandler. And besides the normal party officials spying on me, Alfredo's men are still watching every move, waiting for me to make a mistake. Even with my position, I couldn't get near Chandler without ringing bells in every security department in Havana.

"I can try to meet him again in a different park or location," Pena offers.

I shake my head. "Too risky." I walk in a circle around the fountain, dry now and filled with black leaves.

I stop circling and tell Pena, "I learned years ago that success in the secret police is like playing pool. You have to think indirectly, in banked shots that aren't straight ahead. Actions your opponents won't anticipate. In this case, the solution is obvious: in order to make secret contact with the American without raising suspicions, we must use an indirect method."

"What's that?"

I walk back into my office and return to the patio with my own laptop. Setting it on the small table next to the bushes, I look through my records. Pena has pulled the files on the woman, Raquel Sanchez, and her family. I find them now and scroll down through the pages.

As I read, the memory of the case comes back to me.

Sanchez's husband, Pepe, was a radical and a danger to the party. He conducted subversive activities that I tracked for months. His actions bordered on treason under the Revolution's penal code. I arrested him and, under torture, he confessed. In that process, I also arrested Raquel and interrogated her. I remember an attractive lawyer who admitted she felt the Revolution had failed the Cuban people. Gutsy things to say. I almost admired her for that courage and suspected she was also involved, but I couldn't prove it. In the end, I had to do my duty. Her husband was arrested and was executed shortly afterward.

Is it a coincidence that she's now working with Chandler? Why? I turn to Pena. "Here's an indirect shot: Raquel Sanchez."

"How can we talk to her without bringing attention from dozens of other agents?"

I finish my water and smile at him, as much as I smile at the brilliant idea that came to me. "We wait until Sanchez is away from the American. Then we grab her for interrogation. After all, she has a history of associating with subversives. That's clearly within my area of authority and won't cause any suspicions."

"Uh, why do we want her?"

"If we have Sanchez, we'll get to Chandler."

Chapter Thirty

Pete Chandler
Wednesday afternoon. Three days left

I see the gun come up and the black hole of the barrel. Just before he can fire, I swing my leg out in a precise and deadly taekwondo kick. The gun explodes just as my foot catches Garcia's hand and knocks the pistol up into the air. I scramble to pick it up, but he's faster. By then, Raquel has ducked into the heaviest part of the trees, and I follow her. I hear him shooting away at us, the bullets somehow missing.

We pop out the far side of the trees and look left and right. She rushes me toward the office and the crowd of people next to it across the street. Behind us, I hear the guy shouting, and he continues to fire the gun at us.

We run across the street, and I look back. Garcia emerges from the trees and his planter's hat flies off, exposing his head and Garcia's identity, but he still chases us.

Up on a grassy knoll in front of us, dozens of women dressed in white lead the protestors and face off against a pro-government crowd armed with clubs. Raquel pulls me ahead, and we scramble up the slope beside the building and dive into the crush of people and into safety.

It's chaotic in there, noisy, people shouting, the crowd surging back and forth. But we hide amongst them. I look back to see if Garcia is still following but don't spot him.

"Come on," I urge Raquel. "Let's get back to the hotel."

She stumbles after me, head down, hair limp around her face.

In a half hour, we're in my room, Raquel propped up with pillows on the bed. I stand at the window looking out over the orange-tiled roofs. I turn back to see how she's doing. Raquel is surprisingly composed. "I suspected something was wrong from the start. But I thought if we could get any clue or help, we may as well try it."

"I'm impressed with you."

She looks at me. "That was too close. But thanks to you." Her voice trails off as she stands.

I give her a hug. "It's happened to me a few times. In war zones and, uh, some other places. But we're okay now."

Raquel lets out a big breath of relief. "I was trained, but not for something like this."

"Training helps, but when you're actually in the middle of something like that, it's still scary."

She flips her hand in the air. "Not for me." I smell sandalwood and sweat mixed around her.

I feel the damp press of the breeze through the open window. Both curtains flip casually around the frame.

She lifts her head. "Cubans love a cloudy day," she says. "We have an old saying that it means the sun can't make up its mind." Raquel pauses, her lips compressed. "I'm going to find out who led him to us."

I reach over to squeeze her hand. "Probably one of the dozens of people following us."

"Maybe."

"I'm trying to calm down. From scared to mad to just angry. Deep breathing, you know." I speak in measured words. "I want you to stick close to me from now on. That isn't going to happen again." I've seen trauma like this before on battlefields. It burrows into people and lasts for a long time. I feel responsible for Raquel now.

"Is there somewhere you can go to make sure you're safe? Somewhere out of Havana?"

Raquel shakes her head. "I'm already involved. He came after both of us."

"Remember that I told you when Diego was killed, that was meant for me. But they killed him by accident."

Her expression flattens.

"So, this is my fight, not yours."

Raquel moves to the window, where the breeze brushes her hair off the sides of her face. After several minutes, she turns back to me. "This is my fight also. For years, I have 'kept a low profile,' as you Americans say, to protect my family and myself. I told you about standing up for something that was important. That time, for me, is now. I will probably never see my husband again or feel his touch—thanks to the government and the police. What do I really have to lose?"

"Your life?"

She turns toward the window and doesn't say anything more.

I move behind her and hesitate for a moment. Then, I wrap my arms around her waist, justifying it by thinking that I'm comforting her. She relaxes into my arms and then turns to me, her face close to mine. She leans forward and kisses me. Once, twice, and again.

"This feels good," she murmurs.

I pull her toward the bed, and we settle onto it on our sides, facing each other. We continue kissing and I feel her body stretch along mine, touching me in many places. Part of my mind hesitates because this is such a bad idea. But the rest of me can't stop, and we pull each other closer.

Until I stop. I sit up and look at her. Hair disheveled, face flushed, turned onto her back. She's beautiful, and her body posture tells me she's willing, but this is not a good idea. Not now. Maybe later.

Laughing, she says, "Is it your American Puritanism? We Cubans don't suffer from that."

"Not at all." I run my hand over the curve of her hips. "I'm very interested, but not now."

Raquel sits up and runs open fingers through her hair. "I'll remember that and hold you to it."

Ten minutes later, we cross the lobby and the woman at the desk waves good morning to me. The Sectera Edge phone buzzes, and I open it to find a text from my boss in Minneapolis, my best friend, Martin Graves. Because of security protocols, I cannot use the phone to call him. He's concerned about his brother here.

You must stay and solve this. Frank in danger!

Have you contacted Sonnenfeld? I can't reach him.

In my mind, I see Martin's face. Round, flushed red, with heavy eyebrows. I owe him.

After we're seated and have ordered a pastry, I leave Raquel at the table to walk outside for privacy. Around the corner of the hotel, I pull out the Sectera Edge and call Sonnenfeld. Martin's message reminded me that I haven't heard from Sonnenfeld for a day, even after I uploaded all the diagrams we found. He doesn't answer, so I leave a voicemail. "What have you discovered in the diagrams of the weapon? I know you want me to leave, but with all the people after me, I'm afraid I'll be stopped at the airport again. I can't use that escape route. Do you have the exfiltration plan yet?"

I click off and look across the street. A man bends over, carrying a huge stack of folded cardboard boxes across his back. Brown feet in flip-flops walk blindly into the street, and he almost gets hit by a truck. It's strange for Sonnenfeld not to answer, and I have the impression this mission is his only one. I hurry back into the hotel and tell Raquel.

She nods and lowers her head to finish her croissant, mango jam dripping from the end.

"But I'm not leaving."

"I'm glad for that," she mumbles.

"Oh?"

"This kind of attack on us doesn't occur in my country. I'm not going to let him get away with it."

"I'm dangerous to be around."

She lifts her head and grins. "You give me strength." Her smile jokes with me. "And I'm coming to like you."

My eyes leave her, searching the room to find the comfortable doubts about myself that I've used for so long. They're hiding, and I look back at her. She seems to trust me. So did others, and I failed them. Or they left me, and I didn't try to get them back. What about this woman? I push my hand up across my balding forehead.

"I'll get the car." She wipes her mouth with a cloth napkin and looks closely at me. "Why do you stay, Pete?"

That hit me harder than she knew. Should I tell her? I think of how much she's probably sacrificed just to survive in Cuba. "Well, I've got a duty to—"

"What's behind that?"

I still hesitate to tell her. That would mean opening the latch on the door to ghosts from my past. She waits me out, and I try to start. "In Iraq, I served in the Criminal Investigation Division. Army. I and another officer, Judd Crowe, sometimes had to interrogate prisoners, which I always hated to do. One guy refused to say anything, and Crowe suddenly lost it. His anger exploded, and he pulled out his service weapon." I pause at the memory in my mind, like an old photo that's beginning to fade. "Crowe shot him in the head. Killed him." I take a deep breath. Keep going. "I didn't pull the trigger, but—"

"That sounds horrible."

"Then Crowe covered it up so we weren't caught. I've spent a long time trying to offset that with something good. Something like repentance, I guess."

"And?"

"And it hasn't happened yet." I close the door on the ghosts.

Neither of us talk. From somewhere close, a church bell tolls in sonorous sounds that echo off the stone buildings.

Chapter Thirty-One

Miguel Garcia
Thursday noon. Two days left

Clouds darken the sky, warning of an impending storm. The air seems heavier, or maybe it's the heaviness I feel about the fuck-up at the park. How was I to know the guy could kick like that? Some kind of martial arts. If he was alone, I could've beat the shit out of him easily with my bare hands. At least I think I wounded him. That should stop him for a while. Besides, I've got more important things to do now.

I'm waiting in my limousine on Rosita Avenue near the bus station where Benny said to meet. We need to be trained on the new weapon, and I need to train Benny that I'm the boss.

My cell phone rings, and I take the call from my youngest son, Fidel. I never hear from him, even though I gave him everything as a child. I'm pleased to hear from him until he starts demanding an Italian motor scooter as if I'm Santa Claus. It saddens me, but I agree to find one and hang up.

In ten minutes, I see my cousin limping toward me on the sidewalk. He's wearing a Panama hat and a lime-colored sport coat over white pants. "*Que bolero*, Chucho?" Felipe calls.

"Where the hell have you been?" Ignoring his smile, I yell at him through the open window.

Felipe crosses to the other side of the big car and gets into the back seat next to me. Jose, my driver for years, sits behind the glass wall in front of us. "The air conditioning feels good."

"Shut up. Benny will be here soon."

"*Si, si.*" He waits for a minute, then asks, "You can handle command and control, but I need to know the details for the execution of the mission on the ground."

I look at him. He's too smart to bullshit. I have to be honest with him. "Benny's got a warehouse nearby to practice with the weapon. We both must be able to handle it under pressure, Felipe. In case you, uh, don't get it done, I'll do it."

"*Tranquila*," he assures me.

I don't hear the hum of the Mercedes that slides next to the limo and stops. The smoked window drains down, and Benny says, "You ready?"

He gets out quickly, and the electricity of impatience pops off of him. His cologne hits me just as hard. He looks up and down the street, obviously frustrated with how slow Felipe is moving. "Hurry up, Pepe."

"It's Felipe," he corrects Benny.

Benny says, "Are you jokers finally ready?"

Heat rises across my chest, and I would love to punch this jerk again but hold back.

"You expect me to depend on this guy?" Benny looks at Felipe again. "If you had any idea of the army of operatives behind this, you'd be surprised."

I admit to myself that I have been impressed with the top-level players.

"You got rid of the American spy, Chandler?"

"Yeah, sure." I kind of lie. But if I wounded Chandler, he's probably not a threat for a while. Long enough for us to accomplish what we need to do.

We all get into Benny's Mercedes. He drives around two corners into a quiet street lined with deserted warehouses and storage facilities. The walls are gray and stained from the weather. "Here." He points to a narrow, faded red door, the only entrance to a one-story warehouse. "We bought this a year ago in anticipation of our work now."

Getting out of the car, Benny looks up and down the street again, as if there's someone watching us. He carries a new leather briefcase attached to his wrist with a silver handcuff.

I snort and turn away. "He's the fucking joker," I say under my breath.

Benny opens a shiny padlock on the door, which scrapes across the concrete as we push into the dark interior. Even without light, I can feel its cavernous size.

"Come on, we don't have much time," Benny insists.

The lights flare brightly and we can see to the far end, where several tables sit against the back wall, which is made of corrugated steel, streaked red with years of rust. Steel cases rest on the tables, all closed. Benny locks the door behind us as we walk to the far end.

Just in time as rain hits the metal roof like a snare drum.

Unseen, chirping rats scatter off into the hidden corners. Two water-stained posters hang behind the tables. Under the face of a young Fidel Castro, it says, *Socialismo o Muerte*!

"Fuck him." Benny looks up at the supreme commander. "We'll finally get rid of his memory and replace it with our own."

"I hope you know what the hell you're doing," Felipe yells at him.

Benny raises his palms in the air. "Like I said, I'm working with the B-team here. I hope you two can consummate the mission."

My right fist balls along my side. "Don't worry about us. I want to talk about our extraction and what you're gonna do."

Benny touches the mole on his forehead as he thinks. "This op consists of a network of many stakeholders going all the way to the top of the two governments."

"I know that. Like I said, I want to rendezvous with you outside the hot zone so you can get us out of there."

"Okay. You need to practice with the weapon. We'll talk about that later."

"So, what the fuck is my assignment exactly?" Felipe says. He tilts his chin up.

Latin machismo. I laugh to myself.

"I proved my skills when I hit all those diplomats. The Americans even named it the Havana Syndrome."

"This is a lot more dangerous."

"Oh? We're going to do a hit on the American president?" His eyes glow with team pride.

Benny screams. He looks up into the ceiling as if he's interested in the leaks dripping rainwater. "No! No," he yells. "You are a fucking idiot." He comes toward us slowly, eyes bulging.

Felipe swallows hard.

"The president will not be killed. He'll be attacked and get very sick and live to come after us."

I agree with Benny. "Yeah, that's the whole purpose: to come after Cuba," I say firmly.

Felipe waves his hand. "But I need to know *how* we're gonna bring it down."

Benny stops moving. "You are point, as your cousin assured me."

I nod at Felipe.

He doesn't speak. He looks down at the oil-stained floor, and I smell the steel scent of sweat coming off him.

I gotta keep him in line. "And remember, you get a proportionately larger share of cash. Did you forget the last truckload I gave you?" I lean toward him.

"Sure, but I'm the point. Alone?"

"I'll be right behind you."

"Don't worry. You got the support of my undercover men who will be stationed all around." Now Benny lifts his chin. He flops the briefcase on a table, takes his time unlocking the handcuff, and then clicks it open. Bound stacks of U.S. dollars bulge out of the interior like ripe cabbage leaves. Felipe's face glows as he looks at it. Benny slams it shut. "After you successfully complete your mission."

Felipe takes a deep breath. "But how do I execute the move?"

"When you reach your staging point, you'll receive your final orders." Benny leads us closer to the tables. "This one in the middle has the latest model." He unlocks the case, lifts the lid, and stretches out his hand over the strange contraption as if it were all the gold in Cuba's churches.

"Is it like the one I used?" Felipe asks.

"Better. The scientists improved it. It's much more powerful. You both need training," Benny says.

The rain falls harder, stirring up my uneasy feeling. Felipe seems too confident. I know he's faking it for Benny. Always the money, that makes him so pliable.

Felipe steps up to look into the case. Along one side, three Colt Double Eagle 45s nest beside each other. Gold plated. In the middle sits a square-looking plastic box. "Who made it?"

"Does it really matter to you?"

It doesn't look like much. A white plastic box about nine inches long and three inches deep is attached to a plastic handle grip that hangs underneath it at a fifty-degree angle. It looks like someone's crude carpentry work. On the opposite end, there are ten short silver tubes about two inches deep, each the diameter of a fat cigar, all hooked together in a tight circle.

Felipe studies the wiring and the design. "I'm impressed as hell. It's a deceptive weapon, really. So simple looking, so dangerous in its strange results." He frowns. "That's it?"

"That's it? Yeah, that's it," Benny shouts. "You have no idea the power this bitch can produce." Cradling it in his hand, Benny lifts it gently and hands it to Felipe. After a quick look, he passes it to me. It weighs about two pounds.

Benny interrupts, "It's an ultrasonic sound gun that's engineered to precisely aim the noise. Like a laser."

"Oh?" I turn it over in my hands.

"Since the directivity of a sound wave depends on the size of its source and its frequency, the only way to get a directed beam with enough power is with ultrasound."

"Yeah, that's what I thought," Felipe agrees.

"See, they used a 3D printer to construct the gun-shaped enclosure." He pops off the top to show me. Inside, a tangle of wires and circuit boards squeeze into the box. "These tubes at the end? They're small parametric speakers that focus the sound waves into a narrow beam. It takes all ten of these to create something powerful enough. The sound behaves like a beam of light and can even be bounced off hard surfaces." Benny's face gleams with sweat. "There's a 555 timer circuit oscillating at the right frequency to modulate the audio onto a carrier signal—"

"Hey, Benny, you're as anxious as a kid getting laid for the first time." I follow that with a big laugh.

Benny doesn't laugh. Before I can get my fists up, he stabs one of the golden 45s toward my face. He must've scooped it when I was admiring the new weapon. "Don't fucking upset me." Spit comes with the words.

"Right."

Benny calms down and leaves to get us some water. I check with Felipe. "You up for this, *compadre?*"

"Yeah, man. I got it." He looks down at the floor, shuffles from one leg to the other. "Okay, I'm a little worried." He glances up to see if Benny overheard it. "But, Chucho, you can count on me." He fist bumps me.

I know he's faking that, too.

Benny returns and hands us sweating bottles of Ciego Montero. "Okay, Pepe. I want you to take it and follow me."

Felipe obeys and carries the weapon. "I was hoping for some bigger firepower."

Benny grabs Felipe's coat and flings him to the side. Although smaller than Felipe, he leans forward, eyes bulging again. "You want out? Is that what you want?"

"Uh, no."

"You can get out, but you'll be dead by tonight. And for fun, they'll gut you like a fish."

"Who's they?"

Benny takes a deep breath. "My group is connected to some of the highest-level government agencies in the U.S. And our investors in Miami have poured millions into this project. Of course, they can't be involved in this kind of shit, so they hire experts like us to do the sensitive work. We've successfully been able to change several 'dysfunctional regimes' around the world. We won't fail here."

Felipe's shoulders bunch up with nervousness. "Okay. Show me how it works."

Benny takes the gadget and points it like a gun toward two stuffed bags hanging from the low ceiling. "Those bags are like your human target. In addition, they are wired with several sensors to gauge how accurate your aim is." He hands it back to Felipe. "There's a trigger underneath, and see these two buttons on the top, under my thumb?"

Felipe nods.

"Hook up these two wires first. They connect to the battery. The button on the left activates the wire connection for a sound source. The right button activates the 12-volt battery source and powers up the amplifier. You have to wait a few minutes. Then, you press the trigger."

"Simple."

"There can't be any obstructions between you and the target. Remember from the last job? So, when you're in the middle of a big crowd, you have to remember all those steps."

"I'm going to be in a crowd this time?" Felipe steps backward.

"Yeah, for cover that'll get you close enough to use the weapon."

"Won't there be hell to pay from the Americans?"

"That's the whole point. The Americans will be so angry they'll invade the island to 'install a more cooperative government.'" He looks at me. "That's where your cousin will come in to help us as part of the newly established regime. Which will take orders from the U.S."

Felipe thinks to himself for a while. "So, the target will go down like he's shot?"

"He will feel intense pain in his head. A metallic, grinding sound that will penetrate his body until he collapses. Which is why you have to work fast. Watch this." Benny raises the gun and points it toward one of the bags, which look like stuffed mannequins. After turning on his cell phone and clicking both buttons on the weapon, he presses the trigger. The only thing that happens is a repeating noise that sounds like a cat meowing quietly.

Killed by a cat, I think to myself. I hope these dicks know what they're doing, or Felipe and I will die quickly in the aftermath.

"After the hit, get out by fading into the crowd. Remember, there's no noise with this weapon, and no one will see anything coming out of it. But if something goes wrong, Chucho takes the next shot. Now, I want you to practice here."

Felipe connects a wire to the back of the gun that runs to a battery power source in a gray cloth bag that he loops over his shoulder. He presses the buttons in the proper sequence. For ten minutes, Felipe fires the weapon at the hanging bodies. Benny watches the results on a laptop placed next to the case on the table, which senses and records the successful hits.

After several attempts, Benny pumps his fist in the air. "You're hitting ninety percent of your shots. Maybe this will work, after all. Try again."

I watch Felipe's hands relax as he points and fires.

Finally, Benny says, "Great work, man."

With a flushed face, Felipe hands the weapon back to him. "It's easy."

Then, Benny insists I also practice with the weapon. Although my scores aren't as good as Felipe's, it satisfies Benny, and we stop.

"This afternoon, I want you both to go to Lopez and Sons near the soccer stadium. Pick up your special clothing. They'll be waiting for you, but don't ask any questions." Benny turns to me. "Get the same disguise. And you'll also carry one of these weapons." Benny locks the weapon into the case. Then he curls the handcuff around his left wrist, fastening it to the case containing the cash.

Felipe says, "So when do I get paid?"

"You'll get half when we get to the staging point and half when you complete the mission."

We walk outside and dodge the last of the rain to get in the Mercedes. Benny stops at my limo, where Jose has been waiting. Felipe gets into the limo while Benny sets down the case and grabs my arm.

"I gotta admit, I'm impressed with your cousin," he whispers to me.

I agree but don't say anything.

"So, just to make sure this works, you will also be present at the scene, and we'll be watching you. One mistake and we'll remove both of you so nothing can be traced back to us." He pins his eyes on me. "Quietly, but we take you out."

Chapter Thirty-Two

Ava Alvarez
Thursday night. Two days left

I watch from my office window as the first shadows of early evening inch out from the corners into the small park below. Hunting tiny prey, a crow flits among the trees along the edges. The dying sun catches the tops of Cuban tanks and jet fighter planes mounted in the grass in the park. They were used during the Bay of Pigs invasion, launched by the United States in 1961. Even years later, I still remember how Fidel laughed about the failed attempt and said it was the best propaganda gift the Americans could have given to him. Now, the shadows hide the rust on the weapons.

I finally turn away toward my desk to make the phone call. I'm convinced the American was sent to make contact with me as a result of the message in the painting. Events are moving quickly, and if he can help, I need to meet with him as soon as I can. My idea to use Raquel Sanchez to draw in Chandler is risky. Will she cooperate? Usually, this kind of problem is easy to solve. Intimidation and torture work, eventually.

I dial the phone and give the order. "Pick her up." I'm surprised at how my voice cracks. When I was a new recruit, the tension during a mission was sometimes so high the same thing happened. But with experience, I calmed down. Now, it's back again.

"Who do you want to assign?"

"Use Miller and De Leon. No, use Cortez." I remember his intimidating bulk.

"Delivery point, Comandante?"

My first thought is the secret police headquarters in the green building but realize it would be impossible to seal off this interview from the dozens of snooping eyes there. "Here, in my office. The view is splendid, and I have all the equipment."

"TOA is one hour. For the Revolution, Comandante." The agent hangs up.

I've conducted hundreds of interrogations. Even so, they are never easy, and to steel myself I prepare each step in my mind, the incremental persuasion, what tools will be effective, and, most importantly, the psychological edge to use. In the past, many sessions have been violent and ended with a corpse. I don't dwell on those; most have been for the greater good of the Revolution. But some have been fucking, bloody disasters and didn't accomplish a damn thing.

I take a deep breath to relax the muscles in my stomach.

Another thought tiptoes in from the corners of my consciousness. Hesitantly. Will this be the last time? Maybe the Revolution has mutated into something I don't recognize, something that has already left me behind. Fidel is gone. The old comrades and the old enemies died long ago, their bodies rotting in La Necrópolis de Cristóbal Colón.

I turn back to look outside the window. In the dusk, glittering lights of gold from dozens of windows soften the ancient stones and streets of the city, giving them the appearance of rich comfort.

As always, I'll fight to the end. The country must be saved, or what we fought for will certainly be destroyed. And if I die, at least I'll do what I can to save Tom and his generation of Cubans. But it's still painful to acknowledge that I need help from the capitalists to the north.

I hope this interrogation will be over quickly. I'm sure Sanchez will cooperate but, if necessary, I won't hesitate to use extreme tactics.

An hour and forty-five minutes later, a soft knock on my door interrupts my reading of tedious paperwork. Miller and Cortez lead Sanchez into my soundproof office. They direct her toward a straight-back wooden chair that faces the window.

Cortez' body fills the entire door. Usually, he's so intimidating that I'm surprised to see a red welt on Sanchez's face. I glare at Cortez.

He makes a feeble shrug. "I'm sorry, but she fought like hell. I didn't mean to hit her."

"You two couldn't handle her? I'll deal with your failure later."

"She tried to flee in her car." Cortez gives the usual excuse for kidnapping Cuban citizens.

I direct Miller to pull a cart, similar to the one I use at headquarters, out of a closet in the corner of my office. It has all the same equipment loaded on it with the addition of a rechargeable electric cattle prod. It's about three feet long, so I don't have to bend over, and it was also cheap.

Miller parks the cart just inside Sanchez's line of sight. They fasten her legs and arms to the chair with cloth straps. Then, both of them retreat to a corner of the office and wait, standing at military attention.

"I won't need you this time," I say. They're surprised, and I yell at them to get out. They leave, closing the heavy door behind them.

I walk slowly to the big window and look out, wait silently, then turn and say, "Beautiful view, isn't it?"

Sanchez refuses to say anything.

"Do you know we are sitting in the very office that former President Fulgencio Batista used? Right here, where he ordered the deaths of so many of us revolutionaries. When I first took possession of this office, I intended to remove the phone he used. Then, I changed my mind and used it to order the execution of all his henchmen." I laugh at the irony.

"Why am I here?" she demands

"You're a lawyer and, from everything I've learned about you, you're very smart." I study the woman in the chair. Not beautiful in the Latin tradition, but still quite attractive. Well dressed and graceful and dignified in her confident self-possession. She wears a pair of blue pants, damp with sweat. Her shoes were removed earlier. Barefoot people feel more vulnerable.

"What are you going to do to me?" She clips off her words.

I've read the old file about Sanchez and her husband's illegal activities, and I remind her about it.

"I was absolved of all involvement. Let me go."

"Do you know who I am?"

"I remember."

"Comandante Ava Alvarez." When Sanchez doesn't respond, I continue, "I'm a senior officer in the Dirección General de Inteligencia. I need to meet someone, that's all."

"I can't—"

I lift the cattle prod off the cart and wave it in her face. "This is rechargeable, so I can use it on you for a very long time." I bring the two points close to her face but don't get the reaction of fear or cooperation that I want. While I make sure the chair is centered over the plastic tarp on the floor, I switch on the prod. It gives off a faint humming noise. With her unusual level of resistance, this may take longer than I expected.

Chapter Thirty-Three

Martha Rodriguez
Thursday night. Two days left

The big dude from the president's Secret Service detail cornered me in the conference room of the hotel to yell at me. He tried to intimidate me, but that doesn't work. I've been around too long.

"Do you have any fucking idea what you've got POTUS into?" He's screaming so loud that purple veins bulge in his neck.

"Settle down. You can't talk to me like that."

"You want him to exit the theater and move out into the crowd that'll be assembled in the plaza."

I step back to give myself space. After a few minutes, I assert my own position. "I didn't plan anything except that the president will say hello to the Ladies in White."

"You probably don't have a clue what's developed recently."

I study the guy for a moment. He's got wide shoulders, white face, short hair that is shaved along the sides of his head, and he wears sunglasses, even inside the hotel. His name tag says Munson. Definitely got BDE, big dick energy. But I've handled guys like this for years. "What are you talking about?"

"It's above your security clearance.'"

"You're yelling at me but can't tell me why?"

"Classified."

I decide to fuck with this jerk for a while. "I don't think you know anything either."

He frowns.

"Your clearance is too low, right?"

His shoulders relax and he stands back from me. He twists his neck to the side. "Well, I can't reveal everything I know."

"That's because you're really at a low level."

He forces a fake laugh.

"So, what can you tell me?"

He looks behind me, focuses on me again, and says, "You can't leak this to anyone." When I nod, of course, he continues, "Some high-level Cuban was killed. They found his body in a church."

"What does that have to do with the president?"

"Probably nothing, but this dude was a high-level officer in their secret police. Until the Cubans can make certain it has nothing to do with the president and Raul Castro, they've shut everything down for now."

I nod.

"Our inner contingent is on high alert until the Cubans give us the okay."

"Inner contingent?"

"Those agents assigned to be closest to POTUS."

"Does anyone know who did it?"

"Not for certain, which makes it dangerous to the max." He looks behind me again.

I've already heard rumors about the killing. So much for the classified aspect of his intelligence. "What does that mean?"

Munson takes a deep breath, as if he's digging deep into the secret stuff. "Can't say much, but the Cubans are investigating."

"When will we get the 'all clear'?"

He shrugs.

"Munson, this isn't tough."

"Our people are working with theirs. What we know as of now is that the Cuban security is trying to make sure there's no threat to POTUS or to Castro. After all, they're scheduled to appear together in the plaza after the president's speech inside."

"Do you mean the Secret Service and all the dozens of Cuban security experts can't figure this out?" I'm not surprised, really.

"Of course our guys are on top of things. But this time, it's probably going to be a lot more intense."

I hold my breath for a moment. "A direct threat to the president?"

His body stiffens. "Can't say."

"What can you say?"

"Uh, if I were you, I'd avoid the plaza at all costs. I don't know what shit will go down, but all of us in the Service have been ordered to stay 'frosty.' It's the highest alert I've ever experienced."

"But I'm supposed to lead the president to the Ladies in White for a brief meet."

"Obviously, we're scrambling to develop contingency plans."

"Meaning, the president won't make his speech at the opera?"

Munson shakes his head. "I don't know what will happen."

My stomach twists at the thought of all the work I've done to organize the meet with the Ladies. "He's not going outside?"

"Look, I don't know any more, and even if I did, I couldn't tell you."

"So, who do I talk to?"

"I'd stay in your lane."

My face gets hot, and I want to hit Munson. I've put up with a lot of shit from these young guys over the years. I pause to hold my anger and focus on what I need to do. "Okay, I got it. You be sure to stand tall and do your duty." He actually thinks I'm serious and doesn't catch my sarcasm. I extricate myself quickly. "Gotta run." I turn and make a dash for a quiet spot to call Oliver.

Apparently, he's heard rumors also. "I've heard something like that rumbling around also."

"What?"

"Nobody knows. But I'm sure the president is aware of this and that security is working around the clock."

"But Oliver, it sounds like the president won't come outside to talk with the reporters and meet the Ladies in White."

I could hear him dragging on a cigarette. "I suppose the Secret Service is warning him to stay in the theater while the political guys are urging him to get outside."

"I want him to be safe, of course, but all the work we've done—"

"I just remembered that I promised Berta Soler from the Ladies that she could meet the president. I gave her my personal assurance."

"Take a deep breath, Oliver. I'll check on things and let you know what the chief decides."

Chapter Thirty-Four

Ava Alvarez
Thursday night. Two days left

I face Sanchez and ask her, "Are you a loyal Communist?"

"You know that I served in the Pioneers."

"They kicked you out before you turned eighteen. Not a good record."

She glances at the prod. "I tried." Her eyes move to me, glaring shiny brown.

I wave the prod in front of her. Her defiance wilts with each pass of the tool. I watch her body stiffen in anticipation of pain. Now is the time for surprise. Catch her off guard. "You are working with an American named Peter Chandler."

"He's a trade diplomat, and the bank was contracted to work with him. My boss, well, my former boss, Diego Arnaz, ordered me to work with Chandler. It was not my idea." She blinks a few times. "I'm acting director."

I step in front of her and point the prod toward her face. "One nice thing about this is that it doesn't leave much blood to clean up." I stroke the metal fork at the end while Sanchez stares at it. Scared. I know what's going through her mind. When I click the steel tips along the edge of the metal tray, I tap a rhythm like a clock draining time away. "I have struggled all my life for the Revolution. In my work I have always succeeded." Fear clouds her face, and her body smells faintly metallic. I continue tapping for a few more minutes. Then I lift the prod in front of her eyes again.

Instead of poking her, I reach down to release Sanchez from the chair and lead her over to a low couch along the far wall. I come back with two bottles of water and offer one to her. She looks up at me with a startled expression, and her eyes dart around the room. But I can see the relief that I anticipated. She'll be more cooperative now. I hand her a clean towel, which she uses to wipe off her face and arms.

"Relax, this isn't what it looks like," I assure her. "Because I'm being watched carefully, I have to pretend to use the tools of torture and interrogate you." I can tell from her expression that she's still frightened. "Raquel, you're in a very critical situation now."

Dark eyes expand, but she doesn't say anything.

"What have you done as a patriot?"

Sanchez hesitates, then says, "I work for a bank that attracts the hard currency we need into our country. And I represent poor people in court."

"And I know of your husband's disloyal work in the past."

Sanchez's eyes flash again, but this time with a glint of anger.

"That's not why you're here." I pull over a stuffed chair and sit down. "Have you been loyal to the Revolution?"

"I believe in the Revolution, but it has failed in many ways." Her body stiffens. "I was prepared to give my life until it took my life first. My childhood, my happiness, and finally, my husband."

I pause and look toward the window. In some ways, I can understand and even agree. The Revolution demanded so many things from everyone. I made my choices and don't regret them, except in those lonely moments that seem to come more often now. Doubts that skitter through my brain so lightly they don't even leave footprints, but still keep me awake at night.

I turn back to Sanchez. "Actually, I need your help."

Her voice croaks with doubt. "Huh?"

"Don't worry. I'm telling you the truth." I pause for a moment. All my experience tells me not to reveal anything to this person, but I'm desperate at this point. "I had to set up this torture situation so no one would suspect me of working with you." I explain about my cousin, Rodolfo Diaz, his discovery of the weapon diagrams in the lab at CNEURO, and my secret message that he inserted into his painting. "It was a long shot, but there wasn't any way an officer from the secret police could make direct contact with the American security apparatus."

"Why did you do it?"

"Because the Havana Syndrome is the tip of the iceberg of a plot to destroy our country and give it to the U.S. and some puppets."

"What do you want from me?"

I must be careful at this point. I talk slowly. "It appears that Pete Chandler trusts you. I need to meet with him. Secretly."

"Why?"

"I hope he can help me stop the terrorists here in Cuba."

"What's in it for him?"

"I can solve the mystery of the Havana Syndrome and save his president from a planned attack." I look at her. "You're aware of this?"

"Yes, but I can't control him. He's very independent."

My voice softens. "Tell him I am Rodolfo Diaz."

"How can—?"

"I'm not him, of course, but he embedded my message in his painting."

Sanchez' shoulders quiver, and I know the full implications have finally entered her brain. Now is the time to press for the close. "I must meet with him as soon as possible. There's not any time left." I get up and walk to my desk, open a drawer, and pull out a new cell phone. "Here. Only use this to contact me."

Sanchez takes it and pushes it into her pants pocket.

"You must get to him immediately."

She hesitates but finally says, "How do I know we can trust you?"

"I understand more than you think I do. My femininity was sacrificed for the Revolution also. At the time, I felt it was worth it. Fidel himself caused me—" I realize my relationship with him is ancient history; Sanchez doesn't care. "Let me put it this way; this is the final chance any of us have to stop the attack on the president. That should motivate him." I call for Cortez to come back.

Sanchez nods and turns toward the door. Cortez fills the opening and steps aside to let the woman pass through before saluting to me. "It went easier than I imagined. Take her home," I order him.

Alone, I shuffle back to the window. Gold discs of light glitter throughout the darkness of the city, and even through the glass, I can hear Cuban *son* music echoing from an old stone plaza around the corner while a man's beautiful voice sings "Guantanamera," probably for a group of tourists sipping rum.

I'm surprised that Sanchez agreed to cooperate so quickly. And there was something about her, something that would've made her a good spy. Another successful mission without bloodshed should cause me to feel elated. Instead, I feel hollow and so terribly tired. I've done what I can to get help. Now, it's up to the American.

Chapter Thirty-Five

Pete Chandler
Friday afternoon. One day left

In the lobby of the Ambos Mundos Hotel, I pace to the door and back, waiting for Raquel. She sounded desperate and wanted to meet immediately. I, too, am anxious to tell her what happened to me. I feel personally violated by the attack last night. Walking outside into the mist, I call Sonnenfeld.

No one answers. I call again, and this time a voice comes on the phone. "Hello?"

"Who's this? Where's Sonnenfeld?"

A long silence drags on until the voice says, "Uh, there's been an accident."

"What?"

"Director Sonnenfeld is in the hospital in a coma."

"What happened?"

"I don't have any more information at this time." He hangs up.

Someone touches my shoulder, and I spin around.

"Easy." Raquel smiles at me. "I parked two blocks away so I could sneak in the back door. What's wrong?"

I look at her. Cocoa-colored skin, brown eyes that search my face. Tension radiates from her, and I can almost feel her buzzing. "Are you all right?" she asks. I smell dampness in her hair.

"Last night when I got back to my room, I found it had been trashed again. That's why I carry all my tools with me."

She frowns.

"I'm fine, except I can't let my guard down."

"Did they leave anything?"

"They're professionals. They didn't find what they were looking for."

"Now, I'm worried even more. Someone's getting too close."

"I checked with the hotel; no one there saw anything."

Raquel pulls me by the hand. "Come on. I must talk with you."

I follow her toward the back of the lobby. Next to the lift, a small group of tourists parts to let us pass. Down a short hallway to a door that leads to a rear courtyard. We walk fast through the mist to find Raquel's car. It's parked in a small space, hidden from anyone who may be looking for me. From over the ocean, more clouds with dark underbellies trudge toward the city.

She climbs in, and I go around to the passenger side. Once inside, the windows steam up immediately and the small space warms. I tell her that I've lost my contact with Sonnenfeld. I'm at a dead end for what to do next.

Raquel nods and watches the moisture on the windshield collect into small streams. Finally, she turns to me with a funny look on her face. "Maybe I can help."

"What?"

"Pete, I had a scary but strange experience with the Cuban secret police."

"What the hell?"

"It's okay." She explains the "interrogation" with Ava Alvarez. "Now, she wants to meet with you immediately."

"You think she's telling the truth?"

"How many people know about the painting?"

I think back. "Only a few people. Alvarez must be the control for Diaz."

"But this woman is at the top level of the secret police. Even with your diplomatic protection, I wouldn't trust her. I don't think it's a good idea."

Over the years, I've worked with many dangerous and unsavory people to get what I needed. Alvarez claims she has intelligence that she's hidden but wants to tell us. After all the effort to find the artist, I must make contact, but on my terms. I turn to Raquel. "How do we set it up?"

"She gave me a private phone, and she warned about the danger your president faces."

"What does that mean?"

"Should I call?"

"She wants to meet with me? I'll call."

Raquel taps the speed dial, waits, and taps on the steering wheel with her fingers. Her movements are jerky, and I feel just as nervous. She hands me the phone.

A few minutes later, a woman answers in Spanish. I talk with Alvarez, then click off and turn to Raquel. "She will meet with me. At a house across the entry to the harbor. Near the area where Che Guevara had a home."

"I don't trust her to pick the site."

"Okay. I'll choose it." I open the window and breathe the damp, cool air. It feels refreshing and clears my mind.

"Where?"

"I don't know," I shout. "Give me an idea. I don't want to get trapped."

"Okay, okay, I understand." Raquel stares straight ahead. Finally, she says, "I know of a place. It's a church near the office. They have some rooms for meetings that I think would work, and the priest is always there."

"Sorry to yell at you. Okay, I'll tell Alvarez." I call and talk for a short time. "Reluctantly, she agreed. I'm supposed to meet her in one hour there."

"She'll be alone?"

"Yes." We'll have to be extremely alert. I put my hand on her nervous fingers.

"I've got an idea." She steps out of the car and goes to the trunk, opens it, and returns. "Here, put this on." She hands me the wig I used before and a priest's cassock. I put them on, the cassock hanging around my ankles in black folds.

Forty-five minutes later, we approach the church. The mist frosts the windshield and makes the streets glisten like mirrors. My stomach tightens. All my alarm bells ring loudly. But I have to follow this to the end.

Raquel circles the small neighborhood church to make sure there are no tails. But just in case, I'll still wear the disguise. She stops and drops me off two blocks away. She'll wait for me there.

I try to walk quickly, but the cassock tangles around my legs. Just in case, I'm carrying my gun in the holster in the small of my back. A squat tower rises over the terracotta hump of the church. Small windows glowing with yellow light assure me someone is inside.

I search the shadows from different angles but don't see anyone else. As a precaution, I circle the church. I don't find anything suspicious. I also establish escape routes in case I can't make it back to the car. Thunder grumbles from somewhere behind me.

I pause for a moment. I've gotten Raquel into this situation; can I protect her if this goes badly? My feelings for her have moved to respect and deeper attraction. But this has happened several times in my past. Women I loved have gone out of my life. Will Raquel be yet another one? Will my history repeat?

She told me earlier, "There is a door on the side and several rooms on the main floor. The priest is always there because he lives in a small room in the back. At this time of day, few nuns will be present." Raquel gripped my hand with her own damp one.

Now I walk to a wooden door with a vaulted top. It opens easily when I push on it, leading to a dusky hallway. I leave it open in case I need a quick escape.

I walk down the marble tiled hallway, my feet making faint squishy sounds.

It's silent in the church, and I work my way forward. I'm totally alert, breathing hard, arms and legs flexing.

I move deeper into the church, beckoned by a mango glow from around a corner. I hug the left side of the door and creep into a small room. Candles stand on an altar at the far end. Dull ceiling lights reveal a few benches along the sides of the room, and two tables in the middle also hold burning candles. A slight woman stands behind one of the tables.

I stop about twenty feet from her and wait silently.

Finally, the woman says in English, "Chandler?" She grins. "The disguise doesn't fool me because your skin's too white."

"Yes." I remove the cassock and wig.

"I'm Ava Alvarez. We have much to share, but not much time."

"Okay." I notice a cinnamon smell that hints of countless incense burnings.

"Have a seat here." Alvarez points to a plain wooden chair.

She's middle aged and beautiful. Short gray hair covers her head, which she holds in a dignified manner. She wears green combat pants and a camo cotton t-shirt. Alvarez sits down on the far side of the table, her movements liquid and graceful, as she straddles a chair turned backwards. She's alone as far as I can tell. Before I sit, I make a quick circle of the small room to assure me no one else is present. I assume Alvarez is armed, but so am I. Removing my disguise, I maneuver the chair so that I have a straight, unimpeded line to my escape route.

Neither of us speak.

Alvarez begins, "We don't have much time."

"I agree. Are you the one who sent the message in the painting?"

"Yes."

I test her. "Tell me where the codes were embedded."

Alvarez blinks once. "On the cigars. In the numbers."

"Okay. What can you tell me?" I glance around to the corners of the room but still don't see anyone else.

"Mr. Chandler, I don't think you understand the position you're in. This isn't the United States of America. You're under Cuban law here. And I am the law." Her eyes widen and she stares at me. "Can we work together?"

Although she undoubtedly has lots of blood on her hands, I recognize a professional. Like good officers in the military, I think I can deal with her. Then the candles on the altar shudder in an unusual pattern. Is there someone else in the room? My legs tighten, and I twist around but don't see anyone else.

"Okay. Why did you contact us with the painting?"

"As I'm sure you can imagine, in my position I have to be extremely careful. I have discovered a secret plot that will destroy my country if it's successful. Since it includes some high-level government people, I cannot stop it directly."

"I understand."

"What did you find at CNEURO?" She must've seen the startled look on my face. "I know everything on this island. Well, almost everything."

"I found some old Soviet schematic diagrams for an unusual weapon."

Alvarez nods in agreement. "My cousin, Rodolfo Diaz, discovered the same drawings. What scared us both was the updated version that scientists have perfected. It was used to cause the Havana Syndrome."

"Why?"

"I think the traitors were testing it out."

"Testing it?"

"Yes, which leads to the plot I must stop. It will be initiated by an attack on your president. That's where you and your control in America will come in."

"What are you talking about?"

Alvarez stands up. "Besides the traitors here, they are funded and aided by a covert group from the U.S. I suspect it's Red Dog Associates, a black ops group I know that's been active in Cuba for a few years now, waiting for the opportunity to strike. Beyond that, I wouldn't be surprised if a few of the subversive Cuban exile groups in Florida are also involved."

"I'm not sure about all—"

"Mr. Chandler, I am certain. In my position with the secret police, it's my job to monitor these terrorist cells and smash them."

"But why would our president have anything to do with destroying your country? Instead, he's trying to open up relations between us."

"Of course. My intelligence tells me the attack on the president will cause the U.S. to invade Cuba in some form, eliminate the present regime, and replace it with one hand-picked by the U.S. to be more 'cooperative.' The traitors in Cuba and people like Red Dog Associates have already populated a shadow government, ready to take over."

I lean back in the chair to try and absorb all this. I look at Alvarez, study her steely eyes, and begin to believe her. I run my hand over my forehead. "Okay, what do you want from me?"

"I hate to ask for help from a capitalist to the north," she says without smiling. "Your control in Washington deciphered the message in the painting and understands the significance of it. I need your help to warn your president." Alvarez continues to expound on the details for another ten minutes.

"Uh, I'll relay this information." I thought of Sonnenfeld's disappearance. What could I do without him and his resources?

"Immediately. Your president has been on Cuban soil for several days."

"Where will this attack occur? And how could anyone possibly get through the security screen of Americans and Cubans?"

Alvarez sighs. "I don't know. But my assistant is squeezing all his informants for information."

"That doesn't help me now."

"If we work together, I'll update you constantly by phone. I assume you have an encrypted device." She stands away from the chair. "Because the group of Cuban subversives are operating undercover, my usual assets are unable to penetrate to get the final details. So far, the president has been in small enclosed facilities where only a select security force is present. But besides that, he will be at restaurants, baseball games, tours of art museums, neighborhoods, and visiting the Cuban government buildings. I suspect it will be in some small situation with few people around."

"So, I can always reach you at the phone number you gave?" I hold up Alvarez's cell phone. "And it's secure?"

"Of course."

I stand up, sensing the meeting is closing. I leave her phone on the table. "You're sure of an attack but don't know where or when or what we can do to prevent it?"

"You're very intelligent, Mr. Chandler. I've prepared a response of my own and am prepared to strike, and I'm still receiving updated intelligence. But you also have to strike fast. Contact your control and get him to warn the necessary people in Washington to protect the president and stop this. They must act now."

"Why can't a person in your top position simply contact the Cuban security around the president?"

Alvarez shakes her head. "You don't understand anything, do you? The Cuban spy system involves all of us spying on each other. I was able to shake off the tail following me for this meeting, but usually I'm in the presence of at least one party official to monitor my actions. We all are. So, if I were to approach the Cuban security people, how would I know I could trust them to not reveal what I've discovered? Then the subversives would be tipped off." Alvarez' face darkens. "My only choice is to ask for your help." She scoops up the phone.

"Uh, I'm having trouble reaching my control."

Alvarez' face turns the color of ashes. "You're like an army in a foreign country without supply lines or resources. Do what you can," she sighs. Without another word, Alvarez blows out the candles on the table, leaving only the smell of the smoke as she walks out through a small door in the darkness at the back of the church.

Chapter Thirty-Six

Miguel Garcia
Saturday morning. Day of president's speech

I wait for Felipe in my limo on the street by his apartment. Today we will finally execute the mission, receiving orders from Benny and his group. In all of my juvenile crime capers, I always knew the full plan and the risks. But Benny still insists on withholding the final details, claiming it would breach security and threaten everything. That's bullshit, of course.

I think of Gabbie. I can smell her bare skin and could use a fuck right now. With the work before me, I felt like talking to someone, so I called her last night. I really didn't have anyone else to talk with, but it went badly, as I should've known it would. But then, I don't need her, really.

Felipe plods down the steps from the three-story stone building. He wears a Panama hat and a dull gray *guayabera*. When he gets into action, he won't stand out from the crowd. I don't laugh at him though, because I need him to be positive and strong.

Now I approach the final hours.

Today I don't want my driver, so when Felipe gets into the Mercedes, I pull away from the curb. I drive with my forearm perched on the open window while I draw deeply on a big cigar. The blue smoke fills the car before washing out the open windows.

I grin at Felipe and hand him a cigar. "Nothing better for breakfast." He takes it and laughs.

We settle into the soft leather seats. Usually they feel luxurious, but today I'm too anxious to feel much of anything.

"Chucho, tell me the details of the operation," Felipe demands.

"We got a big fucking day ahead of us," I reply as I thread the car through the crowd meandering in the street. I honk twice and gun the car forward. "You ready?"

"Of course. Where are we going?"

"El Parque de la Fraternidad. Friendship Park. Not far from the capitol."

"Have you got the weapon?" Felipe asks.

I cock my head toward the trunk to answer *yes*.

"How do we conceal the power source?"

"There is a canvas bag that'll go over your shoulder. Inside will be a battery pack and the necessary technology to operate the gun."

"But won't that look suspicious if someone stops me?"

I turn onto Simón Bolívar Avenue and hurry through Chinatown. Double buses wheeze alongside, leaving as much smoke outside the car as we create inside. Small stores line the sidewalks, many painted with a bright red lacquer and gold Chinese characters.

"No problem. If you're stopped, you'll say the gun is a high-tech microphone with the battery pack. Memorize this phrase: it's an ambisonic microphone, capable of picking up even the smallest ambient field sounds."

"Got it."

"No wonder you studied engineering. This information could save your life."

Felipe nods. "So, I'm the point man. Leading the charge."

"Yes. Your cover is an international journalist."

"Will we have headsets, like TV? They call 'em 'coms.' You know, for communications."

I take a deep breath. "Shut up. You don't need a fake headset to give you credibility." I stop at a corner next to a bicycle with a front basket carrying some red flowers. Their aroma sifts into the car. Felipe tosses his cigar butt into the middle and laughs. "That'll be a surprise for them, ha, ha. When they see their flowers smoking." He clenches and opens his hands. "What will we do at the park?"

"We wait for Benny and the final instructions. Timing is everything for this op."

"Yeah, of course. What about the clothing? I got fitted at Lopez and Sons, like Benny said."

"I picked up both of ours. They're in the trunk."

"Pretty clever. It's just like a real photojournalist's vest."

"It *is* a real photojournalist's vest. That's the point. And I've got an ID for you, plus a plastic badge, supposedly issued by the secret police, identifying you as a reporter from Reuters International News. That'll give you access. I predict there'll be so goddamn many reporters no one will notice one more, which will be you." I slap the dash with my palm. "Remember, you're a warrior here. Walk and act like you are the biggest bull in all of Cuba."

Felipe shifts his body in the seat. "I can do it."

"Benny should tell us where the ingress points are. We won't know for sure until we arrive and assess the situation."

Felipe looks at me. "But you don't know where exactly?"

"Shit, I don't. I'm a little nervous," I admit.

"Forget it. We'll be ready."

The light turns and I lurch forward. Dozens of Asian people ride next to us on bikes, most of them piled high with food, furniture, children, and flowers.

Felipe shifts in the seat and asks, "How do I reach the target?"

"Benny will brief us when the time comes."

"But—" Felipe puts his hands on the dashboard to steady them.

"Remember, there are lots of moving parts, lots of support people who must get in place."

Two old Chevrolet convertibles pull in front of us, traveling side by side. Stupid tourists stuff the back seats, laughing and pointing their cell phones at everything.

The crowd forces me to slow down. I glance at the clock on the dash. "Damn it. We can't miss the assembly time."

Felipe's knee bounces up and down with a life of its own. "What if someone checks my 'microphone'?"

"You're an engineer. Give them some bullshit explanation."

"Will you be my backup?"

"Of course. I'll carry the same equipment you have. Once the hit is done, hide the weapon back in the shoulder pack and fade. It'll be simple, huh?"

"Easy to say."

I think of the small shrine in my bedroom. Yemaya has never let me down. Today will be no different. Still, my gut feels hollow.

"And what if that doesn't work?"

I'm getting frustrated with him. "Then, Felipe, you're fucked." Laughing, I reach over and give him a punch on the shoulder. "This is the chance of a lifetime to free our country."

"What if I don't think that'll happen?"

"You'll still get all your money," I assure him. "Isn't that worth it?"

But Felipe doesn't answer.

Chapter Thirty-Seven

Ava Alvarez
Saturday morning. Day of the president's speech

After a quick shower and a change into my pressed uniform, I wait for Pena to arrive. My guard remains outside, ostensibly protecting me. I walk from one room to another, my footsteps echoing across tile floors to the empty walls. Solana's off for the weekend.

From the open windows of my office, I see fog still nestled among the palms and bougainvillea that drape over the dry fountain on the terrace.

Pena has new intelligence that must be reported in person, he said.

From the top drawer of my desk, I lift out the gray Belgian revolver Fidel gave me. It's heavy and smells of sweet cleaning oil. After carrying it for so many years, I feel naked without it. Mendoza became the latest in a long line of executions I had to use it for.

My cell phone rings. Pena? When I answer, I hear the gravelly voice of the inspector general from the secret police. "What are you doing now?" he demands.

"I've been liaising with the Cuban officers who will coordinate security for the presidential party as they have breakfast. All the contingencies are covered."

"I have tragic news."

"What's that?"

"The body of our illustrious patriot, Alfredo Mendoza, has been found in a church basement."

"What happened?"

"He's been killed. Shot at close range."

"Oh, no."

"Do you know anything about this tragedy?"

"No, of course not. I am absolutely loyal to the Revolution, and you know it."

"We have launched an investigation from the highest levels. Nothing will be overlooked to find the killer."

"Absolutely. Good."

"Comandante Alvarez, everyone will be considered a suspect until we solve this crime." He pauses for a moment. "In spite of the American president's visit, we will move forward with our manhunt." He hangs up.

I slump into the soft chair to think. To help, I walk into the kitchen to make more coffee. While waiting for the water to boil, I remember Fidel. But the memories are so far in the past they have acquired brown edges, like old photos that deteriorate and finally disintegrate.

A knock from the front door echoes throughout the house.

I pour the water over the coffee and hurry to let Pena in. He's early, thank God.

He steps into the front room, looking young even though he dresses in the Revolutionary green fatigues with combat boots. He barely salutes as he bursts into the room. "This afternoon. At the plaza."

"What?"

"I have an old informant that I rarely use because he's so unreliable. But we're desperate, so I leaned on him. He was so frightened and hesitant, I had to pay him double the usual price for his information."

"What did he tell you?"

"Something will occur at the Gran Teatro after the president's speech."

I take a deep breath, feeling my limbs tingle in preparation. I tell him of Mendoza's death and the massive investigation. He's shocked at the news. Waving Pena into my office, I bring coffee and a bottle of Havana Club rum from the kitchen. I pour coffee and a generous amount of sweet-smelling rum into each cup. "Do you trust your informant?"

"No, not completely, but what else do we have?" Pena gulps at the drink.

I look carefully at him. My only dependable ally at this point. Could he do it with me? "You've been a loyal adjutant to me, Pena."

"I'm prepared for anything."

"What I'm going to tell you will shock you, but I was able to make contact with the American, Chandler. I asked for his help to alert the security detail around the president. I gave him my phone number and will give him this new intel."

Pena lifts his head. He's silent for a while, then says, "Do you trust either of them?"

I smile reassuringly. "As you said, we have no choice." Changing the subject, I tell him about our weaponry. "I have been preparing for this day for a long time. The technology we will use is easy; the execution of it will be more difficult." I step back to assess his reaction. He seems calm. "I'll show you how it works."

Pena stands and walks in a circle. He runs his hands down the sides of his pants, as if to wipe off sweat. "Can't we just take our service weapons?"

"You know that only the Army will be allowed to carry weapons in the plaza. That's why I prepared the umbrellas. To get around the security prohibitions against weapons." I can tell from his expression that he's doubtful. "We'll be in this together. Our mission will be undetected if we do it correctly." I don't have to tell him what will happen if we screw up. "I'll work the point; you are backup if I miss."

He pours more coffee but no more rum into his cup. "I'll do my best, but—"

Chapter Thirty-Eight

Miguel Garcia
Saturday morning. Day of the president's speech

I'm working hard to keep Felipe in line. "I told you, we have highly placed resources, and they're depending on you to change everything on the island. You'll be a hero."

Felipe sits up. "I know. Here I am, an engineer who would be free to work where I wanted to if the government wasn't so fucked up."

The good feeling we share lasts until we stop at the next light. Although I've committed enough small crimes as a juvenile to get a street sense of the risks, this operation will be the most dangerous. Even with our highly-placed help.

The traffic stops and we wait. I look at the clock on the dashboard and watch the sweep hand inch around the dial. If we miss the rendezvous time, the entire plot will be blown and we could become the targets. Hunted down and killed quickly.

Felipe's past attacks on the diplomats were simple, in crowded areas, within the known streets and escape routes of Havana. This one will be much harder. And I hate to trust my future to these foreign agents, even if they have money and American supporters to finish the job.

"Can you go faster?" Felipe interrupts my thinking.

"I'll try."

Then Felipe remembers the money. He looks me in the eyes. "I get paid at the park?"

"Yes."

"Don't fuck around about this." Felipe's body tenses. "I want my money."

I look straight ahead and lift a hand off the wheel while patting the air between us with my palm. "Easy. You'll get half when we get to the park. It's already in the trunk, not that you can carry it—"

"I want American dollars."

"Of course."

"And the rest?"

"After you do the job, like Benny said. We get the money from him first, then we double-cross that fucking ass." I reach across the seat to put my hand on Felipe's shoulders. "I know you're worried. We all are, but we're Cuban *toros!*"

I turn on the radio and listen to Cuban *son* music. The beat reverberates throughout the car. It's relaxing. As we bounce through potholes, I see a woman walking toward the park. She pushes a stroller, holds a child, and is obviously pregnant with another. In spite of her load, she smiles. I realize people like her don't have a clue that their world is about to change for the better.

"After I complete my mission, what's the plan for getting us out?" Felipe asks.

I look over at him. "That's where the double cross is activated. I insisted to Benny that he extract us two blocks from the plaza by picking us up in his car. It's critical that we get him alone."

"Then what happens?"

"He drives us to my car. I get out first and go to the trunk with our cash. You remain in his car. Engage him in some conversation. Keep him busy while I pull out my Makarov pistol. It's necessary for you to keep his attention so his head is turned away from me. I'll finish him in a second."

Felipe smiles. "I'll keep him talking, but don't let his brains splatter on me."

"I'll try that." He fist bumps me, and we share our secret alone. "During my planning sessions with the top people, I found out that Benny demoted my future position. But I've got assets in the top echelon who agreed to place me higher in the new order. Getting rid of Benny will assure that happens."

"Besides the fact we hate that prick."

I pull the Mercedes into a No Parking spot and stop. Friendship Park is already filled with people, standing and drinking, lying on the ground, and trying to use cell phones. I get out and scan the park.

"Where's Benny?"

"He'll be here. He's a prick, but he's always kept his word."

Calzado del Cerro, the main thoroughfare that runs north through downtown Havana, a block to the east, bustles with traffic. The side-walks are lined with uniformed troops who stand in lazy groups with their arms folded across their chests. A festive feeling floats in the air. A few blocks to my left, someone shoots off firecrackers. The odor of grilled pork carries in the breeze.

Felipe limps in a circle, checking his watch often.

"Get into your uniform."

Felipe opens the trunk. A tan canvas covers everything. He lifts a corner, runs his hand underneath, and pulls out a pair of pants, new shirt, and the photojournalist vest.

He stands behind the meager shelter of an open door and changes. In Cuba, there is no such thing as privacy anyway. No one pays any attention. Actually getting into his role helps to calm Felipe. He pokes his hand into the pockets. In the right front one he pulls out an official-looking card and papers. He turns them over. "My identification documents. My photo looks good on the journalist's card."

"See the gun?"

Felipe glances to both sides. "Quiet. Don't call it that, you idiot! It's too risky. I'll conduct a quick check of the systems." He lifts a blanket and rummages underneath it with his hand.

When he's done, I check my own equipment, including the Makarov with the silencer attached, and get dressed.

We move to the front of the car and lean against the warm hood, waiting. After a half hour Felipe's knees quiver. He stands to steady them, but that doesn't help. "Where the hell is Benny? I wanna get this done."

Just as he says that, I see a car with darkened windows slide next to us. Benny steps out with a big smile on his face. He's wearing a shiny blue shirt unbuttoned to his stomach.

"*Compadres*," he shouts to us. "Showtime, as we say in the States." He comes forward and puts his hand on Felipe's shoulder to calm him. "You are already a hero, Pepe."

"It's Felipe, asshole."

Benny looks between us. "Yeah, yeah, you're right. Here's what you need to know. You'll walk together behind the capitol and come out next to the Gran Teatro. It'll be packed with people since the president's giving a speech inside. There will be security lines surrounding the plaza in front of the theater. You'll find the ingress spot and you both pass through the line, using your press cards. You must arrive in the plaza no later than one fifteen. Move to the side of the opera house next to the second door with the other journalists. Once you're there, wait."

He turns to me.

"Wait for what?" Felipe asks.

Benny's voice drops to a whisper. He leans closer to Felipe. "You'll know when to move. When the president comes outside about one forty, act as if you want an interview along with all the other journalists. Hold the 'microphone' in front of you, pointed directly at him. Don't forget to arm it with the two buttons first." He touches the mole on his forehead.

"Yeah, yeah."

"You two get to the staging area and wait for my call. Only on my call will you deploy. This has to be timed perfectly. And after all the planning and money that's gone into this op, I don't want you to fuck it up." He starts to move away, leaving the smell of his cologne in the air.

"Roger that." Felipe half-salutes before dropping his hand. "And then you get us both out?"

Benny steps back, a frown on his face. "I always save my men." He glances at me. "Just like I told your cousin, I'll pick you up two blocks east of the action."

Chapter Thirty-Nine

Ava Alvarez
Saturday morning. Day of the president's speech

I reassure Pena in words that will reverberate with him. "I'm convinced you are exactly the right soldier for this mission. Your patriotism has been exemplary and, I'm sure, will continue. For the Revolution," I shout. I could simply order him to obey, but considering the importance of our mission, I need a willing partner. "And remember, Ricardo, with your success comes the rewards that will make your family proud of you."

Turning to face me, Pena says, "All right. What do you want me to do?"

"Excellent."

I go to the back of the office and unlock the door of the secret closet. Carrying a long cloth bag back to the desk, I set it on top. Pena comes over. His forehead shines, and he breathes deeply. "Are you sure we don't need backup? A few trusted agents?"

"Absolutely not. Our strike must be kept secret until the last minute."

He opens and closes his hands several times while I unzip the bag. Inside, six blue umbrellas lay like corpses. He starts to laugh.

"Pena!" I command him. "I want to test these Bulgarian umbrellas, and we don't have much time." Laying them in a row on my desk, I continue, "And what do you think of my idea of attaching price tags? Avoid suspicion."

"Uh, I don't—"

"Many other people will use umbrellas, so we shouldn't attract attention." While I inspect the mechanism on each umbrella, I ask, "You help me identify the traitors."

"Of course. Felipe Garcia walks with a limp. His cousin, Miguel, is larger, has big shoulders, and has an arrogant attitude that shows in the way he walks. I sent you their photos."

Hesitantly, he lifts out one umbrella by the handle.

I grab it away from him. "Don't be so scared. I haven't armed any of these yet." I turn it over in the light coming through the French windows. The handle is straight with a trigger mechanism mounted on the side. It looks like a wooden button used to open the umbrella.

"What the hell?" he stammers.

"It's a poison delivery system."

"You sure this will work?"

"Yes. You're not old enough to remember these. So low tech that no one would ever suspect us. It's deadly, but doesn't make a sound like a gun or require the mess of a knife or machete. The perfect weapon for our offense."

I lift the end to show him a sharp point. "This is pressed firmly against the target in order to penetrate the skin. The poison must be injected under the skin to be effective."

"Why is it called a 'Bulgarian' umbrella?"

"In 1978 a Bulgarian dissident, Georgi Markov, defected from the Soviet Union. He was waiting for a bus at the Waterloo Bridge in London when he felt a prick in his leg. Turns out, a Russian spy had used one of these umbrellas to inject poison into his leg."

"What happened to Markov?"

"He died a horrible death." I explain to him, "Inside this handle is a spring that pushes the linkage system to the valve at the end. The entire length is hollowed out to accommodate the apparatus and the poison capsule." I flip over the umbrella. "And the linkage system connects to the valve."

"So where does the poison go?"

"Inside the shaft is a cylinder of compressed air that drives the poison, ricin, into the target. Once I press the trigger, there is a switch just beyond the cylinder that activates the valve, which in turn fires the pellet through the hollowed-out barrel of the umbrella. I put the ricin pellet here." I point to a spot in front of the handle. "I unscrew it and slip it in here." Then I set it on the desk and smile at Pena.

I offer him more rum. He sips this one slowly, probably appreciating its quality. Pouring some into my cup, I shake out my shoulders. He's understanding better than I expected.

"How close do you need to get to the target?"

"You must touch the body with the tip. It will penetrate one layer of clothing."

"Does it kill immediately?"

"No. That's the beauty of this weapon. You wait until the target's in a crowded situation, move in, touch the body, pull the trigger, and fire the pellet into him. It acts quickly by causing difficulty breathing, so the enemy feels like they're suffocating. But the most serious effects occur in about four hours—giving you enough time to escape without notice." I grin at how clever I've been. "And there is no antidote to the poison."

Pena nods his understanding. "You're brilliant."

My eyes dip in acknowledgement. "Come on. We must hurry." I lift the bag containing the ricin poison capsules out of a drawer in the desk. "The poison." Carefully, I place it on the desk and open it. The capsules smell medicinal. "Don't worry. The poison won't activate until it penetrates the target's skin. Still, we have to be careful."

Pena backs up.

After sliding my hands into a pair of leather gloves, I reach into the bag and remove a small plastic box. It's sealed with tape, which I cut using a sharp letter opener. There are twenty-four capsules lined up in two rows. Tom did his work well. Light gray, they look about the diameter of a narrow pen. One end is rounded, the other pointed.

I unscrew the handle from the first umbrella. A slot opens in front of the trigger mechanism. I insert a poison pellet and edge it forward to fit into a slot in the length of the hollow shaft. Next, I place an equally small capsule of compressed air behind the poison. When pulling the wooden trigger, it's critical that the point actually break the skin, so the end of the umbrella must be pushed against the body of the traitor. The insertion takes a moment and will be completely silent except for a muffled woosh of released air. Such a simple but clever weapon.

"Someone I trust manufactured the poison for me."

"Is it made in a lab?"

I chuckle. "It's actually a waste product when castor beans are made into castor oil. It's refined to create poisonous effects in humans. It prevents human cells from making the proteins they need, causing death."

"Nasty stuff."

"We're fighting nasty terrorists."

"Do you suspect other targets?"

"We know the two cousins are working on this. Thankfully, you've already identified them. We'll eliminate them, then see what develops. That's why I have the extra umbrellas and poison pellets."

"When do we leave?"

I look at the grandfather clock in the hallway. "Now. We must be in position in the plaza as early as we can. We can use your car to prevent the spies outside from getting suspicious."

"The umbrellas will fit into my trunk. Should I change clothing?"

"No, we need to look as if we're on an official assignment in order to get access to the plaza. It'll be heavily guarded. And remember, we must act as if we're using the umbrella to shade us from the sun."

"What about the extra ones?"

"Carry two along your side and act nonchalantly. No one will even notice with all the excitement of the president's appearance." I start for the back door. "Hurry."

Pena's face pales and he looks down at the umbrellas. "How are we going to sneak out of here?"

"Pull your car around to the alley in the back, because the spies are too lazy to watch me there. We'll load these in your trunk and leave." As we assemble our weapons, I remember to call Chandler to give him the location of the attack.

He answers immediately, acknowledges the message, and says, "I'm preparing now."

That worries me. "What the hell does he mean?"

Chapter Forty

Pete Chandler
Late Saturday morning

"Do you trust her?" Raquel shouts above the sound of the wind through open windows in her car as she speeds across Havana. "I'm sure Alvarez's the one who killed my husband."

"How do you know that?"

She glares at me. "I know."

"Okay. I don't trust her very far, but the message in the painting was a huge risk for her."

"And?"

"And I think we can trust her about this plot. It fits with everything Benny warned me about."

Raquel squeals around a corner and heads into a straightaway. The buildings on either side of us are lower, two-story and very old. Few trees grow here. Vacant lots with dead cars bookend the corners of each block. "Can you call someone in Washington, like Alvarez asked?"

I shrug. Who could I call now? Sonnenfeld told me if I tried that, no one would know who I am. He *was* my only contact.

"Can you get in touch with the American delegation here? Warn them?"

"I can try to reach them at the hotel where they're staying. But knowing how carefully planned the security and scheduling are for this visit, it will take a long time to get a message through." I pause to think of the nightmare it will be to even get their attention. "As an American, they may listen to me, but I don't have an official position here. I'm not sure they'd give me the time of day."

"We have to try."

"I agree. It's about the only thing we can do. But even if I can get their attention, what do I say? We still don't know the final details of the attack."

Raquel focuses on her driving.

I think ahead to a possible showdown with the enemy. Certainly, I've got weapons, but I don't know how I'll stop them. Alvarez's Belgian umbrellas strike me as a feeble response and probably won't work.

Alvarez calls me on my encrypted phone. I talk quickly and hang up. "Alvarez says they have confirmed intelligence that the attack will occur this afternoon in the plaza next to the Grand Theater."

I open the Sectera Edge and scroll through information about the president's schedule that's now been made public. He will speak inside the theater, then exit out a side door into the plaza at approximately one thirty for a brief stop before heading off to a baseball game. "Forget trying to contact the Americans at the hotel. We don't have time."

"I'm not sure we can get access if you're carrying your weapons."

I agree. "I've got the drone." From my backpack, I pull out a small plastic box and flip it open to reveal the Insectothopter. I pinch my fingers around the body of the dragonfly. "To get airborne, the wings even move like a real insect."

As usual, the traffic is slow. Buses, carts, bicycles, and taxis all fight for an extra inch of progress. My stomach rumbles with anxiety. "How far is the theater?"

"About a half mile, but I know it'll be crowded. When Obama visited in 2016, the Cuban people went crazy to see him. I'm sure this will be the same. That means we have to park several blocks away and walk."

"And I'm sure there will be lines of security to get through into the plaza, right?"

"Of course."

"How will we do that?"

Raquel glances at me as a bus in front of us lumbers forward. "I don't know." She speeds up for about a half block, then stops again.

My head throbs, and I take deep breaths to calm myself. Years ago, in combat situations, I always had intelligence about what lay ahead. We had spotters, snipers, drones, and locals that all informed us of the enemy terrain and their position. Here, we have nothing except a phone and a tiny drone. Not much of an advantage.

Raquel turns a corner, and I see the white dome of the national capitol arching above the treetops. A landmark that we can use since it's next to the theater. She explains, "Between the capitol and the theater is a street and a grassy knoll. I assume it will be packed with people, but the security will keep them back until the president has left."

We reach a roadblock and back up, turn the corner, and come into the old city from the south. This time, tourists clog the streets, wandering as if they are lost. Again and again, Raquel stops and waits for a clot of them to clear a path for her to drive forward. "Did Alvarez tell you who we're looking for? What will happen?"

"They've identified two men and will search for them."

She looks back and forth at the snarled traffic. "I'm going around to the east, by your hotel. We can run from there to the plaza." She spins the wheel and we careen off to the right, but at least we move forward. In ten minutes, she rocks to a halt next to the Ambos Mundos Hotel.

From over the Caribbean, I see dark clouds rolling toward the city. The heavy underbellies are bruised in purple colors.

We get out quickly and hurry toward the dome of the capitol. Raquel was correct: there are hundreds of people moving in the same direction. Many have blankets spread on the grass and are eating picnics. I get a whiff of the sweet smell of grilling plantains. The streets are clogged, so we dodge back and forth when we spot openings in the crowds. It's slow going.

"What's our objective?" she asks.

"We look for the door of the theater where the president will emerge."

"Then what?"

I shrug. I have no idea and I worry it's hopeless, but I don't dare tell her that. And it'll still take a long time considering the crowds. Military trucks line the street to keep people flowing in one direction. We walk as fast as we can.

The Sectera Edge phone says it's noon.

Rows of uniformed guards block the way. "The foreign secret police," Raquel tells me. "The government has probably activated every branch of the security forces."

I hate standing still. Once we get into the plaza, maybe I can find the American delegation. Explain what I know and warn them in time.

We wait in the hot sun, the minutes ticking away.

I dial Alvarez's number and wait. Finally, she answers. I tell her, "We're still trying to get to the plaza. Once we get inside, I'll be able to alert the Americans to the danger. But we have to know where to go and how to get in. Can you help us?"

Alvarez is panting, "With these crowds, it'll be impossible to find you to get you access inside the perimeter."

"You must leave your phone on. Can you hold it up in front of you while you move on the plaza?"

Alvarez doesn't respond for a while. "What?"

"Can you do that?"

"I don't understand, but my adjutant, Pena, can hold my phone."

I look over at Raquel and smile. "We're as good as in."

"Good. We will find you." Still using the Sectera Edge phone, I open the app for the Pegasus program and key in the number of Pena's phone. After a few minutes, it takes control of his phone's camera. I see a blurry shot of a man's uniformed legs and feet.

If he leaves his phone on, we can see exactly what he sees and determine where they are.

And if we can find them, I hope Alvarez can get us all inside onto the plaza.

Chapter Forty-One

Miguel Garcia
Saturday morning. Noon

Sitting on the hood of my car, I drop my head. I'm dizzy and worry that my legs may not work. Two days ago, I bought more tickets from the *bolita* for my Santeria god, Yemaya. Number seven again. He always helps old Chucho; today Yemaya really needs to come through for me. I don't want to die.

"Dammit, why doesn't he call? I gotta get this done." Felipe limps in a circle in front of the car. "The bastard said timing is everything."

A breeze blows a puff of dust across the park. It reaches the car, and I smell all of Havana in it. The ancient stones, cooking oils, and jasmine bushes. The Communist party, the local police, and the secret police are all assembling just a few blocks from us now. And me, Chucho Garcia with the thin hair, will soon change it all.

Felipe lights another cigar and blows a cloud of smoke into the wind. "Have you heard anything?"

"No. When I hear, I'll goddamn tell you."

"Chucho—"

I look across the park as if that would make things happen faster and I walk twenty feet away, then come back. Felipe will take the shot, but Benny insisted I dress in the journalist's outfit like Felipe and accompany him.

In spite of the breeze, I swipe my hand over my face to wipe the greasy feel of sweat off it. Once we get the okay to execute the mission, the two of us will walk up the street behind the capitol, turn the corner, and look for the access point for journalists in the security perimeter. "Simple," Benny said two days ago. But today, it doesn't seem so simple.

Felipe stands with his hands jammed under each armpit. He must catch the look on my face because he stops in front of me. "You okay?" he asks.

"Yeah," I blurt but add quickly, "You?" I drape my hand on Felipe's shoulder. "Pray to your gods?"

"Yeah. Three times this morning."

"Good. You're a big Cuban bull." I lift my eyes to him. "This'll go so fast you'll be surprised. Trust me." I can smell the odor of sweat on him.

"But you'll back me up."

I nod and turn towards the car. "Want some rum?"

"No."

My phone buzzes, and I turn my back to Felipe while answering. "Yes, we're fully operational. Got it. We're going mobile now." When I look over at Felipe, his face gleams. He knows. "We go now."

Jumping off the hood of the car, Felipe straps the canvas bag around his shoulders. Both of us sift through the contents to make sure everything is ready. The battery is heavy and hard and bumps against his back with every rubbery step. "*Vamos.*"

I also carry a canvas bag over my shoulder.

After a break in the traffic, we walk through an intersection and begin to work our way up Industry Boulevard. It runs two long blocks behind the national capitol before it meets the cross street and turns right, finally delivering us to the theater.

Felipe glances behind us and around to the sides but keeps walking forward.

It feels good to be moving, and I have time to think. I picture my mother with her arms forever submerged in soapy dishwater, her life going nowhere. She will be so surprised when I buy her a beautiful mansion.

My skin feels hyper-sensitive to the warmth of the sun across my arms, and it seems like we're plodding through deep water.

Felipe's limp seems to have disappeared. He moves quickly. The immense capitol stretches along our right side, its dirty marble columns stately and imposing and eternal. Surrounding the building on all sides, squares of grass gleam bright green because, in spite of the water shortages, these spaces are always watered.

Will Felipe get close enough to the president? Of course, it will be easy to spot him when he comes out of the theater, but will the journalist cover hold up for him? The effective distance of the weapon is no more than about twenty feet. In order to get that kind of opening, Felipe will only have a few seconds. A few seconds to decide my entire future.

After one block, more food kiosks block the sidewalk. Fried green plantains, tamales stuffed with garlic and pork, and of course, many stands offer *guarapo frio*, chilled sugar cane juice, which Cubans drink as much as they drink rum.

When the various smells make my stomach rumble, I realize I haven't eaten since yesterday.

Cuban flags, red and blue with a white star, flutter from balconies on the opposite side of the street from the capitol. Cars and buses clog the street, forcing bicycles to ride among the pedestrians onto the sidewalk. I dodge them while walking fast. A woman pushing a metal cart loaded with groceries temporarily blocks me.

"Get the hell out of my way," I yell and throw the cart over into the street. Plastic bags and tomatoes tumble over the curb to smash in blood red splotches on the concrete.

I catch up with Felipe, and my legs feel strong now. My breathing comes easier, and I know this will work. I'll make it work with the force of my strength.

Looking at his watch, Felipe calls back to me, "Come on. We're late."

We cover the last block beside the capitol. I glance behind, trying to identify anyone following us. People crowd the sidewalk. Old men with canes and straw hats and groups of young women, their skirts flipping up in the breeze to expose brown legs.

Felipe stops and leans over at the waist. He pants, "My leg."

I move from side to side, waiting, worrying. "Come on, Felipe." I notice black clouds approaching us from over the ocean. I worry that rain will hit us before we complete the mission.

Nodding his head, Felipe straightens and we move forward again. We come to the next intersection and turn right. I see that the wide street on the side of the Gran Teatro has been blocked off with wooden sawhorses and a line of troops. The cordoned area spreads across the street to include the grassy knoll beside the capitol. It creates a plaza-like effect inside the line of soldiers around the edges.

We stop to assess the situation. Felipe looks at his watch as we inch forward.

The outer security line stands almost shoulder-to-shoulder. Inside of them, various Cuban police, secret police, and more soldiers mingle with each other. On the far side is a group of white people, obviously Americans, whose faces glisten with sweat as they stand in the sun.

"Goddammit. This won't work," Felipe says and stops walking.

"You've got your identification papers. You're a journalist with credentials. Keep moving."

"Where's the correct entrance?"

Outside the ring of officers, a long line of the protesting idiots from the Ladies in White march toward the theater. They bunch in a tight group because from every side, men yell at them. A few of the men swing their fists at them but hit only the defenseless air.

"Fucking Ladies," Felipe snarls. "Why can't they forget these demonstrations and just obey the law?"

"Wait a minute." I hold Felipe with a hand to his shoulder. "Over there." I point at a section of the line that has a gate and a sign that reads "Press."

"I hope this works." He reaches into the canvas bag and activates the battery.

When the two lights blink on, one after the other, my chest shivers. I pat Felipe's back and say, "You're good to go, Rambo." I do the same in my bag.

Felipe manages a quick smile and moves off toward the press entrance.

I take a deep breath of relief. I hope to hell he can get it done. I think back to Felipe's training and how my entire future depends on him.

Holding the bag against my side, I follow him to the journalist's gate to show my credentials. I'm stopped immediately by someone from the counterintelligence forces. "What the fuck you think you're doing in here?"

I think of my position and how I could have him arrested. I take a deep breath and reach into the pocket of my journalist's vest with its two dozen pockets and remove my identification papers.

The officer studies them for a long time. Looks up at the sky and reads the papers again. Then he paws his hand through the canvas bag. "What the hell is this?"

"It's an ambi-directional microphone," I tell him.

"I don't know. It looks weird."

"Newest technology." I tense my right hand and, for a moment, consider smashing my fist into the prick's face. Take him down and kick the shit out of him. Instead, I smile.

The guard scratches his beard. "Wait here. I gotta get my boss." He saunters off to the left.

Without waiting, Felipe and I run toward the other reporters mingling at the bottom of some steps. By the time the guard gets back with his boss, I'll be hidden in the huge group of journalists to make sure Felipe does his job. I look around at all the soldiers and security people on the perimeter. I've never seen so many in one place before.

I stop at the low steps beside the theater and pretend to be friendly with other reporters. Some carry cameras, some sit on the pavement smoking, and several young women with blond hair are dressed beautifully, standing in front of cameras. I can smell their perfume even though I'm not close. And, I notice, many of them hold bulky microphones. Just like the one Felipe is going to point at the president.

The crowd of reporters starts to murmur, then call out to each other, then some of them shout, "What the hell? He's not coming out?"

I step up to a woman from Reuters who is standing next to her cameraman. I ask her, "What's going on?"

When she turns to me, I see she's sweating and swipes her face with a sunburned hand. "The president may not come out. Something about security issues, but no one's told us shit, so we don't know for sure."

I fall back a few steps. My breathing comes hard and I have to bend forward, my hands on my knees. I look around but don't see Felipe. Where the hell did he go?

Chapter Forty-Two

Ava Alvarez
Saturday. Noon

I hustle Pena out the back door of the house. Carefully, I place the umbrellas and our equipment into the back seat of his car. "Come on," I yell. "You're driving." My body tingles, and I'm totally alert. It feels like the old times, and that gives me confidence.

Churning through the gravel in the drive, Pena swerves into the alley and turns left onto the street. The car lurches forward. At the end of the alley, he slows down to avoid attracting the attention of the spies waiting in the street. It only takes five minutes to get out of the neighborhood to reach 5th Avenue, which is a thoroughfare into the city.

Pena pokes at various buttons on the dash until the air conditioning gushes out of the vents with a metallic smell. We pick up speed, flying by pink mansions and passing the massive Church of Jesus of Miramar that looks more Italian than Cuban in design.

After crossing the Almendares River, Pena swerves to the left and gets on the Malecon. We race along the road, slowing only for potholes and dozens of old American convertibles. They all seemed to be heading the same direction as us.

As we get closer to the old city, traffic slows. Even more of the colorful convertibles clog the road.

"Can't you get around all these?" I demand.

He bobs his head. "I'm trying. Looks like they're all full of Americans." He honks the horn again and again to clear a path.

I tap my fingers repeatedly on the dash. "Faster."

The wind off the Caribbean is the only thing that has picked up speed, causing waves to crash against the seawall and splatter across the sidewalk. The haze still makes it impossible to tell the sky from the horizon. Rain clouds roll in toward the city.

Pena's good. He dodges to the left and right as he picks through the slow-moving traffic. It takes too much time, but we work our way closer to the old city.

"Turn up there." I point to the right. "You can catch Avenue Salvador Allende, which will take us to the capitol."

"With all the activity around there, it'll be too slow. I'll go all the way to the harbor entrance, then come back from the north side. Much faster."

"Okay." I sit back and toy with the handle of the umbrella sitting next to me. Lifting it, setting it down, feeling the smoothness of the polished handle.

In my mind, I try to picture the street next to the Grand Theater. Although I occasionally have time to watch the Cuban National Ballet performances in the theater, I can't remember the exact layout outside. The published schedule says the president will address the crowd about one thirty. If he and his entourage come out the front of the theater, they'll walk into one of the busiest streets in Havana. No, they must be exiting from the side somewhere. The capitol building sits across the street, so I assume the area between the theater and the capitol will be selected. All the officials will be present there when he comes out. And, I assume, so will the Garcia cousins with their weapon.

I look at my watch again and glance over at Pena and see his forehead glisten. Will he actually be able to provide backup for me? Although I know his heart is in the right place, can I depend on him when we must do the killing?

Pena and I follow the Malecon as it curves to the right, straightens, and threatens to run right into the channel leading to Havana Harbor. Ahead of us and riding low in the water, a Chinese freighter churns forward. Its deep horn echoes back from the ancient walls of Morro Castle of the Three Kings, which the Spanish built to guard the harbor at its entrance.

Pena squeals to the right to perform an excellent U-turn, drives onto the Marti Promenade that runs south through the city, and jerks to a stop.

"What? What the hell is going on?" I shout.

He raises both hands in defeat. "Look. Goddammit!"

I see the snarl of traffic ahead of us. Cars honk, double buses try to edge up on the sidewalk to make progress. The only things moving are the "coconuts" with their yellow curved roofs and bicycles, squeezing between the stalled vehicles. I look at my watch. "We're not going to make it in time."

Pena opens the door and gets out to stand up for a better view. In a few minutes, he's back in again and turns up the air conditioning. "It's mobbed. We're not going to get to the theater in this car." He twists his watch around his wrist several times.

I slam the dash with my palm. "I knew the president's arrival would be big, but this is more than I expected. We can't miss our chance. Dammit!"

"What should we do?"

"Let me think." I've been in tight spots many times before and always figured out a way to complete the mission. "Our uniforms will help."

"That should get us clearance to get through the crowds." Pena wipes his forehead. "But there's still too damn many people."

My official phone rings. It's the inspector general. "Yes?" I answer.

"Where are you?"

"I'm on my way to the plaza for the president's appearance."

"You are ordered to return to headquarters immediately."

"And who the hell is ordering me?" I say sarcastically.

He gives me the name of our top commander.

"All right, but why?"

"I don't know."

"Yes, you do. And considering how long we've known each other, you can tell me."

There is a pause, then he says, "This is all I know. The investigation team checked Mendoza's logs and found he was scheduled to meet with you at the church where his body was found." He takes a deep breath. "Ava, there's a team searching for you to arrest you."

I speak to him softly. "Thanks."

Pena squirms in the seat. "Come on."

"Get out." I spring from the car and reach into the back seat. Cradling all the umbrellas in my arms, I call for Pena to help me carry them.

"What?"

"Get a coconut. It looks like they're moving," I order him. I rush toward a coconut idling about twenty feet to the right. Burdened with the umbrellas, I can't move quickly or I'll drop one.

He waves to the driver. When he stops, Pena reaches in and grabs the driver's shoulder, jerking him out and rolling him onto the ground. Pena calls me over as he climbs into the driver's compartment. Loading all the umbrellas in the back, I squeeze next to him. They lay in a neat pile behind us. "Get going!" I scream at Pena.

"I'll do my best—"

Pena shifts the moped into gear. It burps several times, then stalls. He turns the key repeatedly, but the motor won't start. When he looks down toward the floorboards, he says, "Looks like it's missing some of the parts." We're stopped dead in the street.

Chapter Forty-Three

Martha Roriguez
Saturday. Noon

It's hotter in the middle of the plaza than I imagined. My makeup and hair have been destroyed. But that's the least of my problems. Oliver just texted me: no decision has been made yet by the president about coming out into the plaza.

I don't know what to do. I'm so disappointed.

Behind me, I hear a commotion and turn to see what's going on. The Ladies in White break through the crowds to enter the plaza. They're being harassed by many men who yell at the Ladies and throw things at them. But the first of the women persist and push their way to the center of the plaza.

I work my way over to the group, looking for Berta Soler. I don't see her.

The noise is loud, and from the left side, I hear a band playing music. I feel like I'm at a rock concert. The entire square is cordoned off by police and military people. I've never seen so many in one place.

The press corps has stationed themselves to the side of the theater. I walk over and try to find our "friendlies." I spot several who know me. They call to me, "What's going on, Martha?" I advanced these particular reporters, and they're depending on me to deliver what I promised. It's not my fault, of course, if the president stays inside for security purposes, but I still feel responsible. I loop up into the shaded loggia, walk behind a podium, come out into the sun, and take three steps down to get closer to the press people. I mingle among them, trying to calm them down.

"What the hell, Martha." Joe Cameron from CNN puts his face into mine. "Is he coming out, or did we waste our time here?"

"I'm still waiting for security to clear his plans."

"Well, there are a hell of a lot of people here. It'd look terrible if he hid inside." Joe acts as if it's my fault.

I shrug and move on to talk with some other reporters. I look behind the group and see dozens of other press people streaming toward this area. If the chief doesn't come out, there will be a lot of pissed-off reporters here.

I stop walking and drop my head. The heat is overwhelming, and so is this situation. It's so chaotic, I don't know what to do. Will my entire career crater right here? I hear someone calling my name.

I look up and hurry over to a few of the Ladies in White, looking for Berta Soler. I don't see her. In Spanish, I ask several of the other women about her. No one seems to know where Soler is right now. I worry since the point of them being present is for the president to meet her. What if she doesn't show up and the president is left without this critical photo op?

Sweat snakes down my sides. The water bottle I filled at the hotel this morning is almost empty. And I still don't know what's going on. This is one of the toughest times I've ever had on the presidential trail.

More of the Ladies struggle to get into the square, and I finally spot Soler. I squeeze through the crowd of white dresses and finally reach her. *"Buenos días, mi amiga."* I reach for Berta's hand and grasp it.

Her blouse is ripped across the left shoulder, and something blue has stained the side of her immaculate white dress. Most of her hair has been piled on her head, but tendrils fall all around her face. She looks exhausted already. But she smiles when I say hello. I look at her brown face, lined deeply, and find her dark eyes.

"Martha, *gracias*. I am so happy to see you; I didn't think you'd actually brave this crowd. We are 'running the gauntlet' to get inside."

I'm so impressed by the bravery and determination of these women who have already lost so much. I want to help. She loops her arm into mine and moves me toward the front of the group, now getting larger as more women force their way into the plaza. When we reach the front, Berta asks me, "What do you have planned? When will I greet your wonderful president?"

I take a deep breath. How can I tell her? "Uh, I'm not sure."
"What?"
"Berta, there have apparently been some security concerns."
"What does that mean?"

"Since I have nothing to do with the security, I'm not sure."

"But I'll still meet the president?"

I shift my weight from one leg to the other. "I don't know."

The lines in Berta's face curve down as she realizes the disappointment of what I've told her. Her eyes hold firm, but they moisten. Quickly, she swipes under her cheeks and stiffens her shoulders. "I still have faith. I bet on my favorite *oricha* this morning. She's never failed me."

"Let's hope she won't fail me either." That's about all the hope I have left.

Berta turns to tell the sad news to the group, and I see a collective sag in all the bodies surrounding me. We're all disappointed. Two of the ladies slide next to me and yell at me. Normally, I'd get pissed off, but the longing for some recognition of their cause haunts all of their faces. I ignore the criticism.

I can't leave them standing out here in the hot sun, but I don't know what to do. From over the ocean, dark clouds rumble toward the plaza. I know the forecast is for rain, but it was supposed to hold off until the afternoon. Will all of this get rained out?

My phone vibrates and I grab for it. It's Oliver texting me. I crash-read it and start to bounce up and down. He tells me, "It's decided: the chief is coming outside after his speech."

Chapter Forty-Four

Ava Alvarez
Saturday. 12:15

"Get me another one, Pena," I yell.

As I struggle to collect the umbrellas and our equipment, Pena runs forward to find another coconut. He comes back in a few minutes. "Found one." His face is wet, and he hesitates to help me with the umbrellas.

"You ass. I told you these are harmless until I arm them and pull the trigger. Take these two." I hand him part of the load and follow to a new coconut. We repeat the effort of getting everything inside and ordering the driver out. The whole process wastes valuable time.

This one works, and Pena chugs among the sprawling crowds and vehicles. He can't move fast, but at least we make progress toward the theater. We reach a clot of people blocking our route. Pena guns the engine and we smash into the corner of the group. Several people roll off to the side like falling bowling pins.

By 12:30 we come within one block of our goal. It's so crowded, the coconut can't budge any further. I lead Pena out and force him to bulldoze a path through the people as I follow. Our progress is slow. Stepping from left to right, we work our way to the front of the theater. Ahead of me, he slams into people, forcing them to let us through. I've never seen this kind of determination from Pena, and I'm impressed.

The theater occupies one half of a city block, and its pale marble walls rise five stories. On each corner of the roof, towers rise even higher, each one topped by statues of soaring figures, some of which are women who look like they could fly off the towers at any moment.

I glance to our right and see towering clouds descending on the city. We may need the umbrellas for a different purpose.

We rush around the corner of the building. Palm trees stand along the side, their broad leaves sheltering the facade of the theater. I think of the mission that lies ahead. And I think of Tom and Lucinda. Will I end up causing the death of my son?

On the ground level of the theater, an outdoor corridor, called a loggia, circles the entire building. Arches open in regular spaces to allow the patrons to stroll in and out of the corridor, protected from the elements.

I stop to assess the situation.

To our left, as I anticipated, the wide street is blocked off all the way across to the grassy knoll beside the capitol. A square of military and security officers surround the outside of the plaza. That proves the president will come out here after his speech. I hesitate for a minute. All the security resembles a circus of civilians, military officers, and dozens of dignitaries from both Cuba and the U.S. The soldiers look so young. And in spite of the traditional heat of Havana, the Americans are obvious by their pale skin and formal clothing. They stand in a crooked line on the far side of the space, close to the capitol. Several people carry umbrellas, their canopies popped open in colors that make them look like spring flowers.

For a moment, I can't move. Where to start? How can we find the cousins among the hundreds assembled here? I push Pena ahead of me. "Help me look for them. You say one has a limp?"

"Yes. I'll know them the minute I see them," he assures me.

We reach the edge of the crowd.

Inside the ring of security, I see the Ladies in White. They congregate near the middle of the park, while others continue to come through the security lines. I recognize Berta Soler, the leader. Although I disagree with their tactics, I can sympathize with their pain. Pain which in many cases I caused. But then, how could these simple peasant women understand the greater good for which I worked?

Revolving around the Ladies is a loose crowd of men. Counterdemonstrators, organized and funded by either the Cuban counterintelligence services trying to break up the march or by outside financing and organizations. These days, Cuba is like a sieve. Money and subversives slip back and forth into the country easily.

In the old days, the enemies I fought were obvious. Today, things have changed and become more complicated. All I can do now is to focus on this mission. I step into a relatively quiet cove in the side of the theater and arm a few of the umbrellas with the ricin pellets.

With our uniforms and identification, we enter the security line and are searched for weapons. I carry one umbrella along my left side and hold another with my right hand. At this point, it isn't open, ready for me to strike with it. Pena carries the rest and walks beside me, searching for the terrorists. Although the sun burns down on me, I don't open the umbrella.

All across the space, people mingle by the dozens, maybe hundreds. The noise is cheerful but deafening and confusing.

"Do you see them?" I ask as we search across the space.

"No."

"Maybe they're disguised."

"We've studied their profiles and photos for days. We won't miss them."

Near the side of the theater, a group of journalists waits for the president to come out. I scan the crowd, relying on my training to study each group carefully. For a moment, I feel a twinge of despair. All of my experience, my networks of intelligence, and my preparations may be wasted if I don't succeed. "You search in that direction." I point to the right. "I'll cover this area."

Pena moves beside me, his head swiveling back and forth. "We should get closer to where the president may come out. That's where the Garcias should be also."

"You're right." I lead the way toward the reporters who stand together. Along the back side of the large group, the TV camera people rest their equipment on the ground. Many sit on the ground, a few carry open umbrellas, and some are talking to the Ladies in White.

As sweat streaks down my sides, I hold my umbrella by its handle and rest the shaft in my left hand, like I'm holding a pitchfork back on the farm. Ready to raise it and stab the traitors. I search the crowd from left to right again, looking for a man who limps.

In defiance of the hot sun, rain clouds come closer.

Around us, people laugh and talk. Some hold up signs that read, "*Viva Señor Presidente.*" Small groups dance to music from boomboxes, while pungent cigar smoke drifts peacefully across the crowd with its distinct smell of Cuba. It contrasts with the violence that's about to occur.

Scanning the crowd, I spot the officers from my agency on the far side of the plaza, joined by dozens of secret police sycophants. They don't see me, and I feel protected by the huge crowd. Across the street, the bells of the Church of the Baptist toll in sonorous tones to signal the time. Twelve thirty.

My phone rings again and I don't want to answer it, but I do. It's Chandler calling. He's still not on the plaza but needs help. They remind me of the oddest thing: to keep Pena's phone turned on while he holds it. Stupid Americans, but I need him. I agree to do as Chandler asks. We resume our search.

"Comandante," Pena shouts. "Over there." He points toward the far side of the plaza. "It's that son-of-a-bitch, Felipe Garcia."

"Where?"

"Near the press section. I only got a glimpse, but you can't miss his limp."

"Where's the other one?"

"I don't see him."

Gripping the umbrella with my left hand and carrying it at port-arms, I march across the plaza.

Chapter Forty-Five

Pete Chandler
Saturday Afternoon. 12:30

I watch the Sectera Edge phone as Pena moves through the crowd in the plaza. I see a picture of Pena's feet as he marches forward. We can hear the noise of the crowd around them. Then he stops. The camera jerks to the right, and we spot Alvarez standing next to Pena.

"If he leaves his phone on, we can see exactly what he sees and determine where they are. If that doesn't work, the drone can help."

"The Grand Theater is only a few blocks from here. Usually, we can walk there in a few minutes, but today it may take longer," Raquel says as she looks down the street to the west.

"Let's move it."

We turn to the left and hurry toward the theater. The crowds in the narrow streets and sidewalks slow our progress. We pass the Floridita Bar where Hemingway mostly just drank but made it famous by his presence. The bar is packed with tourists who spill out into the street, spilling Hemingway daiquiris onto the sidewalk. I can smell their suntan lotion while we cross to the other side, where the theater is located, and work our way closer.

I see the immense dome of the Cuban capitol off to the left. In the sun, it glows as if it's a luminescent light bulb.

When we reach the Marti Promenade, a four-lane street that bisects the city from north to south, it's packed with stalled vehicles. We stop. Everywhere we look, soldiers and others in uniforms swarm around the streets. Most of them carry automatic rifles hanging from their shoulders by green straps.

Still, it's a festive atmosphere. People laugh with each other, many push baby strollers, and some stop at the kiosks that sell snow cones in inviting flavors like mango and passion fruit.

"Over there." Raquel points across the street at the Grand Theater.

How could we miss it? I see the large, ornate building that looks like a marble wedding cake, full of people on its left side, near to the capitol. The square is also surrounded by military men and women, although things look calm.

"How can we get Alvarez out here?" Raquel asks.

Pushed together by the crowd, we weave our way among the cars and buses in the street to reach the far side. Sounds come from inside the square: laughter, shouting, music, and orders barked at each other by the soldiers. With hundreds of people, we squeeze along the sidewalk on the outside. The guards stand shoulder to shoulder, some facing out while the others watch inside the square, which is also stuffed with people.

I slow down.

"Come on," Raquel says.

"How the hell can we get inside before it's too late?"

She looks across the crowd and pulls me forward. We step up onto the sidewalk that runs in front of the theater. To the left of the mob, I see a commotion of people; many are women wearing long white dresses. As we round the corner of the security cordon, I watch them carrying signs and surging into the plaza while the military stands by without intervening.

We stop. To our right, the theater climbs into the sky. The soldiers all carry the AKS 74U assault rifle, while others cradle the Cuban Cristobal carbine, which is actually a machine gun. The men and women form an impenetrable wall of green and guns.

The noise is loud. It reminds me of a state fair with crowding and confusion. I check the time on my phone. One fifteen.

"Can you see Alvarez?" Raquel asks.

I look at my phone and see Pena's phone extended at the end of his arm. They're moving across the plaza, twisting between clumps of people. It looks like they're near the middle somewhere, but it's confusing since so many people crowd around them. Where are they headed? Raquel calls Alvarez to get us inside, but she doesn't answer.

Through gaps in the soldiers, I survey the square. A group of American diplomats and officials stand on the side opposite from the theater. Their faces are pink, and they look uncomfortable in the hot sun. If we can get inside, I'll head for them immediately.

I watch through Pena's phone. Suddenly, the two of them surge forward as if they've spotted a suspect and are closing in.

"Follow me," Raquel says and leads me around to the far side of the square. People mingle and form into clots and then disperse to find other groups to join. We approach a demonstration of the Ladies in White and other counter-protesters. The ladies' group is dwindling but still threading its way inside the perimeter.

I respect the women's tenacity. They push their way forward while their leaders yell at the troops, who part as if they're afraid of the ladies. The women flow into the plaza, followed by some of the anti-demonstrators and other stragglers. "I think this'll work," Raquel shouts and pulls me after her. We nudge our way into the mob of demonstrators and begin to shuffle forward with them. "Stay in the middle," Raquel tells me. Before the ladies finish moving through the line of soldiers, Raquel and I slip among the group, surge forward, and pop out inside the plaza.

For a moment, the space around me becomes silent, as if I've been popped into a bubble. I think about the next steps. Making contact with the American delegation is the first thing to do. I watch my phone and see Alvarez making her way toward the side of the theater. When I look up, I see the same view, but we are much farther away. Noise crashes through the bubble, and I grab for Raquel's hand.

She says, "I don't see Alvarez."

We've still got a little time before the president comes out, so I turn to the line of Americans standing in a loose group. I tell the first one I reach who I am and ask for her supervisor. The woman points to a tall man wearing a cream-colored blazer. When I give him my information and the intelligence I have from Alvarez about the danger to the president, he looks closely at me.

"Who are you?" he asks again.

"Pete Chandler. I'm attached to the State Department here. You've got to tell the Secret Service."

"Can I see some ID?"

"Here." I hand him my passport. "But the president—"

"I heard you." He steps back and pulls out a phone. Makes a call, talks for a few minutes, and comes back to me. "Okay. I passed on your message to the agents inside the theater. They'll do what they need to do."

"What's that?"

He shrugs. "I'm just an economist. I don't handle that other stuff."

"But there's got to be a way to warn them."

"Hey, there's about 1,200 people from the U.S. in Cuba today. I'm sure they've prepared for everything." He turns back to look at the theater.

I gather with Raquel. I notice the metallic smell of incoming rain. The dark clouds are building high above us now. "So much for that brilliant idea. Now what?"

"Alvarez seems to know who will make the attack. If we can find her, maybe we can help." Raquel pauses, then says, "I never thought I'd say something like that."

"She's ahead of us. Come on."

We start toward the theater. On that side of the square there are a series of low steps. Several reporters stand there, apparently waiting. It must be the place where the president will come out.

I pull Raquel to a stop and retrieve the Insectothopter. Squeezing the body between my fingers, I hand the dragonfly to her to hold. I scroll through my phone to open the program and suddenly, the translucent wings of the insect are buzzing up and down. Raquel lets the drone lift from her palm.

It takes me a few tries to remember how to maneuver the drone, but I get it down and aim it toward the group ahead of us. Raquel leans in to watch the screen with me. We spot the reporters, the security people lined up in front of the theater doors, and then I reverse it toward us as I survey the situation. It's confusing and chaotic. How are we going to stop whatever will happen in time? Then I spot Alvarez from the drone, and we follow in that direction.

We push ahead side by side. Thirty feet in front of us, I spot Alvarez in her uniform. A man moves along with her, also dressed in a uniform. But there is something odd about her behavior. She carries a blue umbrella, folded shut and pointed forward like a rifle with a bayonet attached to the end.

"What's she doing?" Raquel asks as we close the space.

"It must be her Belgian umbrella. I haven't heard of one being used since the Soviets killed a defector in London. Nevertheless, it can be a deadly weapon." Her movements make it look like Alvarez is hunting the terrorists and has found one.

Looking from the drone, we see her walk calmly toward a specific journalist, wearing a white Panama hat and carrying a canvas bag over his shoulder. He limps forward with other reporters to a large door in the side of the theater. In his right hand, he holds a huge microphone. I've never seen anything like it before.

We're close enough now that the drone is unnecessary, so I let it fall. The sound of thunder rumbles through the streets and enters the plaza.

I sense rustling in the crowd, building louder now as people surge forward to reach the steps below the theater door. I look under the loggia on the side and spot dozens of men and women in dark suits bulging out of the theater. They fan out in a semi-circle and look across the crowd extended before them. The reporters climb the few steps and crush closer to the security people. Someone brings out a podium and places it at the top of the steps. The journalists are allowed to surround the podium at a short distance. Waiting. Excitement builds, and I look at the clock on my phone. It's one forty.

Suddenly, the president of the United States steps into the sun from under the loggia, and the crowd erupts in a deafening noise of cheering and shouting. I've never met the president, but in person he looks much younger than I thought. His smile is wide, and he waves over the top of the people. Then the first secretary of the Communist Party, Raul Castro, comes outside also. A pudgy, stooped man. He shakes the president's hand, turns and waves, and stands to the side. The president takes a step around the podium and leans forward to shake hands while the security detail opens up a space to allow a few reporters access to him.

Elbowing each other to get closer, they call to him, shout questions, and poke dozens of microphones at him. Because Alvarez is following the guy with the Panama hat and limp, I look for him now and spot him about ten feet from the president. His strange mic is extended out in front of his hand toward the president.

Chapter Forty-Six

Pete Chandler
Saturday, 1:45

Although the forward thrust of people stops, Alvarez pushes her way among the reporters until she reaches the one with the limp. I watch as she raises the blue umbrella in front of her. She stabs him in the shoulder. For a minute, nothing happens. Then he begins to cough. His hat falls off while he bends over and wheezes, gasping for air. The other journalists jostle each other to get to the front of the group. They ignore the choking man and surge forward around him like a school of fish regrouping to occupy his space. He staggers back and forth before collapsing on the ground.

Clouds cover the sun and bring a cooling relief, but also the ominous sound of a heavy rain.

Turning her head to check both sides around her, Alvarez backs up quickly into the cover of the crowd. At that instant, a second man charges through the crowd of reporters. I see him and realize it's the same guy who tried to shoot us in the pine trees and calls himself Miguel Garcia. He is also dressed as a reporter and also carries a canvas bag over his shoulder. I forgot how large he is.

He knocks over a female holding a camera as he claws his way to the front of the pack. In a few seconds, he also raises a strange-looking mic, pointing it toward the president. I realize what's going on. It's the weapon that caused the Havana Syndrome.

I wedge my way between the crowd and struggle to get to him.

Before I can reach Garcia, Alvarez darts in from the left of me with her umbrella raised. She stabs at Garcia but misses. Stabs again and this time, he swats it away with a burly arm.

We follow behind Alvarez as she tries again.

At that moment, Garcia points the microphone contraption at her. I don't hear anything but watch as Alvarez drops to her knees, holding her head and screaming in pain. But she's found the terrorists. Garcia starts to turn back toward the president. Alvarez staggers to her feet and makes a feeble effort to stab Garcia with her umbrella once again.

She misses and falls down. Garcia picks up her umbrella and jams it into the side of Alvarez's chest while she's on her knees. From the force of the blow, she sprawls onto the ground. Her head bounces off the pavement, and blood puddles around her head as she stops moving.

Another officer in uniform beside her drops his bundle of umbrellas and squirms away into the crush of people to disappear.

I only have a few seconds. Pushing Raquel behind me, I duck around a reporter to approach Garcia from his blind side. He's trying to turn back to face the president again. I stand sideways, making myself a smaller target as I prepare for a taekwondo kick. The ancient self-defense practice proves that the speed of a strike is more powerful than the size of the weapon: my foot. I begin by relaxing for an instant, then tense my body. I lean to the left, pulling my knee and leg up close to my chest.

Before I can strike, Garcia sees me, slides to the side, and lifts his microphone.

I slam a kick up in the air designed to strike the enemy in the head. I'll only get one chance before Garcia's weapon will hit me.

At the last second, Garcia's head absorbs a glancing blow from my kick and the microphone arcs high into the air. Garcia rocks back on his heels. As if he's moving in slow motion, Garcia pedals backward, giving himself time to regroup.

He looks to find me, puts the microphone into his bag, and this time he comes up with another umbrella. He leaps at me with the sharp point. I step to the side and feel the cloth of the umbrella graze my arm. The confused crowd opens a space around us. That allows Garcia some room to find Raquel. She's facing him and tries to back up but is blocked by the crowd standing around her. She's pinned in place, and I see the look of terror on her face.

The president and the other officials are unaware of the fight going on. Around me I hear people cheering for the dignitaries.

Garcia charges toward Raquel with his outstretched umbrella. She raises her arms in front of her body in a useless attempt at protection.

He lunges, but I'm quicker. From the side, I deliver one more kick to the head. This one cannot fail or Raquel will die. I connect with full power. Garcia staggers, then flips onto his back and he lies motionless on the stones.

I reach down and grab the canvas bag with its strange weapon and sling it over my back.

Now the crowd reverses course and converges to see what happened. When they see the bodies strewn across the ground, they start screaming and pushing to get away. But many stay with upraised cell phones.

The president and Raul Castro disappear behind a wave of Secret Service officers shoving them back into the safety of the theater. Other security forces charge down the steps toward me and Raquel. Many have their automatic pistols pointed at us. I may have just killed a Cuban national. With Raquel clinging to my arm, we back up while I look for an escape. But the soldiers close in from the opposite direction.

I don't have a plan for escape, but I must save Raquel above all else.

We pass Alvarez lying motionless on the ground, and Raquel bends down to touch her. When Raquel stands again, she's got blood on her fingers that she smears across my face. "For once, Alvarez may actually help me," she whispers in my ear. "Follow me."

Instead of fear, I see the look of confidence and control on her face. When we lock our eyes together, I feel a jolt run through me. Raquel is the sleeper cell. She's probably got a safe house somewhere, and she probably has the exfiltration plan so she can get us out of here.

"*Medico, medico,*" she screams for a doctor.

In the confusion and noise, the crowd actually stops moving and opens a narrow space for us. I realize what my role is, and I stumble a few times to make my injuries look authentic. Raquel puts my arm over her shoulder and drags me forward. She whispers, "I have an idea to get us to safety. Do as I say." To the crowd, she yells, "*Ayudanos.*" Help us. Two soldiers who've just arrived part the people to help us.

Cold rain slants down into the plaza and bounces off the stones like oil drops in a hot pan.

"Clear the way," they shout.

I let Raquel lead me toward the Marti Promenade. The noise is so loud it hurts my ears to be in the middle of it. But it helps us escape.

It takes ten minutes to get across the plaza, past the ring of protective soldiers, and out on the sidewalk. Two taxis wait next to the curb. Raquel opens the back door to the first one and barks instructions to the driver.

At that moment, a second contingent of soldiers catches up with us. Surrounding the taxi, they grab for both of us. Raquel yells at them, but they press closer. Then I spot two American security people who squeeze into a space next to me.

"American! Diplomat!" I yell and flash my passport at them. "We need help."

The Americans look puzzled at first but finally agree and push their way to me. Grabbing each of my arms, they begin to pull me away from the soldiers, who argue with them about my leaving the scene. But the security people keep moving me through the rain.

"Don't forget that woman," I plead with them. "She's with me."

I look back and see the Cubans swarm all over Raquel. She twists and fights with them. For an instant, she's free and attempts to reach me. Her eyes lock onto mine. I can't lose another person from my life. Breaking away from the Americans next to me, I make a grab for Raquel. But my hands are wet and slippery. Before I can reach her, the biggest soldier blocks me and uses his shoulder to drive Raquel into the ground. They swarm on her.

I call to the Americans behind me, "Help her! She's one of us."

Instead, they pull me back to safety. I watch helplessly as Raquel is surrounded by uniforms as she lies on the ground. I remember the image of Diego lying in the wet street as rain washed his life away. I twist to the side to get a better look, but Raquel disappears under the soldiers' bodies.

Chapter Forty-Seven

Pete Chandler
Foggy Bottom, Washington, D.C.
One week later

A layer of late spring ice still covers the Tidal Basin in front of the Jefferson Memorial as the black limousine speeds past it, heading toward Foggy Bottom. Mist swirls over the Potomac River on the left to shroud the streets and make driving difficult. The driver ignores it.

I'm alone in the back seat. I'm meeting with some people, but not Sonnenfeld, in twenty minutes at another secret location in one of the most expensive places to live in the United States. My chest feels tight. I have no idea what will happen at this upcoming debriefing.

After a detour from Cuba to Minneapolis to see my daughter, I got on a plane to come here. They will want information from me, but I also have a lot of questions. The first one is going to be: do they have any idea what happened to Raquel Sanchez?

I think of her and worry about the dangers she'll face in Cuba. Probably torture and execution. There's a painful fist in my stomach. Once again, the pattern of my life repeats. I've lost someone I felt strongly about.

Because I was able to retrieve the sonic weapon and the diagrams, American scientists easily reverse-engineered the device and are already working on a defense system.

The limo crunches over ice as it turns into a narrow street. In front of a row of townhouses, the driver stops. "Here we are, Mr. Chandler. They're waiting."

I get out of the back door and carefully walk up the sidewalk. An American beech tree's branches guard the door, budding with a few pale green growths. I hang onto the railing and step up to the yellow town-house. Two stories with black shutters. The door opens as soon as I reach the top step.

"Welcome, Mr. Chandler," the Marine says. He salutes and moves to the side, allowing me to enter. "To the right. They are expecting you."

"Who's 'they'?"

No response.

I turn into a living room at the front of the house. Feeble sunlight brightens the windows that look out over the street. From a couch to the left, a man in a heavily medaled Army uniform stands slowly. He holds onto the armrest for a moment, then comes to me. "Congratulations, Pete. You executed your mission even better than we hoped." With a dry and bony hand, he pumps my hand for a long time. "Come over to the table." He leads me to a round table in the front corner, where two smartphones and several file folders clutter the top. A coffee setting steams on the far edge of the table. Two assistants in blue suits and white shirts come into the room and sit on the couch that the old man just left. They both open laptops.

I sit opposite from the stranger, whose eyes roam over me for a few minutes. "Let me look at the hero," he chuckles. One of the assistants steps up to the table, turns on the recording function of a smartphone, and leaves it in the middle of the table.

"I'm Colonel Jeremy MacMillian. Call me Jerry. You don't know me, but I've been tasked to handle your debriefing."

"How's Sonnenfeld?"

MacMillian's eyebrows drop, clutching his eyes. "I'm sorry to say that he was in a serious car accident. He's still in a coma at Walter Reed."

"What happened?"

He shakes his head. "Later. We have our theories."

"Theories?"

"I read your reports and must say, they were excellent. Nice work. For all the good Cuba may promise, there's still a lot of corruption and problems."

I nod and wait.

"Yes, well." MacMillian clears his throat. "Thanks to you, we avoided a catastrophe. The president is grateful, by the way." He picks up a cup of coffee. "Our operatives have been debriefed, and we were able to assemble the events that occurred."

"I did what I could. So, the terrorists also caused the Havana Syndrome?"

"Yes. A cabal of rebels knew about the Soviet research on sound weapons and were able to get their old schematic diagrams. Then they hired a team to manufacture a new, improved model for the first attack, directed at the American Embassy personnel." He smiles briefly.

"The first attack?"

"Right. They used a couple of nationals, the Garcia cousins, to actually carry it out. When that didn't get the results the cabal wanted, they planned for a much larger attack."

"Against the president?"

MacMillian takes a dry breath, as if to avoid even thinking about the repercussions of the plan. "Yes. At the plaza after the president gave his speech."

"But why? Wouldn't that set off the worst results?"

"Of course. The dissidents knew that the desire for Cuban regime change was very strong by some members of Congress, international American corporations, and many covert groups here. For sixty years, various administrations have tried to do so but failed."

"But how would the Havana Syndrome change that?"

"They knew if something as serious as harming our president occurred, we would react. With maximum retaliation. I don't mean a military invasion like Iraq, but an invasion of some degree that would topple the Castros and the ruling elites. The U.S. would set up a democratic government more friendly to us."

"And the people who plotted this would be in charge of the new government?" I lean forward in the chair. "Who did this? The CIA?"

MacMillian chuckles. "No. Years ago, the CIA was instrumental in toppling regimes in countries to make them more, uh, amenable to our way of thinking. But today, our government outsources these tasks to black ops contractors. That's who masterminded this activity in Cuba."

The conversation stops as both of us consider the permutations.

I look out the window at the icicles hanging from the wrought iron railing. I remember the warmth of the Cuban sun, the music, the shortages of food, and the bright colors. In spite of the corruption and problems, I found good people, including Raquel Sanchez, who risked everything to help me. I know that I did what I could, but I failed to rescue her. I ache for her more than I imagined.

"What's going on in Cuba as a result?" I turn back to face MacMillian. "Ava Alvarez, the Garcias, Raquel?"

He shrugs. "Clouded over in a fog, like they've done for decades. We don't have all the intelligence we'd like. We're sure that Alvarez died, as did the two assassins. At least the attacks will stop and we can work toward a rapprochement with Cuba in the future."

"I met Alvarez. She's the one who made the first contact in the painting."

"Yes. And we're grateful to her. A brutal zealot and, over the years, one of the most successful spies for Cuba against us. You have to respect her. In the end, she died betraying her country in order to save it. How many Americans would do the same?"

There's an awkward pause that signals MacMillian is done.

"But what about Sonnenfeld?"

He bobs his head as if he's considering how much I can legally know. "A strange event. We are quite certain it wasn't an accident."

"What does that mean?"

MacMillian stands and stretches his back. His glance at the two assistants causes them to leave the room. "I'm not authorized to reveal much more to you, but there was an American group of contractors who were probably involved in the plot against our president."

"I think I met one of them. He called himself Benny."

"Did he say he was from 'Red Dog Associates'?"

I nod.

"We've been shadowing them for years. A nasty group of cowboys who work all over the world. They're former military people who are hired to do the dirty work others don't want to do or can't because of political repercussions."

"What do you mean, 'others'?"

MacMillian looks out the window and back to me. "Pete, this intelligence must never leave the room. We can't prove it, but we're certain there are high level people in the U.S. government who paid them and supported this plot."

"Who?"

He shakes his head from side to side. "Unfortunately, they're still embedded in our government and still operating. At this point, we don't have concrete proof to go public with their identities. The continuing battle with our enemies will be fought inside the human brain. Disinformation, propaganda, and the deadly use of new technologies are just the tip of the iceberg." MacMillian sighs.

"Did Sonnenfeld know all this?"

"When Winston hired you, I don't think he knew what you both were getting into until later. As the clues came together and the gravity of the plot became obvious, he was prepared to go to the highest levels to expose it. That's when the 'accident' happened." MacMillian shuffles to the door and opens it to his assistants.

I hear someone coming down the hall. My boss, Martin Graves, turns into the room, brightens when he sees me, and comes over to give me a hug.

"As usual, you did a hell of a job, Pete. You saved our president and probably many others."

That gives me a moment of satisfaction. I think of the ghosts that haunt me and, for a while, they've disappeared. And maybe I will be forgiven for an act committed in the dust of Iraq. "Uh, do you know what happened to our 'sleeper agent,' Raquel Sanchez?"

MacMillian's face brightens. "Oh, I almost forgot. In appreciation for all the aid she gave to you, and to our country, we've managed to get her extradited from Cuba at the last minute. Both she and her husband's parents."

My head pops up. "How?"

"Well, people from Cuba must apply for 'parole process' in order to receive asylum here. Not many are allowed in. Ms. Sanchez, being a clever lawyer, immediately understood the protocol we gave her and began working on it. We had to cut a few corners, but considering how the counterintelligence services would certainly have executed Sanchez and her family, we were able to get them out quickly." He smiles at me.

"She's here?"

"Yes. Now she can apply for citizenship and remain in the U.S."

"But—?"

"If you want to see her, she's staying with her husband's parents at the Harrington Hotel, here in D.C."

I finally release the air stuffed in my chest and look out the window to see the rising sun glistening through the icicles on the railing, melting them into meaningless puddles that will soon evaporate.